Y0-ELK-210

THE
NEW AMERICANS

A Thriller

Kyle C. Fitzharris

iUniverse LLC
Bloomington

THE NEW AMERICANS
A THRILLER

Copyright © 2013 Kyle C. Fitzharris.

All rights reserved. No part of this book may be used or reproduced by any means, graphic, electronic, or mechanical, including photocopying, recording, taping or by any information storage retrieval system without the written permission of the publisher except in the case of brief quotations embodied in critical articles and reviews.

This is a work of fiction. All of the characters, names, incidents, organizations, and dialogue in this novel are either the products of the author's imagination or are used fictitiously.

The New Americans *is available at retail bookstores like Barnes & Noble Booksellers, online at www.barnesandnoble.com, www.amazon.com, or other online bookstores. For more information on* The New Americans, The Eighth Plague, *or the author, Kyle C. Fitzharris, please visit www.kylefitzharris.com*

Because of the dynamic nature of the Internet, any web addresses or links contained in this book may have changed since publication and may no longer be valid. The views expressed in this work are solely those of the author and do not necessarily reflect the views of the publisher, and the publisher hereby disclaims any responsibility for them.

Any people depicted in stock imagery provided by Thinkstock are models, and such images are being used for illustrative purposes only.

Certain stock imagery © Thinkstock.

ISBN: 978-1-4759-9107-9 (sc)
ISBN: 978-1-4759-9106-2 (hc)
ISBN: 978-1-4759-9105-5 (e)

Library of Congress Control Number: 2013908570

Printed in the United States of America

iUniverse rev. date: 6/17/2013

Disclaimer: The use of the great seal on the cover is in no way is an endorsement, sponsorship, or approval by the United States Government or by any department, agency or instrumentality thereof and is in accordance with the guidelines of Title 18, Subsection (a) of § 713.

For More Information Visit:
KyleFitzharris.com

L.O.R.E.
A Division of Life of Riley Entertainment
5310 Oak Park Lane, Suite#118
Oak Park, California USA 91377

Cover Design: Ian Pozin
Editors: Betsy Schell & Terry Rubinroit

Copyright L.O.R.E. 2013

PRAISE FOR *THE NEW AMERICANS*

"Kyle Fitzharris has done it again. His new book, The New Americans is his best novel yet. It literally starts out with a bang and never lets you go! His writing is so visual, and being a cameraman for a living, I can really appreciate his descriptions, and deep dynamic writing that are in this book. He takes you into the characters minds and makes you feel you are traveling the world along with them."

-- Stephen Campanelli, Director/Cameraman- J. Edgar, Gran Torino, Million Dollar Baby, Changeling, Space Cowboys, & over 87 motion pictures

"A chilling, frightening side of L.A. you don't want to believe exists is vividly brought to life by Kyle FitzHarris in this engaging page turner."

-- Kirstin Wilder, VP/Managing Editor, Variety

"Kyle Fitzharris did an excellent job with this novel, I couldn't put it down. The action is cover to cover and the characters are outstanding and truly believable. The conflicts that develop between the Latino Gang, The Russian Mob and IRA remnants are intriguing, suspenseful and memorable. This book has the potential to become a major blockbuster movie!"

-- Roger Burlage, Former CEO of Live Ent., Former President of New World Entertainment/Marvel, Creative Director for the best seller: The 911 Report: A Graphic Adaptation

"Kyle Fitzharris didn't obtain his expertise in a weekend ride-along, he lived it! His experiences are reflected in his writings. His latest action-packed thriller, *The New Americans*, delivers a powerful punch. Buckle up and hang on."

-- Bob Hamer, FBI (retired) Author of THE LAST UNDERCOVER, ENEMIES AMONG US, and TARGETS DOWN.

"The New Americans is extraordinary, riveting and full of suspense. From beginning to end, Fitzharris pulls you in, gives you a bite of the suspense apple, but never let's you go... Fitzharris' first novel, The Eighth Plague was great, but *The New Americans* is even more gripping – I cannot wait for the big screen debut."

-- *Dr. Valarie J. McCall –Government Executive,*
City of Cleveland, Ohio

"I love this book! The New Americans is a fast paced, action packed, intriguing, even frightening thriller you won't be able to put down. Kyle Fitzharris did a phenomenal job creating vivid characters and allowing us into their minds and into the dark underworld of Los Angeles and beyond. This book HAS to be made into a movie, it's too good not to!"

-- *Bas Rutten, UFC Heavyweight Champion, 3-time King of Pancrase*
Champion, Actor, TV Host

"The New Americans is my kind of thriller! It kept me guessing with each plot twist and turn and I especially liked the international cast of characters and how they all coalesced in their world. I read a lot of thrillers, but *The New Americans* is my new favorite!"

- *Anonymous, OSD, DOD the Pentagon, Washington DC*

"Kyle Fitzharris is such a great storyteller in that great tradition of Irish storytellers...his insight into the Irish and Russian mobs in this country and internationally is fascinating ...*The New Americans* grips you by the throat from the beginning and doesn't leave go... "

-- *Timothy V Murphy, Actor, The Lone Ranger, Sons of Anarchy,*
Appaloosa, Shallow Ground, National Treasure: Book of Secrets,
Criminal Minds, CSI LA

"Amazing mental illustration that Kyle Fitzharris has brought to us through his writings. You are able to capture his experiences and different living conditions that you didn't even know existed. "The New Americans" is a must read... and when a motion picture comes out it will be a must-see!"

-- *Jesse Nicassio, CEO, Juke Performance, Former NFL Athlete,*
Inventor of the Mass Suit

To Áine - who lifts me up everyday, shows me the joys of life, and loves me unconditionally...

PROLOGUE

THE SUBDUCTION MEGATHRUST DEEP within the Sumatran Trench manifested itself on the surface of the Indian Ocean as a mere belch from Poseidon. The vertical displacement of seawater above amounted to just inches, but below, a Kraken had been released that would rush, at nearly mach speed, to dispatch a quarter of a million souls.

This part of Asia was unique in many ways, not the least of which was the latitude and longitude of the Indonesian Archipelago's Island of Sumatra. A few degrees north of the Sunda Strait, just south of the Strait of Malaca, flanked by both the South China Sea and the Indian Ocean, it laid smack dab in the middle of the Equator. Sumatra was an easy kill.

This night, Srivajaya, a humble bayside villager, would put the final touches on his *Wayang Kulit Prince* and *Monkey King*. He was a master Shadow Puppet maker who used a white cloth background and the fire he'd made from dried palm fronds on the beach to illuminate his creations.

While Srivajaya finished stretching the water buffalo hide and dabbing gold flake on his masterpieces, the other villagers prepared for the great feast that approached. All manner of food and tropical fruit was dried, roasted, and jerked. The excitement in the air was palpable. But first things first: evening prayers and the giving of thanks for the blessings of Buddha, even some to Mohammed, as the Malay did religiously.

The gentle tropical breeze caused the long dugout fishing boats to list slowly like a hand rocking a cradle, and on the beach the tinkling of bells and tiny chimes at the end of fishing lines signaled another eel or shark.

The evening waned, and as so, the villagers would soon be asleep to dream of their holiest day of the year. Yet this night's dreams would not come, because by dawn's break, the Asian and Middle Eastern developers would smile an evil smile while the Indonesian government would feign grief for the untold loss of life.

Officials would smirk in anticipation of the fortune in illegal payoffs and bribes that would come from finally being rid of the squatters that could not be formerly moved by violence or intimation of any kind.

The prime seaside real estate would now go to the greedy, ruthless, bankers and investors. After all, the successful plunder of over 48% of Sumatra's Tropical Rainforests had not only yielded huge dividends, but also brought millions in donations for the now endangered Tiger, Rhino, Orangutan, and Elephant species. The corrupt couldn't ask for better disasters: earthquakes, fires, civil war, and the greatest of these about to be bestowed upon them this night.

Srivajaya and his wife had already placed their young children in hammocks strung between each corner of the makeshift shanty and blessed their heads. He had thrown wet sand onto the fire for a dead out, and carefully aligned the colorful paints and dyes for his shadow puppets on a flat spot on the beach. He was just about to retire for the evening when he felt a strange, dizzying pressure in his ears. He turned toward the source, and witnessed a horrifying scene the likes of which he had only seen once before as a boy. Water began to rapidly recede from the bay, revealing only bare sand for over a mile out to sea.

Then, as suddenly as it had raced away, a great dark beast arose from the sea blocking even the glow of the large harvest moon. Not believing his eyes, he glanced higher to check the stars and gain relation to the sky, but the darkness now enveloped the stars as well.

A gasp slipped past his lips as he instinctively took a step backward. Then Srivajaya spun around to warn his sleeping family. He wanted to scream but no words came. The monster was too great, too dark, too fast. Srivajaya never took a single step.

CHAPTER 1

THE EARLY MORNING MIST lingered over the quiet green fields adjacent to the flats as the first graying lights of morning crept in.

Although the Belfast projects were dingy from the damp moss that covered the buildings, the emerald tinted Irish grey-green stone walls looked elegant as the mica flakes twinkled in the advancing dawn light.

The streets were empty, with the exception of the occasional stray dog, and the unmarked police car looked like any other car on the street that early morning, except for the two silhouettes inside.

The Royal Ulster Constabulary (RUC) primarily represented the British Protestants in the community, but had established dominance over the majority Catholic populous as a brutal and dictatorial police force. More paramilitary than peacekeepers, they were tasked, among other duties, to locate and capture Irish Republican Army soldiers through any means possible.

British Intelligence officer Charles Tetley waited patiently, sipping his coffee from a paper cup as his partner, Louis Smythe spied through a pair of binoculars.

A light rain obscured his view, and the developing fog on the inside of the windshield from their breath wasn't helping, either. Smythe rolled down the passenger side window ever so slightly to balance out the air pressure and temperature inside the vehicle.

The rain had already glazed the bricked street in front of a stone duplex Smythe had trained his sights on.

"Any sugar?" asked Smythe.

"Nope!" Tetley responded as he looked around the empty paper sack.

"You know I need it for my bleed'n coffee!" Smythe barked.

Tetley turned toward his partner, "Forget the sugar, what are you so keyed up about? Relax, we've done this hundreds of times," he said in a calming voice.

A two-way radio cackled to life. Smythe nearly jumped out of his seat. Tetley looked over at him again.

"What the hell has gotten into you?"

A man's voice burst out of the tiny speaker, "Hold on position – GREEN is GO – Repeat, GREEN is GO!"

Tetley tilted his head to look out of his window and saw a military helicopter hovering over the ghetto housing project. Today was exciting because the British Special Air Service (SAS) was on his joint task force to raid a suspected IRA safe house. He was quite chuffed with himself, as he was team leader and ultimately in charge of the specialized brigade. It had been put together due to his tenacity and diligence, which really amounted to the threats and pressure he'd put on his CIs and other local informants. Yet, it was quite the promotion for an inspector in his mere 30s, and as such, endeared him to both his superiors and his intelligence community colleagues. He really needed to land this big fish.

Tetley glanced down at the manila folders on his lap that read: "DOSSIER" and opened the top file. It was well organized with photos clipped to the left side and corresponding documents on the right.

"Michael McCann, Lieutenant," he said quietly. Smythe glanced over as well as Tetley read on. They both took the opportunity to familiarize themselves with their subjects.

He flipped the next few folders, "Tony Murphy, Billy 'Hammer' O'Brien, Peter Morrissey," he snickered.

"What cliché Irish names," Tetley laughed to his partner. He held up the file, but Smythe had already turned his attention back to surveilling. Tetley closed the file and looked out the window at the prelude to the day's entertainment.

In his side view mirror an Armored Personnel Vehicle roared into the quiet neighborhood.

"Right on time!" Tetley grinned. The APV stopped at the edge of the complex as soldiers deployed quickly, spreading out to their assigned grids. From there, they hopped fences, rolled over stonewalls and began to scour the back and side yards of the dilapidated buildings.

A young soldier clumsily stepped on a small child's toy that lay on a tiny landing. All movement froze. Four SAS Commandoes quietly maneuvered from the flank into single file position with automatic weapons at the ready in front of the other soldiers. They shot to the entrance of the nondescript apartment and reconnoitered.

The Captain nodded his head and flashed his green light toward his men, then at Tetley and Smythe. They quickly exited their unmarked car and hoofed it across the street, crouching behind a hedgerow near the home interspersed within the battalion.

Tetley's voice could be heard in everyone's earpiece, "Hit 'em, hit 'em now with everything!"

The four commandoes raised their guns and each fired large mortar-like shells through the windows. Instantly tear gas and smoke grenades breached the interior of the home. More canisters flew into the already smoke-filled flat. Tetley smiled as the fireworks began, perhaps pondering about what his future held. He was a very ambitious man who knew where he wanted to end up, but wasn't sure how to get there. However, this would be a giant steppingstone.

"We'll be home for tea," he chuckled to Smythe who was still fidgeting like a child with ADHD.

Four SAS soldiers retreated to the front gate and began spraying the house with automatic gunfire. The bullets ripped through the door and aged mortar of the exterior, pulverizing stone, steel and most likely, flesh. Not to be outdone, the RUC soldiers began firing into the home in kind. This would soon become a cluster-fuck of unimaginable size.

A small fire had erupted from the incendiary devices burning the carpet and drapes and anything else flammable in the home. Tetley and Smythe watched safely from over the wall as the house was quickly set ablaze.

"That should sort the rest of those bastards out," Tetley said, titling his chin higher in a Romanesque fashion. Smythe dutifully nodded, but didn't seem to possess the bloodthirsty desperation as his partner had this day.

"AAAAHHHH!" Screams suddenly poured from the home. Neighbors around the ghetto began to shoot to their windows as they could only helplessly watch the horror unfold.

Then suddenly, a large sport utility vehicle crashed through the garage door of the adjoining duplex and barreled out into the street, taking more than it's share of refuse bins, lampposts, and stone pillars. Tetley had not seen that coming.

Tetley could tell from his dossier photo the driver was Peter Morrissey, one of McCann's underlings. He was hardly worth the effort as his inexperience had barely put him on Tetley's radar. McCann was real prize, and Tetley could now see his prey riding shotgun. In the backseat, he could see Hammer and Murphy through the cheap, European window glass. Check, check and check. Tetley signaled with his hand for the commandoes to redirect all their firepower toward the vehicle.

Morrissey fishtailed and skidded, jumping curbs, seemingly to draw fire away from the second home that was now engulfed in flames. The truck shot past the SAS unit as they hauled ass through the center of the gauntlet. Stepping from behind a hedgerow, Smythe rose in front of the speeding truck, took aim with his pistol and double tapped, shooting young Morrissey in the upper torso, then continued to spray the truck with bullets until his magazine was empty.

The truck swerved erratically sending everyone in its path diving for cover. Everyone that is, except for one. Caught off guard, Smythe stood frozen like a deer in the headlamps. The damaged truck careened out of control and slammed hard into Smythe, catapulting his now broken body high and far. He landed hard with a thud a dozen yards away. The truck gasping to right itself, spun sideways and flipped out of control end over end, only stopping when it finally crashed into the army jeeps that were blocking one of the road exits. The collision punctured the lower carriage and caused gallons of petrol to spew everywhere. Amid the heat, bullets and friction, suddenly, the SUV ignited. A fireball quickly rose from the wreckage as black smoke and metal flew skyward.

Tetley, watching as his partner sail through the air, could only run to Smythe's limp body to triage. He shoved his index and middle fingers deep into the side of Smythe's neck. Nothing. He stared into the lifeless eyes. Tetley grimaced, then gently closed his eyelids with the palm of his hand.

The soldiers rapidly advanced toward the wreckage in standard four by four formation. Murphy and Hammer, both injured and bleeding, managed to quickly crawl from the truck and dart through the black smoke and flames, eyeing freedom in the form of a neighboring hedgerow. Suddenly remembering, Murphy reached back into the burning vehicle and managed to grab two black canvas bags. In all the confusion and blinding chaos, they managed to escape over the wall and into the depths of the bleak Belfast alleyways unnoticed -- their partners would not be so lucky.

Bloodied and battered and hanging upside down in the front of the burning truck, McCann reached over, unbuckled his belt first, then grabbed the boy. He pulled and yanked until they both made it through the hole in the jagged broken passenger side window. McCann pulled with all his might and dragged Morrissey's bullet-ridden body from the twisted steel.

"We surrender, don't shoot, we're unarmed! I've an injured man here!" McCann yelled as he struggled to hold upright his young friend's bleeding body. The soldiers advanced and rushed in to draw down on the two.

"We sure gave those Brits a run fer their money, didn't we, Mick?" Morrissey coughed as blood filled his mouth with each breath from the holes in his lungs. Just then, an SAS soldier stepped forward, flipped the toggle from Semi to Auto, and began spraying Morrissey with bullets. The blast had such an impact it tore the teenager from McCann's arms like a demon on high and sent them both in opposite directions. McCann slowly opened his eyes as he lay on the wet road. Dazed and bloodied, he slowly attempted to stand with fire now in his eyes as brain matter covered his face.

"You bastards!" McCann yelled.

But before McCann could swear revenge for the murder of an injured, unarmed teenager, a huge explosion tore apart the home he'd just come from. McCann quickly jumped to his feet, spun around and began to run toward it. But he couldn't escape the barrage of bullets and was knocked to the ground a second time as the soldiers surrounded their kill. From behind one of the commandos, Tetley slowly appeared, grabbed the soldier's rifle, raised it high so as to be as conspicuous as possible, then brought it down hard onto McCann's head.

CHAPTER 2

RILEY WAS ALWAYS GRUMPY after an international flight. He never slept, was always dehydrated, looked like crap, had a three day old beard that was more grey than brown, and his ass was so numb, he could barely feel it when he stood up.

The only glimmer of hope, Riley thought, was there had been no terrorists on board or any bomb threats… this time. He never underestimated his luck and if he were to ever take it for granted, he knew the pooch would be thoroughly screwed.

As Riley rose from his middle seat, or *the coffin* as he called it, he stretched his stiff and throbbing back and knees, reached up to retrieve his laptop bag from the overhead bin, then suddenly caught a glimpse of something heavenly.

A few rows ahead was a gorgeous redhead that was newly tanned, freckles and all, and at an optimal breeding age. An evil grin spread across Riley's lips.

Slyly, he sidled up a few folks behind the redhead as he pretended to check for new texts on his iPhone. That's odd, he thought, a young beauty not glued to her Crackberry. What was wrong with this one? Afterall, he was a crazy magnet, and as yet, no *red flags* were flying. Riley was getting a little insulted as she hadn't yet felt his magnetism and turned to look his way. Okay, Plan B. He began to gently push his way through the crowd waiting to disembark, but realized quickly he wasn't going anywhere. Shit, a mass of Asian tourists. This could seriously fuck up his day. Riley knew he and his fellow Americans were considered amateurs when dealing with crowd control by meager Western standards. The sheer number of people that your average Asian had to deal with on any given day in Tokyo, Hong Kong, or Taipei was mind-boggling. From Riley's face, it looked as though he had long known they were better at advancing through blockades of human flesh and could always get away with it by smiling and ignoring everyone completely.

"Have a nice a trip," a male flight attendant said to the striking redhead, yet seemingly more interested in Riley's approach. Riley peered his eyes as to just make out his name badge: Tim Kesick.

"Y'all watch your step, now," he continued. As Riley got closer, the male flight attendant straightened up, partly perhaps because Riley may have reminded him of his father in some way, and, it seemed, partly to impress. This passenger was one of Tim's favorite eye-candy, but Riley had other ideas as he was chasing different prey.

"Thank you for flying with us, Mr. Riley!" Tim said beaming in anticipation there would be a reaction.

"Take it easy, Timmy!" Riley said as he lightly smacked the steward's shoulder as men do. Riley flew a lot, and although he wasn't gay, the pink mafia loved his ass. And Riley had NO problem with that. This kind of acknowledgment meant better meals, more pillows and the occasional upgrade. It paid to be nice.

"Oh well," Tim sighed to Margaret, his colleague, "I didn't get the tickle, but I got the slap this time!" Margaret gave him a disapproving look then broke out in laughter.

The redhead had just begun her stride up the jet way when Riley saw his chance. An older woman had dropped her purse and, as protocol dictated, someone would have to help her -- someone, but not Riley.

A bottle-neck was just beginning to form when Riley, like a Dale Earnhart, Jr. or any decent NASCAR driver, faked right, then juked left and slid his ass hard against the left hand rail to pass--checkered flag! Still, momentary guilt struck the lapsed Catholic hard.

What the hell am I doing? Riley thought to himself. *I've got a girl back in D.C. I can't be chasing skirt, especially with my track record.* He'd once been accused of being a sex-addict by an old girlfriend, but Riley knew he was just horny, all the time. Maybe it was just abnormally high testosterone levels. *Whatever.*

Nope, she's just a cute girl, no reason to -- he suddenly remembered he had a pair of balls and quickly changed his thought process. *Hey, I travel hundreds of days a year, and hell, I may be no Tiger Woods, but this is Los Angeles, damn it. He had to justify it to himself. After all, a man may be simple, but Goddamn it, we have needs.*

Riley burst out of the tunnel, into the terminal rotund and merged with the mass exodus toward baggage claim.

"She's got to be at the escalator," he chanted his mantra like some brainless Jihadist thumbing his prayer beads before a suicide attack.

The luggage carousels were in a sequence separated by glass doors and when looking down the line, reminded Riley of widened train cars. He scanned the entire area in baggage claim one, then briskly walked to two, and then walked all the way to where his flight ultimately dumped their packs.

A crowd had already gathered around each carousel, and Riley's patience was wearing thin, as he had not yet reacquired his target. *She's my new muse*, he thought.

He arrived at his spot, strode up, took point, then stood shocked as he saw the same group of Asians he had already passed waiting patiently for their bags. *How the fuck did they get here before me?* Feeling a combination of dejection and exhaustion, Riley propped himself up against a concrete column as he knew he was in for a long wait.

Slowly, his chest deflated and he began to relax for the first time since Banda Aceh. Whether it was the fact that he was finally back on U.S. soil, or that he could temporarily forget about the Post-Traumatic Stress he'd been suffering from his last assignment South of the Border. Either way, Riley just took it all in. *Phew*, he exhaled a long breath.

His eyes took inventory as he scanned the airport terminal. *Look at them all, he pondered.* White, Black, Asian, European, Croatian, African, that guy's definitely Venezuelan or at least Brazilian with that metro walk. *Salwar kameez, sarees, that burka looks scary and that one, whoa, there was some serious inbreeding in that family.*

Nowhere else in the world, Riley thought, *has such real diversity... nowhere.* He'd been to Paris, Cairo, Cape Town, Sophia, you name it, Riley covered it, and the U.S., particularly L.A., was the *real* melting pot of the world.

As Riley stood uncharacteristically transfixed, almost hypnotized, a sweet voice suddenly ripped him from his daze.

"Oh, I'm terribly sorry to bother you, but could you tell me if this is the luggage roundabout for flight Double 3-7?"

From over his shoulder, Riley turned to see none other than the redhead he'd been stalking.

"Yeah… I mean, yes, this one's for flight 337."

Riley stuttered a bit like a schoolboy caught staring too long at his sixth grade teacher's angora sweater. He knew he had to recover and recover fast. The redhead was shorter than Riley, but not by much which meant she was strikingly tall and slender. She was right up Riley's alley, which, surprisingly, wasn't hard to be, if you had breath in your lungs and a nice pair of tits. She had crystal-blue eyes, sparkling white teeth and smiled so genuine and meaningful, Riley knew right off she was no L.A. native.

As he raced for a strategy, he leaned forward, but lost his balance, grabbing her shoulder to catch himself. *Shit! Now I've got pervert written all over my face*, he thought.

"Ah, you're grand, just grand," she said in a fine Irish lilt. *Huh?* Slowly, another sly, tightly controlled smile emerged on Riley's face because now, this was his house.

"You're Irish - hmm, and by the accent, I'd say Northern, maybe Antrim, The Derry – no it's gotta be Belfast." He knew she couldn't be from Dublin as Northerners said good or fine, but never grand.

Yet something told Riley this girl was from the North of Ireland. The redhead arched her back and seemed momentarily shocked.

"You've a good ear, yes, Belfast." Riley's brow narrowed like a cat that was about to eat a canary. His renewed confidence caused him to stand up a little taller, straighten his neck, and extend his hand.

"Riley: Terrance Francis Xavier, but my friends call me Terry." If he'd had any, that is. Riley's smile became a weird mix of player, predator, and shades of pedophile.

"Terry Riley, is it? Well I'd say you've got more than a touch of Erin in you."

"Guilty," Riley retorted. "And you are...?"

A slight flush came to her cheeks. "My father always told me not to talk to strangers," she said playfully. Confusion is a dark cloud and it was about to rain down on Riley. *Was this fine young lass flirting?*

"Sorry, Ciara O'Malley," she said laughingly, "It's K-I-R-A with a 'C,' but Americans seem to want to pronounce my spelling as S-I-E-R-R-A for some reason." Riley nodded, knowing the distinction.

There's a middle and confirmation name in there somewhere, but I don't know you well enough, do I, Mr. Riley?" Riley winced in pain. Ouch, she'd dropped the dreaded *Mister* like a brick on his foot. Sure she was ravishing, a bit out of his league and fifteen, no ten, ten-years younger, but pulling the "mister" card, well that was simply uncalled for. Riley looked around for an official. Penalty on the play: *Un-sportsman-like conduct.*

"Please, I told you, call me Terry." *Change direction*, Riley. "So what's a Belfast beauty doing flying to L.A. from Asia, anyway?" Riley continued. "Lounging with the boyfriend on the beach in Bali, perhaps?"

Ciara decided she liked this Riley fellow and, although his flirtations were redundant by no means subtle, she decided to play along with this curious man-child. He looked harmless enough, a little hangdog, but had a puppy-like desperation to him that very few women could resist.

"Well, Terry, isn't that just a clever way to find out if I'm involved or not?" *Busted. Man, I am off my game,* Riley cringed.

"No, it was no luxury vacation, I can assure you," Ciara continued. "I've just come back from Sumatra." Slowly the look on Riley's face changed.

"Oh, Man, that was tragic, I'm coming back from there myself. All that death, and the children..." Riley shuttered, momentarily forgetting his carnal goals. "I think the latest death toll was something like 252,000." Riley scratched his chin attempting the mental math.

"258,000!" Ciara corrected. "All those gentle people wiped away in minutes. It's a great shame... the third killer Tsunami in five years." She made the sign of the cross against her chest, kissed her thumb, and she blessed herself. Riley, of course remained focused on her chest.

Damn it, Riley thought, *I'm off balance again, okay recover, recover.* "Were you there already and got caught up in it?" Ciara dug into her rucksack. It was no Louis Vuitton purse, but it seemed to suit her personality. She retrieved a large pink leather document holder and opened it for Riley's inspection. On one side was her weathered Northern Ireland passport under a dingy plastic cover. On the opposite side, a certification read: RED CROSS DISASTER RELIEF WORKER in red letters with the ubiquitous Red Cross Symbol against a white background. A folded slip of paper slid out and Ciara caught it before it fell to the ground.

"Red Cross, huh? You must've been in the thick of it?" Riley commented. Ciara exhaled "I was in Java distributing rice when the tsunami hit, so I hopped an EVAC transport to Siberut, and made my way down to Southwest Sumatra.

"I haven't been home in over a year," she said, suddenly realizing. *Jesus,* Riley thought, *he hadn't been home in a while, but it had only been about six weeks this trip.* He presupposed she really needed someone to comfort her, or at least buy her a hot meal.

Ciara seemed happy to have the attention of a man who had experienced the same horrors she had and seemed actually interested in what she had to say. Too long had she suffered fools and boys from her town, and the Indonesians were too polite and in tragic circumstances to ever make a pass. She sometimes felt she was sacrificing her youth for the good of others.

"And you, Terry? Inspecting the massage parlors of the Philippines, I'd expect," she laughed. Flirting always caught Riley by surprise, a hangover of being a guilt-ridden Catholic who never seemed worthy of praise. But this kind of flirtation was fun. Irish girls had no fear of throwing it out there -- that was a fact. They blew away their American counterparts, as they would have a conversation with any man: fat or thin, as it was all part and parcel of their Matriarchal culture.

"No. No massage parlors, nothing like that. Don't drink anymore and skanky, postulant Typhoid Marys aren't exactly my cup of tea," He chuckled, well, that may have been a lie. Riley pulled out his new blue U.S. passport, opened it and faced his WASHINGTON POST PRESS CREDENTIALS her way. "I was in China doing research for an article on illegal immigration into the U.S. when I heard the news, so I made my way to Seoul, caught a C17 with the *Devil dogs*, and ended up near where you were to cover the tragedy."

Ciara smiled, "Are we off the record, Terry, or are you trying to interview me for a story?" she toyed "Or maybe I'll end up as one of your numerous, nameless sources?"

Was she succumbing to the infamous charms of Riley? He took a chance and pulled a business card from his wallet, the special ones with a green dot on them that had his unlisted cell phone number. Not the ones for politicians and dignitaries, these cards were reserved for the secretaries, White House kitchen staff, and wayward Irish lasses.

"Look, I'll be in L.A. for a few days if you're in need of shelter -- I'm completely discreet, you know!" Riley was really working it now as Ciara smirked. "Why don't we get a cup of coffee and talk about Ireland?"

Ciara hesitated, afterall she was really quite shy, but the long flight, the exhaustion and the anticipation of seeing Southern California just broke down her defenses. "I'm a tea-drinker, Terry," she said coyly, "but sure."

A loud blast from an air horn above them announced the upcoming luggage dump as the yellow alert light flashed a warning to all the passengers the carousel was about to spin. Riley tried again to be cute and interesting, but the sound of the conveyor combined with the alarm drowned out his quips.

The two smiled one last smile at each other, then Ciara crossed over to the other side to fetch her bags. She turned one last time to throw Riley a farewell wave. *Maybe she'll call -- it could happen.* Suddenly, Riley's ringer App burst, sounding like a bell on an old rotary phone.

"Yeah," Riley chirped into the receiver after being wrenched back from *Never Never Land* and thrust into work mode.

"Riley?" the voice on the other line said.

"Yup!" he retorted.

"I'm pregnant!" the voice blurted out before he could say another word.

Riley ran to conveyer, grabbed his luggage from the carousel, made his way upstairs to the ticket counter on the top level and bit his lip at the notion of doing it all again. He raced to the ticket counter where a line was about to form, stepped to the uniform-clad counter agent, purchased another air ticket, and ran to the outer gates to catch the next flight back to the District of Columbia

He would never have coffee with Ciara, or ever see her again for that matter. Afterall Riley would just be a piece of Ciara O'Malley's recent memory and, afterall, this was her story.

CHAPTER 3

LONG, FILTHY FINGERNAILS SCRATCHED at a lice-ridden beard to quell the itching. The old, stained, frayed tick pillow had long since lost its case and, from the looks of it, had been passed down from prisoner to prisoner for the past fifty years. The man's oily matted hair reached half way down his back. It stuck to his sweaty skin as he tossed and turned on the rust-covered springs of his makeshift bunk.

The man's eyelids fluttered as his mind reviewed miserable days gone by. His dreams always seemed worst at dawn when his sleep was deepest. Sadly, he could never get resolution to the tragic storyline that looped through his head every time he closed his eyes.

A familiar, and gut-wrenching banging began outside of his cell. A normal man would've jumped out of his skin at the atomic pounding of a guard's baton on steel jail doors, but after a decade, he'd gotten used to the traumatic sounds.

"Get yer lazy arse up, convict!" the menacing guard shouted in a gruff Belfast voice.

"On yer feet." A second guard flanked the first as he nodded down the line for the jailer to open the door. The bolt clunked automatically and released as the man, still half-asleep, swung his legs sideways and jumped to the floor.

Although Ulster Irish Republican Army prisoners were ordered to wear orange jumpsuits, which added indignity, because that was the color of their sworn enemies, his clothes, like his comrades were mere tattered rags with filth blunting the color. These IRA volunteers had always been defiant, choosing to ignore prison garb as a rejection of their criminal characterization and forcing their captures to treat them as they saw themselves: *political prisoners*. The man's tatters hung on him like dirty strips of machine shop cloth sewn together, ragged and rough and looked as if it hadn't been washed in years: a prison violation overlooked by the guards all too happy to keep their wards as uncomfortable as humanly possible.

The visual combination of homeless dumpster-diver and grizzled gold miner was not nearly as startling as the stench of his body odor that preceded him. He bent one knee slightly so as not to pass out from military-style attention, then turned to face the wall as he had a thousand times before, stopping six inches from his nose. One didn't dare eye a guard or *screw,* as they were known. This had been a hellhole like Long Kesh Prison or the Maze, but now simply a crumbling structure filled with ghosts ready for *re-purposing.* And whether you were a political prisoner or one of the world's worst criminals, the guards ruled the roost here -- period.

The jail door opened and the two guards entered in uniform fashion. The lead screw orated like an academy drill sergeant. "Michael Ruairí McCann, today you are to be released from your incarceration pending all documentation, are you aware of this?" The guard robotically relayed as if done a hundred times a day. McCann nodded slightly. Suddenly, he heard a chink as four long lengths of chain dropped from the second guard's hand and fell hard to the floor. This was the noise McCann hated most. The chains. Would he be beaten again with them, or perhaps strangled until he was unconscious, only to then be revived, then throttled over and over again?

"You know the drill, convict." McCann knelt to the ground, raised his arms up over to his skull, then interlaced his fingers, placing his hands on the back of his head. McCann wondered if he'd get a last baton beating across his haunches or jammed in the kidneys until he pissed blood as they had done some many times over the years.

Either way, he was used to the pain. He learned he could control it through sheer will power. His pain was his penance, he welcomed it, even accepted it willingly.

The second guard approached and stepped between his legs, spreading them with his feet. McCann felt the click and the familiar clasp of the leg iron. Next, the guard grabbed his right wrist from behind, but surprisingly, didn't swing it hard behind his back. McCann felt the cuffs snap onto his wrist then the broad leather belt wrap around his waist. The guard ran a short length of chain through a large eyehole in the center of the belt, then locked up the left wrist.

"Jesus Sarge, he reeks!" the second guard said as he held in a dry heave.

"Breathe through your mouth," the first guard retorted. The waft of body odor permeated like a force field around McCann's body. It was true McCann stunk like animal, as that is what he had become in this zoo–an animal. He cared not for himself, he merely ate, and drank and slept, and repeated the process day in and day out for over ten long years. He often wondered if he'd even had a soul left.

"It's not our problem anymore," the first guard said. "Our little terrorist is being let go, hopefully this time, he'll blow himself up and we'll all be rid of the cunt! On yer feet, convict."

McCann complied and walked between the guards out and onto the gangway of the parapet. As they marched him down the length of the third floor cellblock, a burst of cheers erupted. This man seemed to be special to the others, even if he didn't see it in himself.

The elevator bell shocked McCann's senses as the car came to a halt. Exiting the secure lift, the guards led McCann into a dimly lit corridor. The scent of mildew hung like rotting potatoes in the basement level, but in this part of Ireland, it was just the way it was and had been for over a thousand years.

After so many years of incarceration, McCann looked like a scraggily yeti or something out of an Asian horror movie. He was lean, sinewy, and gaunt from malnutrition and lack of vitamin D sunlight offers, yet he still had piercing green eyes that had once labeled him handsome. It was difficult taking a regular stride as the shackles weighed heavy on his legs and waist. Osteoarthritis had set into every cracked joint and fissure his bones had suffered from the years of torture, and the dampness of Northern Ireland never helped his condition and prolonged his anguish.

He had limited mobility and the only thought of making a dash for it, would be reserved for an action hero in an American movie. Everyone knew that only happened in Hollywood. It was no wonder the prisoner's favorite movie was *The Great Escape*.

The three men approached a door that read: GUARD'S SMOKING LOUNGE. The guards stopped and flanked McCann as the first knocked. A small peephole in the door opened to expose the thick wire-messed window as the inside guard peered out.

"Right!" the guard on the inside said as he quickly closed the viewing port and with a loud thunk, releasing the slide bolt.

The door opened slowly and the guard inside looked McCann up and down, "I'll take it from here, Sergeant." The two escorts snapped their heels together, released McCann from their custody, turned, and marched back down the hall.

McCann raised his gaze to see a room he'd never been in before. Still careful not to look into the screw's eyes, he wondered *why he was here, not daring to believe for a second they were actually going to release him.* He scanned the room through the greasy strips of peppered hair that dangled in front of his face.

It was a large and luxurious room with leather couches, plasma televisions, snack machines, even a cappuccino maker. This was a room unlike any he'd seen in a long time. A stark contrast from the six by eight he'd called home since before the millennium.

The inside guard led McCann deeper into the room, then passed him off to another man. The man was another prisoner, a large, enforcer-type who spoke to McCann in Gaelic, the real language of the Irish people.

"Conas atá tú?" he said in deep, ancient Irish. "How've you been keep'n, then Mick?" McCann tilted his head to see his mate Joey Costello, an old neighbor from the Belfast projects he'd grown up in.

"Mick, me boy!" a booming voice called out at the other end of the room, jarring McCann's ears to the point of pain. "Today's your lucky day!"

The bellowing salutation came from a gorilla named was Frank O'Malley and, although a fellow political prisoner, Frank was no con -- he was the prize hen. Frank O'Malley was the de facto general of a radical arm of the IRA. So radical in fact, that even *Sinn Fein*, the political arm of the IRA, refused to allow them a name, let alone authorize their actions.

He was a giant of a man with a head on him like a lion, twice the size of most. Although he had been born in the West of Ireland, he'd emigrated as a young lad when his father took work in the North, but that was short-lived. And, like many born in Tralee, he'd come from hardened stock as County Kerry was a place so primitive, so traditional, electricity wouldn't arrive until the late 1960's. Less than one generation of Kerry-men had ever seen a modern luxury.

Frank stood from behind a long table where two other lieutenants sat protecting him. Their arms were covered with dull green prison ink; clovers, the *Free State* Republic of Ireland flag, homemade tattoos the prisoners would design for each other. Jaundiced from poor nutrition, drug abuse or both, they kept their yellowed, Hep-C eyes tight on McCann like anacondas. They knew his reputation, and because of that respected him. But there was a healthy amount of fear that accompanied their suspicions and for good reason.

Frank was sharply dressed and looked like his suit had been tailored specifically for that morning. It was a far cry from what the other prisoners wore. Somehow, Frank was exempt from prison rules or the other IRA volunteer codes. How could a prison inmate get special treatment like that? Frank gestured for him to come closer. McCann dragged slowly from foot to foot as he strained.

"Jesus Christ, Smitty, leg-irons? What the fuck are you lot doing to my boys?" Frank shouted at the guard.

"Sorry, Mr. O'Malley, you know, release day and all, the warden likes to make a statement," Smitty said contrite and embarrassed, not wanting to piss-off his sideline employer. "I've got the key right here."

With that, he ran around McCann, bent down on one knee and quickly released all the handcuffs and shackles to free him. "Will just do the handcuffs when he leaves, sir." McCann glared to Smitty, but it was in appreciation, not scorn – McCann's social skills had been lacking.

"Right, Smitty, give us a few minutes, would ya?" Frank smiled, then looked at Joey. "Here's a little something for you and yer little ones, just a thanks for not being a total arse-hole to the lads like them others... oh, and hit the box on your way out." Joey pulled out wad of blue and white, sliver watermarked Euros from his pocket and handed it to the guard. A surprised look came over him as he bowed, turned and flipped the toggle of an old World War II era radio, and made his way out of the door, leaving McCann and the others alone in the lounge with orchestral music filling the room.

"Sorry about all the *cloak & dagger* stuff, Mick, obviously the screws are still getting their digs in until yer outside the gates." Frank gestured to Joey for a cigarette. "Fuck all that, another half hour you'll be a free man." Warily McCann stood peering at Frank through his that hair still covered his face like a banshee. He knew Frank was up to something, *but what?* This wasn't a simple *Atta-Boy, thanks for taking one for the team, well done and on your way.* Frank had an agenda. Frank always had an agenda.

Slowly, as if he'd just pulled the scab off a fresh wound, McCann began to speak, "Get to the point, sir!"

"Ah for fuck's sake, Mick! Don't call me, sir, we're partners, you and me." McCann stood like a statue as Frank could see he had to acquiesce. "Alright, we need a favor -- I need a favor," Frank said sheepishly.

"I'm through with the organization and I'm through with this place," McCann said finding his speech pattern again. "That's why they call it freedom!"

"This has nothing to do with *The Cause*, you've done your bit, ya did it with great sacrifice and yer a hero to yer country -- this is a personal favor to me." Frank paused. "It's probably nothing, but I just can't take a chance, not with her."

McCann took a step forward, "I've no more time to give to your favors!"

Frank interrupted, "It's Ciara, Ciara, my daughter." McCann stopped, stood straighter and sought the memory of her name in his head like a lost child in a dark primeval forest. He thought hard as he searched the cobwebs of his mind, trying to reconnect synapses that had long suppressed the memories of his past.

"Ciara?" "You remember, your God-daughter," Frank expounded, hoping that would shake McCann from his long sleep. "She's been abroad and I haven't seen her in years." McCann was still not impressed, so Frank continued, "she's heading to Los Angeles and I need to make sure she makes it back here safe. With all the *Peace Treaty* bollocks, anyone could do anything to her and say it was justified, you know, to spite me and all."

McCann tried to make sense of what Frank was really saying. "You're being paranoid, Frank, if she's in America, she couldn't be in a safer place."

Frank took umbrage with the comment. "Paranoid? You're the last person I ever thought I'd hear say that! It ain't paranoia when they're really after ya, is it?" The other men in the room nodded in agreement. Frank tried to calm himself, as he knew he had a long history of having a hair-trigger and he really needed McCann of this mission. "Listen, I've made all the arrangements, what I want you to do is keep an eye on her, that's it! I'm gonna help ya ease back into the world after yer time here in hell. Consider it a *life do-over*, or least a well-deserved vacation in the sun. That's all I'm askin'!"

McCann swept his hair away from his face and began to raise his voice for the first time in years, "Is there something wrong with your hearing, Frank? I said, no and I mean no!" His Belfast Irish was really roaring out now. McCann turned on his heel and looked surprisingly limber for a man of his appearance. Suddenly, Frank erupted and charged at McCann, he had one last chance.

"Murphy's in L.A.!" Frank shouted as he came around to his front. Hearing this, McCann stopped dead in his tracks.

"That's fucking low, even for you, Frank! Murphy and Hammer died in the explosion, along with everyone else. I read the report… I was there!" Frank nodded to Joey for reinforcement. A sly grin stretched Joey's lips.

Joey, one of Frank's lieutenants, stood, opened a dirt-stained manila file and handed it McCann, exposing a number of black and white photos. "We've just found out ourselves. We couldn't take a chance on anyone else knowin', although he's not try'n to keep it any kind of fuck'n secret, is he, the bastard?!" Frank's face began to turn red as though he was going to erupt again.

McCann, still stunned, questioned to himself, "Murphy… alive?" The imagery flooded his mind and wrote itself like a novel all over his face.

Frank had his answer. He knew he'd have to drive home the deal in order for McCann to commit fully. "I bet you've a lot of questions to ask him, well I do too! Like who the fuck ratted you out to the Brits that morning and what happened to all that money you were carrying for us? It took three years of fund-raising to make up the loss and countless transport schedule changes."

McCann took offense at this. "You don't think? No, not Murphy, he's no rat and he'd NEVER steal from the I-R-A."

Frank lowered his eyes and said calmly, "We don't know for sure, all we know is that he's fuck'n alive and we heard neither hide nor hair from the cunt in over 10 years." Frank approached McCann closely and lowered his voice. "You'll have to find out the truth." Frank turned back toward the table and paced. "Quite the entrepreneur, our Murph's become, a real American success story. I've arranged for Ciara to meet some friends at his place for a pint. I want you to go there and just keep an eye on her, keep her out of trouble-like, you know – it'll be the easiest mission you've ever worked."

Raising a finger into the air, Frank pointed to the dingy, yellow-stained fluorescent lights above the men. He then gestured with his other hand and put his index finger to his lips as a Brahms violin concerto rolled over them like a warm blanket. His facial expression told McCann that the room was bugged. "I don't need to tell you who'll be interested in knowing that piece of information."

McCann pondered the situation in light of the new developments. The look on his face, what little you could see of it, was a mixture of confusion, consternation, and anger. He knew now he'd once again be doing the work, the dirty work, for Frank O'Malley.

Frank's timing was always impeccable; it seemed to be his gift. With literally minutes to freedom, McCann was now being dragged back into his clutches.

"Now, let's get down to business," Frank began as if he were running his fingers down a list. "The boys will meet you outside the gates, take you somewhere to get ya cleaned up, and Jesus, you need some deadly cleaning. They'll get ya a proper cup of tea, then it's straight the airport." Frank winked at McCann. "Don't worry, brother, we've sorted everything out for ya, and you'll want for nuthin'!"

But before Frank could put the final nail in McCann's coffin, he balked. "I don't know about this, Frank?" Frank's easy Irish demeanor suddenly took a turn, a turn that many of his enemies had probably witnessed, right at their end.

"Fer fuck's sake, Mick, it's not like you're going home to anything. The I-R-A-'s the only family you've got and Ciara's the only family I've left. You're her godfather, and don't you forget that! That still means something around here." Frank's blood pressure was escalating to an obviously dangerous level. Frank looked around the room at all the intimidated faces, all but McCann's.

"Besides, with all this amnesty business, I'll be out any day now meself, and finally get to hug me wee lass again. I want," Frank corrected himself; "I <u>need</u> you to do this one last thing for me, Mick. She's my little girl." Frank said, not as a military officer, but with the surprising candor of a concerned father.

CHAPTER 4

A STREAM OF NEW ARRIVALS at the Tom Bradley International Terminal at LAX filed down the escalators and queued into the Immigration & Naturalization lines. U.S. Customs, ICE and TSA agents waited patiently, bored to tears, as the next round of émigrés approached. "Next in line!" echoed collectively from each stall.

Ciara happily walked nearer to the Custom's desk one step at a time, her ginger hair flowing with each bounce. She'd been swept up in the exodus approaching the check in stations and had a lingering sensation from the endorphin rush of flirtation with Riley. She'd never felt this way about an older man. But now it was back to business and the plans ahead for the little ones. She smiled at the sudden thought that this might very well be one of the best days of her life.

U.S. Customs agent Viola Williams was heavy-set, post menopausal, and sported the ambiguous asexual cropped hairdo as a badge of honor. She was black, had an attitude, and lived just from up the road in Inglewood. But Viola was the top ICE agent at LAX, a feared, yet respected colleague, and the bane of any in-bound tourist. She took no guff, couldn't care less about your measly life and was a hard-ass in the truest sense. There was no need for Viola to follow the letter of the law as she was the instrument of it and the purest form of *gray area* decision-making the United State's front line had.

As Viola finished her intense interview of a Pakistani traveler, she drew her brown eyes narrow, flipped his passport shut, then sternly handed it back to the man. She held the intense gaze of a python and seemed to lull her victims into a paralytic state of fear.

Without looking up, Viola snapped her fingers and threw up her hand, "Next! Next in line! Come on!" The shrill sound of her voice jolted Ciara awake from her trance-like state as she watched Ferrari after Lamborghini drive past the glass doors just beyond the terminal doors. Ciara hesitantly, but subserviently smiled as she approached the desk and handed Viola her Northern Irish passport.

"Business or pleasure?" Viola rattled off as she had done literally millions of times before.

"Excuse me, Miss?" Ciara said in a soothing Irish lilt.

Viola was in no mood for ignorance. "Have you come to Los Angeles on *business* or *pleasure*?" she barked sharply.

Now under Viola's hypnotic leer, Ciara suddenly remembered something. She pulled out the colorful official visa from her bag. Viola snatched it quickly like a frog's tongue catching a fly and began to peruse it in detail. Slowly, her hard edges began to melt and a real person emerged. "A bit of both, I expect," Ciara answered.

"It says here you're leading a group of orphan refugees?" Viola stood slightly in her chair to peek over the field of travelers. "I don't see any children, where are they?"

Ciara fumbled her words, "Yes, I mean no, Miss. I've come ahead to attend to the arrangements."

Viola was now inquisitive. "*The Tsunami Orphan's Project*?" Ciara smiled every time she heard those words, as she knew the children were going to be safe in their new homes.

"We're to bring nearly 100 children to live with host families here. They're <u>so</u> excited to see America," Ciara said with a sudden surge of joy, then playfully lowered her voice, "... and frankly, so am I."

Since Viola's conversation was now cutting into her usual *churn-n-turn*, a crowd was beginning to gather behind her station. But Viola was intrigued with this precious young woman and, if she'd had two cups of coffee, would have invited Ciara to sit and chat like two girlfriends.

"You're one of them Catholic nuns or a Mormon missionaries, aren't you, honey? Viola said smiling, exposing perfectly white, flossed teeth.

"Oh, Heavens, no! I'm just a volunteer. I wouldn't take a dime to this work, it means so much to so many people." Viola tilted her head as if to ask for more explanation. "I feel it's my duty and now I have a chance to bring them here, to be safe." A tear began to form in the corner of her eye. "Those children wouldn't have a hope in heaven if it weren't for the kindness of your families here, ya know? No one else in the world has stepped forward to help them," she said matter-of-factly. "And for that, I'm truly grateful to you."

Viola nodded her head slightly, "Girl, I know what you mean. I volunteer for my church in Atwater Village and if we weren't doin' it, who the hell would?"

Suddenly, just behind Ciara, an agitated man rocked back and forth on his heels. He shook his head in frustration and yelled into his cell phone, all the while chomping on an eviscerated cigar butt. He was the quintessential Hollywood wanna-be with no concern for decorum and completely devoid of class.

"I don't care what Cameron says, I need $300 million for it to work. 3-D? I'd don't give shit if it's in 5-D, I can't do it for less than $300 million!"

Viola looked over Ciara to gaze at the man, but Ciara hadn't noticed him, "How can you not care, they're just wee little children, aren't they!" Viola reached out and patted Ciara's hand. Obviously touched by this woman, she was not afraid to show it.

Suddenly the man behind Ciara slapped his phone into its holster and focused his frustration on Ciara and Viola. This was not a smart move. "For God's sake, come on already. Unlike you people, I do have life, you know!" the man yelled, startling everyone in the queue. The business travelers always used Viola because she was quick and by-the-book. But they also knew she never, ever, took any crap. This guy was toast.

Ciara lowered her eyes apologetically, but Viola was having none of that. "Shut your impatient hole!" Viola shouted at his rudeness.

"Sorry to take so much of your time, Ma'am," Ciara contritely said. Viola took her large silver-polished plunger and began stamping all of Ciara's documents.

"God bless you, baby! You have a wonderful time her in L.A. and if you need anything, any help with those babies, I mean anything at all, you call here and ask for Viola, that's me, they'll put you right through!" Viola yelled across the sea of custom's desks, "Shanikwa, let this sweet baby go on through." Ciara melted Viola with one last smile as she nearly bowed, then walked ahead.

The agitated man goose stepped forward and threw his bags down hard to the ground in frustration while giving Viola a dirty look. "Jesus Christ, lady, let's just do this thing, already."

But before the man could get out another word, Viola snarled, "You disrespected Viola, and now you're gonna pay, Motherfucker! Strip Search!" Viola bellowed. Suddenly, two monstrous Custom's agents appeared behind the man to carry out Viola's orders. The color immediately drained from his face.

Viola smiled devilishly and said, "Gentlemen, drag this son-of-a-bitch into interview room one, and bend him over the table... I'll be doing the full body-cavity search myself." With that, she pulled out a pair of exam gloves from below her desk and a familiar thwack startled the man as she snapped the latex over her wrist.

CHAPTER 5

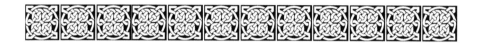

A DEEP PRIMAL CRY EMANATED from the monster's deep dungeon-like cave *as he roared.* The guttural utterances echoed as they resonated off the concrete walls. The beast was in pain.

A group of men jabbed and zapped a long cattle prod again and again deep into the dense forest of fur hitting flesh each time. They stood around laughing as they toyed with the ferocious animal knowing the exact length of steel chain, having drawn lines on the floor to make sure they never got too close to the claws that, with one swipe, could lop their limbs off.

Alexei Rostov laughed with a demonic snarl as Oleg Rostov, a smaller, uglier, and punier version of his brother slobbered his food. "Hit him again, A-lexi-a-vich!" Oleg blurted out as he shoveled Chinese noodles into the hole in his face. His Russian accent had not diminished one iota since leaving the motherland decades before. Oleg turned and laughed like a court jester as the other men followed in lock step.

Alexei's gang was comprised of thugs, enforcers, and ne'er-do-wells from all over Russia, Ukraine, Georgia, every rat hole he could find them in. They'd all grown up poor, hungry, and neglected, yet would gladly lay down their pathetic lives for their psychotic leader.

Conversely, Alexei and Oleg were sadists. They were rich, spoiled and void of any conscience either collective or individual.

They sought out short-term gratification like a junkie with ADD and ratcheted up the evil with each new victim. Their father and patriarch, Victor Rostov, had indulged them, brought them up with cold, emotionless feelings, but wanting for nothing. They were what true sociopaths with grandiose narcissism aspired to be. Alexi zapped the beast again.

Ursus arctos middendorffi was the wretched victim du jour. The poor animals fate was sealed the day Victor Rostov bought him from a black market smuggler specializing in endangered Alaskan grizzlies.

As a youth, Alexei had begged his father to get him a bear after seeing one on an obscure television program about nature. He had grown tired of cutting the heads of his toy soldiers and mutilating little girls Barbie dolls in the school yard and wanted something alive that would react to his *special treatment*. Alexei prodded the great beast again.

Rasputin was a Kodiak, the largest bear on earth. He was larger than the Polar bear, and not just any American brown bear. He stood nearly 10 feet tall when on his hind legs, weighed over 1,700 pounds, and was larger than any Alaskan grizzly ever raised in captivity. His fur was blondish brown, thick and strong as nature had built for him to survive the cold Arctic winters. His zygomatic arches, the width of his head from cheekbone to cheekbone, measured nearly 35 inches, making the size of his massive cranium bigger than most car tires. He could easily devour a full-grown man… that is, if he could just reach one.

His giant iron collar weighed heavy around his neck like a yoke and the thick, dense chain did nothing to improve his demeanor. The agitated bear began to shift from side to side near a pile of animal bones and filth. Bears were, afterall, territorial and this was Rasputin's home. He let out another roar as a warning.

Alexei stood in front of the bear, fearless, or stupid, or both. He laughed at Rasputin and taunted him with a stick as he whacked him again. Although Kodiak's have thick skin and heavy hides, a hit with a long stick stung like it would a man. He struck him again.

Rasputin let out another roar as Alexei tightened the leather wrap around his wrist that held the stick steady. Oleg and the other men were quickly tiring of this mindless game, when suddenly Alexei grabbed his video camera from a nearby table. Although it was a sickening display of animal cruelty, Alexei couldn't resist capturing it on camera to replay over and over again.

As Alexei edged forward toward Rasputin, he held a piece of raw meat in front of him as a peace offering. Rasputin hesitated for a moment, then cautiously advanced. The enormous bear began to sniff the air until he caught the scent of the meat, then and only then did he open his mouth to accept the offering. As Alexei teased him over and over again, pushing the meat closer, then pulling it away, he finally dangled it just out of Rasputin's reached. The bear came forward until the end of the chain pulled his collar backward. He was choking now trying to get at the food. Alexei zapped him once again. Rasputin flew backwards as 2,000 volts from the cattle prod shot through his body like a bullet.

Alexei, knowing he had but a brief instant, ran toward the fallen giant and zapped him again. He jumped back and watched how the second jolt caused the bear to seizure. As a result, the tortured creature's bladder opened and he urinated all over himself. Rasputin cried in pain, quickly got to his feet and stood on his hind legs. His massive frame seemed to stretch past his 10 feet height as his presence filled the entire room. Alexei's men jumped back quickly, well beyond the bear's reach, yet fearing this monster could somehow break his chains, *then what*?

Rasputin lunged at Alexei, teeth bared, fangs protruding, saliva dripping. He raised his large paws and began to swipe at the Russian, tilting and lowering his head, flattening his ears and rumbling a low roar. With only so much length, the chain pulled taut, nearly snapping the bear's neck as he charged again and again in revenge.

Alexei stuck his neck out just at the edge of the Rasputin's outer limits and smelled the foul breath. His facial expression revealed his malevolence after every violent assault on the great beast. Alexei was truly evil.

CHAPTER 6

ILES OF CONCERTINA COILED barbed wire capped the twenty-foot high stonewalls. It was not your standard, four-walled jail, but a high-tech, multi-angled modern prison that had guard towers and turrets placed strategically around, atop and across the entire compound. It was a labyrinth of stone, steel and pain.

Since it was late morning, the yard was filled to capacity with inmates playing soccer, poker, weightlifting, the usual routine of a prisoner's day.

Slowly the large iron double doors opened, as McCann was lead outside by two guards. Always a spectacle and the only ray of hope the prisoners had, they quickly began to gather at the fence as they realized it was a final farewell.

"Go get 'me, Mick!" shouted an inmate from the yard.

"Kick the shite out of them Fuckers!" another shouted.

"Send the Bastards home, Mick!"

Without looking up, McCann kept walking, nary eyeing a soul. Slowly a chorus of an old Irish song, *Our Day Will Come* rose above the yard. His comrades sang in Gaelic, like a group of altar boys, as they sent their old friend back into the world, broken, but not beaten. It was futile for the guards to attempt to stop the singing of the freedom ballad, or any formerly outlawed rebel song for that matter. They had learned long ago it would only be met with retaliation outside the prison walls, and every guard had families locally, so they looked away to keep the peace all the way around.

The air was bitterly cold, as evidence by the plume of exhaust pouring from the car as the engine ran hot as it idled for nearly an hour. The walk was long for McCann, but as he approached the final set of double doors, he could see a familiar face in a grey suit. It was Charles Tetley, and he was no friend of McCann's.

Due to new protocols, Tetley was unable to get too close to his sworn enemy. After all, Tetley had lead the Belfast raid that caught the former IRA volunteer, even though he felt no responsibility for the death of his own partner in the melee. Tetley was part of the old guard and he blamed McCann -- he blamed him for everything.

"Wherever you go, I'll be right behind you, ya murdering bastard!" Tetley half-whispered over the shoulders of the prison guards unlocking the gate. Tetley's hatred for McCann, whether misguided or valid, was not worth a suspension if the press had gotten wind of how he really felt. The United Kingdom had the most voracious and scandal-creating yellow journalists in the world, and Tetley valued his position. A position that he saw could help with a long-term plan to exact his revenge.

With his head still low, McCann refused to look up and acknowledge his old nemesis.

A long low creak of steel resounded through the air as the guard opened the outer gate. Suddenly, a burst of shouting erupted from the dozens of reporters. "McCann, will you to return to the IRA?" One reporter yelled.

"Mick, are you repentant?" another added.

"Will you honor the Peace Accord?

Will you visit your family?" Each reporter tried to get their question in at the expense of the others as they clambered over one another.

The PSNI or Police Service of Northern Ireland had been dispatched early to the prison gates in anticipation of the controversial release and were doing a fine job keeping the reporters clear of the front gates. They were used to throwing up barriers and attempting to keep the peace since the first shots of the thousand year protracted hatred were fired on *Bloody Sunday*, nearly 40 years ago.

McCann, so long conditioned, lumbered from side to side as though his shackles still cut deep into his ankles, even though he was now free from his pinnings. He peered through the forest of hair in front of his eyes as the large car doors opened and four men exited in unison to stand by McCann. As one respectfully opened the back passenger door, the others helped McCann into the vehicle. They quickly hopped in to flank McCann in the back seat and slammed the doors hard to make a statement. The men threw a glare at the prison guards, and all shared a moment of mutual hatred for each other as the cycle of hate and disrespect continued. Then, the car sped away, stopping again for nothing or no one.

Tetley, not finished with burning his image deep into his memory, followed McCann outside the prison gates and had taken a position at the barricade line. A short squelch popped as he spoke into a handheld walkie-talkie, "Keep three cars on that bastard at all times."

CHAPTER 7

PALMS IS AN AREA of West Los Angeles that is old, but still holds a lot of the charm of the 40s and 50s. South of Santa Monica, east of Venice, west of Mar Vista, and just outside the madness of L.A. proper, or as the local rental ads would have you believe, <u>Beverly Hills Adjacent</u>. Though a quaint little area, it had had its bouts with the drug induced 80s, gangs, and low-income residents, yet for the most part it was just a quiet place to retire.

A great deal of credit for Palms being a safer place of late went to Los Angeles Police Department Detective Kevin Fitzpatrick. He had purchased his smallish bungalow in the late 70s, for a fraction of it's current value, when he was still a rookie. He'd spent most of his days and nights working while investigating nothing but murders. His marriage was brief because of it.

One night, when he was actually at home about to crack a beer after a practically difficult day, a neighbor woman knocked on his doo. Ausanat Cheu-Len, a former beauty queen from Thailand whom he'd always had his eye on, stood illuminated under his non-energy efficient lit stoop and was obviously in distress. She began pleading to him for help.

It seemed a local Thai gang, known as the *Mother Phukers,* (their version of humor while paying tribute to their hometown, Phuket,) had slithered slowly into the area under Fitzpatrick's radar as his attentions were generally elsewhere. They had begun by first engaging in minor gang activity, typical for new, bored immigrant 1st Generation-ers. These low-level crimes entailed hassling people for change and rousting geriatrics at the convenient store. Next it was the odd *B&E*, where they'd pawn the stolen loot amongst each other. But lately, the *Mother Phukers* had grown harder and emboldened. It seemed, more crimes were being committed against the now predominately Asian residents and it was dangerous, not only for them, but all the residents of Palms.

Ausanat told Fitzpatrick she had a young daughter in middle school and the *Mother Phukers* had been harassing her to the point of ripping her clothes. This type of roughhousing never sat well with an *old school* detective. He knew it wouldn't be long before there was a rape or molestation. He also knew it would take an act of Congress to get a Gang Task Force into play and as it happened, in those days, they were all restricted to the federal level. But luckily Fitzpatrick was a key player in the newly formed Special Investigations Section SIS of the LAPD based right around the corner in Santa Monica.

Fitzpatrick knew how to stop these hoodlums before they took over the entire grid, so he simply asked a couple of cop buddies from his unit to come by and play poker one Saturday night under the guise of interdepartmental fraternization. This was code for the boys in blue, as they all knew it really meant *cracking some heads*!

The guys sat down for a nice evening of poker, drank some suds, shot the shit, then some time around midnight, Fitzpatrick and the others heard the clichéd screeching of tires just outside on Venice Boulevard. Next, the stereotypical shouts of intimidation, and finally, gunfire. His men slowly placed their cards on their host's poker mat: a combination tv stand, computer desk and dining room table down, checked their ammo and exited his house through the back door. They hit the alley and disbursed like a swarm of bees. By the end of that night, the Thai *Mother Phukers* were all but extinct: 27 in custody on prior warrants or trumped-up charges; three dead-the idiots that thought they could out shoot the police; and the neighborhood was back to its old peaceful setting. The word was out: *don't mess around in Palms!*

Fitzpatrick was honored, quietly and unofficially, of course by his very close brothers of the badge. He had successfully driven out the organized crime element that had reluctantly decided to relocate to a northeastern valley suburb, which was no longer his problem.

The gang members feigned victimization, accused Fitzpatrick of hatred and bias, using racism as a defense, in typical Californian style. But thankfully, the judges weren't listening that day and every *Mother Phuker* was convicted.

Fitzpatrick could only laugh at the irony: as he wasn't anti-Asian -- he was anti-everybody! And, truth-be-told, he secretly liked the fact the United States still took in the tired and weak. Afterall, he was a kid from Kansas City that had come West after a stint in the military and was fascinated by unique cultures and characters. He could speak a little of many languages and he prided himself on being able to relate to several groups of people, even if he didn't do it well. It was one of the deciding factors for him to become a cop, although these days, he hadn't felt very nostalgic. He hadn't had a decent case in years, something he could really sink his teeth into. So he spent most of his time playing *Words With Friends*, hunting for memorabilia on the internet, and taking his sister Katie's kids to see the Angeles, Ducks, Clippers, or Galaxy. He was no fair-weather sports fan -- he was a diehard fanatic, and a serious sucker for the underdogs, so Los Angeles was the perfect place.

Fitzpatrick opened his eyes from a rare deep sleep as his antiquated phone began to ring. He only seemed to get real sleep from seven to eight a.m., and had no guilt about sleeping (what he considered) late. Afterall, he'd earned it as he was on the verge of retirement.

Fitzpatrick lifted the hissing plastic nasal pillows from his nose and unstrapped the Velcro that encircled his head. He brushed back the cowlick the headgear always kicked up and smacked his tongue against the roof of his dry mouth. He flicked the six foot long copper and plastic tube off the bed and swung it, in one motion, back into it's cradle. He depressed the blue button and the unit went silent.

Fitzpatrick was a large man, north of six feet four and well over 245 pounds. He'd been diagnosed with a sever case of sleep apnea five years prior when he'd fallen asleep at the wheel and crashed his third government-issued Crown Vic. The outcome could've very well saved his life as the department forced him to take a sleep study where his malady was diagnosed, and ultimately a remedy prescribed. Since then, he dutifully crowned himself each night allowing air to be constantly forced into his sinuses through an expensive, claustrophobic, and cumbersome CPAP machine. Secretly, from the first night he used the machine, he knew it had saved his job and his life. He wasn't about to drop 40 pounds at his age, and, as long as he kept it hidden when entertaining a lady friend, which he was hoping would happen soon, he was happy to have it.

His nocturnal issues aside, Fitzpatrick was known for two things: his love of movies, and his unpleasant demeanor -- not necessarily in that order. He had gained the reputation of being a real bastard with a bad attitude during his sleep deprivation days, but even after getting better, he still got more compliance out of those who still feared him. *Why then change*? Larger than most of the cute and cuddly new breed of men in Southern California, he didn't *man-scape*, he had fists like anvils and was truly one of the last of the *old timers*. He was the kind of guy Clint Eastwood would call up to have drink. He was grumpy, he knew, but it was the one saving grace that kept him at the top of his game. And his game was about playing dirty with the filth of L.A. He had one job, and one job only that he wouldn't wish on anyone -- getting justice for the dead.

CHAPTER 8

CIARA STROLLED UP OF the terminal gangway with her luggage in tow. She could see family members waiting for loved ones to emerge from Customs. A sense of joy and relief permeated the area as parents and children rejoiced at being reunited to the point of nearly clogging up the works at the top of the ramp. Occasionally, though, people just trying to vacate the terminal or catch a cab, could walk right past the crowds unimpeded. Even the John Wayne and Marilyn Monroe impersonators LAX hired as greeters, circled the crowds, forcing openings to keep the cattle moving.

A row of black-capped limousine drivers lined the walk holding signs, some in bold black marker, others in colorful prints. Still others held placards for the pre-packaged tourist heading to their pre-ordained hotels. A handsome, salt and pepper haired man in a nicely tailored black suit held out a sign that read: CIARA O'MALLEY – RED CROSS-BELFAST.

Ciara's eyes lit up with excitement as she ran towards the man. "That's me! That's me!"

The man tipped his cap, "Miss O'Malley?" he said, just to be certain. "My name is Kenny. I'll be your driver today."

Kenny took Ciara's bags out to the curb and loaded them into the trunk of a polished ebony pearl stretch limo. As he did so, Ciara stepped out of the shadows of the terminal and let the warm Southern

California sun wash over her formerly alabaster face. When she saw just how large her transport was her eyes widened to the size of saucers. Kenny raced around to beat Ciara to the door and opened it quickly, tipping his cap once again and bid her enter.

Overwhelmed with the elegance, Ciara ran her fingers along the smooth wood finish, and the Baccarat crystal decanters and flutes. She touched every foreign-looking button that new technology had to offer.

Kenny looked into the rearview mirror. "Please help yourself to anything back there, Miss O'Malley -- it's all complimentary. Should I turn on the television for you?" Stunned Ciara shook her head yes. She was speechless.

A large dark panel slowly descended to reveal a flat-screen LED television. Ciara's mouth nearly dropped. "I haven't seen TV in so long, I can't even remember."

The deep voice of a local newscaster began at the top of the hour:

> *"Another body was found today, brutally raped*
> *and murdered, bringing the number of victims*
> *to 12. Women's groups around Los Angeles are*
> *demanding authorities step up the search for the*
> *killer..."*

Kenny's face grimaced as he suddenly realized this wasn't the kind of welcoming fare a young traveler should hear on her first trip to his city. "Sorry, miss, the news here is always glorified crap, if you pardon my French." He thought he'd better try and cover up his faux pas. He immediately turned it to a music video station.

Ciara, still uneasy at the luxury being foisted upon her, squirmed a bit in her seat. "Excuse me, sir, are you sure there's not been a mistake made here?" she asked sheepishly.

Kenny smiled as he answered, "Call me, Kenny, we're not formal here in the L.A., and no, miss, there's no mistake. A bunch of the parents got together and thought it'd be nice if you were given a little a comfort during your stay here in L.A., afterall, you've been knee-deep in it for quite a while, if you don't mind me say'n." Ciara looked around the spacious back area of the limo as Kenny continued, "First time in a limo?"

Ciara blurted out without thinking self-deprecatingly, "first time in a car with four-doors, more like!"

Kenny grinned, "In that case, just wait 'til you see the hotel."

The limo meandered through the streets and freeways of Hollywood as Kenny had been instructed to show Ciara everything worth seeing before dropping her off. As they passed under the Hollywood sign, onto Sunset Boulevard, then through the tunnel off the 10 Freeway in Santa Monica, the Pacific Ocean revealed itself in deep blue and turquoise. Ciara's mouth stayed agape the whole time.

Loews Hotel rose above the Pacific Coast Highway by at least 100 yards, quite a feat for any beachside property in Southern California. The hotel was on the *Cliffs of Erosion*, as they were known, and had some of the most spectacular views in the U.S.

The limo driver slowed as he turned into the circular drive and up to the reception area station. A cadre of valets swarmed the limousine like locusts. Momentarily caught off guard, Ciara was startled as a valet briskly opened her door and numerous hands bid her exit. Kenny jumped out and made his way through to Ciara. As the valets helped her out, she couldn't help but fantasize for a brief instance, feeling like a celebrity about to walk down the red carpet.

"You're all checked in, Miss O'Malley," Kenny said. Ciara, knowing the American custom of tipping for good service, dug into her change purse for a gratuity. Yet all she could find was the odd Indonesian Rupiah or Tiger unc coin after so long in Asia. Kenny saw what she was attempting to do and quickly stopped her. "No, Miss O'Malley, thank you, but it's all been taken care of: the room, the food and beverages and especially the tips!" Kenny looked over the valets, "And don't worry about the bellmen, they've been taken care of as well."

A few yards away, an older valet was directing three younger ones as Kenny raised his hand to get his attention. "Andrea!" Kenny shouted. The older valet popped up his head, acknowledged him, and hurried the others on their way as he immediately attended to the limo driver. Kenny took this opportunity to hand Ciara a small, decorative package.

She looked at him and smiled. "Miss O'Malley, this is the Bell Captain, Andrea… Andrea, this is Miss Ciara O'Malley."

He bowed low and gracefully, "Ah, Miss O'Malley, we take care of you bags, don't you worry about a ting!" Andrea said in a heavy Italian accent. "You go up and rest after you long journey. I gonna take care of every ting for you!" With that, he snapped his fingers and three more bellmen appeared and rushed to unload her luggage.

Kenny always got a chuckle saying Andrea's name as he used to wonder why anyone would name their son after a woman. It wasn't until he learned that Italian men have an *A* at the end of the names, unlike other cultures that place an *O* there. Still, you wouldn't see him doing that with his son.

As Ciara watched in wonder at all the fuss being made over her, tears began to flow down her face. Out of character, she suddenly leapt toward Kenny and threw her arms around his neck, kissing his cheek.

"No one has ever… I don't have the words… thank you, thank you so much!" Overwhelmed himself with her kindness, Kenny could only tip his cap, trying like hell not to well up. Andrea, knowing passion all too well, took Ciara's hand and began to lead her into the foyer like a princess.

CHAPTER 9

THE ROOM WAS DARK and the bed messed from a long nap as Ciara stepped out of the bathroom after a long, relaxing shower. Upon arrival she had found the complimentary basket filled to the brim with pristine California wines and cheeses, crackers and an assortment of fresh fruit. She donned the heavy cotton bathrobe that hung on the hook behind the door, then wrapped her wet hair in an equally thick towel.

The curtains allowed only a sliver a light to illuminate the room, but Ciara could make out the path to the bed. She had no problem navigating. The room was filled with music emanating from a small Bose unit on the nightstand and Ciara couldn't help but strut to the lively tune as she headed for the balcony. She threw open the curtains with dramatic flair as she'd seen in a movie once. The brilliant sunlight almost blinded her as her hand felt its way to the lock behind the valance. The sliding French doors were so heavy, Ciara had to pull hard to begin the momentum and move the door on its tracks like a caboose separating from a train.

Ciara stepped out onto the balcony, and the warm ocean breeze splashed over her. Her eyes opened wide as she gazed in amazement at the deep blue of the Pacific Ocean combined with the brightness of the sun. The palm trees swayed in the breeze while Ciara watched roller bladers, tourists and cruisers, peddle, skate and walk the Strand just below her window. She secretly wished to be down there with a group of friends, laughing, playing volleyball, feeling the ease and relaxation that she envisioned most Americans felt.

Her envy lasted but a brief moment. She allowed herself that. Knowing she was part of something bigger, something truly important to nearly a hundred children who would live long and privileged lives because of all her dedication and hard work. She knew that this generation of new Americans that came from tiny Sumatra would grow up safe, healthy, and happy. Sure they might end up being spoiled and eventually forget the suffering they had endured, their loss of everything, or where they'd come from, but she knew these kind-hearted Americans and they would love them as their own.

Ciara knew the love and opportunities bestowed on these children could hardly be rivaled the world over and that they would now have a great life. She thought for a moment about her own life: growing up poor in a Belfast project, her unit next to the trash containers with the stench of the filth permeating her life, thanks to Great Britain.

She thought of how her father, the biggest and most kind-hearted man she'd ever known protected her and her family from the freedom fighting dealings he was involved in. She remembered walking nervously to school with British soldiers on every corner, their automatic weapons trained, hating the duty of protecting the likes of her. Her mind raced back to the mud and rocks that were thrown at her as she walked to school through the wealthy Protestant areas and how those parents would allow their children to be cruel to them just because they were Catholic. She never understood what the difference was: we both believed in God, we both believed in Christ, we believed in almost everything, so why were they so hateful? How could the small Northern Irish minority of Protestants rule the enormous majority of native Catholics with such tyranny?

As she thought of how she grew, her country continued to suffer from The Troubles. Bombers regularly blasted local pubs, killing unsuspecting victims, while garrisons of soldiers were massacred by IRA Volunteers. She had always felt a kinship to children from broken cultures and broken worlds as Ciara felt she was broken herself -- but now she meaning, she had a purpose, and she was on the mend.

Taking one last look at a couple kissing on the giant solar-powered Ferris wheel, she sighed in joy. Ciara waltzed back into the room and over to the bureau near the bed. There, a large vase filled to capacity with red roses released an aroma she'd only experienced one other time as a child in Ireland.

She picked out the card from the center of the bouquet, it read: *Welcome to Los Angeles, Darl'n – Can't wait to see ya – Come to the club tonight & we'll catch up! Love, Danny.* The card slipped from her fingers as she threw up her arms in excitement. After retrieving it, she noticed her card file. In it was a dossier of each of her wards complete with photo and vital statistics. She smiled as she inhaled the aroma of the roses again.

Suddenly, she leapt onto the California King bed and began to scream, "Jesus, Mary, and Holy Saint Joseph, is this really happening?"

Grabbing a bottle of champagne well chilled in a sliver challis, Ciara popped the cork as champagne began to fly everywhere.

CHAPTER 10

CHAMPAGNE WAS NOW SPLASHING the leather seats and windows, everywhere except into the cheap plastic cups being held by multiple pairs of hands. The black Hummer limousine was ostentatious, enormous, and not exactly environmentally friendly, but it suited the men inside and some would say, an ironic depiction of their character.

The Humvee was packed with Alexei's men, rowdy, roaring, laughing, clamoring over each other. Suddenly one of them raised his partially filled cup of champagne for a toast.

Alexei was lean and muscular with a square jaw and sinewy features. He had a jagged scar on his forehead, a deep gash over his brow and chunk of flesh gone from his chin. His hair was dirty blonde and seemed more slimy than clean, yet none-the-less, his body was honed to a sharp edge. Although in his late thirties, he appeared much older. If first impressions told everything about a person, then Alexei Rostov was an uneasy, enigmatic, power-hungry psycho who would stop at nothing to get what he wanted. Oleg was just short and round, with dark circles under his eyes from an iron deficiency and drug abuse. He was thoroughly disgusting and sat across from his brother as the other men horsed around.

Alexei pulled a small high definition digital video camera from a satchel and began shooting his crew in action. The men, seeing this, began to flip off the camera with obscene gestures for their fifteen minutes of fame.

"Come on Alexei, put down camera!" Oleg said in his broken English. Suddenly, champagne flew from somewhere and all over Oleg. "You fucking idiot, you spilled champagne on my five thousand dollar Armani suit." Oleg lifted a large compact mirror up to his face, but realized it was now sopping wet. On the mirror was a slurry slush of an eight ball of cocaine, hundreds of dollars worth of drugs ruined.

The others scrambled to try and salvage the illegal substance as gaudy gold chains and Russian Orthodox crosses swung back and forth against tacky nylon tracksuits. Alexei just laughed at the others, as he couldn't care less about them or the drugs. There were always more of both if he'd wanted.

"Shut up, Oleg, you pussy!" Alexei yelled. "You have fifty more in your closet." Alexei began to bang on the smoked partition that separated the driver from the occupants in the rear of the enormous Hummer. "Where are the fucking bitches, Ivan?" Alexei ranted. "You were supposed to get whores for us tonight. It's my brother's fucking bachelor party, you asshole!"

The darkened window slowly dropped and a large, ugly, thug of a man shrugged his shoulders as he turned his head to answer. "All the whores I could find were two-bit skanks, Boss!" Ivan retorted in a simple-minded way. "You don't want to give your new wife *bitch diseases*, do you, Oleg?"

The other men howled like a pack of hyenas ridiculing Ivan. "Take us to a fucking bar or something, WE NEED BITCHES!" Oleg shouted.

The men begin to chant: *"We Need Bitches, We Need Bitches!"*

Just then a loud ringing sliced through the festivities like a samurai sword. Ivan turned to look before pushing the button. The men scrambled, covering the drugs and straightening themselves. A true look of terror filled their faces as they readied themselves for something akin to a lashing. Even Oleg had a look of concern on his face, everyone was worried -- everyone that is, but Alexei.

The ringing became ever louder and added to the tension. Oleg gave a quick nod to Ivan, who only then pressed the button. Slowly, the flat-paneled television rose from near the partition and a snowy satellite signal gave way to a clear, crisp picture. The powder blue and white *Skype* logo appeared at the bottom of the screen.

A massive, graying boulder of a man appeared. His face was pockmarked from a childhood disease and over half a century of smoking thick Cuban cigars and yellow Russian cigarettes, hadn't help. He was Victor Rostov, hardened by long Moscow winters with an attitude to match. He dressed in a dark suit and held a large Havana between his sausage-like fingers. His eyes were as cold and deadly as the personality that had resided inside him.

He spoke in Russian, his voice deep and hoarse, "Are you boys taking it easy tonight?" A guttural sound bellowed from Victor. "Remember we have a meeting with Yuri and our investors before the ceremony."

Oleg, always the little ass-kisser, spoke first. "Yes, Papa, we're just being guys, you know?" The other men nodded obediently, eyes wide. "I'm relying on you two to keep everything under control until this deal's done and stop shoveling that shit up your noses!" Rostov roared.

Alexei, knowing his father was shrewd and cunning, knew it was equally as futile to argue with the man, "Yes, Papa." Taking a cue from his brother, Oleg agreed, "Thanks, Papa."

Rostov grunted in disgust, then his hand filled the screen as he reached toward the computer's camera, and the feed was suddenly killed. The men, still frozen to their seats slowly began to thaw. Then, after a moment, they sighed with relief.

Oleg picked up the camera to capture everyone's expressions. "You bitches!" he cackled, as a ceramic Chihuahua bobble head danced up and down in the rear of the back window.

CHAPTER 11

IN ALL OF LOS Angeles, the West Side was the only place anyone really wanted to live. And by West Side, that didn't include Mar Vista, Culver City, Playa or even West L.A --was Santa Monica. And Santa Monica was an anomaly, even by L.A. standards.

While the San Fernando Valley could peak at 118 degrees Fahrenheit in March, Culver City hosted race riots, Mar Vista and Venice raised gang members like cockroaches, while Lakeview Terrace and Watts just kept the body count at record levels. Santa Monica in contrast was serene and ideal. It was always a perfect 72 with clear blue skies from morning until late afternoon and rivaled such destinations as Monaco or the Canary Islands. Santa Monica might max out at 83 only two weeks a year, yet it was always prime tourist time. Humidity was a term that was as foreign here as deep-fried ice cream.

This particular evening the on-shore flow came in early, dropping the temperature from a comfortable 72 to almost chilly 61. The fog rolled in even as the sun was still low in the sky and the yellow low sodium lights created a haunting halo effect up and down Montana Avenue.

Santa Monica was not only known for it's pleasing weather and post-graduate professionals, but for the fact that every light-skinned illegal alien could seek shelter without immigration even batting an eye. If Los Angeles was the melting pot of America, Santa Monica was a microcosm of the world.

For the Brits, Santa Monica was called - *The West End*, the Aussies - *Sydney North*, the French – *Le LaLa*, and South Africans – *Es-Capetown*. But one thing Santa Monica had more of than anywhere west of the Mississippi River was Irish pubs.

From the Brentwood border at Bundy, it was a straight shot down Wilshire to the beach and one could hop from Bar*Food to O'Brien's to Sonny McLean's to Fair City to Stephen's Green to Patrick's Roadhouse and never blacken the tread on their shoes.

Even with British pub rivals like The King's Head, The Mucky Duck, Britannia, The Cock & Bull, or George V's, the Irish ruled here. And, like the sea-side atmosphere itself, the only tensions you'd see among former European, African, and Scandinavian rivals would be over someone's poor choice of music on the juke box or a FIFA Champion's Cup for that matter. Everyone came to Santa Monica, everyone, whether they stayed the night or for a lifetime.

CHAPTER 12

URPHY'S LAW LAID SMACK dab in the middle of town and boasted the largest square footage of any pub for miles. Even though it was ordained with provincial black and white framed photos of turn-of-the-century Dublin, pictures of fields of heather across the Irish countryside, Murphy's Law was still a business… and business was booming!

It had a pub area replete with a thatched roof imported from Athlone and hand-carved draft pulls for the perfect Guinness. A menu of corned beef and cabbage, bangers and mash, and lamb stew kept the old-timers and tourists on their stools and drinking. But the real moneymaker at Murphy's Law was the entertainment. Acts, originally tinker groups, folk singers, and slapped together trios, filtered their way to Murphy's Law, since U2, Enya, and Colin Farrell had popularized everything Irish. This simple pub had now become a huge success.

Danny Doyle, a young entertainer in his 20s, shook his locks spraying the ecstatic 20-something girls with sweat after his long set. He was the only one on the West Side that could wear a wife-beater T-shirt and not look like a total tool. Additionally, his back shoulders and forearms were covered with ink, but the kind of tattoos that depicted Christ on the cross, Celtic designs, and morose Irish poems in Latin. Actually, they were quite tasteful.

The drummer ended the set with a mini-solo and the crowd

clapped and screamed for more. Danny jumped down from the stage and tried to make his way through the throngs of females, but found he'd have to get a little forceful to make headway.

At the bar, Ciara O'Malley sat rosy cheeked and excited that her old friend had seemingly *made it* and was being lauded in a new land by new people. Just then, a tall pint of stout was placed in front of her.

Ciara looked up and smiled. "Go raibh míle maith agat!" she said in her native Irish to the bartender. The bartender took a step back; not expecting to hear his long lost language, then smiled wide. "Well, you're very welcome, my dear!"

Tony Murphy was everyone's favorite bartender, but everyone just knew him as *Murph*. He was a long way from Belfast and the IRA, and, since he was older and wiser, decided that part of his past was a lifetime ago. Murph was not only the bartender, but also the owner of the fine liqui-torium. He was still devilishly handsome, as many men from his part of Ireland were. He stood well over six feet tall, had broad, yet thin shoulders, like a swimmers, and large head atop them. He had chiseled features, but not hard like those that stayed on the farms or worked the cold Irish and North Seas for fish. Deep blue eyes that always got what they wanted and, although he had crow's feet and crags in his dimples, they were perfectly symmetrical. Upon first glance, you just knew he wasn't American.

"Put that to your gorgeous lips and tell me if it's as good as the stuff back home," Murphy said in a finely tuned accent that was considered by L.A. standards as *Mid-Atlantic*.

Ciara took a long sip and placed the pint glass back down, knowing full well her lips were covered with the thick foam. "Ah, now that's heaven!" She half-turned back toward the stage and the frenzy that was just abating. "I still can't believe I'm here," she said as Murphy leaned two elbows on the counter, ignoring other thirsty patrons. "It's like a dream," she surmised as she turned back to the bar. "You must be so happy here."

Murphy had now warmed to this beautiful creature and was smitten. Every night he'd serve lovely lasses from around the world, but this one was special, something about her was special. He'd bedded more than his share as well, but he'd be content with putting Ciara on a shelf, *perhaps she was the next Ex-Mrs. Murphy?*

"Darl'n, are ye on your own this fine eve?" Murphy said with the sincerity of a pit viper. "It be a sin if a rose like yourself were void of good company -- and it just so happens that I'm <u>very</u> good company!"

Ciara was used to this kind of attention in Ireland, but she hadn't had it for a long time. Although she didn't consider herself a beautiful woman, she knew she had a unique look, at least unique to the places she had been traveling since leaving home.

Before Ciara could respond, Danny suddenly appeared through the crowd behind her. Realizing the predicament she was now in, he decided to interrupt, "Easy Murph, she's with me," Danny explained. "Watch yourself with that fella. There's a trail of broken hearts from Belfast to Barstow with his name on it."

Murphy stood straight up and playfully took offense, "Jesus, Danny, you don't even give a fella a chance, do you?" Danny smiled a knowing, but respectful smile, then looped his hand under Ciara's arm. "Come on, Ciara, I've got one more set, then we'll grab some tea with the band."

Ciara felt like a young public school girl again who'd had a crush on Danny since before she knew what a crush was. She dutifully followed, but was careful not to divulge her long, concealed feelings for him. Danny began to romanticize, "We'll stay out all night and watch the sun rise like old times, how 'bout that, then?"

Ciara wanted nothing more than to spend as much time with Danny as she could. When they were friends, so long ago, it was puppy love, but now they were adults, albeit young adults, and she had direction and purpose. Ciara desperately wanted to spend quality time with her young suitor, but knew she couldn't -- at least not this night. "Ah, Danny, not tonight, I've to meet the parents in the morn. We're to work out the little one's schedules you know," she said in a disappointed tone.

Danny's face showed the dejection, as his thoughts were similar to hers. Even though he could have the pick of any girl in the pub, he wanted Ciara. He had always wanted Ciara. Looking at his puppy-dog eyes and not wanting it to be years before they met again, she decided to compromise.

"Alright, we'll have a cup of cha when you're through."

A smile widened on Danny's face as he breathed in renewed confidence, expanding his chest like a peacock. "Right -- I'm on! Can't keep an adoring crowd waiting, can ya?"

Danny ran back through the crowd and leapt onto the stage in a single bound. He grabbed a guitar from its stand and threw the strap over his shoulder. The band counted down: "*three, two, one,*" then blasted out another song. The crowd simultaneously began dancing and singing along.

Ciara felt a warm sensation ripple through her breast as she unconsciously began to sway with the rhythm of Danny's song while kept time by tapping her hip. She looked around and realized she liked this place, L.A., she could get used it here.

CHAPTER 13

THE RAIN HAD STOPPED, but the stone streets still glistened under the graying skies. The weather was of no concern to the crowd of eagerly awaiting friends and family. Hours before they had filled the streets waving Irish flags and freedom posters as they could hardly contain their excitement. McCann, despite his long incarceration was a local hero, and the years away had only grown his legendary appeal. He was no prisoner, no murderer to them, quite the contrary; he was a freedom fighter who fought the occupying forces with everything he had, but who had paid the ultimate price for loyalty to his country. Unfortunately, McCann's friends weren't the only ones waiting to get a glimpse of him.

The cunning reporters and paparazzi knew the best place to be was here, at McCann's welcoming celebration, and not the prison where they'd get nothing for their efforts. From as far as Donegal, Armagh, and Mayo, people infiltrated the crowd as cameramen and journalist jockeyed for position. Various aunts, uncles, distant cousins, Sinn Fein representatives as well as splinter group recruiters checked smart phones and iPads for the latest updates on when their man, McCann would arrive.

A banner waving above the street read:

Fáilte_A_Chur_Roimh_Dhuine - *Welcome Home Michael McCann – Political Prisoner of War For 10 Long years.*

A young girl waved a flag as she sat on her father's shoulders.

Suddenly, the dark sedan came screeching around the corner and into the town square. Tetley's men followed at a discreet distance, leery of getting too close and exciting the mob. Yet crowd or no crowd, they had a job to do. If McCann's car stopped, then they'd stop, if it turned, they'd turn. They would be undeterred.

The celebrants began to cheer, as McCann got closer. His car raced toward the masses, then quickly slowed as it penetrated the horde of people. The crowd banged and tapped the hood, roof, quarter panels, then boot of the car as it passed to welcome their hero home.

But McCann was still out of sorts; he kept his head down and didn't dare make eye contact with any of his adoring fans. He was just not ready. Afterall, he had been tortured, segregated, dropped in a hole of solitary confinement, and left to die. But he hadn't. He was understandably anti-social, as he had not been exposed to any version of *society* for nearly a quarter of his life.

Besides he hadn't been among free people for over a decade, he knew they wouldn't recognize him, and his appearance might cause them to riot the police with calls of mistreatment. Either way he was going to stay anonymous for as long as possible.

Slowly, the crowd enveloped the car as more and more people brought up the rear. McCann's car made it's way deeper and deeper, through the roundabout, past the stores and churches, and deep into the town. The streets were so overrun by now, not even a tank could get through if it had wanted to.

Tetley's men soon realized they were in danger of letting McCann get too far ahead and tried to breach the back of the crowd. It was a futile attempt to catch up, but therein lay the rub.

Catching a glimpse of an official tag on the lead tail car, a woman yelled, "They're following our Mick -- stop 'em lads!" With that call to arms, the crowd suddenly turned ugly. Children were sent quickly to the sidewalks and the adults began to attack the three trailing vehicles. Banging on the cars, kicking, and rocking them back and forth, the crowd refused to let them pass. From every aerial angle, stones began to fall, smashing the front and rear windows, then sticks, then weapons came from nowhere. Younger men dropped to one knee and began to jab at the car tires, puncturing each one with metal spikes they carried up their sleeves for just such an event.

Tetley's men shouted from the inside of their cars, "Get away! We're on official business! Get away, I say!" It was useless, they were outnumbered, out gunned, and out of time. Tetley's men had no choice but to call in a *Mayday.*

Ahead, at the end of the street, a large pub with another welcome banner and a group of well wishers waited to buy McCann his first pint. Many knew how tough it was in prison as they themselves had spent time in the Maze and other penal towers. They raised their glasses and put the hands on their hearts. McCann's driver nodded to them as they slowly passed. The patrons nodded back and understood what had to happen next.

When the driver hit the sharp turn, he quickly downshifted and hit the accelerator hard. The car lurched forward and began racing through the narrow streets like a Formula One leader. Swerving to escape notice, the car maneuvered in and out of alleyways, tight turns and short blocks, through bleak, empty lots, and single lane roundabouts. As the car careened around the corner of a dead-end passage, a single garage door opened and the sedan raced in and skidded to a stop. The door quickly slammed shut.

Five men instantly appeared at the car like phantoms arising from the mist. Slowly the door opened and the men bid him exit. McCann looked up at the unknown faces. They all seemed so young and inexperienced. He'd never had the pleasure of fighting with them, but knew they held him in high esteem.

Without a single word, the guardians led him down a passage to a tunnel under the repair shop. Pushing aside a false wall, McCann was brought into a large room with a small, lighted area in the corner.

By now he was finally starting to ease up a bit and out of curiosity lifted his head to see what was ahead. He glimpsed a barber's chair; massage table and portable shower under a single spotlight. Under the glow of the last light near the corner, he could see a buffet table filled to the brim with food. Even as far away as he was, he smelled lamb, fruits, vegetables, and as cliché as it was, his favorite, potatoes. Someone had gone to an awful lot of trouble. His stomach began to rumble.

Two large men helped McCann into the barber's chair as he was still getting used to life without shackles. He lifted his head once again to scan the personnel and this time saw a number of what he called *civilians*: those regular people the IRA were always fighting for. Two men and a woman: a tailor, masseuse, and stylist.

Eamon, his massive bodyguard approached passing the others and stepped up to McCann who now sat awaiting the next move. Like McCann, Eamon was not loquacious, not prone to conversation. Men like them never needed to be. He simply handed him a thick envelope.

McCann pulled the red velvet ribbon to open it and dumped the contents unto his lap. Bringing it closer to his face, he inspected: a first class airline ticket, *Aer Lingus*, a stack of U.S. currency, just enough to last a week or so, a disposable *burn* phone with an international calling card, and to top it all off, a brand new blue passport: *an American Passport.*

Suddenly a tall, thin, well-manicured man stepped forward. He was well adorned with thin gold chains and bangles. His light linen shirt was certainly not the norm in this part of the world, with accoutrements so as to accessorize; he always wore a Tommy Hilfiger jumper or Kenneth Cole pea coat. His name was Teddy Rawlings, but he insisted everyone call him by his Christian name, Theodore. He was as fierce as they came, and even in the desolate wind-swept regions of the North, Theodore was no victim to provincial sentiment or prejudice. In fact, Ireland itself had a long history of openly gay men and women as, so prodigious as the Irish were, the sheer numbers of children in each family gave them a higher percentage and home-field advantage.

Theodore stared at McCann, eyeing him up and down, side-to-side, stem to stern, then finally lowered his eyes in disappointment. "Oh my dear God, someone call Amnesty International, this man has been tortured!" Theodore protested. "Jesus wept, just look at the state of him!" Teddy stepped up slowly, carefully, he whished McCann's hair away from his face, then rolling his thumb over his fingers as they were now dirty. "Where did you find this man, hiding in the Wicklow Mountains like Rip Van Winkle?" He was careful not to grab McCann's hair, but instead ran his fingers under and through it with a disgusted look. "Just look at the state of him," he repeated. "I may be a gifted, but I am NO miracle worker!"

"The-o-dore!" Eamon said in a low, serious paternal voice.

Theodore had momentarily forgotten his place, but quickly acquiesced. He straightened up, reluctantly accepting the enormous task at hand, and began pointing to the others. "Right, I'll need all of you... you, hand me that bottle of shampoo, the big bottle, we'll need all of it. You, over there with the shoulders and the dreamy eyes, heat up some towels, get me the straightedge razor and the leather strap, you bring lots of hot water... and you, dear boy, hand me my special clippers. This is going to take a while."

CHAPTER 14

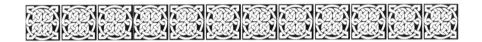

ALEXEI THREW OPEN THE double doors, almost smashing the beveled glass that had been imported from a cathedral in Estonia, and entered like a bad debt. By now his crew had been partying for days on end and had nothing but hedonistic ideas being fueled by narcotics and a primal drive that would stop at nothing to satiate their carnal desires. Alexei, Oleg, Ivan and the rest of the crew were completely out of their element and seemed misfit for the zip code they had now entered.

Men like these should never have traveled west of the 405 Freeway. They were better off in Odessa or Little Armenia in Glendale, Arcadia or even the Moreno Valley than here, but unfortunately for everyone, Alexei didn't give a shit about other people or what they thought.

A young drunk couple kissed in an oak booth by the front window when Alexei approached. "Fuck off, we need this booth," Alexei shouted over the din of music and laughter. The couple didn't miss a beat and continued intertwining their tongues. "Get the fuck up!" Alexei yelled as he grabbed the boy and threw him hard to the ground. The young girl screamed and cursed, jumping to the aid of her beau.

Alexei looked around as a number of patrons that suddenly stopped what they were doing and focused on this strange aggressor. Not wanting to be 86'd from yet another establishment, Alexei reluctantly reached into his pocket and pulled out a wad of bills. He threw it hard at the boy, whose lip was now split and bleeding slightly.

"Here, get the hell out before I change my mind and fuck your girlfriend while I make you watch."

With that, the girl quickly scooped up her man who was now more concerned with collecting the bills from the floor. "Babe, this will pay for drinks the rest of the week!" he said smiling with blood red teeth.

Alexei's crew jumped into the booth and spread out making themselves at home. He himself would sit on the end facing the door as he was paranoid from a cocaine bender and he knew he had many, many enemies. You don't get to the top, albeit the top of the lowest level of thugs in Los Angeles, without cracking a few eggs... and skulls. Oleg followed suit and covered the other side of the booth, flanking his brother.

By now they were so amped on coke, booze, crank, amyl nitrate, and an assortment of unnamed substances, they couldn't see straight. Alexei had all his drugs couriered from a friend in Siberia, as he knew it would be top quality and never cut. These guys were trouble, and trouble followed trouble wherever they laid their hats.

"Alexei, what are we doing in this fucking place?" Oleg complained. "There's nothing here but faggots and stuck-up bitches." Alexei was thinking the same thing and contemplated standing to leave, when just then the crowd of dancers cleared and Ciara appeared from across the room like a drug induced vision of Venus.

"Oleg, give me the fucking camera," Alexei yelled over the music. Oleg gave his brother a strange look, but none-the-less reached into the bag and retrieved the HD camera. Alexei turned it on, flipped the eyepiece out and slowly zoomed into an extreme close up of Ciara.

Starting at her long, perfect legs, Alexei, like a starved voyeur, began to pan up to her hips, midsection, to her chest, finally stopping at her face. Oleg pulled something out of his pocket, put it up to his nose like a nasal inhaler and snorted. It was an oversized *bullet* used to carry cocaine for quick hits and it was nearly empty. Oleg was never discrete about it either.

"Hey, Oleg, are you going to Jew all the yayo?" Tomash objected.

Oleg scowled, then reluctantly pulled out a small grinder used to granulate the drug into a fine powder. The other men began to salivate like Pavlov's dog as Oleg untwisted the cap and dumped the five or so grams on the table. It was instantly a feeding frenzy. The men lurched forward and plunged pre-rolled dollar bills into the fray. The ghetto straws roared to life like a Dyson vacuum. The men inhaled as much as they could, as quickly as possible.

But Alexei couldn't keep his eyes off Ciara. He was fixated on her as she sipped her Guinness and swayed to the music on the dance floor. She was like a fawn and Alexei a hungry wolf. He turned to see the other heads buried in the mound of cocaine like hyenas on a fresh kill.

Raising his hand, he smacked three of them across the tops of their heads. "Assholes!" He shouted in Russian. Alpha male had spoken. The men quickly backed off the pile whimpering as Alexei leaned in grabbing one of the rolled bills unraveling on the table. Taking the side of his hand, he scooped a long, thick rail of powder away from the pile and placed his straw at the end. A long and loud snorting followed. Alexei sat back in the booth to let the drip set in after the powder absorbed through his nasal membranes and shot directly to his brain. "Ah! Mother-fucker, that burns!" he yelled. The others snickered and nodded knowingly.

Alexei suddenly jumped up from the table and stood above the crew. "I'm going in," he exclaimed. With that, Alexei flipped his stringy hair back out of his eyes and straightened his shirt.

"Those bitches don't have a chance, brother!" Oleg screamed as everyone roared with laughter.

Alexei shot across the dance floor and entered the crowd, pushing and shoving his way in, hyper-focused on his target.

Ciara was reaching over the post to place her pint glass down on the railing as she continued to move to the rhythm of the music, when suddenly, she felt something odd and bulging against her backside. It was Alexei. She spun around to face her offender, half-expecting to find some young drunk kid, only to see this totally abhorrent creature. He had pressed his crotch against her, to which she was instantly repulsed. She immediately stepped backwards to avoid additional contact of any kind.

Alexei was wasted, obviously, unkempt, reeked of some fowl odor and had an enormous herpetic sore on his upper lip. This guy was anything but harmless. But, since Alexei thought himself God's gift to women, he unabashedly continued. He attempted to move and sway with Ciara, but only embarrassed himself by stumbling awkwardly and fumbling like an idiot.

"Hey baby, you want to go to my place and dance for reals?" he slurred. Ciara heaved up a smattering of vomit in her mouth.

Her expression said everything she needed to say. Not thinking she could be offended any more than she already was, retorted politely, "Thanks, no! I don't think my boyfriend would like that very much." Ciara turned her gaze toward the stage and to Danny. From the stage, Danny caught her glimpse and winked at her. She smiled back lovingly -- wrong move.

Ciara's action did not sit well with Alexei as his mood suddenly shifted. "Fuck him! I'm talking about you and me. He can go straight to hell!"

Now she was truly offended beyond measure and free to express it. "Excuse me?" She shouted. She saw her escape and took it, losing herself in the crowd as she advanced toward the stage. Alexei watched in anger as he saw her sashay to the foot of the stage, Danny leaned down in typical rock-star fashion and began to serenade her with song.

Ciara's rebuff was too great an insult to Alexei's thinly veiled ego. *No one fucks with Alexei Rostov*, he thought to himself. Slowly, he became enraged by the snub as now Alexei was forced to watch another man receive the attention he demanded of this cow. *No one disrespects Alexei.* The Russian looked around the dance floor, then suddenly remembered something he had buried in his pocket.

Slowly, his hand retrieved a small, lint-covered gel cap and let it hover over Ciara's pint glass on the railing where she had last placed it. He took his thumb and forefinger and broke it open as yellow powder sprinkled from the small capsule. "I'll show that cunt," Alexei mumbled.

CHAPTER 15

IT WAS A DREARY day in Belfast as it was most of the year. Yet, this northern city had a beauty and a history and a sadness that was rivaled by few others on earth. Forever dank, Neolithic stones covered in moss enhanced the landscape, pulling it together as one large, intertwining environment. The outskirts of Belfast were especially wild, mysterious, yet never dull.

The dark sedan roared over the rural single lane country road without a lorry in site on a mission. As it crested a steep hill, McCann could see a lone cemetery sat at the edge of a windswept cliff. The car pulled off to the side and into a tangle of overgrowth that virtually hid it from view. The driver, knowing British protocols, already suspected Tetley had dispatched more cars to pick up their tracks and find them. He watched in his side view mirror as each unmarked vehicle pulled off the road less than a kilometer behind them. Each of Tetley's officers communicated by radio, but never exited their vehicles, while McCann's entourage intercepted each message over their sophisticated scanners. But Tetley, knowing how aggressive *The News of The World* and other British rags were about catching cops in the act of wrong doing, ordered his men to simply observe and report -- for now.

McCann's men jumped out of their vehicle and took up positions to secure their package. After a moment, he slowly exited wearing a hoodie and large, draping clothes to cover his new identity. The four others, there to protect, advanced with him, but McCann motioned downward with his hand, they slowed, then froze at a spot meters behind him.

McCann carried a large bundle in his arms and was careful not to drop it over the wet grass and rocky outcroppings. He slowly made his way through the battered and rusted gate into the ancient graveyard that had housed the dead for hundreds, if not thousands of years.

By now, the sun was slowly peering over an onshore cloud formation as McCann turned his face skyward. It was the first bit of sunshine he'd felt on his now bare face for too long and it meant all the more as he was finally a free man, and now back with the only ones he cared about.

Making his way across the flat stone graves and around the ancient mausoleum, he took long, deep breaths as the air tasted sweet. His mold-soaked lungs seemed a little clearer, and a strange sensation crept up on him: a mixture of adrenaline, fear, guilt, sadness and joy. A mix he had never felt and could not reckon.

Just then a light rain began to sprinkle as he followed what seemed to be a predetermined path to three white headstones with Celtic crosses atop each one.

As he stopped in front of the crosses he dropped to his knees. He beat the stones until the skin on his knuckles opened wide and blood flowed freely, staining each stone, claret and crimson. His escorts could only watch from afar as they all knew too well what he was going through as they, themselves had felt that at one time or another.

McCann's eyes filled with tears that poured onto the graves, his face contorted in grief. He kept pounding his fist until he could feel pain no longer. He sat on the ground and swung his legs forward as if to have a chat.

He was home, as here; Colleen his wife, Nuala his beautiful daughter, and Seamus his playful young son, lay at the cliff's edge for all eternity. Reverently unwrapping the brown paper covered bundle, McCann spread the bright, full, colorful flowers across each graves. They lay in shocking contrast to the grey and green of this morose place. McCann sat perplexed, unsure of how to deal with these new emotions.

He had never truly grieved his family's death and in typical Irish tradition, bottled everything up inside, becoming unable to release his feelings. *"AAAAHHHH! AAAAHHHH!"* poured out of McCann.

After a moment, he bent over and rolled his face into the dirt as the damp soil began caking his lips and face. He began muttering ancient Pagan and Latin prayers in Gaelic, first quietly, then screaming louder and louder until the voice he had lost over a decade ago was reborn. He was mad with grief and finally, finally after ten long years, he was beginning to exorcize his demons. *"AAAAHHHH! AAAAHHHH!"*

Frank's men tensed and refused to look at each other, as men will do when emotions are involved. Frank had purposely ordered his men not to give McCann a weapon of any kind, not just then anyway, as he knew what a man in his grief stricken state was capable of doing. McCann would be in no rational state and had he a weapon, even the smallest shard of glass; he'd join family then and there.

"AAAAHHHH! AAAAHHHH!"

By now even Tetley's men, sworn enemies of the IRA, shuddered at McCann's laments like a banshee on the bogs. At that moment, all of the men Irish or otherwise, took stock of their own family and would bear down hard not to allow a single tear to fall.

AAAAHHHH! AAAAHHHH!

After what seemed like hours, McCann finally stood bloodied and emotionally spent. He was careful to mark each headstone with a kiss and a touch of his bloody hands, then slowly turned to walk away. Tetley's men focused their long camera lens on McCann's face, but were unable to get a good look at his new identity as he was covered in mud and grass and looked like an unholy specter haunting the cemetery as moved past each gravestone. The onlookers shuttered at his transformation.

McCann stumbled toward the cliffs overlooking the Irish Sea as his four bodyguards lunged forward to prevent him from throwing himself over. Just at the edge, McCann changed his direction, only to see his men surround him to take him safely back to the sedan. He turned for one final look, then McCann entered the back seat.

CHAPTER 16

C IARA LAUGHED AND WHIRLED, she was tipsy, more from exhaustion and jet lag than drink, and danced back through the crowd to the railing where she'd left her beer. There were other pints around, but Ciara always had a system to place her drinks in odd, inconspicuous places for easy access and no confusion. *Afterall, backwash was gross!*

Beads of sweat had formed on her brow, as the room was now hot from all the warm bodies dancing. She picked up her large, thick glass and inspected it for any foreign matter such as cigarette butts, gum, or even spit. All clear. With a great thirst, she took a long gulp, then another, then another, polishing off her last drink for the night as she had important business in the morning. And, as customary, she retrieved a cigarette from a pack in her back pocket and popped it in her mouth.

A simple, convenient store lighter glowed hot as she was about to light the fag. "You can't smoke in here!" a shrill voice screeched.

Ciara turned quickly toward to source. "Sorry?" she said questioning as she turned to see a pair of leering eyes connected with a bad hairdo staring judgmentally at her.

Some young, bitchy girl, half-coed, half-hippie, a brunette with the raised eyebrow began to cackle, "It's against the law, haven't you heard, L.A. is a NON-SMOKING city!"

Being away from Western civilization so long, Ciara had forgotten decorum and took for granted that most of the pubs in other parts of the world still allowed smoking. And, spending so much time in Asia, well, it was just a shock back to reality for her to say the least. "Jesus, I'm sorry," she said genuinely. The young brunette tossed her matted hair as she turned and walked away.

Ciara looked around the large pub, half out of desperation to validate her frustration with a witness, half looking for an escape, she the caught a glimpse of an exit sign down the back hallway. *Out back, that's okay,* she thought. *It was too far to walk out the front, fighting the crowd, besides there would be a gang of smokers off the back like everywhere else – maybe she'd make a new friend?*

She headed down the long corridor past the restrooms, but suddenly lost her footing and stumbled. As though she'd been hit upside the head with a Limerick brick, Ciara felt something powerful overwhelm her. Her body slowed as she pushed the bar to open the exit door, then it hit her again. She stumbled again as she heard the old metal fire door slam behind her. She knew something was now terribly wrong -- she struggled to compose herself. She slowly put the cigarette to her lips and fumbled with the lighter. *Maybe she was dehydrated, exhausted from the trans Asiatic flight, perhaps?* All she probably needed was one good toke off a cigarette to get the nicotine flowing in her bloodstream again. And like a thousand times before, Ciara felt if she could just take a few drags, she could relax and ride out this temporary rush.

She looked down and noticed her hands shaking strangely as she tried over and over again to flick the lighter. She heard the metal door open, then close behind her, but was too paralyzed to turn. Then, from behind her, a shadowy figure appeared under the canopied light above the brick wall. Even in her sickened state, Ciara could sense something ominous. She could just make out a hand entering her field of vision. A flame ignited from a large silver Zippo and illuminated the figure. Ciara's eyes tried to focus. It was a man, she thought, maybe a man. Then, for a brief minute, the image became clear. It was Alexei. As soon as she recognized him, his face began distorting, shifting fluidly, liquefying, changing like a gargoyle. She suddenly felt a wave of dread surge up through her body and knew that it was no coincidence she was unable to collect herself.

She'd felt a less intense version of being out of control once when she tried mushrooms and the time a schoolmate had laced her joint with something. Realizing now she'd been drugged, she knew she was in trouble. As her mouth gaped open to breathe, the cigarette fell from her parching lips and over the railing onto a car hood. Her legs began to give way as she collapsed, but Alexei quickly wrapped his arm around her waist. His expression now mimicked that of a Jeffrey Dahmer or Hannibal Lecter as his eyes turned black, almost shark-like, but death inside them.

A screech could be heard at the end of the alleyway as the Hummer limo raced up the back and came to a halt under the stairwell. Carefully hoisting her up and to his chest, Alexei nodded as the others opened the back door, screaming and howling like a pack of rabid dogs. Ciara, barely conscious, was now acutely aware of what was happening and began to scream; yet nothing came out of her mouth. She heard it in her head; it was a primal, and instinctive reaction. Just keep screaming. But now she was nearly paralyzed, and completely vulnerable.

As careful as Alexei was putting Ciara into the limo, once in, he merely tossed her limp body onto the back leather seats. He stood and admired his new possession as the others peaked around him to admire their new plaything. Ciara knew she had to act quickly, so she mustered up enough strength to reach up and touch the back window, attempting to pound on it for her life. Alexei admired her perfectly rounded ass and the flesh that just peaked out above it as her shirt rose when she tried to crawl up the back of the seat.

Cotton and lace dug into her skin as she began to feel her clothes being shredded. Every stitch and corner of her garments lacerated her skin as the men ripped and tore into Ciara like lions with an antelope carcass.

She suddenly felt cold on her body and realized she was now naked. But she also felt the warmth of her own blood as it trickled down her skin. She knew what was happening and knew what was to come. She had been near this point before, but thankfully it had never happened. She began to pray that she'd pass out, pray that God would spare her from this inevitable assault. But her prayers were not answered since now the drug had stabilized in her system and her thoughts were clearing the confusion. She was like a patient awaking from surgery, only to find her body limp, her muscles flaccid, but her mind fully functional.

With room to stand, Alexei stood and was the first to undo his pants and strip down. He began to stroke himself, as he was not yet hard due to countless drug-induced days. He knew this might happen, so in preparation he'd popped two Viagra tablets, if for no other reason than to impress the others. He would be rock hard and ready to go for hours.

Alexei came at Ciara from behind, wrapped his fingers of his left hand and made a fist through her hair. He tightened his grip and yanked her head back towards him. "No one denies Alexei Rostov, you cunt!" Alexei whispered in her ear.

Just then Ciara felt a sharp pain as he entered her. Nausea overcame her by this new violent violation. Alexei wrapped his right hand around Ciara's throat and began to squeeze, almost crushing her larynx as he rammed his cock into her.

Ciara's brain was beginning to shut down and she knew she was passing out, but just before, Alexei twisted her head around so she could face him. Ciara opened her eyes one last time only to see Oleg and the rest of the Russians standing naked, advancing towards her. As they began to close, a single tear fell from the corner of her eye.

CHAPTER 17

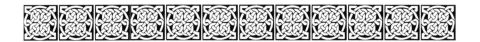

FRANK O'MALLEY WAS A smart man and smart men don't make mistakes. He knew that Tetley would have the RUC covering every airport, railway and bus station in and around Northern Ireland for at least a fortnight. But Frank also knew Tetley had fuck-all for leverage or control south in the *Free State* Republic of Ireland.

Frank's men had done their job well. They'd driven McCann the 175 kilometers from Belfast to *Aerfort Bhaile Átha Cliath* in Dublin. They had driven all night through lashing rain, changing vehicles innumerable times to avoid detection, even putting on hats and trench coats like spies of the 40s. The best tails in Europe would've been shaken early on, but Frank wanted to be sure McCann was on the first flight out to America. He knew the Brits would never suspect McCann could be on the move so soon, let alone leave the city, certainly the country for that matter, as he had never been more than a few miles away from… no way!

The black sedan pulled up outside of Dublin airport at the terminal that housed Aer Lingus, Ryan Air, and a host of international, intercontinental, and intra-European airlines. Just then security officers passed by the sedan and gave suspicious looks.

"This is where we leave ya go, Mick," said Eamon as he turned around in the front seat and handed McCann a small leather bag filled with some clothes and toiletries. "Good luck in Americ-a, *mo chara*," he finished.

The men stepped out of the car and opened the door for McCann. Eamon walked up, wrapped his large arms around McCann and gave him a big bear hug. Hugs, let alone any real sign of affection between men, was a relatively new concept in modern Ireland, it just wasn't done in earlier times. McCann had been away for a long time and had the recent realization that he would have to go with the flow in order to fit into society again. He reluctantly hugged Eamon back.

"Go dté tú slán!" Eamon said, wishing him a safe journey.

"Slán ábháile," McCann responded in kind, knowing he would probably never see him again.

McCann stepped up to the Customs and Security counter. "Passport please," the agent said. He opened the blue pedigree passport and gave McCann the once over with a cold, dispassionate look.

McCann was no longer McCann. That is to say, he looked very much like the old version, the McCann no one had seen in over 10 years, but this man, this new man was different. He had cleaned up very well. His hair was short, but just long enough to retain the waves and keep the grey in check. He was dressed in a smart looking dark suit, obviously custom cut by Frank's tailor. Besides the obvious scars from torture and prison fights, his skin looked remarkably fresh and toned. He'd had an hour-long massage, manicure and pedicure and really felt like a new man. But still showed signs that he didn't feel he deserved any of it, yet he knew he had to play along to get on the flight and finish his mission.

The Customs agent checked McCann's photo once more, then handed it back, "Thank you, sir, have a nice trip."

Dublin airport was heavily patrolled by An Garda Síochána constantly sweeping for bombs with sniffer dogs, under carriage mirrors and sensors, but that was just routine since 9-11 and the new austerity protests. Any normal man would have been sweating through his clothes, but McCann was no ordinary man. He passed a final round of security and the Irish Police easily allowed him to enter the gate area where he was welcomed by two comely ticket agents in green uniforms and pill box caps.

They smiled genuinely, ripped the stub from his ticket, and handed him the boarding pass, "Have a nice flight, sir."

McCann made his way down the gangway, into the ship, down the narrow aisle, found his seat, tossed his small satchel into the overhead bin, then tentatively settled into his luxurious First Class leather seat. He couldn't help but run his hands over the plush softness of the arm rests and gazed around at all the buttons and levers that gave the seat the ability to fully recline, play movies, draw a blind, and totally encapsulate him. He felt like the world was beginning to creep back into him and he thought maybe he'd no longer keep himself so closed off from the world, even if it had forgotten about him.

"Would like some champagne, sir?" a sweet voice chirped above his ear. McCann looked up from admiring his surroundings to see a beautiful brunette flight attendant. She had jet-black hair and crystal blue eyes. She was Black Irish. There was a hint of deep blue just beneath the whites of her eyes -- that was the dead giveaway. McCann had an uncanny way of reading people, even before he perfected it with the prison populace. He knew that, though Irish, she was of Portuguese extract, a result of nearly every country invading Ireland at one time or another throughout history, and that she was probably from Galway or somewhere deep in the Ring of Kerry. His mind wandered, remembering as a child seeing the two galleons shipwrecked in Dingle Bay and that their masts were visible at low tide. They were still there someone had recently told him.

"Sir?" she was holding a large glass of champagne over a white linen napkin. McCann nodded, as he never needed to answer, his eyes always said it all. Yet he flight attendant had a secret of her own as well, as she too, could read McCann. She looked deep into his transfixing eyes, over his person, his easing rigidity, and knew this was the man's first time in first class, maybe the first time he'd ever flown at all. He was handsome and fascinating in a strange, mournful way. She was definitely going to keep an eye on him.

McCann slumped his shoulders, then settled in as it was going to be a long trans-Atlantic flight. He was sure he wouldn't sleep in such a strange environment, but luckily no one had the seat next to him, and. oddly enough, most of the first class cabin was empty. None-the-less he would try to relax and strategize a game plan.

The roar of the engines and the elevators uplifting filled his ears and after take off, McCann reclined the seat to its full extension, just to close his eyes for a moment. Although he hadn't consciously realized it, this day had been highly stressful: afterall he'd been released from jail, given a full makeover, had seen his family for the first time in a decade, and was now leaving the land of his birth under an assumed alias. He took a single, long draw of air, then exhaled like a man taking his last breath. As he did so, he slowly closed his eyes and began to dream:

McCann's mind fills with images as his body floats past Crumlin Road, scaling rock walls, past the murals to his red brick home on Arydone Road.

He sees himself a younger man asleep next to his wife Colleen as their daughter Nuala, tosses restlessly in the next room, mumbling to herself as seven year olds do.

McCann feels the sensation of smiling to himself as he watches his four-year-old son, Seamus, flushing the downstairs toilet, then stepping over three sleeping bags where Tony Murphy, Peter Morrissey and Billy Hammer snore loudly.

But then McCann's happy dream begins to darken. Next to the sleeping men lay a host of armaments. AK47s, C4 plastic explosives, Czech-made guns all sit near duffle bags filled with stacks of cash. The image of a tattooed arm resting on one of the bags with an I.R.A. insignia slowly comes into focus. The dream darkens further.

From the kitchen a brown dog snarls, then growls as British soldiers surround the house and move up quietly. The images appear in slow motion as Murphy and Hammer jump, then snap to, fully alert. They grab their guns and peer out the window to see the soldiers upon them Peter, groggy, rises slowly.

McCann can hear Murphy whisper upstairs to them, "Get your arse up, Mick! The place is crawl'n with Brits!" From the banister, McCann is already dressed, carrying Nuala to their bedroom. Seamus follows with a thumb in his mouth. "Is it another raid, Da?" Seamus asks innocently. McCann gives a reassuring smile to his son, "Don't you worry now, Shamey. Just lay quiet with your Mam and I'll see yaz later." ...and darker still.

McCann could feel himself getting angry in his dream. "You used the phone, didn't ya?" he yell-whispered to the men downstairs. "You used the fuck'n phone. Now we're fucked!"

McCann could see Colleen racing into the hallway now dressed in a large terry cloth bathrobe. He ran to her, squeezed her tightly, looked deeply into her emerald green eyes, kissed her cheek, then quickly hugged each child.

He sees himself racing with the other men pulling out a large .454 Casull pistol, bolting a round into the chamber and pushing the other three men through an opening in a closet door, through a hidden passageway, to the adjacent apartment.

McCann could hear himself shouting to the soldiers, "Don't shoot fer fuck's sake, we've women and children in here, don't fire, we're coming out!"

McCann sees himself, Murphy, Peter and Hammer jump into an SUV and break out of the adjoining unoccupied home as British soldiers pursue. He feels the violent end of their escape when the truck crashes and the soldiers advancing, leaving his friends to die a fiery death.

His images change direction as he hears glass breaking when SMOKE GRENADES fly through a window. His house fills with tear gas and SAS soldiers spray the house with bullets before readying to SMASH through the doors. He hears something from the second floor bedroom as Colleen and the children SCREAM in fear. This sound blasts into McCann's brain, as his dream becomes a nightmare...

McCann sees Tetley and Smythe crouched under his front wall as Tetley radios in slow motion, "Give them everything you've got!"

FLASH GRENADES EXPLODE inside the house as a SMALL

FIRE ERUPTS from the incendiary devices. THE FIRE ON THE GROUND FLOOR BEGINS TO GROW.

Out of an upstairs window, his wife Colleen FRANTICALLY SCREAMS, "For God's sake! Save my children!"

McCann sees himself rushing through the hail of gunfire to get to his family. He feels the sensation of being shot, the bullet tearing through his flesh and bone, then shot again as his body begins to fail him. He stumbles and falls as he's tackled and forced to the ground by SAS soldiers. In his painful memory he watches helplessly as Tetley approaches. McCann remembers the feeling of crawling, broken and bleeding across the coarse gravel in an effort to save his family all in vain.

He hears a low, agonized utterance emit from his lips, "Colleen!" Feeling an excruciating pain, McCann turns his head to see Tetley stomping down on his wounded leg. He locks eyes with the inspector as Tetley raises the butt of his rifle, "Shut your fucking face, Paddy!"

It is then McCann watches helplessly while his red brick house EXPLODES into a million pieces. He CRIES OUT... then blackness.

CHAPTER 18

SANTA MONICA, CALIFORNIA HAS a strange microclimate. It sits on a bight, not a bay, and is sunny most of the year, but can get cloudy or fogged in at a moment's notice. Even as the rest of Southern California bakes in the arid sun, Santa Monica can easily be 20 to 30 degrees cooler than just a few miles inland. It has an ideal Mediterranean climate and never gets too hot, too cold, too wet, or too dry.

As Murphy busied himself rubbing down the long, varnished mahogany bar, the others readied the pub for the upcoming event. *Murphy's Law* wasn't the oldest established public house in Santa Monica, but it was certainly the most popular. There is something to be said about an area that can host Irish and British pubs as well as the likes of Indian and Pakistani restaurants, adjacent to one another.

"Jesus, Liam, you're a fucking carpenter, can't you hang a simple banner?" Murphy barked in frustration. Standing amid half-opened boxes of plastic leprechauns, four leaf clovers and other Irish decorations & paraphernalia, four men stood consternated.

"Murph, could yaz stick your nose up someone else's arse? I mean, for fuck's sake, I'm a professional. It's delicate business we've got here." Liam retorted.

"The operative word is <u>business</u> lads and Paddy's Day is the biggest pay day of the fucking year for this place! If you don't hang them decorations right, you can forget about being paid!" The men looked at each other confused, "You don't pay us anyway, ya cheap bastard," was there response. Murphy scowled as he continued polishing the bar.

Just then, a large figure with bags under his eyes to match his demeanor entered the bar. It was Detective Fitzpatrick. He was in bad mood, as usual, but seeing the boys attempt to adorn the pub, he couldn't help but be cheered up by their failings. He wore a lightweight jacket that barley covered his barrel chest, thick biceps and forearms, but it had been cool that morning, so he'd decded to dress accordingly.

Although his badge was buried deep inside his coat pocket, the bulge from his police issue Glock 19 and handcuffs on his belt easily gave away his profession. After a chuckle at the lads expense, he walked toward the bar as the four men continued to bicker about placement, height, and overall composition.

"Top-O-The-Morn'n to ya, Murph. How's it hang'n?" Fitzpatrick shouted, startling the entire establishment with his booming megaphone of a voice. Hearing the familiar tone, Murphy's demeanor equally improved. He immediately stopped drying a crystal beer mug, threw the towel over his shoulder and turned to greet his friend.

Fitzpatrick slammed his hand down hard on the bar. "Gett'n ready for Paddy's Day, eh?" Kelly, an older bartender who had probably been inherited along with the pub, walked behind Murphy toward the back wall to clean the large mirror against it.

"Look what the cat drug in," Kelly said as if an old enemy had suddenly appeared at his door. Murphy gave Kelly a disapproving scowl.

"Kevin Fitzpatrick, one of L.A.'s finest. How are ya, Detective?" Murphy added happily.

"Murphy you shanty-Irish bastard!" Fitzpatrick smiled and snickered back. The other men paid no mind, as the test of an Irishman's true character was how much abuse he could take as well as give out.

"Well, ya know the *Fitz* in your name doesn't just mean *son*... it means *bastard son*!" Fitzpatrick always came into Murphy's Law when he wanted a pint, a history lesson… and a laugh. These two could do this all day.

"What'll ya have there, Fitz? And don't go giv'n me that, *still on duty* bollocks. You've been a friend with the Guinness family for some years now, as God is my witness!"

Fitzpatrick smacked his palette in anticipation like a salivating dog. "Guilty as charged… well, I guess one wouldn't hurt."

With that, Murphy grabbed a large pint glass and began to pull a draft. The heavy black, stout poured thick as it slowly rose. Murphy stopped short of the top in order to let it settle. It's said that to pour a true Guinness takes over 5 minutes, and Murphy was a slave to tradition, especially with his friends.

During the summer tourist season, he'd not stand on formality and quickly pour the pint to the top, letting it settle in front of masses of paying customers. This way he made more money, poured less beer, and had hardly a hassle.

Fitzpatrick, remembering why he'd come in the first place, changed direction and began a not so subtle line of questioning. "So, Murph, is Danny Doyle coming in tonight?"

Murphy took a wooden spoon and scraped the first foamy head off the pint and continued to pour. It was definitely a process to pour a perfect pint. "Well, that depends," Murphy said, not missing a beat.

"Depends on what?" Fitzpatrick said on the verge of being annoyed.

"Depends on what he's done now, doesn't it?"

Fitzpatrick curled his lips and laughed the only Gaelic he knew, "póg mo tóin!"

Murphy chuckled, "begg'n the LAPD's pardon, but your ass is a little too big to kiss!" He nearly cradled the full pint and set it on top of a dry beer mat. Fitzpatrick reached into his back pocket and pulled out a black leather case. He flipped it open as to retrieve one of the $20 dollar bills peeking out its slip.

Murphy would have none of it. "You're money's no good here, Detective," he said as he raised his hand to stop his friend.

"Now with all the corruption like in the City of Bell and Vernon and what not, you know I can't accept something for free," Fitzpatrick explained matter-of-factly. The two men stared each other down, neither willing to give an inch, when suddenly they burst out into mutual laughter. "Jesus wept, Fitz, ya almost had me there." Fitzpatrick chuckled as he took a long, deep gulp of Guinness. "That's my serious face, I like to use that one on the perps during interrogation!"

Fitzpatrick flipped the other side of the leather wallet to reveal a detective's gold shield. Cops never really spoke about it, but the difference between silver and gold; police and detectives, was vast. You automatically won the pissing contest flashing gold. No gray area.

On the opposite side of the wallet, a Los Angeles Police Department photo identification card with large red letters spelled out, *SPECIAL INVESTIGATIONS SECTION.* He pulled out a photograph from the sleeve and looked at it for a moment. "You ever seen this girl? Her name is Ciara. And don't give me *that depends* bullshit!"

Murphy took the photo and began examining it. As he studied the lines, his eyes perked up. "Yeah, she was in here the other night." He smiled. "And Holy Mother, she was something else, too. A real Irish rose, she was, but sweet like, you know. Why, what's happened?"

Fitzpatrick's unusually pleasant expression mellowed to his work face. "Nothing so far as I know, except maybe got herself misplaced.

"Lost?" Murphy sniggled, squinting his face.

"She's been organizing this group of children from Indonesia to come live with host families here," Fitzpatrick said as he took a swig. "Problem is, she never showed for the final meeting with the parents."

Murphy had begun folding linen dining napkins, but was now becoming intrigued. He shrugged as though a young girl not making a meeting in L.A. was no reason for concern.

"Katie was supposed to meet her as well, but no one seems to have seen her since the other night." Fitzpatrick ended.

Murphy searched his thoughts... wait, Katie? "Katie, which Katie?" Murphy asked questioning.

Fitzpatrick took another, longer gulp of stout. "You know, my sister, Kate."

Now Murphy was really confused. He momentarily stopped folding. "How in the hell does your sister, Katie, have any connection to Danny Doyle or this Ciara girl?"

Fitzpatrick lowered his eyes in mock frustration. "Kate is one of the host families. She's adopting two children who lost their parents in the Tsunami -- try and keep up," Fitzpatrick playfully shot back. "Kate practically organized the whole thing at this end. She'd never met Ciara, but spoke with her often over the computer -- what do they call that, *Shite* or *Skype*, or some shit like that? Anyway, from what I'm told, there's no way <u>that</u> girl would've ever missed a meeting with the adopting families. And as far as we know, she never checked out of her hotel room, either." Fitzpatrick was really starting to enjoy his first beer of the day.

"So when she didn't show to the meeting and no one could get a hold of her, Kate called me." Fitzpatrick rummaged around a wooden bowl of assorted peanuts, cashews and Chex Mix -- bar food: *The Breakfast of Champions*. A thick foam had formed on his upper lip and now Fitzpatrick looked like a lush from the 70s.

Murphy turned to another innocuous duty, "Ah, I wouldn't worry, Fitz! She looked like she was hav'n a right good time the other night. She'd only had the one drink, I know since I served her, and ya know how cheap the Irish are, but sure she was dancing up a storm." Murphy pulled up the long, rubber bar mat that collected over spills and drained it in the sink. "She's probably at Disneyland gett'n the first sunburn of her life."

Fitzpatrick, perhaps searching for a reason to ignore his sister's request, thought it plausible for a moment. "Normally I'd agree, but this one seems different," Fitzpatrick retorted. "She's real dedicated, I guess. It just doesn't fit the bill, her going missing like that." Fitzpatrick took one last swig of the black stuff and placed the large pint glass back on the bar top for Murphy to collect. As he began to gather the items from his wallet, he mumbled, "Where the hell are you Ciara O'Malley?"

Murphy stopped dead in his tracks. He shot up from below the bar and grabbed the photo of Ciara before Fitzpatrick could stuff it back into his wallet. His demeanor suddenly seemed dire.

"That's little Ciara O'Malley? Jesus Christ, I never…"

Fitzpatrick, seeing the sudden change in Murphy took note. "You never what?"

Murphy owed his friend an explanation, "Anyone from Belfast, or Ireland for that matter, knows the name, O'Malley." Murphy, now rising to a panic, began to interrogate the interrogator. "Tell me now, if this was the last place she was seen, then we've got to get to Danny Doyle's, here, I need to use that picture, I can Photoshop a poster and we can get it out to the news stations!"

Fitzpatrick raised his hands, "Whoa, slow down McGruff, I'm the detective here, remember?"

Murphy took a breath. "You're probably right, she's most likely just out sightseeing."

"There's nothing to worry about at this point. I'm gonna check a few things out first." With that, Fitzpatrick pulled out a business card and scribbled something on the back. He handed to Murphy as though he was just another interviewee.

"If you hear anything else, you've got the number to my desk, here's my cell, okay? I had to get one of those new fucking smart phones, so I'm not sure how the goddamn thing works yet."

Murphy took the card with a bewildered look on his face. "Yeah, yeah, Fitz, okay! Thanks." he said concerned. As Fitzpatrick turned to walk out of the pub, Murphy shouted, "Keep me posted, you'll do that, won't ya?"

A beam of sunlight suddenly cut through the entry of the pub as the front doors opened, then shut quickly, before Fitzpatrick could exit. The others could barely make out that a man had just walked into their establishment.

It was McCann. Temporarily blinded by the stark contrast between dark interior and bright exterior, Fitzpatrick accidentally bashed McCann's shoulder with his chest when he passed.

He squinted as his eyes adjusted, "Oh, hey, sorry pal!" Fitzpatrick grabbed McCann's shoulder with his catcher's mitt of a hand in apology. McCann reacted in a split second, nearly tearing the offending hand from his person, but stopped short, as this wasn't another prisoner trying to get over on him. McCann looked straight into Fitzpatrick's eyes, then nodded in respect without saying a word. No need for a fuss, this was merely an unintentional act that happened to every normal person in the outside world.

McCann cautiously made his way toward the bar. He kept his head low and wanted to make it well into the center of the main room unmolested or noticed, when something suddenly fell in front of him.

The banner the boys had been working on slipped from their hands and cut through the air, just missing McCann's face. He stopped, startled, nearly jumping out of his skin, but controlled himself, quickly assessed the situation and identify the source, to determine it hostile or not. He'd read of American soldiers experiencing Post Traumatic Stress Disorder (PTSD), and knew he had either that or something akin to sheer pent-up rage. This was a strange new world – he knew he'd have to control himself.

"Hand us up that, will ya, fella?" A voice shouted down to him from above in a clear, Irish brogue. McCann knelt down grabbing one end of the thick banner. Deep, jagged scabby, scar-covered knuckles stretched white and pink as he gripped it hard enough to pick up the vinyl banner in one go. He hardly looked up, merely a glance, for fear the men would become overly suspicious. As he stood, he stretched out his arm to hand up the banner and saw four men on two ladders: Liam, Sean, Johnny, and Hammer. These men knew McCann, and he them. Hammer's face suddenly paled as if he'd seen a ghost.

CHAPTER 19

THE LARGE INSULATED METAL door stood agape with the help of a heavy steel barrel. Frost had developed on the outline of the door and the cavalcade of cold air could've been mistaken for smoke if it weren't for the obvious sub-zero temperatures surrounding the back bar.

After grabbing the ragged parka from the hook just outside the freezer, Murphy threw it on and entered to begin his daily ritual of the keg count. The days delivery had just arrived, been stowed, and invoices signed. It was now time to spend the coldest 10 minutes of his day taking inventory. The large freezer held slabs of meat; blocks of ice and emergency supplies, as well as being jammed packed with kegs of beer from every maker. It was no use grumbling as it was a necessary evil that Murphy was used to after all these years. He never trusted Kenny or any of the other lads with this important duty, employees or just regulars ready to lend a helping hand, so he always did the count himself -- always.

He could not have sensed the presence of another, as the condenser for a freezer of its size was loud and throbbing. Murphy couldn't have seen the figure cross between the plastic drapes that kept a large percentage of cold from escaping, even with the door open. He wouldn't hear the ice pick being shimmied, then plucked from a large block of ice or the figure now approaching him from behind. Murphy liked to pride himself on his acute awareness of his surroundings, but he was older now and not *high alert* every minute of the day. What he did finally notice was the needle-like pain and the cold steel tip that startled him as the ice pick pressed hard against his neck.

Murphy's instincts kicked in, but he suppressed his reaction to panic. He stood as the stranger behind him lifted him silently. He had one, maybe two plays, so he wouldn't blow it. "Listen, brother, I don't have much, but the key to the register is under the bottle of Peach Schnapps. You're welcome to it, no judgments, times is hard, just take what ye want. I'm sure ya don't want to spend a minute in jail or the likes of me."

No response came as Murphy searched his thoughts for a secondary plan. The deep throbbing of the compressor heightened the drama. "Sibhse bastardaíocht!" was all Murphy heard.

But what he heard was in Irish, and since he hadn't spoken Gaelic in so long, it was hard for him to remember. "Wha, what?" Murphy said nervously.

"Who did you call that night, you bastard!?" Murphy felt the puncture of ice pick as it dug deeper into his neck as he felt the second layer of derma being pierced. His eyes widen and he gasped for air. Then he felt was his body being hurled across the freezer as it landed hard against the back wall atop a pile of frozen bags of breaded cod. He had to push hard against two kegs to get them out of the way. He slowly stood gain his composure.

Murphy strained as he peered to see through the cloud of freezing air. "Jesus Christ, Mick, you're alive!" Murphy shouted as his terror quickly turned to joy. He smiled a smile that was quintessentially Murphy. He advanced toward his old friend, "Come give us hug, brother."

McCann stood his ground and the hate-filled expression on his face didn't waver. "Shut your gob, and don't you *brother* me." Murphy slowed his lunge to embrace his mate cautiously, but his smile grew wider and wider none-the-less. "I haven't decided whether to gut ya, or kick the shite out of you yet." McCann fumed.

Murphy gingerly stepped closer and lowered his head apologetically. "Ah, Mick, we're family, you and me! Colleen was my sister for God's sake," Murphy said as he made the sign of the cross with his right hand and kissed his thumb as though a rosary was attached to it. " I swear I didn't know them phones were tapped. I just called Siobhan for a little sexy talk, like, ya know, for two minutes -- two fuck'n minutes, Mick! Ya gotta believe me!"

McCann's cold stare began to subside as that was, or at least had been, Murphy's *modus operandi* – it was all part of his charm. McCann's anger lessened and his thoughts began to turn nostalgic. Murphy, seized the opportunity, crept in and slowly embraced McCann. First a light hug then squeezed to a full bear.

Murphy pushed them both out of the freezer, still in a tight embrace like they were dancing the tango, "Ah, you're looking fit, Mick." Murphy was lying as upon closer inspection, his eyes began to inspect the many scars that dotted McCann's face and hands. He could just imagine what trauma the rest of his body had endured.

Just then from around the corner of the freezer door, Hammer and the other lads appeared, oddly concerned for Murphy's safety. A collective sigh of relief could be heard as Murphy led McCann through the hallway and back out into the bar.

In a deep Donegal accent, Hammer began, "Ah, Jesus, I don't believe it. Mick, it's good to see ya." The four others closed in for hugs and handshakes of their own, as McCann had no choice but to loosen up.

"Sure it's Michael McCann in me bar, can yaz believe it, lads?" Murphy said proudly.

Murphy suddenly bolted behind the bar reached up and grabbed five shot glasses. He then hurriedly searched behind the rows of liquor with his hands, finally scooping up a bottle of 30 year Irish whiskey. Uncorking it with his teeth, he spit the cap onto the floor, and began pouring shots high and wide. He slid the thick crystal shot glasses in five different directions, until they came to rest in front of each man. Then, solemnly, he lifted his and proposed a toast. "To Mick, whom the good Lord has seen fit to bring back to us. God bless him!"

The other men raised their glasses. "To Mick, Slainte!" They shouted in union.

After a few moments of more shots and proverbial backslapping, and remembrances, a questioned was posed.

"What brings you to America, Mick?" Johnny asked innocently, but fearing an ominous answer. McCann placed his empty glass down on the bar as Murphy promptly refilled it.

McCann slowly lifted it to his lips, "Frank," he said in a low voice. A collective shutter ran through the other men. "I've come to keep my eye on his daughter, Ciara. Frank's worried MI6 might try and spook her."

Suddenly, Murphy's eyes widened as he remembered, "Jesus, Mick, your man… he just left."

McCann, thinking quickly retorted, "the big fella? Whatcha mean?"

Murphy quickly downed another shot. "Detective Fitzpatrick -- I mean Fitz, he's LAPD. He was here asking after Ciara."

McCann stood back from his bar stool. "Ciara, Frank's Ciara, why would a cop be ask'n about her?"

Murphy nervously looked to the other men. "Mick, Ciara's gone missing," Murphy, said almost ashamed.

The pleasant feeling of camaraderie quickly faded as the hair on the back of McCann's neck stood on end. He closed his eyes momentarily to hide his concern and searched his mind for a solution. He began to rub the back of his neck slowly, then, unaware of the stress building inside, rubbed furiously. The others took notice and slowly backed away a small bit. This man had been incarcerated for over a decade and had troubles the likes that no ordinary man could imagine – and the lads knew it. He could explode at any time, and with his past reputation, there was no telling what would result.

McCann opened his eyes and sighed. Not a sigh of relief, but one of surrender. He reached into his pocket, dug around, then retrieved a cell phone. "I gotta call this in," he said coldly.

The others eye's lit up as Murphy stepped from behind the bar. "Mick, ya just got here, brother," Murphy said gently as he approached, wrapping an arm around his shoulder. "You're jet-lagged. There's no use gett'n all worked up over nothing right now. Call Frank later."

Murphy could be very convincing when he wanted to. "Besides, even your man Fitz thinks it's nothing to worry about, well, just yet." Murphy looked over McCann's shoulder to the others, raised his eyebrows and tightened his lip. Message received.

Murphy's voice changed from empathetic and understanding back to his playful self. "Come on Mick, we'll get ya sorted at my place, unless you've reservations at the fuck'n Four Seasons or something?" The other men began to laugh, but McCann was every bit as serious as he had been when he'd first stepped through the pub doors.

McCann gazed at Murphy with cold eyes, not yet knowing if he could trust this man. And Murphy knew the score. There'd be no real homecoming until he could prove to McCann that he was innocent of any smear campaign the IRA had imposed against him or whether his loyalty was still questioned.

Then, a small miracle emerged as slowly, an uneasy ripple, barely a smile appeared from McCann. It was a tempered smile, he could see no teeth or sign of joy, but it was the slightest smile and he'd take it. Murphy knew it was all he was going to get, so he led McCann back down the hallway and out the back as the others followed in tow.

Murphy turned his head to shout back toward the bar. "Kelly, hold down the fort! I don't know when we'll be back." As they flowed out into the alley, they could just barely hear Kelly mumbling as he threw a bar towel over his shoulder in frustration.

CHAPTER 20

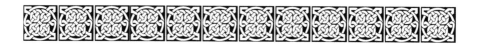

A LTHOUGH THE SUN BEAT down in Marina del Rey, there was always a little cloud cover to keep temperatures cool. The docks glistened after just being hosed by the maintenance crew, swayed with every departure of small watercraft. The bay was filled with dozens of pleasure boats as more were launched every few minutes. Even though hundreds of boats entered and exited the channel, they never, ever left a wake as the harbor police here were considered just right of the Nazis.

Unlike Key Biscayne or Kennebunkport or Puget Sound, L.A. really only had one, tiny marina where a precious few hundred sailors could afford the slip fees. It was the perfect place to hide in plain sight. And an Irishman was good at hiding.

Murphy jammed the worn key into the large deadbolt on the tall, gated fence and opened it. He lifted his head up slightly, signaling for everyone to follow down the slipway as they carried cases of beer, coolers and bags of barbeque briquettes.

Murphy led his ragged crew past multi-million dollar yachts, sloops and fishing trawlers. "How 'ya, Morty?" Murphy yelled as he waved to a geriatric in a captain's hat rubbing clean the orbed compass next to the wheelhouse.

"Ahoy, Murph, how are the seas today?" the gray haired man shouted back.

"Fair seas today, Captain, but watch that cross wind past the point." Murphy winked, tipping his cap. He knew Morty rarely left the docks, but always played along as it seemed to be the highlight of the old man's day when he saw his neighbor.

"I know what you're trying to do, you know," McCann whispered angrily at Murphy as to not signal to the other lads. "You've got a lot of explaining to do, you know that!"

Murphy, who was walking astride, just smiled and pointed to the sea. "We're a long way from home, brother, you can relax now. Nothing bad ever happens here."

Just then, McCann looked up to see a dozen beautiful women dancing atop the deck of a sleek 50-foot Hunter. Music was pumping, and although it might have been considered rude, the neighbors would be doing the same thing if they weren't already doing the same thing. McCann visually lost himself temporarily in an ocean of bikinis as Murphy turned left and led him down the length of the ship. He caught a glimpse of the boat's name: *THE LIFE OF RILEY* it read -- *how apropos,* McCann thought.

Murphy jumped into the fray of double D's, "Ladies, are ya ready for a day at sea?" They all encircled and jiggled their natural and unnatural breasts over him as though he were Hugh Hefner. McCann would've been sickened by the display if it weren't for the fact that he had hardly seen a woman, let alone half-naked Venuses, in over 10 years. Strange feelings began to arise in him, but he tried hard to suppress them as best he could, afterall, he was here on a mission.

Hammer pointed to Liam and Johnny to stow the cargo as they prepped the boat for launch. He checked the engine first, tapped the fuel gauge and spun the wheel forward and back to insure proper motion. He nodded at Murphy through the window. All set.

Murphy hopped aft to the bridge and without having to, Hammer moved to the side as *de facto* second in command. McCann found himself still on deck in the middle of tanned, young rhythmic flesh. It didn't seem quite fair. This would be a true test of his mettle.

McCann's eyes were immediately drawn to a beautiful brunette sitting on the sun-bleached cushions looking out to sea as the others frolicked. He was about to make a move toward her when he heard a scream. Instantaneously he turned toward the source, a voluptuous girl under the shower on deck being spanked by another. She suddenly took notice of McCann and set her sights on him.

"So when was the last time, *mo chara*?" Murphy shouted down in Gaelic.

McCann shot him a look. "It's been so long I wouldn't know where to start," McCann shouted back in their native tongue so the women couldn't translate. The others hardly took notice, after all, this was L.A., everyone spoke with some kind of accent, and in their first language, from time to time, but careful not to alienate others.

Liam popped open a number of cans of Guinness and handed them around until one got to McCann. "The women here are deadly! Jesus Christ, Mick, I think I'd go insane if I hadn't had a ride in years. Fuck'n unbearable!" Murphy chuckled.

CHAPTER 21

THE MASSIVE KEEL CUT through the blue water effortlessly as a pod of dolphins rode a pressure wave ahead of the bow.

Murphy, relaxed at the helm in his typical jovial style. "Sun block, Mick!" McCann looked oddly at his old friend. "Sun block. It's lotion that keeps the sun from fry'n that paste you call skin. Put it on fast or you'll be as red as a bare-arsed goose in 15 minutes." Murphy knew his friend had never been out of Ireland and all this must've been a shock to the system, but he also knew Mick would have to be kept in check as well – he had too much at stake now.

McCann sipped his beer and a somber look came over his face as he stared out at the deep blue of the Pacific. Tunnel vision closed off the thumping and bumping of *house* music that seemed to now be coming from the distant shore. The girls gyrating slowed and garbled and McCann's sorrow took him back to when he was young. The waves weren't deadly here and didn't come in multi-sets, and the water wasn't as black as the sea could be off the northern coast of Ireland. Yet, McCann had always loved the ocean. He did not know why, but he felt it deeply. Every Irishman did, it was in their *DNA*, it coursed through their blood. The Portuguese, Africans, and most notably the Vikings had all invaded Ireland from the sea at some point in history and the blood that coursed through his veins always drew an Irishman back to the water -- for better or worse.

McCann turned to see the dolphins popping up, charging and racing the sail boat, staying just ahead as they seemingly led the journey.

"They're beautiful, aren't they?" a soft voice said startling McCann from his dreamlike state. He turned quickly, embarrassed, to see the brunette whom he'd eyed when he first boarded. "Hi, my name's Tracey, Tracey Vogel." she said extending her hand. Like all men, he was trained to take a snapshot of what was in front of him, but his look lingered unashamedly, inspecting every curve and soft ridge of her perfectly sculpted body.

Any other woman would have been uncomfortable, but for some strange reason, Tracey knew McCann was special. He sat by himself as his other mates took dance partners and chugged beer bongs. He looked out of place and the closer she was to him, his difference became more and more apparent.

He admired her tall, lean, typically Californian figure. She had striking green eyes. Green eyes set against tanned, freckle-less skin and jet-black hair. He thought her Sioux, Black Foot, Pawnee or from one of the numerous Indian nations across the United States he'd read about as a boy and seen in the movie picture houses.

McCann was seriously self-conscience, but was slowly beginning to regain some semblance of self-confidence. It seemed like an eternity he'd been staring, although it was merely an instant.

She plopped down next to him. "They mate for life, you know." Tracey said not realizing she was now flirting. This would surely knock him back to reality.

"Sorry?" McCann said definitely taken aback.

"Dolphins -- they mate for life," she repeated, this time aware of the double entendre.

"Yeah, and the only thing they do is eat, swim, and fuck all the day!" Murphy yelled out, breaking the moment. Lisa, one of the young women, slapped Murphy's shoulder, feigning embarrassment, then jumped into his lap for a kiss. Murphy leaned over and whispered into her ear. Lisa began to giggle as they both turned to look at

McCann with devilish eyes. McCann, sensing one of Murphy's ill-timed shenanigans, shot him a leering sneer.

"They're certainly more intelligent than we are," Tracey continued, trying to keep McCann's interest.

"That doesn't seem too much of a stretch," McCann fumbled. It was the first conversation he'd had with a proper woman in a long, long time. He hadn't quite found his footing.

Tracey smiled as she realized McCann was trying to communicate and decided he was worth the effort to get to know. "You must be one of Murphy's friends, I can tell by your accent."

McCann took a swig of beer and turned slightly so she wouldn't see the hatred in his eyes. "Yeah, we go way back," he responded sarcastically. She smiled wider now as she, too, began to feel more confident.

She had a Midwest sensibility and, unlike most California women who were unfriendly and never dared approach a man unless he was a celebrity or calendar model, could converse with any man. "Did I mention my name was Tracey Vogel?" she said again, this time demanding a response from this odd character.

McCann ran the name through his database and surmised she was probably of German extract, but somewhere down the line a Native American jumped into her genes. Perhaps the beer had kicked in and the shots of liquid courage from the pub funneled through his mind. He began to straighten up.

"Michael McCann - - call me Mick!"

"Mick, isn't that a bit derogatory?" she said playfully.

This loosened him up. "Yeah, *Mick the Mick*, that's me." He said as the first true play on words crossed his lips in eons. A slight rush of endorphins blasted his brain. Just as he was deciding that he liked this girl in front of him, something overshadowed and killed the moment.

"Hey, Mick, Lisa needs a hand below deck with the food," Murphy interrupted. "How'd ya like a thick juicy *Omaha Steak*?"

At that, McCann's basic urge: food, eclipsed his second basic urge: the desire to mate. The conversation abruptly ended. *Steak, a real steak?* With Pavlovian response, McCann's taste buds began to pop as his mouth watered. He reacted as though he were hypnotized, but kept himself from uttering, "I haven't had a steak in…"

Slyly Murphy was at his side, slapping him on the back. "Go on now, you, go get a piece." Murphy said as he turned to wink at Hammer. "Don't you worry, Tracey's in good company, she's not going anywhere." Tracey smiled an uncomfortable smile, as she too had known Murphy for many years and suspected he was up to something.

McCann also knew Murphy always had an ulterior motive, but he looked at his waistline and the baggy pants that draped off his frame and knew he had to put some weight back on. He had been under nourished, underfed, and under another man's thumb for a great percentage of his life. He carefully headed down the first set of steps and disappeared from the top deck. Tracey leered disappointed at Murphy as he began to chuckle uncontrollably.

He scooted over next to her. "So how ya gett'n on with our Mick?" he said in an oddly misogynistic way.

Tracey skewed her lips, wrinkled her face and huffed, "Well, thanks to you, I may never know."

As McCann came to the hatch, he thought of the years of beatings and how abuse can create paranoia in any person, especially an ex-con. McCann cautiously went below deck into the hold where a large, ornate kitchen stood. It was elegant and looked like something out of *Lifestyles of The Rich & Famous*. He followed the scent of cooked meat. As he cornered the breakfast nook, he could see Lisa with her back to him, cooking a large T-bone steak in a skillet. He took a moment to smell the air, taking in the aroma and the rush of instinctual, carnal voracity. Lisa spread a glob of butter on the steak, flipped it once more then forked the slab of meat and slapped it down on a beveled china plate. Taking a designer Japanese steak knife, she slowly carved a piece off the bone and seductively offered him a bite. She drew into him closer and brought the plate to her chest, just below her voluptuous breasts. Now, McCann was looking doe-eyed down a double barrel of trouble. He now realized that both of his base needs were about to be met.

Lisa slowly pushed the steak into his mouth as he lost all resistance. "Tell me how good this is!" she whispered, entrancing McCann like Delilah herself. As McCann chewed, his eyes rolled to the back of his head in ecstasy. He sighed deeply, this time as his brain remembered the taste of real meat, not the maggot-ridden gruel he'd been fed in prison. Without even noticing, Lisa lured him slowly backwards as they passed a large steel locker, across the polished mahogany floor and through a thick, varnished wooden door.

This goddess led McCann by the arm to the forward cabin and the master bedroom. Like leading a dog with treats, she continued to hand feed him steak until they reached the berth. "I've got more goodies for you in here," she said, now appealing to his primal instincts. And like a dog that had been starved for years, Mick gobbled and gobbled, nearly finishing the entire slab before he'd walked the length of the hallway. McCann was now acutely aware that Lisa had bolted the bedroom door shut and was standing in front of him with an empty plate. She took two steps back, placed the knife, fork and plate on a shelf and smiled. McCann slowly savored the last bite as though he were a spectator at the opera. Lisa reached behind her back and pulled the spaghetti tie as the entirety of the tiny lingerie-style bikini dropped to the floor. McCann quickly gulped the last chunk of meat, fearing he would choke. Not only had he never seen a woman as perfect and beautiful as Lisa, he had never seen a woman as perfectly clean, perfectly shaven. He marveled at the *Aphrodite* in front of him and she let him take it all in.

Murphy had already briefed his team player on McCann's situation and Lisa thought it her duty as an American, an ambassador of good will… if you will, to provide this poor, downtrodden guest to her shores, the finest welcome imaginable. She also loved Murphy so; she would do anything he asked. It certainly didn't hurt that this guy was cute and besides, he looked like he was practically a virgin anyway. It wasn't a stretch for her to justify and disregard any objections.

McCann, overcome with testosterone and passion, lunged at Lisa.

He grabbed her around the waist and pulled her close to him hard. He'd long ago given up hope of ever having another erection after years of torture and guilt, but now, *Holy Christ*, he'd win the blue ribbon if he were in a contest now!

Lisa was taken aback at the strength of this lean, sinewy man, and suddenly became just as excited at the prospects of more surprises. She would not be disappointed.

CHAPTER 22

ONLY HIGH-RANKING GUARDS WERE allowed in the basement offices and lounges at the prison. Nights in Northern Ireland were cold and damp, and as such, this night seemed more of both. The stars shone bright in the clear sky and it gave the minimum-security prisoners a chance to glance skyward. Although they weren't exactly windows, the rooms had a single narrow vertical slat covered by three inch thick plexi to allow light in during the day and, provided it was relatively scratch-free, some chance to dream at night.

Wilson was the lone guard tromping down the quiet concrete hallway after *Lights Out*. His footsteps echoed and bounced against the solid walls as they announced his arrival at a door that read: GUARDS LOUNGE.

He entered and headed straight to the back toward Joey and two other men who were playing poker with Frank O'Malley. Frank threw his cards down hard as he folded. Grunting, he looked up. "Wilson!" Frank shouted happily, "How's the little one at home - - Aoife, isn't it?"

The guard nervously smiled and nodded. "Ah, thanks for ask'n, Mr. O'Malley, she's grand, just grand."

Wilson slowly reached into his pocket and retrieved a small packet. He glanced it momentarily, then handed it to Frank with a slight look of sadness. He took a deep breath and smiled at Frank, "Well, it's official, you're outta here in the morning, sir!" He cautiously checked Frank's face for a reaction. Frank, never trumped easily, sat frozen to his chair. Wilson knew he needed to say something to prod this man back to reality, as this news would shock any man after years of incarceration.

"So how does it feel to be a free man -- well, almost free?" Wilson chimed. Frank had hardly breathed since Wilson's announcement and, even though he'd been expecting the news, he hadn't yet prepared himself. Frank started to rise, but slipped as his hand pressed against the back of the chair. Joey and his other lieutenants lurched forward to grab him in case he collapsed. Frank righted himself, found his feet and stood tall. He waved off any assistance and allowed the gravity of his newfound freedom sink in. He slowly opened the packet and withdrew the hard-stock card that read in red letters: OFFICIAL RELEASE: FRANCIS CONOR O'MALLEY. Although he'd regained his composure, he was still at a loss for words.

His men gathered around him and began to rejoice, slapping his back and lightly punching his arm. "Good man, yourself, Frank!" Joey said. "Fair play to ya, Frank!" One said.

"You showed 'em, Frank, they never broke ya!" another proclaimed.

Frank began to tear up as the thought of finally being free sank in. "Jesus, lads, I didn't think it'd be so soon," Frank whimpered. He turned and looked back at Wilson who had stepped aside knowing full well this was their celebration, not his. Frank looked to him and said, "Wilson, where's that Poitín you've been hiding for special occasions?"

Wilson's face lit up and he headed toward the dartboard and removed it from the wall. With one hand he placed the corkboard wheel on the ground revealing a small hole in the wall.

One of Frank's men grimaced, "Why ya sneaky, Proddy bastard, it was under our noses this whole time! Ah, sure that's even low for the likes of you." Wilson turned his head and smiled at the others as he reached into the hole in the drywall and retrieved a bottle of clear liquid, unmarked and unlabeled. *Poitín*, or po-tcheen as it's pronounced, was a deadly mix of yeast, brown sugar hops and treacle -- pure Irish Moonshine. It had been outlawed since 1661 because of its volatility and propensity to explode, taking with it anyone nearby, not to mention it's deadly consequence, such as blindness and insanity, if too much was ingested.

In a rare moment of unity, both prisoners and guard shared a jovial moment. After all, if it weren't for Frank and his men, Wilson's family wouldn't have the little the new solarium or the luxuries they had as no one could live on a prison guard's wages alone. And, if it wasn't for Wilson and guards of his ilk, Frank and the boys wouldn't control the cell block they were in or have the little luxuries other prisoners could only dream of.

"Right, Wilson, get to pouring those shots and don't be stingy like a Protestant!" Frank roared.

CHAPTER 23

WILSON POURED SHOTS FOR everyone as they toasted to Frank's good health. It was the beginning of a long, fraternity like session, when Frank's secure cell phone suddenly began buzzing. Frank always had it set to vibrate, but either way, you could always hear the hum. Joey reached back over to the table and grabbed it.

The *Orange* logo appeared, then words: *McCann* followed. "See Mick, those bastard's even took our phones!" Joey joked referring to the telecom company. "Yeah, okay, hold on a minute, he's just here. I'll get him." Joey shouted over the din of celebration and laughter, "Frank -- Frank, it's McCann!"

Frank's eyes lit up as he too, was lit up by this time. He grabbed the phone from Joey as he handed him his drink. Frank couldn't have been happier and he wanted to share his good news with his favorite soldier. "Mick how's sunny California? Ya giv'n it to Pamela Anderson, yet?" Frank barked.

There was a pause on the line that Frank mistook as cell site interruption. All he could hear was a faint, "Frank."

Frank yelled into the receiver louder in case McCann couldn't hear over the riotous noise behind him. "I'm out tomorrow, Mick! Can yaz fucking believe it, tomorrow like!?" Frank could hardly contain himself. "Now I can finally see my baby girl after all these years." Now there was cross talk.

"Frank, listen!" He could hear McCann as he pushed his large index finger into his free ear. Now everything McCann was saying came through loud and clear. Frank listened intently as Wilson handed over the bottle of poitín.

Slowly, Frank's cheerful mood turned ugly. His face began to swell and turn bright red and looked very much like he would explode. "What?" Frank whispered into the handset. There was a pause then Frank hurled the highly volatile and explosive bottle across the room. Everyone in the room froze. "What the fuck do you mean, she's gone missing?" Frank screamed into the phone. "I don't give a shit, Mick, you find her. You do <u>anything</u> it takes to find my little girl now!"

Frank attempted to punch the cell phone off button, but his fingers were too fat and couldn't hit the precise key. He raised it over his head to smash it on the ground, when Joey suddenly grabbed his hand and slowly took it from him. "My baby girl's missing lads," Frank blurted out as his eyes welled with tears.

CHAPTER 24

A MC-MANSION IS A PEJORATIVE term coined in the 80s for over-the-top, enormous eyesores built in neighborhoods, supplanting smaller older homes. It began in Southern California during the housing boom, but caught the eye of frustrated residents and disgruntled city councils. Like a corporate franchise, wealthy homeowners would find an upscale, yet provincial neighborhood in Beverly Hill, Santa Monica or West L.A. and demolish the existing structure just for the lot. Older lots, especially in Beverly Hills, could span the length from block to block or street to alley. It was a perfect way to build a monument to any self-absorbed ego, eclipse whatever ocean or mountain view others had, and create envy where there was once bougainvilleas.

The Rostov mansion was no different. It laid nearly at the edge of a rocky cliff overlooking the Pacific and, although tacky and ostentatious, it sat on a good piece of property with Kentucky blue grass, acacia trees, and lots and lots of gardens.

This fortress-like castle even had a basement. Something that was all but outlawed in California due to the frequency of earthquakes, yet somehow Rostov was able to pay off the inspectors and add the additional 10,000 square feet he needed to house whatever illegal activity or merchandise he procured was never included in the formal design plans. Most people outfitted large basements, say in Kansas or Minnesota, as rumpus rooms for the kids or man-cave sports-themed hideaways for frustrated, sex-starved house husbands replete with pool tables, flat screens, even stocked bars with couches and *Lazy Boys*. But this basement was different. This underground lair was scary and foreboding, calling this dungeon a basement would be like calling a great white shark a guppy.

It looked like the ground floor of an old Vegas casino. Long hallways introduced winding corridors and weird, dark rooms off to the sides. At the end of one passageway hung two large flags, one: a red with a yellow hammer and sickle, the other blue, red and white. One symbolizing Communist Russia, the old guard, the other, the Russian Republic, the new regime. Below the flags a heavy chain capable of holding a tanker at sea lay slack on the floor. A large steel eyehole brace was anchored to the wall with numerous bolts. After perusing the wall and seeing this odd fixture, you'd follow the chain to its logical end... Rasputin.

Victor Rostov had named the bear *Rasputin* after the mysterious, mad Russian monk, who was said to have been both saint and sorcerer. Rostov likened the bear, as well as Russian court confidante, to himself. The bear for his own size and strength, the holy man for his courage and survival. Rostov had always fantasized himself the embodiment of the iconic Rasputin. After all, he ran a successful organization: albeit illegal prostitution, drugs, gambling, kidnapping, extortion, the usual operations of an American businessman.

So prolific was Rasputin, Rostov knew, that he bedded thousands of women, including, it is said, Tsarina Alexandra Romanova, rupturing her uterus in the process with his powerful endowment. But what fascinated Rostov even more was the fact that this legendary priest had cheated death like a demon.

Rasputin had survived a series of murder attempts that began with him being gutted by a knife-wielding prostitute, only to survive and meet a more sinister end.

After being lured to the basement of a Russian noble's home under false pretenses, Rasputin was fed cyanide-laced cakes and poisoned vine. When his assassins realized he was completely unaffected by this, they shot him through the back four times, beat him unconscious with clubs, severed his penis, then rolled his limp body in carpet and threw him into the frozen Neva River. Somehow Rasputin miraculously escaped his bonds and broke free, only to finally succumb to drowning in the frozen river after hours of exposure.

Rostov felt the menacing strength his prize pet possessed and wanted it cultivated, so he left it to his sons who were all too happy to create a monster of this enormous creature and please their patriarch.

CHAPTER 25

THE LAPD HAD RECENTLY moved into their new facilities in Parker Center, downtown Los Angeles, but SIS headquarters hadn't yet made the move and were still located near the beach on the Westside. SIS Division seemed out of place in this paradise, as Santa Monica was not what you would've called a haven for criminals. Sure, you had your occasional pickpockets and con artists on Venice Beach and a shit load of homeless, but all in all it was pretty peaceful up and down the coast.

SIS was established in the late 1980s after the *Venice Shore Line Crips*, VSLC, had started a violent turf war with the *Bloods* and were wreaking carnage over what was always a predominately white, upwardly mobile community of wealthy corporate people, artists, celebrities and tourists. Yet, the City of Los Angeles, in their infinite wisdom, chose to put two large apartment complexes in the center of Venice as low-income housing. Venice was the perfect location as most were of the mindset of charity, helping the homeless and less fortunate, but no one thought the denizens of these housing projects would actually organize and take over the area through violence, intimidation, murder, drugs, and gang activity. It got so bad that the city was forced to paint large numbers on the roof tops of the apartment complexes, just so LAPD, Sheriff's and U.S. Marshall's helicopters could narrow their nightly searches for offenders. Residents were in so much danger, that once a four-year-old boy pointed at the house of neighbor and was shot by the gang on the corner thinking he was somehow a threat. Venice bordered Santa Monica and the SIS Division straddled both cities. Thankfully, the gangs were no match for the SIS.

The old police station had given way to modern technologies and ambitious architecture. It had glass windows and was now more like the set of a Hollywood forensic crime scene drama than a working law enforcement bureau.

Through the opened door, anyone walking by could see the placard that read: SIS CAPTAIN TOM BRINK. Brink was a dashing officer in his early 50s and looked like a cross between a young Clark Gable and George Clooney. He was the face the department used when the camera crews arrived for updates and press conferences as the *powers that be* downtown knew the love affair Angelinos had with leading men. With graying side burns and peppered short hair, he was less paramilitary and more Viagra commercial, complete with a trophy wife that Angelia Jolie would envy.

Brink marched into his office with a strange looking man in tow. He was oddly dressed for SoCal weather and covered up like an anorexic on the hottest day of summer. As Brink made his way around his desk, the man waited patiently. It was British Intelligence Inspector Charles Tetley. Tetley, who'd just arrived from London, was in Los Angeles on a mission of some great secrecy.

"Inspector, it's nice to meet you, I'm Captain Brink," the seasoned officer said extending his hand, and actually meaning it this time. "Please let me know if I can be of any assistance during your stay here in Los Angeles. The LAPD is at your disposal." Tetley, knowing this man was certainly not his equal in rank, felt he'd give him a modicum of respect, as he was, afterall, his liaison in the States.

"Sorry, forgot my cell phone. Come on, his office is down the hall, we can walk and talk," Brink said in a matter-of-fact, staccato fashion like his character had been written by Aaron Sorkin. Brink never liked formalities, but he tried when he could, to show pleasantry.

Fitzpatrick was leaning back in his old, leather, high-backed chair with his office phone buried in his head. He was senior enough to have an office, but it didn't matter, his booming voice carried, unless his door was closed tightly, so everyone at SIS could hear him.

No surprise, Fitzpatrick was making yet another friend. "You're all a bunch of morons!" he screamed during a heated phone call. "I put that son-of-a-bitch away twice, and your office set him free both times." Fitzpatrick was passionate about three things: college football, professional football, and police work. He had passed himself over for any promotions, any advancement that would take him off the street and away from being directly connected to crime. He knew he was close to forced retirement, and with all the budget cuts, corrupt city council members, and police chiefs, Fitzpatrick's days were numbered. This made for an unusually surly detective.

"I don't give a fuck about <u>his</u> civil rights! What about the rights of those girls? If I see that shit stain on my streets again, he's gonna end up a statistic! ACLU? Oh, God, I'm quaking in my Florsheims." Fitzpatrick slammed the receiver down hard and shook off the stress of his job. He closed his eyes, inhaled through his nose and exhaled slowly out of his mouth. A trick he'd learned from a gal when he took his first, and only, yoga class at 17th and Montana Avenue.

Fitzpatrick glanced up at two sets of shoes standing in his doorway. Brink could only shake his head in disgust. "Work'n on that promotion again, aye, Fitz?" Brink said sarcastically. Fitzpatrick held his hand up like a ghetto diva, "Don't start with me, Skipper." Tetley shifted slightly in his shoes behind Brink as he caught Fitzpatrick's eye. He gingerly stepped to the desk, gave a smug look as he searched Fitzpatrick up and down. Tetley was clearly not impressed.

"Oh right, this is Chief Inspector Charles Tetley, he's with British Intelligence," Brink started. "He's here on some sort of special assignment, so I need you to show him around, answer his questions, get him anything he needs. This is coming from the Commissioner's office, so try not to fuck it up." Fitzpatrick's face fell, "Skipper, I don't have time to baby sit Sherlock here, I'm up to my ass in back logged cases."

Brink's leading man good looks quickly changed, the kind of change that insured he'd stay captain as long as he wanted to. "Clearly you've mistaken me for someone who gives a shit. I'm not ask'n, Fitz. You <u>will</u> assist Inspector Tetley for the duration of his stay. Am I making myself clear?"

Fitzpatrick acquiesced, "Yeah, crystal."

Begrudgingly, Brink huffed, then turned and exited his subordinate's office. Tetley stepped closer and loomed over the detective's desk. This was not going to be a match made in Heaven.

Fitzpatrick jumped up in an attempt to change his own mood, walked past Tetley, out his door and through the precinct toward the coffee machine. He could smell the simmering brew, but not whether it was fresh or not. He grabbed a Styrofoam cup, poured it half full and cautiously drank as to not burn his lips. *"Blahk!"* Fitzpatrick cried as he powered down the thick, dark roast. "This designer coffee is for shit!"

Tetley folded his arms in pompous British fashion. "Maybe you should switch to tea, Detective?" he said arrogantly. Which was ironic because Tetley, although his name did lend itself to wealth and position in the world of tea, was not posh at all, in fact he came from a very impoverished upbringing. And even though he was from a lower caste, he'd always felt himself superior to others.

Fitzpatrick had already dusted off Tetley's comment and shot him a dirty look for good measure, when his phone suddenly rang. He always seemed to fumble with the tiny receiver as his hands were too large and his fingers too thick.

"Yeah, when? Okay, be right down," Fitzpatrick said matter-of-factly. He charged back into his office, grabbed his jacket, and bolted out the door, leaving Tetley standing alone like an orphaned child. After a moment, he stopped, backtracked, turned around and reentered, "Come on, Tea-Bag."

CHAPTER 26

L EGALLY, THERE COULD BE no basement floors in Los Angeles, yet older structures; especially government buildings, always seemed to have lower levels. They weren't fooling anyone that these below ground floors still constituted *death traps* as the slightest shaker over a 4.5 temblor could bring the building pancaking down like the Trade Towers. Yet no one ever seemed to want to talk about that.

The halls here were featureless. It seemed that the modern, but certainly bland design, was a product of lazy architects who chose instead to assign lower levels to be used for storage, since no one really paid any attention to them.

A pale fluorescent bulb eerily lighted the examination room. The new energy efficient, low sodium's were yellowish, but in this room they used greenish LEDs so as not to produce heat and ultimately hasten decomposition.

Although the area had been redesigned and looked somewhat updated, no one here could truly appreciate it. This, afterall, was the morgue.

A number of stainless steel autopsy tables filled the large room. The tables were elongated and wide to accommodate long and large bodies, had a drain at the bottom and a high-pressure movable faucet overhead to flush the excess blood, tissue, and gore. It looked like the scene out of movie, as the bodies, covered with pristine white plastic sheets, lay silent. Surgical instruments were organized with precision perfectly aligned on a small portable cart between each table.

In long white disposable gown, mask, and double exam gloves, the Medical Examiner, or ME as he was commonly known, spoke softly and methodically into a microphone hanging from the ceiling.

Dr. Vincent Chang had spent many years obsessively documenting every case he had before him like a Supreme Court Justice. He respected each body, as he felt he was their physical and spiritual guide over the River Styx and the metaphoric *Ferryman* to the next world. It was his job, not only as an ME, but also as an investigator to find the true cause of their demise and offer the final decision on who or what took the life of that soul.

The self-sealing double doors burst forth as Fitzpatrick entered in his usual Neanderthal fashion. "Fitz..." Dr. Chang said admonishing. He pointed to the table and as Tetley followed behind, to the box of shielded surgical masks. Fitzpatrick nodded and made a quick cut right and grabbed a mask, but no gown. He continued to the table where the doctor was working, leaving Tetley to fend for himself. *This caveman was a bull in a china shop*, Tetley deduced.

Fitzpatrick, almost out of breath, walked up behind Chang offering no salutation. They were old friends, colleagues, but it would've been awkward for them to exchange handshakes at this meeting. That was simply not going to happen in this environment.

"What's up, Doc?" Fitzpatrick said over his shoulder.

"The reason I called you down is it looks like our boy has struck again." Dr. Chang said in a curious, but interested way. He turned slightly to face Fitzpatrick and the stranger behind him.

"Don't worry about him, Doc, he's kosher," he said regarding Tetley.

Dr. Chang nodded, grabbed the white sheet with two hands, then slowly uncovered the body. It was a woman's body. Although during her life she was perfectly sculpted with perky breasts, lean rib-protruding sides and alabaster skin with freckles strategically placed across her form, she was now a rotting corpse. Her body had been dumped in the ocean and decomposition had accelerated rapidly. Eliminating the fish and other sea life frenzy over the soft tissue parts of her body, the only recognizable trait left was one green eye. Marine life had a habit of attacking soft tissue as it was easily managed, and everything else left for the larger creatures. First, they attack the soft skin, eyes, lips and cheeks. Next, it's onto the muscle and tissue, then finally digging deep into the body and eradicating the organs until the bones are stripped clean. What was still visible, ironically enough were the contusions on her upper thighs and between her legs. Fingernail scratches and purple bruises revealed to the veteran investigators, this girl was probably raped, and forcibly at that. Her formerly beautiful eyes were now blood red from petechial hemorrhaging, and only one remained. A single green eye remarkably untouched. It clearly belonged to Ciara O'Malley.

Tetley squirmed, shifting from foot to foot as Dr. Chang began his examination. Although a seasoned inspector, Tetley never could get used to this part of the job as forensics per se was, until recently, still in the American's wheelhouse. No one could blame him, afterall, he was taught in a typically English public school, and was from another time. He was brought up not to express emotion or be effected by *common* traits that Americans seemed to lavish.

Tetley pulled a monogrammed handkerchief from his jacket pocket and placed it over his mask to further filter the rank air. "Good Lord!" Tetley said in disgust. "That poor woman."

"Jesus, Doc, this one's torn up worse than the others," Fitzpatrick said studying her wounds. Dr. Chang, realizing he was not used to dealing with the living that often, offered his apologies.

"Oh, I'm sorry, would you like some balm? It's mentholated." Dr. Chang said to Tetley as he removed his gloves, then retrieved a small round bottle of what looked like Carmex. He took the balm from the cart, untwisted the cap and offered it to both men.

Tetley reluctantly agreed and dipped his finger into the waxy gel that contained, among other things, a mix of menthol, camphor, phenol, and a host of other acids and lanolin. He and brought it to his nose to smell. "Uhm, yes, menthol, that will do nicely."

"Just dab it in under the nostrils and breathe through your mouth, or I could offer you a drop of peppermint on your mask for the same effect?" Dr Chang continued. "Either way, it helps."

Dr. Chang dipped his finger in and smeared some balm under each of his nostrils. He offered it to Fitzpatrick who waved it off. After decades in his business, the seasoned detective was used to the smell. He felt that the stench would settle in his nose to be retrieved later. He determined that if he should ever lose interest in a case, or become complacent when following up with the family of a victim, the smell, that acrid, decomp smell, would be a constant reminder to him to be at his best for those who could not seek justice for themselves.

Dr. Chang began again in earnest. He defined each relevant point that needed to be covered, although there would be no need as the *Chain of Custody* stopped with him. He didn't need to justify himself to anyone, that is, anyone but a Grand Jury.

"Besides the obvious mutilation of the body, Jane Doe here had large quantities of what was probably seminal fluid in her vagina, stomach and rectum, suggesting multiple perpetrators," Dr Chang said in a tutorial manner. "She was tortured, brutally, and was probably alive throughout the entire ordeal. There are ligature marks and patterns consistent with her being bond, tearing of the muscles, tendons, and ligaments " Dr. Chang stopped for a moment and looked over his bifocals at Fitzpatrick. "You'll get *Special Circumstances* on these guys, Fitz." Who nodded in response. "As you can see, there's no *Y-Incision*. I haven't done a full autopsy yet." Fitzpatrick looked at Dr. Chang curiously as if to ask why. "A Preliminary toxicology screen showed doses of a synthetic form of Rohypnol, or *GHB* as it's known."

Fitzpatrick interrupted, "Doc, this was no *date rape!*"

Tetley, now feeling a little more confident, decided to chime in. "Doctor?"

Dr. Chang stood up, and turned to the two men. "Let me explain," he said. "It's synthetic, really sloppy stuff. Whoever made this crap probably flunked basic chemistry." Chang turned back towards the body. "Sadly, this poor girl would've died anyway! It may have taken up to 12 hours, but this shit was designed by a monster to keep someone alive just so long, then it fries the brain of the victim like an LSD overdose."

Fitzpatrick took off his mask and threw it hard to the floor. "This day's gone from shit to worse!"

CHAPTER 27

T DOESN'T MATTER THAT the Port of Long Beach is the second busiest container port in the United States or that, combined with the Port of Los Angeles, it's sister port, makes one of the busiest trade routes in the world, it was still a huge cesspool of corruption. Oh, the port and harbor were clean, relatively speaking; afterall it had won accolades and awards from the EPA for its pollution control and strides in reduction therein. But the graft, the union strangleholds and illegal black market cargo, even with Homeland Security breathing down their necks, made wealthy the right people who knew how to get things done. The two seaports imported and exported more cheap Asian goods and manufacturing, that if one was so inclined, they could acquire literally anything – there was nothing that couldn't be had.

Behemoth shipping vessels lumbered across the horizon and would have to be *stacked and racked* on a busy off-loading day. Oil tankers, freighters, General, and Dry Bulk carriers, container ships, super-cargos and super-tankers would slow and even full-stop as they waited to unload their payload.

An enormous warehouse near Dock 32 was stockpiled with various metal containers waiting their turn to be loaded and sent to sea. This day, it looked as if the owners were putting it up for sale. The concrete floor that ran the length and breadth of the warehouse was immaculate: recently hosed down, then manually swept dry. The sunlight that peaked in from atop Signal Hill illuminated the gigantic room and everything was in its proper place.

The *clunk* and *chip* of a heavy limp resonated and was recognizable as Victor Rostov's as he proudly lead a group of Russian investors on a tour of his holdings.

Unlike his usual maudlin and serious personality, today Rostov was somewhat excited, albeit still controlled, as the group passed each container.

"Gentlemen, what you see before you are hundreds of shipping crates. Inside these containers are millions of sixth-generation cellular phones. The latest in smart, wireless, voice-activated lightning-fast cells complete with satellite communications," Rostov orated like a politician. "Each of these phones cost pennies to produce and can be sold for hundreds of times our cost. Yet, even at such a small price, we undercut the American wireless market by 50 percent. This means our phones are affordable to every *Third World* nation and to the smallest corner of the globe. We will undercut the Chinese on their own soil and be able to practically give them away to our friends and comrades in Russia." The group of investors looked to each and mumbled.

Rostov continued to lead the group slowly, deliberately pointing out each example of his investment idea. At the center of the warehouse, he approached a number of large, burlap tarps that covered long, cylindrical objects. Looking up to a crow's nest high in the upper corner of the warehouse, Rostov nodded to an operator in the control room. As the signal was given, the man flipped a switch on his console and floodlights burst bright, illuminating everything below.

"You are all here today to invest in what will be one of the largest, single business ventures in our 50 year history." Rostov motioned with his hand. "We all go back a long way, Comrades: some of you from East Berlin, some of you from Chechnya, Romania, Hungary. What Mother-Russia could not give us, we take from the West's *Free Market Economy.*"

Rostov nodded again to the operator in the booth who pulled a large lever that initiated one of the trolley wheels. As mechanical and electrical sounds grew louder, the cables holding one of the tarps, began to reel in follow the rotating wheel. As the tarp rose, the floodlights revealed a large fuselage of what appeared to be a rocket. It was enormous, like that of the space shuttle or an old Cape Canaveral Titan missile from the 1960s. Yet, this was merely one of four pieces.

Gasps could be heard, followed by *oohs* and *aahs* that flowed freely from the investors. Slowly, two hands began to clap, then four and soon all of them applauded furiously at the wondrous sight they now beheld… yet one man tempered his excitement with patience.

The missile was painted bright white and was polished to a high gloss as though 50 men had spent weeks working it with hand buffers. At every spot where the floodlights reflected, it beamed and sparkled. There were obviously more sections to the rocket, but each was hidden for now, to be revealed only when readied for pre-launch. And no one, not even the scientists or engineers could come close to them for fear of accidents or tampering.

This giant could have easily been confused with some kind of militarized weapon or rogue missile as a well-funded group of terrorists might have created, except for the exterior markings.

Meeting all current guidelines and specifications, Rostov wanted his new prize to be above reproach. Two red, white and blue flags adorned it: one American, one Russian, and in deep red letters with yellow trim, the name: ROSTOV COMMUNICATIONS ran down the length near the ubiquitous tail numbers. *The only thing that would have made this rocket complete,* Rostov thought, *would've been a hammer & sickle.* But those days were long gone.

Each nut and bolt had been thrice inspected with every serial number documented as Rostov knew this was the last shot he and all his comrades had at winning the ultimate prize. They'd been waiting five decades to legitimize their illegal activity into one spectacular, albeit legal, business venture. This was truly *The American Dream.*

Rostov's investors were sold. They stood jittery in anticipation, whispering and nodding excitedly to each other while smiling confidently at Rostov as to not pull up their skirts too soon. The sole holdout, the buzz-kill as he presented himself to the others, was none other than Yuri Klaugin, *Capo di tutti Capi*: Boss of Bosses. Yuri looked like a miniature Russian tzar. He was shorter than the others, bald, but with a good, solid, well-shaped head and deep, carved crow's feet when he squinted. Feared by many, but respected by all, he was a man who carried tremendous weight on his shoulders, but could cut, slash and chop away at anything at anytime. While in his presence, one would be forgiven for feeling simultaneously impressed as well as frightened.

As the applause from the investors wound down, Yuri stepped forward to Rostov. "Are you planning to bomb the competition, Victor Vasili?" he said using the endearing term for his old soldier. "Remember, the Cold War is over," Yuri now said half-jokingly. Although cold and calculating, Yuri did see the opportunity for levity on occasion. But his intent was to test Rostov, push him to make sure his idea was sound and vetted through and through.

Rostov, in anticipation of just such criticism, nodded once more to the man in the booth. The operator pressed his thumb down hard onto a green button on the console and held it there for a moment. Yellow lights on either side of the warehouse lit up and a horn blew loudly as the enormous double door of the warehouse hangar began to open.

As they did, the investors turned toward the water to see a large freighter dockside. This was no ordinary cargo ship, no this ship was modern, high tech and looked as though it was outfitted to raise the Titanic.

"Gentlemen, I give you, *Sea-Launch*!" Rostov was beginning to embrace the showman buried deep within each of us. His decades of cold and bitter lack of emotion would not serve well with these men, as he had to convince them of his dream, he just had to. "*Sea-Launch*, a partnership of superior Russian and American technologies bringing us well into the Millennium," he said proudly. "That ship, Gentlemen, will sail to the equator and fire our satellite rocket into space. Once there, it will begin an indefinite geosynchronous orbit 60 miles above our earth. Then after we power up our satellite, we will control all communications for the new Russian Republic!"

Impressive. The looks on the investor's faces clearly illustrated their imaginations as visions of dollars, Euros and rubles, danced in their heads.

Even Yuri was starting to warm up. "How is it done?" asked Yuri, now more curious than skeptical.

A grin, not a smile, a knowing grin, began to form on Rostov's face. He knew if he could convince Yuri and get his blessing, the others would follow without hesitation, as loyalty was the currency in this man's game.

Rostov pointed to the vessel. "There, there in the center of the ship's belly, the stages of the rocket will be assembled horizontally and mated with our satellite." Victor began gesturing with his hands. "It is brought to a launch platform, much like an oil rig, in a secret location in the middle of the Pacific Ocean at the equator. Then the rocket is raised vertically on a platform and shot into orbit on a fully automated laser targeting system. Everything is pre-assembled, pre-packed, and nearly pre-paid. Gentlemen, at the end of this year, you will be able to call anywhere in the world, surf the web, download pictures of your grand children, pay your bills, or summon your mistress for the monthly price of a loaf of bread. We will make billions!"

The investors nodded in agreement and stepped closer as if to touch Rostov for his revolutionary ideas to rub off on them. *And now to the Q & A.*

"So, WE own the satellite, and WE provide the service to the people?" asked one investor.

"And WE own the phones that WE just sold to those people who will be using our service!" interrupted another.

"*Ah,* A Vertical Monopoly! That's what the Americans call it! This is brilliant, Victor" said yet another. The excitement was beyond containment now.

"Capitalism… Communism… it's all economics and market share now, Gentlemen," Victor saged. The others continued to nod like a colony of penguins as Rostov waved them to a long table near the back of the warehouse.

Each investor had at least one aide, some had more than one, but each carried with them a large case which looked like those carried by soldiers transporting weapons or computer equipment or even cash… lots and lots of cash.

Each aide followed the next in military fashion as they rounded the corners of the long table and placed the cases atop it. Each investor stepped up behind their case as their aide jumped to cover their flank. Security was no problem as the entire warehouse and surrounding area was covered with armed bodyguards. Even the seagulls seemed to have been silenced this day.

Already in front of the cases on the table were large binders with clear covers. "Please, Gentlemen, take a prospectus and peruse the contents. As it outlines, the cost of this enormous operation is $500 million dollars. The $5 million dollars you should have in each case is the second installment for the launch. The total investment so far is $250 million and the remainder of the money will be expected from you after the satellite is in orbit."

A concerned look came over an investor's face. "What is our guarantee? What if something were to go wrong? Some of us are investing our entire fortunes, obviously we cannot afford any mistakes."

Just then, Yuri interrupted as the other investors began to question Rostov with their eyes. "You all know that I would not be involved if I was not certain of this project's success," Yuri spoke calmingly, but then added a single, shivering caveat. "Besides, we have Victor's *loyalty oath* as our guarantee, isn't that right, Victor, Vasili?"

The investors were slowly pacified as Yuri's convincing comment was the blessing they'd all been waiting to hear. Now it was full steam ahead. The investors began quickly opening their cases, hoping to be the first to impress with their offerings. Some used keys to unlock a pad lock, others twisted the metal opener, yet all were eager to bestow their millions first to Rostov. After opening the cases some ran their hands through the money as to show there was nothing hidden: no small bills or blank stacks, the investors proudly stood awaiting Rostov's approval.

Rostov strolled the edges of the table like a military officer and smiled. This was his day -- finally. Any doubts he'd had about himself in the past would now be erased. The incident in Odessa in the late 60s or the investigations of the early 80s, all that was behind him now. No more strip clubs, prostitution and drug dealing. He had truly arrived. He was quietly being honored for his life's achievements and he wasn't about to let it slip away. As he began shaking congratulatory hands with the investors, he glanced one last time to Yuri for acceptance, or acknowledgment, or even just a nod. Instead, Yuri's eyes went black like a doll's and the look on his face was foreboding.

CHAPTER 28

SUNSET BOULEVARD CUT ONE of the oldest and longest swaths through Los Angeles, running from Olvera Street Downtown for over 20 miles. Sure it meandered through unsavory areas, but it also swung through cities like Beverly Hills and Brentwood, and eventually ended at the Pacific Coast Highway and the big blue of the Pacific. Along the way, though, Sunset offered visitors and patrons alike the opportunity to get dirty -- down and dirty. From the Body Shop to the Hustler Store, *The Strip* was a popular destination for those wanting a thrill and it's pseudonym seemed *apropos*. Yet the majority of Sunset wasn't as clean and tidy as the parts near Doheny & Kings Road. Most of Sunset was home to head shops claiming to be medical marijuana pharmacies, tattoo parlors and strip joints you wouldn't want an Iraq combat veteran to visit. This is where the Rostov's knew money could be made, the seedy side of L.A. Junkies, perverts, tourists, everybody ended up on this side of town for one reason or another and the Rostov's would happily be there to take everything they had.

The New York Strip, or *NYC's* as it was known, was your typical titty joint that flourished in desperate times, like the Recession of 2011and 2012, and the oncoming Depression of 2013, it was always in full swing. It was on East Sunset Blvd., far from the tour buses and preschools, but accessible to frustrated businessmen and curious college students. It was housed in an old building with apartments on the upper floors complete with Chinese laundry and a Falafel restaurant at street level.

The deep bass house music pumping from NYC was so loud it rattled the glass window display that posted the latest showcase dancer. Thick red velvet curtains ran from floor to ceiling, and were all a passerby could see if looking through the windows. Even if you were bold enough to enter, you'd have to pass through a divided sheet of black duva-teen: dense, sound-absorbing theater drapes that were common in the 40s and 50s and abundant in the old Hollywood antiques shops and local boutiques.

Bare-assed strippers in pasties and G-strings spun around shiny poles as others strutted in different directions on and off three different stages that rose above the seated audience. Yuppies, dregs, Charlie Sheen-wannabes, all threw $1s, $5s, $20s, dollar after dollar, to keep the sirens on stage and shaking their stuff. The dancer's sets were short, usually only four to five minutes, precisely the length of an extended rock ballad or trance hit from Ibiza.

On stage things seemed to move smoothly, but off stage, down the corridor in the changing rooms, it was organized chaos. Half naked, fully nude and Goth-Shock-clad girls dashed between each other darting in and out of the costume room. Chain-smoking fitters tried desperately to fasten one last hook as the dancers broke like linebackers toward the stages. It could've easily been confused for a Broadway play or Hollywood movie scene change if it weren't for Rostov's men. They were thugs in the truest sense. Talk about sexual harassment in the workplace, these men didn't just slap asses and grab boobs, they would chose their victims daily: rape, sodomize, objectify and generally mistreat any girl at any time they wished and NO ONE would ever say a word.

"Davai, Davai!" Oleg screamed at the girls like they were cattle. "Move your ass, you fucking sluts!" he'd say just to keep his voice in the forefront of their terrified minds. The atmosphere was even less pleasant here then on the stages. Most of these girls came from Eastern Europe: Poland, Ukraine, Belarus, and Budapest. They were sold a bill of goods by their families or friends, and were now, each one an indentured servant. Some were conned by Rostov's men back home, others were brought over to pay a family debt. Others still, would have paid for passage to the U.S., then held for ransom until family members could buy their freedom.

It was the cruelest kind of slavery as the girls were forced to strip night and day and most to whore themselves out until the Rostov's decided to give them their freedom... a freedom that would never come.

In the Champagne Room, each girl, either fit, lean, busty or saggy was forced to dance. Even the newly arrived had been taught by the lifers, strutted and undulated for 18 to 20 hours sometimes. Lap dances were just the beginning, then it was off to the *Closets,* as the girls called them, private rooms where the high rollers could get more than what was on the menu.

It was a busy night at NYC's, so no one heard the glass break in the old storage room as an object shattered the old pre-tempered window.

A dark-skinned hand ran a crow bar around the four corners of the frame to clear the tiniest shard. A long piece of cardboard from the dumpster behind the club was flopped down to keep knees and hands from getting lacerated.

In the dim alley light, three worn leather jackets crawled in through the window. The three men looked more like a splinter biker gang than the young Mexican thieves they were. Carlos, Miguel and Juan had had it in their minds for the past weeks to make a spectacular gesture to the man they admired most, and NYC's would be the perfect gift of which to present.

As the men climbed in with ninja stealth, they were careful to lightly touch their surroundings. In the dark anything could fall, smash, or generally give away their position. Carlos reached into his back pocket and pulled out a long, slender object. He pressed the small silver button on the black, polished wood when a long blade suddenly appeared and snapped into place. He brought it up to his lips and could hardly contain his excitement. "Okay, Vatos, here we go," Carlos said nearly bursting with laughter. He turned the deadbolt from inside the storage room and slowly opened the door. He cautiously poked his head into the hallway and peered down the length of both sides. All clear. He turned and winked at the others.

The storage level of the club was rarely used for anything other than liquor, food surplus, and the occasional liaison. When Oleg or Alexei got board with banging the girls in the closets, they'd move to the kitchen, onto the stage, in the dressing rooms, or in their offices. Nowhere was out of bounds for them. Despite being evil bastards, they did enjoy a healthy dose of diversity.

A single sliver of light shot from under the office door in stark contrast to the darkened hall as the three men slinked forward through the shadows.

It was late as Ivan and Gregor, two exceptionally large, yet not particularly interesting Russians, sat nearly eclipsed by the night's take of streaming cash stacked atop stacks. The Rostov's kept every dime the club brought in: the door, the bar, drug sales, prostitution, even the strippers. The girls were not allowed to keep any of the tips they made on stage or in the closets: that was a crime punishable by broken limbs or digit removal. The Rostov's knew a bitch had to be as physically attractive as possible, but even in a cast or a large bandage, the Rostovs knew some man would fuck her. They kept corporal punishment limited to hands and feet in order to keep the face, hair and bodies pristine. It was a judgment call.

As lumbering as Ivan and Gregor were, they were surprisingly good at counting money quickly and accurately. Once they'd finished a mound of cash, they would sort it into large and small denominations, create equal sized stacks, then push them to the other end of the table for storage. A safe that could hold three men was open behind them. Inside were even more piles of cash, drug paraphernalia and large plastic zip lock bags filled with pink and blue pills, white powder and green leafy buds. But on the top shelves of the safe were stacks of mini HD digital videotapes with writing from a black Sharpy, and production quality video cameras. The guns and AK47 magazines sitting next to all the pirate booty was just sheer overkill.

"Would it kill them to buy a fucking money counter like the other clubs?" Gregor grumbled. "Who else on this side of town deals with so much cash, I ask you?" Ivan, his lip raised from the endless count, shrugged and agreeably nodded. "I'm just saying, banks have digital counting machines at every window, we're like bank, da?" Gregor continued.

A smile pursed Ivan's lips, "Yeah, we're like a bank, a sperm bank, heh, heh." Gregor, not a man prone to showing a humorous side; burst out laughing.

It was at that moment the Mexicans decided to make their move. Carlos crouched on the ground and slowly opened the door with his hand at the bottom, while the others covered the opening with their guns drawn like a *SWAT* team. They had to be careful not to allow the music to pour into the room as they crept in. "Fuck, Ivan-Ivan-o-vich, that was a fucking good one! I'm going to tell Oleg that one." The two continued to laugh as the moment slowly died as they returned to their routine, unaware that the three men were already upon them.

"I think we can help you with your little problem, Amigos!" Miguel said drawing down on the two Russians. Startled, Gregor dropped the cash he was counting and began to jump up, but Miguel was too young and too fast. He stepped forward and with a *bam*, pistol-whipped him. Miguel smashed him with an overhead shot to his forehead, then continued on his face and head, knowing the shock to his face would probably knock him out. Gregor, grunted from the blows, then crumpled to the floor unconscious.

Carlos and Juan flanked Ivan before he could push his chair back. Realizing his fate, and knowing how intolerant Oleg and Alexei were to mistakes, Ivan narrowed his eyes to a cold stare. He burned the image of the three young men deep into his brain, knowing, if he were to live, he'd be required to recall their faces at the drop of a hat and in great detail.

Slowly stowing the .38 snub-nose into his waistband, Juan pulled out a thick silver object and began flipping it in front of Ivan. It was a butterfly knife he had ordered from a mercenary magazine after seeing one of the countless Rambo movies in his native Jalisco. He placed the razor-sharp blade to Ivan's throat, then slowly moved it under his jacket. He sliced something, but Ivan didn't move. *Could this monster from the Volga Mountains be that imperious to the pain of being stabbed or was it a delayed reaction the men were waiting for?* Juan thought. Suddenly, a thick, leather shoulder holster containing an old Takarov machine pistol, fell onto the table.

Ivan slowly sighed. "This is Alexei Rostov's club. Do you know who you filthy *wetbacks* are fucking with?" Ivan said regaining his composure.

"Si, we're fucking with you, puta!" Miguel quickly slammed the butt of his gun onto Ivan's temple, not wanting Ivan to prepare himself for the blow, or turn his head to force a graze. He caught him quickly in a vulnerable place. He knew he could easily kill Ivan with a blow to the temple, but these kids were willing to take that chance, as the *Risk/Reward* option seemed balanced.

They quickly pulled out a number of rolled up duffle bags from their coat pockets, unraveled them, snapping them in mid-air, then began scooping, pulling, packing and piling the cache of cash, drugs and guns into them. The three boys were in and out in mere moments.

As they cautiously slunk back toward the storage room to escape, two more of Alexei's men were entering the hall to retrieve a case of watered-down vodka the Rostovs used for their high-end bottle service clientele upstairs. The boys had to think fast – *the dressing rooms?*

Oleg was on a tear, the disc jockey was missing cues and overdubbing and smash-cutting house music with 70s funk. He was losing his mind, more due to the wear and tear of prolonged drug use than mere annoyance, so instead of choking out the dj, Oleg decided to grab a stripper ready to go on stage and drag her downstairs for a quickie. As he passed the office, he slid his hand under the stripper's Catholic schoolgirl plaid skirt and began to fondle her.

At the doorway, Oleg suddenly threw her to the ground as he looked in to see Ivan and Gregor bound and gagged. They were bloodied and still unconscious from their beatings. Oleg quickly reached behind him and drew his pistol. He searched the hallway with his eyes, then caught the last split second of Carlos bringing up the rear as the three attempted to escape.

Oleg squeezed the trigger again and again as bullets zinged past Carlos as they dove into the strippers' dressing room. "Go get Alexei and the others -- Bitch, now!" Oleg kicked the stripper in the ass hard as she stood to run back to toward the stages.

Hearing the gun shouts, Alexei and the others quickly appeared from all corners of the club. "Shoot, Goddamn it!" Oleg shouted to the others, who needed little prodding. Thus began a *Shoot-To-Kill* campaign of indiscriminate killing as the Russians unloaded magazine after banana clip at the fleeing Mexicans. Bullets flew everywhere randomly hitting men and women repeatedly.

Carlos, Miguel and Juan ran serpentine down the aisle, as the girls were having their hair teased or costumes changed. A bullet tore through a middle disc in Juan's spine. Miguel caught a shot to his scapula, which glanced off the hard bone and tore into his lung. Blood spatter shot high and low, over the girls and across the lighted mirrors that lined the salon-style room. Carlos, unscathed, was the only one who returned fire, hitting two of Alexei's men.

The three little thieves, though bloodied and injured had successfully shot their way out the back exit and made it to their awaiting car, the entire contents of their grab unchanged.

CHAPTER 29

THE MARINA WAS CALM and peaceful at night. Moonlight danced off the ripples in the bay and the tiny wakes late night trawlers would produce upon their return from a day at sea. Hardly a sound could be heard except for the bells and wind chimes on each boat that signaled a change in sea or wind currents.

Many owners lived on their vessels due to divorce, nostalgia, the economy, or for the fact that they could walk to any one of the numerous pubs and restaurants dockside and not have to contend with a *DUI*. It was paradise for the right-minded person.

McCann lay in the forward berth. The only light that came in through the darkness was from the opening in the hatch above the hold. He had opened it just a little to allow the smoke from his cigarette to rise and escape. He still found it hard to believe that things had changed so drastically, that virtually everywhere in the western world saw smoking as dirty and uncouth. He took a long drag off the cigarette, a pack Murphy had left in a little care-package for him.

McCann lay on the soft pillow with his left arm behind his head. It was the first time in over a decade he felt as though he was starting to relax. His right hand lowered to his side, still holding the lit cigarette. As he slowly exhaled, he focused on the distant foghorns at the mouth of the harbor, then drifted off to sleep.

[*The early morning mist lingered over the quiet green pitches as the first graying lights of morning crept in like a fog bank. Although it was bleak and bleary, the Belfast projects had a charm with stonewalls surrounding it like a fort, the architecture of the flats and the narrow, stone streets. British military convoys surrounded every block and were always present, always surveying the area, hassling the residents, looking for the proverbial needle in a haystack. Luckily, all the haystacks around this province were filled with IRA volunteers protected by their friends and families.*

There was no reason for McCann not to go about his life, so, like most nights, he got his four hours of sleep next to the missus and prayed for the health and happiness of his children as his head hit the pillow.

In his dream, McCann floated through his tiny, two-story flat and hovered over his own bed. He was a young man then, still in his 20s, still an ideologue. His young wife, Colleen slept soundly, wrapping one leg over his torso as she did ever night, giving him comfort and stability, even in the repressive, survival-at-all-cost environment they were forced to live in.

He hovered over to the other, smaller cutout they called a bedroom and watched his eight-year-old daughter, Nuala, who tossed and turned as she dreamt of kittens and dinosaurs. And his littlest one, Seamus, who'd just turned four, squeezing his stuffed cowboy as he kicked his sister who lay next to him in the small bed.

McCann drifted to the staircase and above his comrades who slept in the den, deserting their security post as they did ever night. He flew out of the window and around the red brick building that housed far more families than should have legally been allowed, then over the armored personnel carriers and half-tracks that rumbled through the streets in the dead of night. Over the roadblocks and border crossings into the Republic of Ireland manned by security forces. He soared beyond the sea of green-mountains and dales and fields full of heather. As he began to float out to sea, west toward the Americas, he suddenly felt the wind bump him, tussling his body...]

McCann woke suddenly with a start. The cigarette had long since dropped from his fingers and had burned itself out on the linoleum tile. It was the sudden rocking of the boat that screamed at his subconscious, *WAKE UP!*

He reached back behind his head and under the pillow to retrieve a large, .45-caliber pistol. He could see the shadow of legs passing the window and could hear the footsteps that someone was going to a lot of trouble to minimize. McCann kept the pistol under the pillow as he bolted a round into the chamber to keep the action soundless.

Slowly, the cabin door opened and a dark figure began to cautiously climb down the steps to the polished wood floor. McCann was already in position, up and crouched above the kitchen, his legs spread-eagle on either side of the back of the breakfast booth. He wedged his back against the ceiling and shelves and squatted his neck to become as small a target as possible if he were to be discovered before he could pounce.

As the figure crept silently toward the forward berth, McCann waited, waited, waited, then sprang from above. In one fell swoop, he had managed to jump behind his attacker, pass his right arm around the neck and under their chin while simultaneously wrapping his left arm at the bicep, inverting it in front of his right. He then took one step back and with all the leverage, cranked his arm and began a chokehold worthy of a boa constrictor. *This perpetrator had no chance –it was lights out!.*

Gasps and gurgles followed as, in an instant, McCann realized the neck was small and lean and that the body was slight and slender. "Urgh, Mick, it's me!" The tiny female voice coughed. It took another second to process as McCann was used to large, sweaty, hairy men saying the same thing as they'd tried to take advantage of him during his early prison days.

"It's me, Tracey," the voice rasped one more time as McCann knew her eyes were beginning to role back into her head and her brain was shutting down from lack of oxygen and blood cut off from both her carotid arteries.

McCann quickly released his death grip as the sound of Tracey gasping to inhale filled the cabin. He never even needed the pistol.

He moved his strong arms to her shoulders, and then spun her around. Still dizzy, she collapsed into his arms. He recognized her quickly and knew she was from Murphy's party. They'd had a moment and he was glad she was there, but why was she there?

McCann stroked her long black hair and touched her face to stimulate sensation and consciousness. He was a hard case, but this one could soften him.

"Mick," she said softly. McCann smiled at her, as he looked deep into her eyes. "What the HELL are you doing?" she screamed as she came to. McCann, not expecting all the commotion, stood slowly as not to frighten her anymore than he had. "You scared the shit out of me!" she shouted as she punched him in the shoulder. He tried not to laugh as the blow felt more like a tap on the shoulder than a punch.

Still in the darkness, McCann slid the pistol in a drawer he was leaning against so as not to scare her further. "I should be asking you that question, I'm supposed to be here," he said in retort. McCann flipped a switch and an overhead light burst bright.

Tracey now became concerned with her appearance, flipped back her hair and straightened her dress. "Well, I'm sorry I scared you," she said diminutively. "You're right, it probably wasn't a good idea to just sneak in without announcing myself, but I thought you might have been sleeping."

McCann's eyebrow rose with that comment as ironically, he was. "So were you just going to climb in bed with me, or did you have something more sinister on your mind?" Tracey, shocked by this comment, realized she was *way* out of her league on this one.

"Oh, Mick, no, I mean, I wasn't…I mean," she said flustered. He turned and walked back toward the forward berth. Confused, Tracey followed still attempting to justify her actions. McCann stood at the door with a welcoming smile on his face. *Now she was really in deep water*, she thought.

"Murphy said you'd be here and to just walk in as it would be cool and since we really didn't get a chance to talk the other day, and

I thought maybe you hadn't eaten and maybe I would come over and take you to dinner and, --," she rambled.

McCann put his index finger up to her lips. "I'm just mess'n. I'd love to come to dinner with you," he said genuinely. His expression was deep and meaningful and slowly calmed Tracey.

"That's the first dinner invitation I've gotten in America," McCann said, easing her tension. Tracey saw a look of what she perceived as relaxation on his face and something else in his eyes, something sweet, but forlorn that she was now drawn to.

McCann's smile was soothing to Tracey, yet knowing herself and knowing her past, she straightened up proudly, stuck out her chest and said, "But it's my treat!"

CHAPTER 30

I T WAS HARD TO see the beauty of the Pacific Ocean at night, you could see the lights glistening off sailboats and fishing trawlers, but for the most part it was pitch black and endless.

Tracey meandered through the curves and straight-aways of PCH as McCann, reclining, happy to let this beautiful creature do the heavy lifting, felt the cool salty air rush over him in the small convertible. Tracey always liked Moonshadow's Restaurant at night and thought it to be the perfect *first date* spot.

A valet ran up to Tracey's car as they stopped, he opened her door, she jumped out, then handed him the keys. McCann couldn't help but question her judgment. "You're just giving that man there yer car?"

Tracey smiled, "Sure, he's just the valet. Almost all the restaurants have valet service in L.A., silly." She continued as she briefly explained the service.

McCann was confused at this strange custom. "So let me get this straight: you give your man there your keys, he takes the car to God knows where, then you pay him to bring it back to you?"

Tracey thought a minute, "Well, when you put it that way, it does seem pretty stupid. Come on, let's get our table." McCann began to chuckle, then shrugged it off.

The two were ushered to the back patio and bid onto the white vinyl couches above the crashing waves. The couches were more like settees, the kind you might see in a coastal European resort or a Moroccan village restaurant -- very comfortable and very welcoming.

After a few moments Tracey suddenly got a chill as the temperature began to drop and the ocean breeze kicked up. "Here, let me," McCann said as he removed his black leather long coat and swung it over her shoulders, just missing the couple behind them. Now that was a noble gesture.

Tracey got another chill from this, but this time it had more to do with her emotions and the fact that no man had ever done that before. McCann, just plopped back down, unaware that Tracey's face had flushed, and continued to take it all in as he sat quietly.

He wasn't used to the company of a woman, especially an American woman, so he pulled an old Irish 50 pence coin from his pocket and began to roll it across his knuckles. It was a nervous habit that McCann had developed in prison to calm himself and focus on the task at hand.

After the order had arrived, McCann sat listening to the waves crash against the rocks below while the candlelight flickered. He'd all but tuned out Tracey, not because he was disinterested, but because he knew she was as nervous as he and was really just talking to get him to talk more. He wasn't that type of chap.

"... I mean, I don't know much about Ireland, except that it's green and beautiful and U2 is from there," she said digging deeper into her seafood salad. "Oh, and I think it rains a lot. My family's German, we really don't have any Irish blood in our family. What city are you from again?"

McCann rolled the 50P coin back and forth, back and forth, as Tracey almost became transfixed at his undulating hands. "I'm from the North of Ireland, there's two Ireland's ya know," he said, not to be nasty, but informative. *At least he was now talking.*

"No, I guess I didn't know that," she said happily. She thought for a moment he might actually be interested in her.

McCann nodded and leaned closer to the candle. "And, although I'm from a city, as it were, it doesn't resemble a city like this; I guess they're more like villages and provinces to you," he continued. "I'm from Belfast, but not a very nice part of Belfast."

Tracey decided to push the conversation a little harder. "So, is it me, or are you naturally shy talking about yourself?" Tracey stopped chewing, unconsciously awaiting his response.

McCann reached down, picked up his pint glass and took a long, inescapable sip. "I'm sorry, I don't mean to be, I'm just not used to -- well, female company." McCann finished off the rest of the pint and searched the patio for the waiter. He thought, *goddamn it, where's that waiter?*

"Do you mind if I ask you a personal question?" Tracey said curiously.

"It hasn't stopped you yet!" McCann said teasingly.

She wanted to answer back in a smart-alecky tone, but this was serious. "Is it true that you're an ex-convict?" she said, not knowing whether she really wanted him to answer or not.

"I was a <u>political</u> <u>prisoner</u>!" he said sharply. "There's a difference." Tracey wasn't expecting that. "I was a soldier, fighting an enemy that's invaded our country, occupied it, split it in half and continues a campaign of terror and oppression against the Irish people." McCann continued passionately. *Where the fuck was that waiter?* He needed to rein it in, he thought.

Tracey sat frozen by McCann's words and if there were any concerns over his past, they were now beginning to fade away. "But that's all in the past, you're in America now!" She said optimistically sitting up straighter and full of confidence. "You can start a new life all over again, you know, like a *do over!*"

McCann was now curious about this one, she wasn't like the girls he'd known, well he hadn't really known a woman in over a decade, maybe he was being too hard on her, maybe this is how women were in this day and age. He eyed her curiously and she felt every scan of his eyes.

"Are you married?" she asked inquisitively as she quickly looked at her salad, feigning as if it were merely another question. Americans

135

had an impetuousness that was usually forgiven by others in the world, but would be considered rude by some.

"I was," McCann said hesitantly. *Jesus Christ, I'm going to kill that fucking waiter... oh here he is.*

"Sir, are you ready for another one?" the waiter asked. Nervously he nodded and held up two fingers to double his order, gritting his teeth as though the waiter should stand close and keep them coming.

"Oh, you're divorced, aren't you? I guess ten years is a long time to be apart from someone," Tracey said oblivious to what was percolating in McCann's brain. "I thought I read divorce just recently came to Ireland?"

Frustrated, McCann knew the only way to change the subject was to just bite his lip and tell her. "It's not like that -- Colleen was her name."

"Oh, that's pretty name," Tracey interrupted as her ADHD was beginning to peak.

"My wife and children are dead - - it's just me now," McCann forced out the last words like he was expelling a demon.

Tracey dropped her fork hard on the plate. Her jaw dropped open at the realization of why this man was the way he was had suddenly become vivid.

"Oh, God, I'm, -- I'm so sorry, I had no idea," she said horrified as a wave of dread came over her. She was mortally embarrassed now and took an inventory of all the stupid things she'd asked him and how she had been so nonchalant to this man who'd obviously lived a very different life than her. She was wading in unfamiliar waters and could only do one thing -- she reached out and took his hand.

CHAPTER 31

YELLOW CRIME TAPE NEARLY encircled NYC: beat cops, cruisers, detectives, forensics, even a couple of off-duty CHP's were all milling about the crime scene.

Blood, bullets and bodies were strewn everywhere. Ironically, the music was still pumping and some of the girls were still dancing as their mascara dripped down their cheeks for all the tears for their fallen girlfriends -- and favorite clients.

Fitzpatrick lumbered into the strip club holding a Styrofoam cup as Inspector Tetley dutifully followed behind, though still not comfortable in his temporary surroundings. It hadn't helped that his new relationship with Fitzpatrick had not yet improved. In fact, their relationship seemed to be very much on the rocks.

Fitzpatrick stopped short and Tetley nearly ran into the back of him like Laurel to his Hardy. He began watching two strippers still jumping on the poles and sliding down in circular motions. Tetley couldn't believe Fitzpatrick would be so uncouth as to ogle and objectify a young woman in the middle of a murder investigation.

"Detective, you are a professional, avert your eyes!" Tetley huffed. Fitzpatrick turned and sneered at his English counterpart, then turned back toward the dancers.

"Ladies, why the hell are you still dancing?" Fitzpatrick shouted over the blare of the music.

One of the girls looked toward the other, inspected the room with her eyes, then meekly said, "We are told to keep to dance, no matter what!" She spoke in a heavy Ukrainian accent.

"Yah, if we stop we are beaten," the other said in broken English.

Fitzpatrick bellowed at one of the many civil servants standing around with their thumb up their ass until their orders came down, "Turn off that fucking music!" Fitzpatrick screamed like a blow horn. Everyone froze as they knew that particular tone, a tone that was, like many of their father's, loud and deep, strict and merciless. Now, no one was moving for fear of violating something in his eye line. He fiercely pointed up at the spinning disco ball and the big Bose speakers overhead, "Somebody shut off that fucking music... are you deaf?"

One of the sergeants grabbed a rookie and threw him toward the dj's booth up the stairway, mouthing, "You heard the detective, shut off the fucking music!"

The rookie was confused, so many buttons, so many cables. After a moment, he decided to pull the plug on four power strips and the room became quietly manageable. Fitzpatrick turned back to the girls still air dancing even though the music had stopped. "Ladies, please stop. Go over there and talk to the officers and give them your statement." Fitzpatrick smiled a paternal smile, as he knew the girls were probably illegal aliens, mules or junkies since Rostov had gotten a hold of them. He had a real soft spot for the disregarded and downtrodden, but couldn't afford the emotional baggage of getting involved that came with sympathizing. The girls smiled back thankfully, then quickly jumped off stage and toward the boys in the blue.

Fitzpatrick turned back to Tetley, "Come on Sherlock, time to get our hands dirty." He barreled through the club walking over evidence and bumping past techs and other lower level crime scene processors.

Bounding down the stairs every other step, Fitzpatrick, with his bulky size and questionable attitude, flattened officers with complete disregard to get to his destination. Tetley followed, gingerly taking each careful step and apologizing to the offended that had just been squashed by his counterpart.

Fitzpatrick spotted a forensics team down the corridor in front of the entrance to the changing room. It was a bloody mess. One of the team members, Tina Jansen, a young, sturdy woman in 30s was still dressed in her street clothes. She was normally very *by the book*, but had obviously been called in at the last minute from dinner or a date. Pretty in a bookish way, but sharp as a tack and unusually witty. She moved smoothly over and around the bodies, always careful and respectful. By this time her exam gloves were smeared with the blood of the deceased. She pulled off the pair, tossed them in the portable Hazardous Materials barrel and retrieved a fresh, latex-free pair.

Jansen's partner, Claude Washington was a cut up. He never, ever told people his first name, as he was embarrassed because of what his Haitian parents had named him, as it was a death sentence to a child. In Haiti, Claude was considered a name to be envied, here, not so much.

Washington was tall and lean and constantly had to fight his coverall garment as he was too thin for city-issued garb.

As Washington rolled over the body he had just begun inspecting, Fitzpatrick sniffed the air as he Tetley walked up. "Jansen. Washington. A little early for the Goon Squad, isn't it? Jesus Christ, this place smells like the Artesia shooting range with all the cordite in the air." Washington examined the half-nude body of the victim. "What a waste of a fine look'n *sister*," he tutted, shaking his head.

Jansen could only shake her head as she stifled a laugh, "I hope Washington's wife gives birth soon or I'm afraid he's gonna start bang'n these vics." Jansen playfully smacked Washington on top of his head.

"Hey, watch the fro," Washington snapped back as he tried to straighten any messed curls from his tightly trimmed Afro. His forearm tried to comb down any strays while he purposefully kept his bloody gloves away from his head.

"Jesus Christ!" Fitzpatrick snorted. "You guys are gonna need a month to dig out all the bullets." He always carried an array of disposable pens he'd steal from the supply room closet just for these situations. He took the pen from his lapel pocket and began to lightly probe the holes in the wall.

There were so many bullet holes, the wall now looked like an oversized pegboard. The detective probed each hole to different degrees, some bullets were shallow, some deep, and others penetrated right through the studs.

A young officer approached Fitzpatrick as he calculated each of the bullet's depth and trajectory. "Sir, the witness over there says that a Mexican gang came in and shot up the place." Fitzpatrick never missed a beat as he continued. "Sir?" the officer repeated, dangerously close to bothering his superior.

Fitzpatrick stopped momentarily, stood upright, turned to the officer, then looked past him. Sitting on the stage was Ivan, bandaged from his wounds and nursing his head with a paramedic's ice pack. "That fucking Ruskie over there is lying!" Fitzpatrick said without giving it a second thought.

Just then he dug out a small caliber bullet as the young officer, now intrigued, stared over his shoulder. Fitzpatrick popped two more bullets out of the wall, then two more and another.

"Indra!" Fitzpatrick shouted over his shoulder. A head popped up from below a table and acknowledged.

"Yes, sir!" He leveraged his forearm against the table top, stood, and quickly ran over with a giant baggie of shell casings. With each step, the bag jingled like Christmas. Officer Indra sidled up next to Fitzpatrick and slid the baggie into his hand without being asked.

"Look and learn, Rooks," he said as he turned back toward the men. Taking his pen, he rolled each bullet gently in his hand so as not to smear any fingerprints. "You see how this slug is smashed to shit? 5.56 millimeter. This is soft lead, crappie material for a bullet, but effective at close range, like a dumb-dumb, immediately flattens on impact and concentrates the force of the blow," Fitzpatrick edified. "This one, this big fucker here, this is from a machine pistol or submachine gun, probably 7.62, maybe 9mm." The other officers began to gather around, as Fitzpatrick was known for his knowledge of bullets. "Do any of you know what these slugs have in common?" Fitzpatrick waited a moment for a response, then lifted up the baggie and shook the shells to prompt any spark of memory. "Of course you don't, because these are all from Russian guns." He opened the baggie and gently dug through with his pen until he found a shell and picked it out." This shell here is from a Markov, this from an old Takorev or an AK, but this piece of shit is an Izhmash AN94, very new, very deadly, and very Russian." The collective gasp was audible from the other officers, even Tetley, who had begrudgingly stepped up now hung on Fitzpatrick's every word. He knew of the Russian mob existed here as they had in England, but was unfamiliar with the type of armament they used to kill with.

All were transfixed as they eyed each of the bullets. Fitzpatrick dumped them back into the baggie, the slugs, the shells, everything and tossed it back to Indra. "Bag 'em and tag 'em, Indra!"

The officer, obviously used to his gruff manner caught the bag before the contents could spill everywhere. "Sir!" he shouted dutifully.

Fitzpatrick bowled his way through the crowd that had now gathered and made a beeline for Ivan as Tetley followed in his wake. Various officers began making their way toward him in an attempt to ask his opinion, but stopped short, as they knew he was on a mission. He marched up to the stage and loomed over his next victim. Although LAPD and paramedics surrounded Ivan, they all knew the score when Fitzpatrick was on a rampage. They exited the area quickly, getting out his field of vision because something was about to happen and they weren't going to be the ones to rat him out to Internal Affairs, that is, if they valued their teeth.

Fitzpatrick snapped his hand open so quickly; you could barely see the smack to the side of Ivan's head, yet the sound was unmistakable. "Hey Boris, where are your scum-bag bosses?" Ivan had been smoking a yellow cigarette, indicative to black market Russian contraband that had now flown out of his mouth and half way across the room.

"Argh!" Ivan gasped, not expecting the blow. "Vat the hell you doing-k, cop?" Fitzpatrick bent down over Ivan again, this time pushing his hand between Ivan's clavicle and throat. He began to dig his wrinkled, corn-flaked thumbnail deep into the soft tissue that housed untold nerves, veins and arteries.

It was like Mr. Spock giving Andre The Giant the *Vulcan Nerve Pinch* as he bore further into Ivan's flesh. "You must've taken a helluva shot to the head, cause I think you're hearing has gone," Fitzpatrick leaned in once again and began shouting in Ivan's ear to a deafening decibel. "Where the <u>fuc</u>k are those pillow-biting Rostovs?"

CHAPTER 32

AST L.A. HAD ALWAYS had a reputation for gang violence, but over the past 20 years, the LAPD Gang Task Force had done a decent job of cracking down and cracking heads. You still wouldn't be caught dead wandering Boyle Heights or Geraghty Street after dark, but for the most part, the gangs kept things behind closed doors. However, they plotted new frontiers and territories to open all the time and, like the mafia, diversified and expanded where need be. Now, bingo parlors, bodegas and the back rooms of barrio clubs hosted *members* for an extended game of dominoes or *Digital Poker*, the latter incorporating butterfly knives, losers losing fingers, or worse--whole hands.

Pepe's was considered the finest Mexican social club in the barrio. It had a clean, frontage, fresh neon and would've been mistaken for little Tijuana by an unsuspecting tourist dumb enough to wonder up to the street taco vendor for a snack.

Music blared from speakers too nice for a place like this and unscrupulous Latinas, old and young would dance with a counterpart or solomente, to whatever mood they were in.

Card tables were strewn across the dingy tile floor as average men in Horchata-stained wife-beater T's, slapped down hard the small oblong domino *bones*, besting their opponent. "Oy-ye!" the shouts would resonate from muchachos here and vaqueros there -- it kept the club lively.

The odd drunk couple would bump and grind to the mariachi's accordion attempting the perfect tango, yet still this was a place for community.

The large ballroom was awash in yellowed fluorescent light, just the way the old hideaways in Mexico City would have them. Above the dancefloor a mirrored ball bounced red, blue and green colored beams from the strobe around the entire room.

Suddenly, out of nowhere, the tables began to tremble, and the dominoes danced nearly on end from the thump, thump, thumping that got louder and louder.

The patrons immediately thought *Earthquake!* That is until the penetrating light of the 10 million-candle halogen spotlight of the Sheriff's helicopter bore through the tiny cracks in the painted windows and the turbo prop-wash nearly blew out the walls.

A rumble of muffled shouts ordering a legion of SIS Commandoes grew with intensity as they got closer and closer. There was a moment of eerie silence, then a *BAM* as the thick, Belizean mahogany doors burst open. *First Unit Assault Team* in full riot gear blasted the doors at center-mass with a steel ramrod. *Second Unit* poured with dozens of laser-sightings dotting each patron, accessing, then acquiring their correct targets.

In a mercurial fashion, the commandoes inserted themselves, then split the room down the center, making an aisle all the way up to the bar.

Oddly, the Mariachi music was still blaring as the whirlwind of activity quickly ceased and everyone stood or sat frozen awaiting the next move. From the dust and debris, and through the bluish-white light, Fitzpatrick appeared, unprotected, wearing nothing more than his gold shield on his belt. He marched in and headed directly to the back. Tetley followed, sheepishly, in full gear, oversized and falling off his thin frame.

The commandos stood at the ready preventing anyone from moving, their mirrored face visors reflecting the strobe lights and lasers like cyborgnetic robots from the future.

Fitzpatrick marched up to a table of men, their domino play

unaffected by the dramatic entrance of the police. A lean man with black greased-back hair slapped down a bone and smiled, revealing a single gold front tooth. He took a sip from the coffee cup next to his stake.

He was *El Cid*, leader of the *Vato's Locos*, a powerful Mexican drug gang. Unimpressed by the LAPD's display of force, he sipped loudly as he slowly cocked his head and looked up at Fitzpatrick.

Not in the mood, and rarely showing respect, Fitzpatrick grabbed the back of a folding chair and whipped it around, sitting even before it had stopped moving. Somehow, when the detective wanted to, he moved like a young man. He had plopped down next to El Cid as Tetley took a position in a neutral corner away from anyone with darker skin than his own.

"Oh, El Cid, L.A. ain't as big a town as you seem to think it is," Fitzpatrick said sarcastically. "You just can't waltz over to the North Side without folks knowing it! Why is it you always think we white people are stupid?" El Cid looked over the dominoes, plotting his next move. Fitzpatrick leaned in, brought his face nearly nose-to-nose with El Cid, "I know it was your men that hit Rostov's strip joint," he whispered. "I know because the idiots shot everything they weren't aiming at!" El Cid smacked his lips, but a small chink appeared in his armor. "You're go'n down this time, *Jefe*," Fitzpatrick whispered again into his ear.

El Cid's eyes widened slightly for a second, then closed to a slit as he picked up a domino and placed it gently next to his opponents. "I think we can come to some sort of an arrangement, Detective."

CHAPTER 33

YOU WOULDN'T THINK, WITH all the controversy and infamy the LAPD had, they would put one of their most highly secret and most lethal divisions one block from the beach inhabited by nearly as many skateboarders as grains of sand.

The Special Investigations Section, or SIS precinct was a modern building, built in the 50s, rebuilt in the 60s, left to decay in the 70s, but revitalized in the 80s and 90s, then finally destroyed and rebuilt in 2008, just before the economic bubble burst.

It had more high-tech infrastructure than a U.S. embassy abroad, and, surrealistically enough had daily tours available, as all good Los Angeles attractions did.

The walls were fabricated from a special mix of urethane and clear plexi with a Mylar inner and outer coating to deter laser microphone surveillance or any other type of cutting-edge eavesdropping. There were cameras positioned everywhere, some even over-lapped each other so nowhere was there a blind spot. This put any TV crime lab or secret agency to shame as the reality had become better than fiction.

The foyer was actually a rotunda and probably conceived by Eli Broad as it was more art than function and looked suspiciously like a Hollywood agent's digs rather than a police booking, holding, and processing tank.

El Cid sat quietly in a small interrogation room alone with his thoughts. A large plasma monitor filled the entire wall, but didn't fool El Cid, he knew the cops were sweating him as they drank cool drinks and ate their doughnuts in the other room.

Fitzpatrick and Tetley observed El Cid through a one-way mirror. "I don't know how you guys do business in the U.K., but over here, we don't have to torture them to get what we want," Fitzpatrick said sipping a soda.

Tetley's face wrinkled as he said, "Ab-U-Grab! That's all I have to say about that!" Fitzpatrick, contemplating a justification, decided against it, and redirected his anger instead.

Perps always jumped slightly and El Cid was no different as Fitzpatrick barged into the interrogation room. He pointed Tetley to a safe zone as he entered. He'd psyched himself up like a football player about to take the field, and grabbed the sole item on the table in front of El Cid, which was a small universal remote. He pressed a button and the plasma screen burst bright. El Cid sat quietly, he was used to being rousted over the years, and he thought himself immune to police pressure since he popped his cherry at 12 years of age. But he absolutely did not like Detective Fitzpatrick. There was something about this man that intimidated El Cid, *Fitzpatrick was too much like, like, his father, El Patron.* And El Cid knew, deep in the recesses of his psyche, this pain in his ass could possibly break him.

The lights automatically dimmed as Fitzpatrick pointed the remote toward the scanner on the wall near the door. The lights slowly faded and the room lit up blue as the DVD warmed up. After a moment, the screen filled with jumping images and muffled noises. Then the real show began.

Preceding the graphic images, the room suddenly echoed agonizing screams and pleads for mercy. Much of what then happened was unintelligible, but after moments, everyone in the squad room seemed to know what was now being played. El Cid never appeared shocked, in fact he looked indifferent, but Fitzpatrick knew it was all a macho front. El Cid was a drug dealer, unsympathetic to the wanton desires of human addiction, and unfazed by pleas for more or less, but this was no drug deal. What was being shown was a gang rape and murder and it was long, monstrous and inhuman, at least, that's what the detective was betting El Cid would see it as.

Russian voices poured in from every direction in the scene. They laughed and high-fived each other as they took turns raping and sodomizing their victim. These were Ciara O'Malley's last moments of life, an eternity of pain and suffering at the end of her short time on earth. She died at the hands of monsters, far from her home and far from the loving arms of her friend's and family.

Tetley grimaced as a sickened look eclipsed his face. Fitzpatrick, already having viewed its sin over and over again, became understandably enraged. Unfortunately for El Cid, the detective's emotions would be directed towards him.

In a split second, Fitzpatrick was on El Cid. With almost unbelievable speed, this larger than life middle-aged man scooped up the thin Mexican, one hand around his throat, the other smashed into his crotch, lifted him in one motion off his chair, then slammed him up against the clear plexi wall for all to see.

As Fitzpatrick smashed and mashed his face into the glass, El Cid could hear his gold tooth scraping the mirror like nails on a chalkboard. The heat from the fiction of pressure and movement against the mineral sent a shot of pain into his jaw like a dentist drilling into a raw nerve without anesthesia.

"Who the fuck was holding the camera, was it you Cid?" Fitzpatrick shrieked into one of his ears. Fitzpatrick pounded his head against the wall again. The other detectives outside the room could hear the thud as El Cid's head ricocheted off the wall.

It was protocol to immediately intervene when a policeman got out of hand with a suspect, but everyone knew Fitzpatrick and knew why he was leaning so hard on his suspect. They quietly went about their business as if nothing was wrong: filing papers, processing bank fraud suspects, but tilting a head and eyeing the dinosaur detective's *old school* ways of interrogation.

"I asked you a question, you piece of shit!"

El Cid, his cool façade now crumbling, shouted, "Hey, I brought this to you, *gabacho*, remember!" Fitzpatrick was an unusually strong man, especially for his age, and he meant business – he did not suffer fools.

At the same time this was happening, from outside the interrogation room, six officers were attempting to drag a large suspect into the processing area. Upon closer inspection, it was an enormous black man, out of control and handling himself well for having half-a-dozen uniforms trying to subdue him.

The cops knew this perp well and had dubbed him Tiny Tim. They were used to seeing him in psychotic fits of *roid rage*, but every one of them hated the idea of having to engage him on any level. But it was the only way they could keep him off the streets, temporarily at least, and away from innocent people. A former pro-football player who'd lost all his money on what were now known as *Charlie Sheen Weekends*, Tiny Tim was a Baby Huey on steroids, wearing only diapers, a cowboy hat, and snakeskin boots. He was truly a slave to fashion.

After a few moments, Tiny Tim seemed to get bored of playing with others, so he decided to kick it up a notch by throwing the officers off him one by one until the entire precinct was now involved.

One of the smaller detectives began to bang on the window for help. Another barged into the interrogation room shouting in desperation, "Fitz, give us a hand! Tiny Tim's back and he's got a bad case of diaper-rash!" Fitzpatrick normally hated being interrupted, but a devilish smile suddenly slipped across his lips.

From the open door, El Cid watched as Tiny Tim began tossing male and female officers around like swatted flies. Marquez, one of Fitzpatrick's favorite detectives, even though she was female, pulled out her stun gun and zapped Tiny Tim. Nothing. Marquez looked at the gun, checked the charge, it was good, then ran around the room. She locked eyes with Fitzpatrick who squinted his eyes and threw his face forward. "Hit him again, Marquez, this time with feeling!"

Tiny Tim was like the *Terminator*. He'd already taken hundreds of thousands of electrical volts and, even though they should've coursed through his being and knocked him on his ass, it only seemed to make him madder. Marquez thrust the stun gun into Tiny Tim's spine, leaned her body forward, pressed hard on the trigger and locked it down.

Slowly, Tiny Tim dropped to one knee, then the other, as a thin line of smoke rose into the air from his burning flesh. After he collapsed, the dozen or so officers were able to drag him to the temporary cell in back of the room. He was stunned for sure, but began to recover almost immediately. This was no ordinary man -- if he were a man at all.

Wrapping his enormous fingers around the back of El Cid's neck, Fitzpatrick squeezed until he knew his prisoner would go anywhere he wanted him to. He dragged El Cid out of the interrogation room and into the center of the precinct. "Cid, I'm thrown'n you into lock-up with Tiny over there if you don't stop jerk'n my chain, I shit you not!" Fitzpatrick shouted over the din of the riot. "That Chickenhawk has torn a new *Bagina* on every one of his cellmates for the past three years."

Tetley, confused by the term blurted out, "Did you say, *Bagina*, Detective?"

Fitzpatrick leaned back and turned his head, "Yeah, I'm gonna tell Tiny that ole' Cid here is a child molester, and he's gonna turn Cid's butt into a vagina and tear it up like it was happy hour at the *Bunny Ranch*! And Tiny has a prodigious reputation, he loves going for hours and hours – and he gets off on the screams," Fitzpatrick laughed devilishly.

El Cid, still refusing to answer the question, was easily pulled across the carpet toward the holding cell by the back of his neck. He remembered his papa used to do the same thing when he was in serious trouble. Fitzpatrick nodded for two of the officers to unlock the cell door. They each held separate stun guns, tasers and even a beanbag shot gun. They may have been armed, but they did not want to be in front when Fitzpatrick opened that door, so they bolted to the side to watch the 'ol pro work his magic.

Suddenly, Fitzpatrick swung El Cid's hands behind his back and cuffed them together then he tossed him into the cell. A pall fell over the room as everyone stopped what they were doing and shut the hell up because there was about to be an explosion the likes they may never again see in their lifetime.

Fitzpatrick was one of the few officers that could control Tiny Tim. Oh sure, he practically matched him with size and strength, but it was the added fury that gave each man mutual respect of the other, he was by no means intimidated by this prisoner.

"Oh Tiny, here's a little somethin' from all of us, call it a belated birthday present -- it's your new bitch, Cid!" Fitzpatrick called Tiny Tim out, but had to try hard to contain himself from bursting. Just then, Tetley left the safety of the interrogation room and walked up behind, at a safe distance, of course. He was simultaneously awe-struck and repulsed at his counterpart's methods. Yet Fitzpatrick, now seemingly nonchalant, walked right over to the coffee machine and began to make himself a fresh cup-o-Joe.

Feet scuffled; muffled cries arose as a commotion ensued in the cell. The other officers in the room quickly assembled to watch Tiny Tim gather his faculties and began to advance on his quarry. Unintelligible grunts and groans emanated from Tiny Tim while he licked his lips as he nodded in approval of his new toy.

Just then, screams rang out and the sound of tearing clothes and slapping flesh filled the air. "Wait til your crew finds out you rolled over and went fag in one day, Cid!" Fitzpatrick shouted lifting the pot to top off his cup. "Uhm, we're outta *Stevia!*" Fitzpatrick remarked searching the table with his eyes for more natural sweetener.

"Alright, alright, Jesus Christ, I'll tell you! I'll tell you!" Fitzpatrick sipped the piping hot coffee slowly, then looked at the two officers at the cell door. "Hold up, give him another minute or two so he doesn't decide to change his mind later."

Tetley stood cross-armed with a disapproving look on his face. After a moment, the officers wrestled El Cid away from Tiny Tim using a cattle prod, then pulled up the whimpering mass of flesh and hauled him back toward the interrogation room. Tetley followed Fitzpatrick who now followed the officers as they dragged El Cid and sat him gently back down onto his chair, careful not to disturb his fresh wounds. El Cid was sweating profusely, as he tried to wipe the froth from the corners of his lips with one hand, while using the other to cover his crotch to hide the urine stain that was still growing in his pants. El Cid had been broken.

"Okay, last night some homeboys got into some mischief and had a little business go south on them, comprende?" El Cid said, now in an unusually obliging mood. "They grabbed some cash, some recreational pharmaceuticals, and those DVDs."

Fitzpatrick looked over at Tetley, sneered a combination of *fuck you and I told you so,* then back to El Cid. "Get to the point!"

El Cid squirmed in his seat, "Those Russian locos have been pushing into my hood, ya know? Maybe somebody wanted to even the score a little, ya know, hit 'em during business hours and such -- make it hurt, send a message!"

Fitzpatrick, getting frustrated, knew his blood pressure was beginning to spike again. "Cut the crap with the somebody shit - You ordered the job!"

El Cid, taking umbrage and not getting any traction for his bargaining chip retorted, "That tape's worth a walk and you know it, Fitzy!" El Cid said with a macho attitude. "Besides, you got dick on El Cid! No probables, then there's that whole illegal-search thing. I'll call my Jew, lawyer-up and be outta here in an hour, ya know I'm talking verdad."

That was his last card to play, and El Cid knew it. But Fitzpatrick was an old hat at this type of negotiation. "Sorry tough-guy, you're my inside man now, and only my friends call me Fitzy!" he said as he laid down the only deal that was going to be made.

"I want everything on Rostov and you're gonna get it for me." Fitzpatrick raised his arm and half-turned to point back toward the holding cell. "And if not, there's your motivation for keeping your ass virtuous. Don't forget, Tiny over there can do more damage in an hour than a Marine platoon can do in a week."

CHAPTER 34

URPHY WAS BUSY WIPING down the bar with a stout-darkened rag while Kelly washed the last of the pint glasses before their doors opened. It was just another ordinary day as Kelly mumbled and grumbled at the list of chores that awaited him while always managing to forget something important that would cause him grief later. A tremendous banging on the front window caused the older Irishman to nearly jump out of his skin. Murphy seemed unaffected by the noise as the homeless often did this when the passed by on their way to the beach, but just to be on the safe side, he tossed the wet bar towel over his shoulder and headed towards the front.

"Jesus wept!" Kelly shouted, "Who the hell is bang'n to wake the dead?" Murphy made his way to the front door to unlock it. He peered through the security eyepiece to see Fitzpatrick and and another blurred figure looming outside. Fitzpatrick tried to look in the eyepiece from the other side.

Murphy undid the bolt and happily swung open the large door. He smiled as he bi his friend enter, but his smile quickly turned to scorn as he came face to face with the stranger. "What the fuck is <u>he</u> doing here?" Murphy spit pointing at Tetley from behind the door. "Like fucking <u>hell</u> am I'm letting him in my establishment!" Murphy shouted louder this time. "That bastard killed my sister, my niece, my nephew, and everyone I loved -- I should do him where he's standing!"

Fitzpatrick could hear Murphy fiddling with something against the door, probably a small caliber pistol, or a Louisville Slugger 9. He was actually taken aback as he'd never seen this side to his friend Murph, and would never think him capable of such vitriol and savagery. *Maybe he didn't really know his friend that well afterall?*

"Whoa! Murph, wait, I'll explain everything," Fitzpatrick interjected putting his massive frame between the two men as he scooped Tetley around him to bring him into the bar. "You gotta trust me on this," he pleaded, realizing this mild-manner barman just went from zero to psycho in under two seconds. Slowly, cautiously, Murphy closed the door behind the two men and stowed whatever weapon he had behind his back, blocking it from view.

"I swear if he gets outta line, I'll kill him myself," Fitzpatrick whispered to Murphy just loud enough for Tetley to hear. The door opened quickly. It was obvious Murphy was hiding something that could surprise all of them, so Fitzpatrick put his hands in the air to show he was unarmed, slowly reached around Murphy's back and discretely disarmed him. He then made sure that he put himself between the angry Irishman and the smarmy Englishman all the way back towards the bar until Murphy could cool down. These two were natural enemies, and his experience told him they weren't about to kiss and make up.

Fitzpatrick marched the two others toward the back office like a water buffalo, letting nothing slow his pace. Murphy's jaw was still clenched and his knuckles whitened as he stayed a half step back at Tetley's 5 o'clock. He raised his right arm up high to bring it down hard on the back of Tetley's neck, but Fitzpatrick shot him a look. With different chemicals and emotions running through his brain, he could hardly contain his rage and murderous thoughts. Tetley, acutely aware of Murphy's anger was altogether unimpressed at the bravado, but none-the-less knew he was in the Irishman's kingdom now and would be forced to govern his tongue. *This will be tough,* he thought.

In the back office, Fitzpatrick slammed the DVD into the player, clicked the remote and queued it up to the spot he needed. He pressed the remote continually and freeze-framed a shot of the limo.

"Listen, Murph, you're a good friend, so do this for me. It's not gonna be easy, but I need you to identify the girl in the video," Fitzpatrick said calmly. "Look at her closely, just tell me if she's the one that was here the other night... and Murph, Brace yourself, this isn't going to be pretty."

Murphy, found the detective's tone curious, and decided he's play along, but suddenly looked a mixture of intrigued with murderous madman. He shot one last evil glare at Tetley as Fitzpatrick hit the play button on the remote. Each man turned their attention toward the screen and watched intently.

With every scene more disturbing than the last, Murphy began to cringe, lowering his shoulders in disgust at the futility of his own helplessness. He'd suddenly been drawn in by compassion, but horrified to the point of revulsion as he watched Ciara O'Malley attempting to fight off her unseen abductors. When he could no longer take it, he averted his eyes, even as the young woman's screams grew louder and louder.

Unbeknownst to the three men, a dark figure had slowly crept up toward the back office from the unlocked alley entrance. It was McCann. From the long corridor, he spied Kelly sweeping the front bar. Kelly reached up to wave and shout a salutation, but McCann instantly placed his index finger to his lips. Kelly touched his own finger to the side of his nose and nodded in compliance. Kelly smirked, seemingly to reflect on the old rebels days and the code: *say nutt'n til ya hear more.*

McCann slinked up and peered through the crack in the back office door. His eyes widened in shock, then narrowed in rage as he watched the horror on screen.

"That's her, Fitz!" Murphy shouted at the television screen. "Sweet Mother Mary, that's Ciara O'Malley. Ah, Jesus wept, what bastards could've done a thing like this?" he cried out in what could only be described as real pain. Murphy took his hand and made the sign of the cross, blessing himself.

"I'm sorry Murph, You know I can't say anything about a case," Fitzpatrick said, almost ashamed.

"But Fitz, she one of ours!"

The detective snarled in what seemed like contemplation for a moment, then nodded his head.

Tetley, witnessing the obvious breach in protocol interrupted sternly, "Detective, you cannot break protocol!"

That was all Fitzpatrick needed to hear. "Russian hoods, probably the Rostov's," Fitzpatrick said sneering, brushing off Tetley's by-the-book whimpyness. "You can hear them in the background." Fitzpatrick pointed to the screen, "There, that one. That douche bag was *Spetznatz*! You can tell by the Russian Special Forces tattoo on his forearm. Definitely Russian mob as they like to keep those guys on their payroll."

Fitzpatrick wriggled his thumb and depressed the remote to freeze the frame, then pressed it two more times to zoom in tighter. Murphy pounded his fist onto a table in anger, unconcerned with the pain and swelling that would surely develop with each traumatic contusion. Fitzpatrick stepped up to the table. "You've known me a long time, Murph, so trust me when I tell you -- let me do my job!" Fitzpatrick said with fatherly sage. "We know who these guys are and I'll have them in custody in a week -- and I guarantee you they'll get *the needle*!"

Murphy now seemed more nervous than angry as he searched the room with his eyes. "I've gotta call Frank, Jesus, I gotta call Frank!"

Tetley jumped into the fray, "Frank?

You mean her father, Frank O'Malley? I knew it! The girl was a courier," Tetley said in disgust. "He sent his own daughter here to set up an operation."

McCann, having infinite patience from over a decade in prison, wanted to interject and beat his nemesis to death with his bare hands, stopped short as knew now wasn't the time for *his* revenge.

"Shut up, Tetley, you don't know dick!" Fitzpatrick snapped back as the tension was now rising exponentially. "Murph, these Ruskies are ruthless, well-financed and have zero respect for life. I know you're connected, but I'm warning you, no, I'm begging you, don't fuck with these guys -- L.A. ain't Belfast!"

Murphy stood and lunged toward the door as he shot Tetley daggers with a deathly leer. Fitzpatrick raised his hand, "don't bother, he's not our concern. Let's go."

Fitzpatrick grasped the metal bar on the back door and threw it open. He, too, was upset with what he'd seen, and he'd thought he'd seen it all. It never got easier when you were a detective. Homicide, rape, brutality, *for God's sake, he was still a human being*, he screamed inside his head.

Tetley followed close like a scared puppy awaiting a rolled up newspaper, as somehow he'd even managed to piss off Fitzpatrick more than he already had. "Are you fuck'n nuts? What's with all the '*oh, she's a courier* bullshit'? This *Tsunami orphan's* deal has been in the works forever and it was set up through the U.S. State Department," Fitzpatrick couldn't stop shouting at Tetley. "Ciara O'Malley was no fucking courier, she was a innocent girl!" Tetley knew when to speak and when someone was just venting, so he held his comments back. "Jesus, I feel sorry for that poor thing, but it's nothing like what'll happen to the Locos," he said changing the subject.

"What do you mean?" inquired Tetley.

Fitzpatrick talked as he walked, "Rostov'll want payback for the strip club hit in a *big* way. It'll spark an all out gang war."

Suddenly, Fitzpatrick got a strange tingle in the back of his head. He snapped his head around like an angry gorilla. Seeing this, Tetley followed suit. It was McCann and he had appeared behind both men out of nowhere like a poltergeist.

Fitzpatrick, not easily startled, was suddenly unsettled by this stranger's stealth. "... And who the <u>fuck</u> are you?" he barked as his defense mechanism kicked in.

McCann leered coldly at Tetley, his crystal eyes becoming dead like a shark's just before a kill. "Your man Tetley knows who I am -- I just had to be sure it was really him," McCann said with the lulling spell of a serpent.

Tetley, recognized the voice as Northern Irish, but confused as how someone 6,000 miles from his home would have the vaguest notion who he was. He studied this strange man's face. He studied the grooves and the pox, the ridges and the scars as he was trained to do in a split second. It wasn't until he concentrated on the man's piercing eyes that he realized. *"McCann?"* Tetley shouted in a combination of fear and realization. He stepped back and instinctively spread his legs shoulder-width and brought his hands up into a combat-ready position. His adrenal glands opened and shot fluid like a bullet throughout his brain -- it was fight or flight.

McCann, fought hard to control the murderous thoughts he'd been entertaining, then turned his head toward Fitzpatrick, while keeping Tetley in his peripheral vision.

"Detective, you're a friend, but this one isn't," he said in a low tone. He turned his eyes back to Tetley. "Like you said, 'L.A. ain't Belfast!" McCann, driving his point home, slowly backed up and cautiously glided down the alley, but not before shooting one last glare at Tetley, "remember that, murderer!"

CHAPTER 35

T
HE GUARDS AT THE old prison were exhausted from all
the amnesty about. They had been pulling double-shifts and
nearly tripled the squads by dipping into the guard pool from
H Block. Since this was a political prison about to be shuttered, it
was held to different standards from those of a minimum, or even a
maximum-security facility. But just the same, those differences also
lent themselves to unusual release scenarios. It was a far cry from
the days of Bobby Sands and the hunger strikes, but none-the-less,
it was stressful.

It's bad enough the cons were getting special treatment, the
guards collectively thought, but the bloody press and sympathetic
media were causing problems at home, even to the point of having
their children hassled at school by reporters. The guards wanted this
whole *Good Friday Accord/Belfast Agreement* shite over and done
with so they could go back to their jobs of keeping the lunatics from
running the asylum.

Frank O'Malley was under heavy guard this day. Tight security
was required with each release, but was now becoming merely
a formality, as none of the prisoners would be dumb enough to
jeopardize their release, or any of their fellow inmate's. It had become
more like a party and it was the one thing the guards knew not to
mess with. They had better treat those prisoners squarely on the
inside as they, too, had families on the outside.

Frank was led through the *Gen Pop* corridor, smiled and waved like a diva after a performance. He even shook the hands of the other guards, as he was led into the yard. All the men cheered. Frank look just past his fans and could see his newly waxed sedan just outside the gates with his four large bodyguards waiting to take him to the closest pub, or brothel, or to maybe just a park and let the light of freedom warm his face. As the sergeants opened the outer gate and made the transfer from prison guards to bodyguards, Frank turned back for one more look. A last wave surged the cheering crowd to a crescendo.

Frank's bodyguards stayed in tight formation as reporters clamored for an interview with the former IRA leader. Afterall, Frank O'Malley was big news, he could have easily jumped on his soapbox and made a political statement, chastised the RUC, or condemned the prison system, but instead he declined all interviews like a gentleman. He said nothing; he just waved, and smiled.

As they secured Frank into his car, one of the men handed him a cell phone. From the window, others could see him laughing at first, then stopping, listening intently, and for one brief, dramatic pause, his face seemed to age a lifetime.

"Ah!" Frank's screams of emotional pain could be heard for blocks as his men quickly drove him away.

CHAPTER 36

THE ROSTOV MANSION LOOKED like something out of the old television series *Dark Shadows*. The old stone-block frontage was graying now with mold and hard water stains since it faced away from the east and the sun's rays. It was an odd choice for Southern California, but perhaps made the owner feel closer to his dacha in the Volga Mountains of his youth, giving it that little, miserable, touch of home.

Fitzpatrick flew through the neighborhood past a line of limousines that could be seen as he crested the hill. They sped past a group of limo drivers, *Slavs* the lot of them, and searched for an opening close to the mansion. Since the limos took up all the real-estate in front of the home, Fitzpatrick slammed the brakes down hard on the Crown Vic, and blasted the gearshift into *park*. He had his foot out the door before the vehicle ever stopped moving. The car was now in the middle of the road, strategically blocking anyone's entrance or exit. He didn't bother to signal to Tetley who was now getting used to the fact that if he didn't keep up with this ogre, he'd just be left behind.

Security was extra heavy this day as it was the day Victor Rostov's youngest son, Oleg, was to be married. Guests by the dozens were escorted from their limos into the mansion usually with the escort carrying a large, ostentatious gift.

Armed guards with dogs roamed the enormous property walking

in and around the perimeter of the grounds, hunting and pecking for any suspicious activity.

Two cars in the minefield of limousines just didn't stand out. They were unmarked and unassuming, but Fitzpatrick had caught a glimpse of them none-the-less. His brain had not registered a hazard, so he didn't give them a second look and felt no immediate threat, yet he should have -- they were Feds.

Tetley mindlessly followed Fitzpatrick as he cut a trail across the perfectly manicured lawn, as the detective took the opportunity to create divots and wreak havoc in Rostov's pristine grass, and with each dig of his heel, he put a little twist on it... a little *fuck you* for good measure. He was becoming quite chuffed with himself that in some small way, he was able to screw up something Rostov was probably very fond of. That pleasure would abruptly cease when suddenly four federal agents surreptitiously blocked him from taking another step toward Rostov's home. A short, stocky man in his 40s with jet-black, slicked back hair, approached. He was Special Agent Michael Mancuso and his fuming shot out of the top of his head like a cartoon character as he marched toward the two.

"And where do you think you two are going?" Mancuso yelped, trying to control the volume of his voice as to not alert Rostov's men. "These guys are under surveillance -- *federal surveillance!*"

Fitzpatrick, having no patience, especially for ambitious federal agents, broke through the barricade of men. Tetley followed hesitantly. "I could give two shits, Mancuso, you fucking brown-nosier!" Fitzpatrick barked. "The Rostov's are murder suspects now, and I've got fucking jurisdiction, so get the hell out of my way."

Mancuso, seeing the futility of trying to negotiate with an extra-departmental agent, turned to one of his men. "Kenny, call Detective Fitzpatrick's commanding officer, it's Brink, right?" Mancuso said pointing to a now slowed detective. "Notify him that the FBI is attaching murder charges to the list of federal indictments." Mancuso clasped his hands together in a conclusive way, "Well, that's it! It looks like you and your little European friend here can take an early lunch -- Stand down, gentlemen!"

Tetley, who had yet to stop, turned toward Mancuso now remembering U.S. federal authority trumped the local police any day of the week. He suddenly seemed relieved.

Not so much for Fitzpatrick. He spun around and made a beeline back toward Tetley. "Call Mother Theresa for all I fucking care about your federal authority. This is L.A. fuck-stick, so shoot me, cause ya ain't got balls or anything else big enough to stop me from walking inside!" Fitzpatrick reached out like a boxer, grabbed Tetley by the lapel, and in one motion, dragged him the rest of the way up the lawn. "Come on, you."

CHAPTER 37

THE TIMING COULDN'T HAVE been more advantageous. While Mancuso and the other Feds were busy harassing Fitzpatrick, all eyes were on the wedding party.

Wedged between the line of limos in the back service entrance, a large flower delivery van had pulled up coinciding with Fitzpatrick's arrival.

An odd looking delivery man in a tight green smock and ruffled white collared shirt jumped out of the driver's side cab. He kept his head down and averted his eyes from any contact as he tried to adjust his wardrobe that seemed far too small and mismatched for him. He hummed an unintelligible tune going about his business, carefully opening the double doors at the back of the van.

Gently, he extracted an enormous *Bird of Paradise* flower arrangement, then peered through the bouquet that was covering his face. It was Murphy. His arms bulged through his shirt and the tie erratically hung around his neck. He looked almost out of place -- almost.

Murphy placed the flowers on the street, then jumped into the back of the van and closed the doors behind him. He pushed aside a group of vases filled with tall plants to reveal a young man, bond and gagged, amid the commercial flora. Murphy reached over and slowly pulled the duct tape off the teenager's lips being careful to not damage his face.

"Don't you worry, fella," he said slapping the shirtless boy lightly on his cheeks. "There's a bigger tip in it for ye, than these rotten bastards would ever give ya!" Murphy pulled out a wad of hundred dollar bills as thick as his hand and flipped through the stack, proving they were all legitimate. He brought it to the boy's eyes and once again flipped through them like a deck of cards. The young man's eyes lit up, as he smelled the currency.

Murphy snickered, then shoved the wad of cash into the young man's bare armpit. "That should take care some college courses, eh, son? But this is all hush-hush like, ya know? If we find out you mentioned this to anyone, well…! " From the front of the van, Liam, Hammer, and Sean turned around intimidatingly and stared down the lad. Still reeling from the size of the wad of cash, the boy grinned wide and gleefully nodded in acceptance. "You guys are cool!" Is all he respond.

From the van window, the men peered out at the front lawn only to see Victor Rostov himself waving a large fresh salmon in the air while proudly displaying his enormous Kodiak bear.

Rasputin stood on his hind legs slowly, cripplingly and tried to dance with each clap of Rostov's merciless hands. The old bear was riddled with arthritis in all his joints as he'd been terribly mistreated, lacked sufficient vitamins or sunshine, was malnourished, and had suffered endless beatings. But the creature had one advantage… he remembered everything!

He may have been a tortured prisoner whose sole purpose was to act like a trained monkey, dancing for his keeper's pleasure, but with the scent of fish, he remembered his days in the wet forest, in the cold streams and the taste of spawning salmon. Rasputin wanted to roar out in anguish at his suffering, but he knew he'd get the lash or worse.

As the giant animal stood painfully on his hind legs fully erect, Murphy watched in disgust from afar. Just then, Yuri, and the investors arrived to round out the sideshow.

CHAPTER 38

IN THE BACKYARD OF the palatial estate, three young boys took turns playing with a remote controlled airplane. They wondered at the colorful instrument panel, pulled the toggles backwards for the aircraft to rise, then pushed forward for it to nosedive. They seemed far too adept at the task that demanded manual dexterity, the likes that only young people today could show at their age. They watched for hours as the radio-controlled airplane swooped and spun, shot skyward and buzzed the guests annoyingly. This was truly a young boy's dream come true.

Since Rostov's mansion was high above the ocean, the boys flew the plane out over the water, along the sea cliff, back over the crowd in the yard, down into the canyon. There seemed no better fun to be had on a sunny day.

It was a drone model *X-WingBR*. It had a homemade primer grey paint job and whined and whinnied at a high pitch when its gas-powered engine throttled up. It was loud, noisy and obnoxious, but was tolerated by the guests, as the boys were part of Rostov's family.

Murphy had slid past the guards and appeared from the side gate carrying the huge flower arrangement. He was careful not to draw attention to himself, but was seemingly walking in the wrong direction. Then, he began to curiously take interest in the boys flying the model plane.

For a moment, he wandered back in his memory to when he was a boy. He'd always loved toys and laughter and games, but where he was from, they never had anything so exciting. All he and his friends had when he was a boy, were sticks and stones. Their idea of fun was hurling flaming debris at the British troops and the RUC or whoever was occupying their country at the time.

As he reminisced, his odd behavior suddenly caught the eye of the wrong person: Alexei Rostov. Already on high alert and artificially paranoid from an insatiable appetite for cocaine, Alexei yelled across the yard, "Hey, asshole, bring the flowers to the front. Can't you fucking idiots follow orders?"

Murphy merely smiled and bowed his head in a *mea culpa* sort of way. He then attempted to pour on his charm as he lifted the flowers higher to cover his face. "Sorry, sir!" he said in his best dorky American accent.

Alexei scowled at Murphy. "Fucking immigrants!" he mumbled.

Ironically, the security guards that swarmed the property never gave a second glance at the help. By now, Murphy had maneuvered toward the house and slinked in through a side door of one of the eight garages. He was in.

As boys with toys do, they began to fight over their turn at the controls and the model plane circled higher and higher in the melee. At full apogee, it lost control, went into a tailspin, and finally crashed, landing in the coyote brush amid the other chaparral near the cliff's edge. The boys screamed a collective, "Shit!" They knew the plane had probably been damaged.

From under the wedding canopy fashioned for the patio the boys were summoned by an old woman, "Davai!" she shouted. The boys, as boys will do, had now completely forgotten about their plane, dropped the remote control where they stood, and bolted for the buffet table filled with food and sweets.

Just below the edge of the cliff on a rocky outcropping, an unseen hand reached down behind some sagebrush and carefully picked up the downed model plane.

CHAPTER 39

THE DRAWING ROOM AT the Rostov mansion was every bit as cliché as the rest of the enormous compound. The foyer, rooms and library were mahogany and dark wood-lined from top to bottom. Wooden walls, cabinets, books shelves, desks, credenzas, even the floor was made of the most expensive hardwood. The shelves were filled with books, or so it seemed, as Rostov was, in fact, a bit of a phony when it came to appearances. And, as appearances go, it could be deceptive since his bookshelves looked to be filled with priceless first-edition classics from Shakespeare to Tolstoy -- yet it was all a cleverly crafted façade.

Rostov, having neither the time nor inclination to read, had paid a small fortune to have the shelves custom-made by a Hollywood prop outfit in the northern San Fernando Valley. Each book spine was molded and fastened to a large wooden board that could be inserted into the shelving frame. Each faux cover was hand-painted and aged with crackle resin to resemble each classic. It was the height of vanity and hubris, but since people did look up to Victor Rostov, he felt it was his duty to continually impress them. The desired effect had not failed yet. Thankfully, none of his colleagues seemed to care much for reading, either.

Rostov was in an unusually good mood this day. His youngest son, Oleg was marrying the wispy and gorgeous supermodel, Ivanka Ivanovov, who had promised to give him many sons. He was of course, concerned with his son's excess for all things excessive, but knew, if need be, Rostov himself could perform the procreative duties, insuring his realm would continue unabated for generations to come.

The old man was equally confident as today his investors were all with him, enjoying his hospitality, to celebrate the blessed event. Of course, like so many other things in Rostov's life, this was all a front. He knew it was his last-ditch-effort to raise the funding for his grand scheme. Now, by *Vore z vacone* tradition, they were required to front the money needed to complete his epic operation.

After an extended tour of his mansion proving to his fellow comrades he was not about to jeopardize his fortuitous lifestyle, Rostov led the investors into the drawing room for a traditional cognac.

Yuri Kalugin had never been to Rostov's home, but was no taking in all the excess, yet the shrewd old sable was not easily impressed. He was himself incredibly wealthy, although humble in comparison to his comrades, and the lyubov for his beloved deceased wife, Elenochka, kept him grounded, yet more to the point, off the radar of the U.S. Treasury Department or the I.R.S.

Yuri knew Victor was, like many of his countrymen, extremely insecure about where and what he had come from, and to flaunt his wealth and success was merely a sign of his deep-rooted insecurity. Yet Yuri was disturbed as this clearly presented itself as weakness. Still, Yuri thought, Victor was a good earner and no matter what the malady or poor taste, he produced for the good of the organization. Yuri had long overlooked Victor's flaws because they had never interfered with business. The only thing that ever worried Yuri about Rostov was his offspring: Alexei and Oleg. *They were vile, loose canons.*

Alexei suddenly appeared in the hallway and pranced ahead of Rostov as a child would, while the old man bid the investors to the conference area. Like a hawk, Alexei realized something about the room was now different. On a long wooden table there was a small package tied with a blood red bow sitting next to an ornate vase overflowing with orchids. *Hum, orchids are bad luck,* the Russian thought.

A manservant followed closely behind Rostov holding a large, and seemingly heavy, humidor. As Rostov walked behind each investor now seated at the conference table, the butler would pop open the humidor for their inspection. Each man searched the box choosing carefully. Some rolled the cigars under their nose to smell the freshness, still others only concerned with the label. *Romeo & Julieta, Machanudo, Davidoff, Graycliff, Cohibo pura Dominicana Robusto,* the list was endless. All the cigars were said to have been hand rolled on the sweaty thighs of teenage virgins from Cuba, Central and South America. They were extremely expensive, the best quality, and only top-shelf.

By now Rostov too, had seen the floral display and gift, but since it was his son's wedding, thought nothing out of the ordinary, merely, perhaps, in the wrong place. *Yet who could have left a present there,* he wondered?

Waiters, butlers and servants abounded. They scurried in and out of the drawing room with bottles of brandy, cognac, and premium Russian vodka for the die-hard nostalgist.

As the investors happily partook of Rostov's generosity, Alexei curiously opened the strange package. "What is this, Papa?" Alexei said in piss poor English, untying the bow and tearing the paper like an ape with a flower.

"I have no idea, Alexei, Alexa-i-vich," he said in a low tone as not to offend in case anyone in the room had left the gift.

To the father's, and son's surprise, the package contained a single DVD. There was no label, just a clear plastic jewel case. The only instructions came in the form of blacker marker that read: PLAY ME. Rostov looked across the long wooden table to see Yuri nod ever so slightly as it was time to begin. Rostov lost all interest in the DVD and turned to his investors.

But Alexei's interest had piqued. He walked to the wall where a small media center lay replete with a large flat screen television, *blu-ray* player and all the hi-tech gadgetry men do so enjoy. He hit the remote button that simultaneously popped the disc open, turned on the LED and fired up the theater system. He dropped the disc into the machine.

Yuri slowly stood and raised his brandy snifter. "To Oleg on this blessed day," Yuri began the toast in an unusually pleasant manner. "May he have many strong and healthy children, God willing -- Ura!"

The others raised their glasses and toasted, "Nostrovia!"

Alexei hit the *play* button with the remote and almost instantly the screen burst to life with screams and the appallling images of Ciara O'Malley's vicious rape and murder. Momentarily entranced, Alexei began to snicker and smile at his handy work. *Which asshole from his crew had played this practical joke on him?* He thought to himself. What he didn't realize was that behind him, everyone's attention was suddenly drawn to the disgusting act being played out for all to see.

There was no time to stop the DVD before everyone in the room saw the happening as it was purposely cued to the right spot. Alexei, his brother Oleg and the other men in their so-called posse, were clearly seen raping, torturing, sodomizing, and murdering the young life on camera.

Some stood and protested, others waved their fists, but all were stunned. The investors couldn't take their eyes off the screen as each scene became more unsettling than the previous. The mood in the room irrevocably changed and mumbling broke out amongst the others.

"Smut, on your son's wedding day?" Yuri barked. "Tasteless Victor, tasteless." Victor lunged toward his son, grabbed and tore the DVD case from Alexei's hand. He fumbled with the package as a small envelope taped to the bottom appeared.

In one motion he swiped his finger, opened the letter and pulled out a card that read: *"HAND OVER THE MURDERERS OF THE GIRL OR WE WILL HOLD YOUR ENTIRE ORGANIZATION RESPONSIBLE."*

Seeing his father's displeasure, Alexei quickly shut off the DVD player. "Sorry gentlemen, that was from Oleg's bachelor party," he said sheepishly, "things got a little out of hand with a whore!" Rostov glared at his son. Alexei's face had turned red in anger realizing his father was somehow now displeased. Seeing something was amiss with Alexei, Yuri pushed hard against the wooden chair, arose, then turned and exited the room in frustration. The other investors, giving the father/son duo a sneer, followed suit by standing and exiting in military fashion one by one.

It was at that very moment Detective Fitzpatrick burst into the mansion through the large front door and into the foyer as two large bodyguards ripped from their complacency, rushed to stop him.

Fitzpatrick was like a wrecking ball on a rusty chain, no one was going stop him today. With the investors and other wedding guests crowding the hallway, it was the perfect distraction for Fitzpatrick to uncouthly plow his way past them towards the drawing room. He was so single minded, he didn't even bother to notice that his Irish friends from his favorite pub: Hammer, Liam and Sean, were wheeling large equipment crates into the mansion, unmolested by the guards. Murphy slowly popped his head up from behind a crate while still hiding his face as he literally brushed past Fitzpatrick. *Phew, that was close!*

Back in the drawing room, Rostov raised his hand and smacked Alexei hard across the face for his idiocy as Fitzpatrick barged into the room. Tetley had politely excused himself through the gathering crowd and was late to the party, as usual, but safely brought up the rear.

"Let me get in on some of that action!" Fitzpatrick shouted for additional effect as Rostov smacked Alexei again.

The guards, who had been mired in the human wave of guests, suddenly appeared in the room behind the detective disheveled and panting from exhaustion and embarrassment. Quickly, Fitzpatrick pulled his badge, flashed it to the room, and shook his head. "Ah, Ah, Ah, everybody relax," he said implying any molestation of his person would meet with serious repercussions. Rostov nodded to the extremely annoyed guards that were primed now and ready to kill

Fitzpatrick for humiliating them, but they knew they'd be able to deal with him later. "Bye, bye!" Fitzpatrick taunted the guards as he waved them off like a little schoolgirl.

"I am sorry, officer, it is not <u>convenient</u> for you to be here," Rostov said in a low, and questionably sarcastic tone.

"It's <u>Detective</u>, asshole, and it wasn't convenient for those girls to die at the hands of your evil spawn!" Fitzpatrick growled, gritting his teeth. "Your fucked-up offspring are about to be charged with murder, among other things, and I'm gonna make 'em pay." Alexei's lack of impulse control caused him to take immediate umbrage at this man's brazen insults, regardless of the truth in his statements. He bolted toward Fitzpatrick, but before he could cross the room, Rostov, as cool as a cucumber, threw his arm out to stop his son from making a very big mistake.

"These are serious charges, Detective. I presume you have a warrant?" Rostov responded.

"He doesn't have shit, Papa! These fucking cops have nothing better to do than hassle us because we have money," Alexei barked like a yapping poodle. "Just like O.J.! You pigs are just fucking jealous."

Fitzpatrick made his way over toward the bookshelf. *Hey, why not take a minute and do some investigating while you're antagonizing a suspect?* "Your two whack-jobs are linked to over a dozen rapes and murders," he said to Rostov as he inspected the bookcase. "I just thought you should know. I'm hoping they're still here when I come back with the warrant."

Rostov and Alexei were momentarily confused. Was this a bribe? Was this law enforcement officer here to offer a freedom for his two sons for a price? Now things were getting interesting. Alexei and his father loosened slightly. Money was easy for Rostov. He could always negotiate, that was the currency of his life, negotiations.

"And why is that, Detective?" Rostov said in a playful, open-to-comprise sort of way. Fitzpatrick ran his fingers over the faux book covers on the shelves. He flicked a warped corner like he was picking the dried end of a scab. The wood gave way just a little to reveal the façade. *Wow, even this guys books were bullshit,* the detective thought.

He turned back around and faced the Russians. "I'm hoping they won't be here so I can track them down and shoot 'em like the rapid dogs they are!" Fitzpatrick said succinctly. Rostov's temper transmogrified his face, but somehow he contained himself.

"Good day, gentlemen!" Fitzpatrick had made his point; nothing more needed to be said. These were men of action, not talk, they all understood each other and knew that then and there was not the place it would happen… but something definitely would happen!

Fitzpatrick nodded to Tetley who had been standing idle, just listening to his American counterpart. *These guys are bleeding crazy,* he thought. They turned and began to exit the drawing room. *Whoops, one more thing,* the detective thought. "You know, Rostov, those two pussies of yours had to drug all those poor girls just to get laid 'cause no woman in her right mind would ever sleep with open wounds like them voluntarily." Fitzpatrick added. "You're gonna wish you stayed in your little dacha in Russia, you fucking commie!" Fitzpatrick turned back to the bookcase, slowly grabbed the warped wooden corner with his enormous hand and tore off a quarter of an entire section, leaving a gaping hole lay in its wake.

As the two left the same way they came, Alexei started to follow, but Rostov interceded and swung him around with one hand, smacking him again in the face with the other. "I'll deal with you, идиот, later. Until then, you do nothing! There is too much at stake for any problems, now."

CHAPTER 40

FROM THE BOTTOM OF the long winding staircase, Murphy looked up and winked at Hammer as they passed each other: one upstairs, one down. He whistled gleefully as though he owned the place, but inadvertently caught the attention of one of the guards.

"Hey, stop whistling," the guard shouted, "It is bad luck to whistle in house!" Murphy nodded and immediately stopped the unconscious habit.

"What the fuck does that mean?" he whispered under his breath. Afterall, he was a naturally happy-go-lucky fellow. *So why was it bad luck in Russian to whistle -- and why can't they use proper English with articles like 'the' house when they speak?* Murphy shrugged off the notion of the superstition and made his way down a long hall. While Murphy busied himself probing for opportunities and weaknesses downstairs, Hammer checked all the upstairs doors to see what was behind them.

Hum, let's see, hall closet, bathroom, towel storage, bingo, he opened a door and suddenly startled two security guards as they monitored a bank of closed circuit televisions. Screens showing the grounds, the wedding guests arriving, the driveway, the foyer, the patio, almost every inch of the estate was covered by these *Eyes-The-Sky.* The guards whipped their heads around and leered disapprovingly.

Tempted to smile back for what he was really thinking, Hammer instead apologized. "Sorry boys, just look'n for the Box, you know, the little boy's room," he said convincingly, yet insincere.

"Back downstairs, Paddy," one of the crusty guards snarled. Oh, *Paddy, is it,* Murphy thought? *You're on me shit list now, Boyo.*

As Hammer made busy, Sean searched another area of the upstairs quarters. He, like his fellow Irishmen, had been posing as one of a countless wedding day servers, florists, plumbers, any cover identity to gain access to as much of Rostov's property as possible. Sean may have had the toughest cover as he was forced to carry a large black canvass bag that held the equipment needed to do his particular job. It was big and bulky and, although Sean was tall and lean, he still had to hoist and swing it when rounding a corner. *Frankly, it was a little embarrassing,* he thought.

He entered Rostov's master bedroom like he was walking into an office. Um, nice plush carpet, but white? *Who's your decorator,* he thought.

Sean, too, had a song stuck in his head since listening to Pandora on his iPhone, humming it joyously as he took great pleasure in his work. "Hmmm, hmmm, hmmm," Sean happily hummed, unaffected that he was in enemy territory or that his friends constantly gave him grief about his idiosyncratic behavior.

"Ah, here would be good," he said quietly as he set down the bag behind a nightstand. He opened the tote to reveal a well-organized surveillance superstore. Sean had everything available to monitor, eavesdrop and surveil anyone at anytime, anywhere. He thumbed his way through burst-transmitters, wireless earpieces, light bulb bugs... ah, here it is. He grabbed a spring-loaded screwdriver, popped it into the outlet on the wall and pulled off the faceplate. He carefully opened a tiny plastic box in his other hand. He pinched a red and blue wire and gently clamped a listening device to the 220V power supply. He checked the needle on a small hand-held meter. *We're hot! Who needs batteries when Comrade Rostov pays his power bill?*

Sean sat back down against the bed and searched the opulent room. "Now where to put my eyes?" he muttered under his breath.

Oh, that'll do nicely, he thought as he locked onto a gaudy oil painting of Rostov and his wife above their conjugal bed.

Sean continued his work in earnest as down stairs, Murphy seemingly meandered like one of the help. It was highly unusual for Los Angeles, but Murphy had a perpetual smile glued to his face. He realized that L.A. really was a place where no one actually showed true happiness or had any joy to speak of, but his personality could just not be beaten down. Not in Belfast, and certainly not here among these lightweights.

"How's it go'n?" he said in a playful way wheeling his crates past a kitchen filled with Polish caterers and kitchen staff. They were beautiful young women and each knew instantly Murphy was trouble, but the kind of trouble they'd happily jump into after their shift was over. Murphy winked again as he passed the large pantry and out of sight. It was there at the end of a long hall near the lift: a basement stairway.

A basement or cellar in Southern California was seen by most as nothing more than a sure tomb during an earthquake. But even Murphy knew that the mansions built nearly 100 years ago, still conformed to turn-of-the-century craftsman standards. He parked this payload at the top of the stairs, quickly worked out the physics of getting it down in his head, but before he descended to begin his search, he saw a large electric dumbwaiter, almost the size of an elevator.

Murphy carefully, cautiously made his way deep into the belowground vault. It would be difficult to explain why he was there, so he thought about his excuse if he ran into any trouble. *The bathroom excuse was getting old.*

At the bottom, there was a maze of doors and a host of options on which way to go. *Typical of rich scumbags with evil intentions*, he thought, yet he knew he was in the right place. Anyone like Rostov would do all his dirty business as far away from his family as possible.

As he walked into a main chamber, Murphy came upon an illuminated scale model of the Rostov's communications satellite project. He took a few moments and studied the multi-stage rocket, the componentry, the aerodynamics. He pulled apart the coupling fuselages, studied the interior, and popped off the capsule to inspect the payload mock up. *It was really quite beautiful,* he thought. He took another moment to pull more sections apart, digging into each section, studying its design while making a mental schematic in his head. Well, onto the next room. He walked further down one of the corridors and happened upon two large metal doors. He grasped the *L*-shaped handles and yanked them down revealing a battery of arms. *Whew,* he thought to himself as he admired the cache of weapons: AK47's, shotguns, revolvers of all makes models and eras, C4 plastic, Semtec, M18As, Claymores and host of other explosives. *Who the fuck were these guys? This kind of hardware could supply a small army for a coup.*

"Oh, come to Papa," he groaned in mock orgasm, reaching for an AA-12 shotgun, an M110, SASS, and the jewel of the massive assault and urban warfare crown, an XM307.

The new XM307 was so light, barely 50 lbs., that it didn't need sand bags to hold it down as the recoil was slight, and you wouldn't even spill your pint of beer if you set it on top of it while you shot. *Bonus,* a case of 25mm airburst grenades! This was convenient because these munitions would kill everybody in the room, yet leave the room intact. Sustainability is the *Green Way* of killing, after all!

Murphy began a new shopping list as Christmas had just come early. More curious than serious, now, he made his way further into the basement until he came to a large, locked door. Let's see: *fireproof door, airtight, blast-resistant, this should be good,* Murphy thought.

On the wall to his right, an electronic keypad light blinked red. *Nobody's getting in here.* Murphy searched his chest pocket for something and pulled out an unusual looking key card. One side was white and looked like a normal parking or office security card most people carried. But the opposite side of the card was metallic with a small electronic circuit board. Murphy loved his little gadgets.

He fiddled with the metallic side, then swiped the card, pressed a few keys on the pad, then waited. Red, red, red, after a moment, it blinked green. Open. *A piece of piss.* He was in.

Murphy pulled what looked like a pair of swimmer's goggles from his back pocket, but were actually night vision glasses. He carefully opened the door so as not to trip any additional security measures such as a laser matrix, thermal imaging, or motion detector. *Wow, was that it? It's always the rich ones that skimp on good security,* he thought. *I mean, after all, any decent criminal could rob them blind -- although, no one had ever accused him of being decent.*

Hitting the light switch, the fluorescents trickled on gradually, eventually illuminating the entire room. Big deal, it was just a big storage room with 10 steel cases sitting on a large table.

Murphy wandered up to the first case and blew on his fingers, drying them for sensitivity. He inspected the locks on each case. Okay, standard locks, tight, tamper-proofed and had a hard outer seal, but probably a soft rubber gasket interior lining. He reached around to his back pocket again and produced a small rake and a tension bar. He used both hands to manipulate the lock picks, digging deep into the reset openings. Around the other side of the steel lock, he prodded the tension microbar until he felt something springy and mechanical. A tiny clink told him he had it in record time. *Cheap bastards.*

Murphy stepped to the side and slowly opened the top in case a dye packet or some Russian surprise might await him. But this case was just a case. It may have been one of 10 cases, but its singular function was to carry one thing and one thing only and Rostov's investor's had given it over to him for safekeeping. Murphy's eyes slowly lit up as he opened the first case and gazed on what lay before him.

CHAPTER 41

FITZPATRICK IRREVERENTLY PUSHED PAST the two bodyguards still seething awaiting his exit. He jumped down the entry stairs, off the landing and onto the flowerbed below. He traipsed across every colorful flower and plant until all were crushed beneath his size 13 shoes. Tetley, who had said nothing for nearly and hour followed like a duckling chasing his mother.

From across the lawn Mancuso caught sight of Fitzpatrick and made another direct heading to intercept. The federal agent's cell phone was pinned to his ear as he attempted to talk and yell at the same time. "That's it, Fitzpatrick, you're taking early retirement, I'm making sure of that, now!"

Behind Fitzpatrick, the wedding party was arriving through the side gate toward the patio. The blushing young beauty, still in her early 20s, was a mixture of excitement and nerves as she was about to marry Oleg Rostov and enter into one of America's premiere Russian families, and her family couldn't have been happier.

Leading the way was a Russian Orthodox priest in full headdress, robe and flowing vestments. If no one knew any better, they'd think it was the priest's big day.

As the altar boys followed like trained marines, they swung smoking incense lamps to the tempo of the priest's blessings. The burners went forward and back, laying a heavy cloud of incense that dripped like dry ice in a Hollywood horror film.

It was perfectly average for Los Angeles, 72 degrees with a slight breeze, just another fucking beautiful day. Skies were blue and cloudless and the Pacific was a deep, almost black color as a light wind blew white caps in the distance. Rostov's mansion sat atop a mountain peak smack dab on the border between Malibu and Pacific Palisades. Mel Gibson and Bill Clinton couldn't have pooled their resources to afford an estate so opulent. It was so perfect a location; Rostov himself had hired an agency to fend off daily inquiries from location scouts and movie producers. He wouldn't have his pristine sanctuary sullied by commoners. Besides, he was a secretive person and never, ever called attention to himself or his family. Anonymity was crucial for a man in his business.

All work ceased and the servers stood their ground while the wedding party entered the backyard. The acres of lawn had been manicured to perfection as Salvadoran and Guatemalan gardeners stood and removed their hats in respect. *It was quite a spectacle*, the arborist's thought, this Russian wedding.

Alexei stood next to his younger brother, Oleg as they both eyed the endless friends and fellow Ukrainian models that were present to send their friend off. They were both wearing designer tuxedos, but somehow couldn't pull it off right. It was extremely difficult to look slovenly in Wang and Dolce, but after partying for days and not bathing, the brother's Rostov, as well as their band of merry men, looked like a month of bad Vegas weekends.

Alexei's men were greasy, not used to being out of their usual tracksuit attire, and completely wrong for a formal function such as a wedding. They couldn't wait for the simple ceremony, so they all carried flasks with cheap booze to extend their cheap buzz.

Alexei was nothing but bored and was still irritated by Fitzpatrick's earlier visit, but, like all sociopaths, wanted to satiate his short-term needs. His brother, unfortunately, was cut from the same cloth.

Oleg licked his lips at a small group of barely legal Czech girls knowing as soon as he consummated his marriage, he'd be back at the bar and ready for something new. It was only out of respect for his parents who needed an heir, did he marry. He had no intention of settling down, ever.

It was only Victor Rostov himself and his glamour-obsessed wife, Anastasia that seemed to belong. They had handpicked the paparazzi and videographers and kept a tight control over how their family was to be perceived and published.

The photographer's snapped every moment at every angle, catching all the drama and emotion for the highest readership. This pleased Anastasia very much.

The priest led the precession over the tiled slab and onto the patio where Oleg and Alexei waited. After a final Russian hymn, he joined Oleg and the bride's hand together and blessed their heads. Alexei looked at his brother and sneered. Oleg's face took a down turn and now looked more like a condemned man than an ex-bachelor. *What a puss.*

Just then a small whining came from below the cliff face behind the wedding. The priest looked up to see the small radio-controlled plane the boys had been playing with earlier. The plane zipped up and around the wedding, then made mock dives over the wincing crowd. Alexei laughed, knowing the boys were probably even more bored than he, if that were even possible, and they had decided to wake bored wedding guests up.

"I am going to wring their little necks," Rostov whispered to his wife. He searched the crowd, then suddenly locked onto his grandsons fidgeting with their tiny tuxedo collars. But if they're here, who's flying that…?

Rostov looked at the model plane as it passed overhead again, this time he spotted the bulky payload secured with duct tape to the fuselage. He just caught the letters: C4 and instantly knew it was from his basement stash. But before he could call out to the crowd, a flash of light blinded him. Then came the secondary shock wave. The drone exploded into a trillion pieces as tiny shards of metal and aluminum showered the wedding party. Fragments tore into flesh, into hair, through clothing. It was a bloody mess.

Rostov was knocked hard to the ground by the downward force

of the blast, and the concussion to his inner ear rendered him dazed and confused for what would be at least a half an hour. As he tried to regain his composure, he crawled over to help his wife to her feet and slowly found his footing and stood.

Chaos ensued. The guests began to panic. *Was this the act of Chechen Separatists, the one's that killed the hundreds of Russian school children or the group behind the Boston Marathon bombings? Could it have been Al Qaeda? Who could perpetrate such a crime?*

The explosion was dramatic, chaotic, but, upon closer assessment, it was far from lethal. It was, however, incredibly messy. Designers and stylists would be horrified at what had become of their customized wedding party creations, but no one had been seriously hurt. In fact, the entirety of the event amounted to nothing more than shattered nerves and a few cuts. It seemed this was a personal message and it had been sent well. *Stop those paparazzi from taking any more photos!*

Rostov had to quickly compose himself; he then began to bark orders to his security guards. Just then, in the thick of it, his cell phone ring tone burst through like a shot. He could only hear it faintly at first, then the sound became louder and louder.

"Da!" Rostov screamed into the tiny handset microphone. There was a moment of silence, then a low, gruff voice spoke, "this is your only warning, either hand over the others, or deal with our brand of justice!" The voice on the other end ceased and the line went dead. Rostov looked at the phone in disbelief, then slammed it to the ground, smashing it into millions of pieces. He gazed over the stunned and frightened crowd, then his eyes landed on his captain as there, across the patio, stood Yuri bloodied and furious. He cast his evil eyes on Rostov whose blood suddenly ran cold.

CHAPTER 42

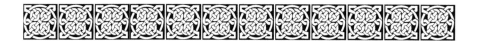

A CROWD OF CHILDREN WAS led down the long gangway at the Bradley International Terminal of LAX. The little ones were so excited they could hardly stay in their skin. Most of the children had never even seen a plane before, let alone flown thousands of miles in one. Yet to see the wonders of modern technology and to witness a clean, modern city of millions of people, this was all beyond comprehension for young ones.

The flight from Sumatra was long and arduous, but children are resilient, even handicapped ones. Most of the nearly 100 orphans had some injury or impediment and all of them had experienced profound losses.

When Ciara O'Malley first arrived in Sumatra and saw the devastation, she bled herself dry dealing with relief organizations, as well as U.S. and international adoption agencies to get the children safe passage from all parts of the ravaged country. She fought so hard for the lives of these children, the locals called her *merah dipimpin angel,* or *the angel with red hair.* She oft times would hike days on end into the jungle when hearing of a single, parentless child. Ciara only had to look into the eyes of these little lost lambs and she could move mountains to get them to a safe place.

Most of the Sumatran children had lived in squalor, were homeless, hungry, or dying of whatever disease du jour was currently attacking the island streams and drinking water, even before the tsunami or

Ciara's arrival. Ciara had *Herculean* tasks just to stabilize most of the minors before she and the other volunteers could put together an action plan and get them to families who would love them forever.

Some were missing limbs, some were wheelchair-bound, still others missing eyes, disfigured, most were in some way, un-whole. These were some of the thousands of children left broken and battered and orphaned in this world. Their government didn't want or couldn't care for them, if anything they were viewed as leeches of the State like the parasites their parents were. The Sumatran government wanted them to simply disappear... and miraculously, that's just what happened! The Irish girl knew what to do.

These children would be Ciara O'Malley's legacy and you would never know to what extent they had suffered for one moment from the glow on their faces. It was as though they had been reborn once they took their first steps onto American soil.

The volunteers and chaperones led the band of brothers and sisters under a large banner that hung in the *Arrival* atrium that read: *WELCOME CHILDREN OF SUMATRA*. A special customs line had already been arranged in advance and U.S. Custom's Agent Viola Williams was ready to receive them all in her official capacity.

Unofficially, Viola's eyes were still not dry from crying at the thought of poor Ciara and her sacrifice to bring these children to their new world. Viola thought fondly of that poor girl ever since their conversation and feeling, after nearly a quarter of a century on the job that she had actually connected with another human being. She'd spent countless hours weeping for that girl after hearing the fateful news and only later found out her own business card: *VIOLA WILLIAMS – U.S. ICE AGENT* would be the only item discovered near Ciara's dead body. It was protocol to interview any federal agent if they'd been in contact with a murder victim, but Viola could hardly stay composed during the entire process. After she learned of Ciara's tragic end, Viola made a special trip to the Inglewood Indoor Gun Range, burning through thousands of rounds and of bullet casings and shells, just to try and assuage her grief. Viola wanted payback.

On Viola's desk still lay a copy of the Los Angeles Times with the headline: *Irish Red Cross Aid Worker Brutally Raped and Murdered*. But now was no the time for such thoughts. Now was the time to rejoice in what God had blessed her with.

Smiling, happy faces of the children filled Viola's heart as she anxiously watched them as they queued up in her line. She shot anyone else approaching her station a frightful *momma bear* glance, but grinned widely for her new arrivals. She checked her face in the compact mirror she had squirreled away in her purse and straightened her uniform: *hair good, check, makeup good, check, freshly brushed teeth and minty-fresh breath, check*! It seemed as though every one of the children were smiling just for her. She said a quick prayer for young Ciara O'Malley and promised to do her best to continue where her young friend had fallen.

"Come on children, this way... this way to Viola's line."

It was at that very moment when, from the *Down* escalator behind the group of Tsunami orphans came the opposite of sights: a lone figure, ogre-like and gruesome, hunched over from fatigue and stress, carrying little more than hate and sadness in his heart. It was Frank O'Malley. He had come to America to take his daughter home.

Frank lunged quickly down the steps, bounding two steps and at a time as now he was on his own mission. He didn't know, nor could he be bothered to care that the children right in front of him would be his daughter's legacy that would carry her name across the lips of first hundreds, then later thousands for her sacrifice. Years of arduous work in the jungles of South East Asia would produce an act of generosity that people worldwide would remember *ad infinitum*. But Frank couldn't care less about those children, or anyone else for that matter, except his own child, Ciara -- and the bastards that had killed her.

At the bottom of the escalator, he split right past the group of orphaned children, pushed aside a porter, and searched for the exit to street with his blood-shot eyes. Frank was single-minded and even the devil couldn't stop him now.

CHAPTER 43

THE LOS ANGELES COUNTY Morgue was located on Mission Road deep in the heart of downtown. Los Angeles wasn't known for it's downtown, because Los Angeles had in it's past no real city center to speak of. It certainly had a seat of power, as the L.A. City Council held sway over millions of legal, and an equal number of illegal, citizens. Downtown L.A. was not like Chicago or New York, where flocks of people gathered to centralized areas and city centers, but it was improving with the advent of *L.A. Live, Staples Center*, and gentrification – there was even talk of a professional football stadium to be built there.

L.A. still had its crime, and an enormous homeless population, not to mention the serious gang problems. But in the past years, L.A. had made a push to create the downtown it had sorely lacked.

Cab fare from LAX to downtown was no cheap ride. Frank dug deep into his pockets and pulled out a huge wad of dollars, Euros and pounds. At least he had come prepared. He arrived at the government building, hopped out of the cab, slammed the door, tossed the driver well more than the fare, and marched to the entrance.

Frank passed through security, the full body spectrum x-ray machine, assumed the position, and got the wand for his belt buckle and some non-descript metallic pocket litter. Frank didn't get upset as he not only knew the guards were doing their jobs just like in prison, but that he had a single direction to follow and he was merely existing in a perpetual state of blind shock.

He crossed the freshly polished marbled floor of the old government building toward the elevators to the lower levels. The building was vacant due to government cutbacks and sequestration, but it gave him time to prepare himself for the upcoming event.

When the elevator finally opened, Frank found himself at the end of a long, sanitized hallway. He was forced to take a hard whiff and could smell the hint of formaldehyde and would've wretched if it weren't for his steel composure for the task at hand. He made his way past the windowed labs and freezer compartments, well down to the end of the corridor.

A sign on the door read: LOS ANGELES COUNTY MEDICAL EXAMINER – DR. VINCENT CHANG. Fitzpatrick and Tetley had wisely arrived early and stood on either side of the coroner's office as suddenly Frank burst in. Tetley absolutely did not want to be in the same room as his old enemy approached, so he stood against the dark, unlit part of the back wall, as a bead of cold sweat formed under his hairline. He braced himself, as this was the first time these two men would be in such close proximity since Frank's trial in a British court. One would not relish the thought of being alone with Frank O'Malley if he didn't like you, let alone wanted your freshly ripped heart still beating on a platter for his tea.

As it were, Frank was barely able to comprehend who else might have been in the room as he marched toward the only man in the room he could see. Undeterred, grief-stricken and getting worse, this was not going to be a good day to be near Frank O'Malley.

Dr. Chang was a tall, lean, good looking Asian man, fastidious, proper and very professional, but had a flare for the European and often had a small cup of highly caffeinated expresso on his desk. His name always caught people off guard as when they heard it, they imagined him a more, well Asian person. Dr. Chang understood the irony, and actually appreciated it. His mother was a bit of a *black sheep* and had been obsessed with old Italian movies, and thought Vincent would be a fine, strong name for a first generation American.

Since Dr. Chang was the only non-white, non-Irish looking fellow in the room who's official badge read: DR. VINCENT CHANG-LA COUNTY MEDICAL EXAMINER, Frank surmised he was in the right place.

Fitzpatrick eyed Frank up and down, forward and back. This guy was big, as big as himself, perhaps bigger. He knew that when big guys tussled, bad things happened.

He reluctantly stepped into Frank's path. "Mr. O'Malley?" Fitzpatrick said calmingly.

"Frank," Frank said without acknowledging the detective.

"Frank, I know you've come a long way and I'm sorry to have to put you through this," Fitzpatrick continued as necessity dictated, "but we're going to need you to identify the body, if you would please, sir."

All three men stepped to the polished metal autopsy table, with Tetley reluctantly joining, and stood two aligned. Fitzpatrick leaned forward and gently grasped the pristine white sheet that covered the body. With the nimbleness of a neurosurgeon, Fitzpatrick drew back the sheet, but stopped just after the head was revealed. "Is this your daughter, Mr. O'Malley?"

There was no doubt it was Ciara O'Malley. Her face was angelic, her trauma minimized by Dr. Chang's superb scalpel and cosmetic skills. He had literally reduced, softened and eliminated Ciara's facial contusions, lacerations and other evidence of the brutal attack. He had worked off a photo that the Irish government had provided when he first contacted his counterpart and searched their databases. Although it was an old photo from her public school days in Belfast, she still looked every bit the angel she was now.

Frank studied his child's face. Her nose seemed a little different, he chalked it up to age, but in reality, Dr. Chang had spent a great deal of time on it. He gazed at her perfect ear lobes and the sheen of her lovely red hair and the smallness of her lips. Fitzpatrick was wise to keep the sheet over the *Y* incision that cut from the top of her shoulder blades to her bikini line. It was the job of the ME to cut from the clavicles, past the sternum, then use the large spreaders to expose and excise the organs inside which would be weighed, measured and assessed to make his report on *cause of death*, then return them to the body and sew them back into the cavity.

Fitzpatrick had no intention of causing this man any additional grief. After all, Frank was a devote Catholic and every detective knew the idea of a body being desecrated could drive some to kill.

Frank stood over his daughter motionless. "Frank, is this your daughter?" Fitzpatrick repeated, this time just a little louder in an attempt to draw him out of his state. Frank felt a sudden shock in his chest, but it was no heart attack. It was the crystallized realization that his baby was dead. He became unglued.

Tears burst forth as a guttural cry came from deep within him. "Aaahhh," he screamed. His large frame fell over Ciara's body and huge hands clutched her head. He began to wale like a coven of Arab women as he drew her in tighter to his chest. "Ciara, a chailín mo chroí my darling, Ciara!" Frank cried.

The other men knew not to make a peep, not just yet. Let this large man grieve, they would expect no less from each other. Let his emotions take over and exhaust as much of the hatred for the despicable act out of him as possible. He'd feel liked he'd been beaten with pikie's axe handle afterwards, but it would calm this monster down. "She's still my wee little girl, my poor, poor angel."

Frank cried and cried until he had nothing left to cry with. His face was stained with tears and snot flowed freely from his nostrils. After what seemed like hours, he slowly released his tighten grasp on Ciara's head and gently laid it back on the table. He rose slowly from her body as though he had already buried her, looking up slowly to face the other men, and suddenly locked eyes with Tetley.

As though a switch had been flipped on in his head, Frank's features distorted, transmogrifying him into the monster they all feared. He began to shake uncontrollably. Frank bolted from the other side of the table, rushing Tetley. "Bastard!" he cried in a weird, Pagan tone as he attacked. "You did this!"

Fitzpatrick shot a look at Chang and knew he wasn't going to be of any help. For a split second, he felt like giving Frank a few, uninterrupted seconds with this pain-in-the-ass, but also knew that Tetley was merely a thorn to him -- he was the devil to Frank.

It looked like a Tokyo sumo wrestling match as Fitzpatrick intercepted Frank to protect Tetley, both goliath bodies slamming each other, tree trunk arms and limbs flying everywhere. The scrawny Englishman wouldn't have lasted a three-count.

"Mr. O'Malley... Frank, he's not the one to blame!" Fitzpatrick shouted over and over in his ear, nearly deafening Frank. "Don't spoil the memory of your daughter like this. Let us do our job and I <u>swear</u> to you we'll get the killers responsible."

Tetley's face began to quickly turn blue as Frank had reached out one of his huge mitts and wrapped it around his throat, <u>all</u> the way around. He looked like an anaconda, squeezing the life out of his prey. "<u>He</u> doesn't care who's responsible," Frank shouted as he continued to wring Tetley's neck. "His kind doesn't understand <u>justice</u>!"

As strong as Frank was tired, Fitzpatrick could now feel him giving in to the sadness. Fitzpatrick wrenched and wriggled, then slowly pushed Frank's arm away from Tetley's throat and down to his side. *Phew, that was close!* He thought.

Tetley, his face now pasty from lack of oxygen, crumbled to the ground gasping for air, but no one really seemed to care or wanted to help him, as they were both attending to Frank. Fitzpatrick eventually looked down at his colleague on the floor and opened up his hand as if to say, *I know you got throttled, but let it go or it'll get worse.* He settled Frank down as best he could, "Let me give you a lift to a hotel," Fitzpatrick said soothingly.

Frank shoved Fitzpatrick back as he wiped the tears from eyes. He was embarrassed, but couldn't be bothered with that. "Leave me! I want to be alone with my daughter, now," he blurted out.

Fitzpatrick threw his head in the air, a signal to the others to exit. Dr. Chang had already begun to help Tetley up and was helping him out the door when Fitzpatrick backed out, yet careful to keep a keen eye on Frank.

From the hallway, he watched as Frank leaned over his daughter's body once again. He had sympathetic eyes for Frank, now weeping, whispered into Ciara's ear. What Fitzpatrick couldn't see was the small scalpel Frank had taken from the medical tray. Nor could he see him slowly cut a locket of Ciara's hair. Frank fell onto Ciara's body one last time and wept uncontrollably until his heart finished breaking in two.

CHAPTER 44

EAST L.A. WAS DICEY enough in the daytime, but after sunset, you were taking your life into your own hands. Some streets in the barrio were quiet and sedate, akin to their suburban neighbors, but not this area.

It seemed a little out of place so late in the evening, but a mariachi band blared festive traditional tunes as each member of the band took turns howling and yipping.

The Mexican Social Club was packed and this night seemed to be an exception as the patrons danced, and sang, and drank like it was *Dias De La Muertos*.

A crowd began to form in front of the door. Murmurs became raised voices, which became screams of joy as El Cid suddenly appeared under heavy guard and waltzed into the bar. He was the *Hombre of the Hour*, like it or not.

Even as the patrons hooted and slapped El Cid on the back, there was no mistaking the look on his face. He was pissed! He didn't bother to stop and shake hands, or even acknowledge their presence. He was focused and that focus was revenge.

El Cid made his way deep into the crowd, then continued through the hallway to toward the back offices. It was a long corridor that was heavily guarded at all times. No stray drunk or curious abuela would be making their way here.

El Cid stopped at an innocuous looking door at the end near the storage room. He waited for a moment as his security team took up a post: two to stand behind him, two to open the door, one entered, and one held the door.

Inside, a single energy-efficient lamp swung slightly over the heads of Carlos and Miguel. The two men were seated and tied to their chairs. Miguel, wounded from the Rostov strip club debacle, squirmed uncomfortably. Carlos sat upright and alert.

Carlos knew they were in deep shit, but showed enough respect for his boss by not showing it or showing apologetic signs of any kind.

El Cid entered the room like a Roman emperor, then slammed the door in anger. He scanned the room. "Where's Juan," he said to one of his security guards. "I wanted all of them." Carlos took the opportunity to attempt to alleviate the tension and perhaps ingratiate himself to his employer. Big mistake.

"He's dead, Jefe," Carlos blurted as he immediately realized the error.

El Cid paced side to side, "Putas! What the <u>fuck</u> were you thinking?"

Carlos thrust his face forward as his eyes widened. "They weren't showing you respect, Jefe!" he said loyally. "It's our city. I thought, *send a message*, you know... we didn't expect any trouble."

"Trouble? Trouble?" El Cid screamed. He lunged forward and slapped Carlos hard across the face. A large welt in the shape of a handprint immediately began to swell on his face. "Who the fuck are <u>you</u> to make a decision like that without getting my approval?" El Cid shouted as saliva sprayed Carlos' face. "Nobody pulls a job without <u>my</u> permission, Comprende, puta!"

El Cid dramatically pulled a pistol from his waistband, cocked it and placed it on Carlos' temple.

Just then, Miguel spoke up, pleading for Carlos' life. "Jefe, por favor, there, there in the corner is the rest of take," Miguel pushed his nose in the direction of the bookshelf where, at the base were duffels filled with the cash and coins the boys had, well overlooked when they first offered their tribute.

For an instant, it seemed that El Cid might warm, as the gesture of 100% tithing was now strong in these two men. Yet, unluckily for them, El Cid was not in a generous mood. They would die.

As El Cid began to squeeze the trigger, everyone in the room cringed for the predicted report. Suddenly, a loud bang filled the air, but it wasn't El Cid's pistol. From inside the club an explosion of gunfire eclipsed the Mariachi band.

A hail of bullets flew indiscriminately piercing walls, doors, windows, and people. Screams began to compete with the gunfire. Rounds impacted the office door where El Cid and the others were. They all dropped for cover, all of them that is, but Miguel and Carlos who were still tied up.

From the entrance of the club, an earth-shattering crash burst in, not only the doors, but the side walls as well. It was Alexei. He had driven his enormous Hummer at full speed into the bar.

It was a natural instinct, but relatively futile, as the patrons scrambled, leaping over booths and counters to escape the onslaught. Panic ensued as bodies, sober and floating, ran for their lives.

Alexei exited the SUV and pulled back the slide on an automatic weapon as his men took up positions at all sides of the club. Alexei, having too much fun to wait for everyone to get into place, opened fire, spraying everyone with skull-smoking hot lead. "Hola, amigos, it's fiesta time!" Alexei shouted unloading banana clip after banana clip.

Around the back of the club, Oleg, not missing an opportunity to wholesale slaughter, had driven his Humvee around and opened fire on those trying to flee through the back alley exit. He seemed even more bloodthirsty than his brother, laughing like Tony Montana as he strafed midlevel for maximum kills. *After all Scarface was his favorite movie.*

A woman holding a child flew out the back door and fell at Oleg's feet. "Por favor, Señor, Por favor," she cried cradling the child.

"Really, that's all you got for me, Bitch? Suck my dick!" Oleg said as he depressed the trigger, unloading an excessive amount of bullets into them both.

In the distance, sirens could be heard as they seemed to all be converging on the building. That's a first, LAPD responding quickly in this neighborhood?

El Cid and his men flew out the back door to escape in the alley. Not so fast! Oleg couldn't believe his luck; El Cid was running right to him, *the fucking idiot. This was like shooting fish in a barrel*, Oleg thought.

He didn't even need to take aim, so he hung his gun low and was about to shoot from the hip at El Cid's security team when they clogged the doorway. They had been trying to protect their leader, but after pushing their jefe outside, they realized it was absolutely the wrong move.

Oleg clipped one of the guards, just for fun. The others pulled back inside, slamming the fire door. This left El Cid all alone at the hands of the other Russian whack-job.

As Oleg drew up on El Cid, he pulled out a small walkie-talkie. He pressed the open mic and laughed, "Alexei, davai! I'm in the back alley. I've got the beaner!"

Suddenly, slowly, from around the brick corner, like a serpent, a gloved hand appeared. In all the commotion, nobody bothered to check the perimeter for any other partygoers. El Cid's eyes widen as he saw a strange blue flicker light up the alleyway. An electrical charged burst forth, then, headed for Oleg's neck. It touched him near the nape, just below the ear and immediately dropped him to the ground where he began to convulse, as his body contorted and seized.

When Oleg fell, El Cid could see Liam and Hammer behind him holding a large stun gun. The two men from Erin smiled, then pressed their fingers to their lips. El Cid stood frozen in amazement as the Irishmen scooped up their victim and loaded him into the back of his own Hummer. Hammer stood on the foot rail and whispered, "We were never here, fella!".

Seeing a once-in-a-lifetime-opportunity, El Cid turned and raced the opposite direction into the darkness just as Alexei burst out of the back of the bar with the other Russians in tow. They swarmed into the alley, but it had already gone quiet.

"Where the fuck are you, little brother?" Alexei put his walkie-talkie to his lips and squelched it, "Oleg, Oleg?"

Suddenly, the men heard something in the alleyway and began to run toward the source. They kicked at trash and refuse bins, flipped up discarded newspapers, nothing.

"Oleg, Oleg, where the fuck did you go?" Alexei continued. As he did so, he began to hear his own, muffled voice. He walked over to a puddle of oily, brackish water near the dumpster where the Hummer was supposed to be parked. There in the darkness, he saw Oleg's walkie-talkie.

CHAPTER 45

LOS ANGELES PROPER USED to have nothing to brag about. It was miles and miles of old industrial buildings and manufacturer's warehouses, but with the beautification push of late, little by little, L.A. was creating a centralized city.

However, Fifth and Clover was not part of the gentrification plan anytime soon. It was a 10-block area of abandoned buildings and factories from the *Hey Days*, circa 1920s-70s. It was the perfect place to hide a body or muffle a scream or have a quiet, *Come To Jesus* meeting to correct someone's behavior. If one was so inclined, they could do anything to anybody for as long as they wanted and no one would ever know.

This particular warehouse had been abandoned longer than the others. It was centrally located in the *Dead Zone*, as city officials called it and was such a blight, it was too expensive to redevelop, at least until they could heap the cost onto the next administration.

The back end of Oleg's Hummer was barely visible to anyone creeping around the facility, which meant it was safe as nobody would be caught dead here before or after dark.

It had interesting architecture, though, as a row of deco sky lighted louvers could be opened or closed to let in the sunniest of L.A. days or the clearest of harvest moon nights. This evening a wide moonbeam shot down illuminating the entire floor of the warehouse where Oleg's body sat in an old metal desk chair and propped up by two dark figures.

The resounding, obnoxious sound of something heavy being dragged across a concrete floor was overwhelming. Slowly, Oleg began to awaken from his unconscious state to see a large wooden table come at him. He snorted through his bloodied nostrils to clear his head. *The table seemed to be attacking him.*

The two men standing either side of Oleg pulled him to his feet, kicked the metal chair away from under him, and presented his sweat-drenched body to the onslaught of the furniture. It was heading right for his crotch. "What the fuck?" Oleg said in a groggy-voice as though an ammonia capsule had been broken under his nose. The table moved closer and closer until the shot to his groin completed the awakening from his electrical dream. His eyes bulged with the pain when suddenly Oleg caught a glimpse of a shadowy figure. He tried to move, but realized he was being held from both sides by large figures.

He struggled to see their faces, but to no avail. "Is this a fucking joke?" Oleg began. "I just got married, it's my wedding night." Movement continued around him, but no one answered. "You assholes obviously don't know who I am!" Oleg barked as his tone changed from bargaining to outright threats. "I'm Oleg-Fucking-Rostov, Goddamn it!"

In the darkness, Oleg finally heard a noise, but not a noise he wanted to hear. From the distance, faint screams became louder and louder and the glow of a small object grew brighter and brighter. A laptop computer appeared. The mysterious hand brought it closer, placing it softly on the table to face Oleg.

On the screen, the video that Oleg, Alexei and the other Russians had taken as they raped and murdered Ciara O'Malley, played in horrifying digital surround sound. The graphic images of the crime were so extreme, quiet grunts and groans from the others in the room told Oleg they were sickened and that he was outnumbered. Screams for mercy echoed throughout the vast warehouse and down the empty chambers and corridors. Tensions could be felt rising, as

Oleg seemed more bored and annoyed as the prolonged torture of the Irish girl continued.

"Blah, blah, blah," He yelled into the blackness. "Who the fuck cares?"

The hand appeared out of the darkness after the evil deed was completed, plucking the laptop from its cradle. For a moment, Oleg wondered if that was the only point that was going to be made... that is until he heard a quick, sharp sound. From the shadows, the menacing figure pulled a switchblade and pressed the button, quickly releasing the long blade. The steel glimmered in the night light as the figure stepped into the light to reveal itself. It was McCann. He brought the blade to Oleg's face, carefully caressing it against his cheek, his ears, around his orbital bones, his eyes, probing his nostrils, chin, and around his lips.

McCann then slowly, deliberately, brought the blade down from his neck, past his chest and further south to his crotch. McCann tensed his grip, raised the blade as if to slice Oleg, then slashed his belt and trousers in one movement. They dropped to the floor effortlessly. Now, the Russian stood before his captures naked and vulnerable. McCann threw the switchblade down hard onto the edge of the table, just out of reach of Oleg. The point buried upright in the hard wood from the force of the thrust.

From Oleg's blind side, Murphy appeared with a stoic look on his face. He said nothing as he leered at Oleg, then suddenly slammed something hard on the table. "Who the fuck are you guys?" Oleg said with genuine confusion.

In the moonlight, he could just make out a large ball peen hammer and a sixty-penny nail. The six inch long, thick metal spike looked ominous: thinner and a tad shorter than a railroad spike.

Oleg began to sweat more and more profusely, and once he started, he could not stop. "Okay, okay, yeah, you guys are businessmen, I can see that," Oleg shouted into the darkness, acquiescing to the implied demands. "You made your point, you want money. I know this because I am Russian. It's always about the money." There was only silence, no response. He seemed to be talking merely to hear his own words, to comfort himself, as the silence was beginning to drive him mad.

Slowly he began to realize the gravity of the situation and felt one more tirade of threats might just do the trick. "Okay, that bitch," he yelled, "she was nothing more than a whore we got a little rough with… that's all… what is big deal?"

Suddenly, from the Russian's peripheral vision, he could see Johnny dousing the warehouse with liquid from red plastic containers. After a moment, the stench of diesel fuel rose up from the floor and filled Oleg's nostrils. *Now he was in some deep shit*, he thought.

"Okay, okay, ha, ha, you win. Let's forget the whole thing," he said as he began to freak. "You know my father will pay you assholes a shit-load of money, so give me a cell and I'll have the money wired to your account… no questions asked, like the kids from the milk cartons."

Oleg's pleas floated aimlessly into the air like dust from the warehouse exhaust returns. What Oleg didn't know, what he could not have perceived was that McCann and the others were not *about the money*. These men had lived, and died by a <u>code</u>: they were about Ciara O'Malley, they were about the *underdog*, and they were always about justice. As the other Irishmen doused the walls and floor of the warehouse with the highly flammable liquid, Oleg worried that one spark would ignite the dust, fumes, and ancient timber that were propping up this decrepit warehouse. It would flash fire like a back draft in a split second.

In the half-light, a red light caught Oleg's eye. From experience, he knew that he was being videotaped. Okay, at last, their demands. *Phew, they had him going there for a moment.*

Now Oleg heard rapid footsteps as McCann approached from the darkness and suddenly splashed him with a bucket of fluid in the face. "Ah!" He screamed as his eyes began to burn and his throat seized from diesel fuel exposure. He began to spit and gag. "I will fucking kill you, bastards!" the still defiant Oleg yelled as he panted harder and harder, choked and wheezed as his tracheal airway became more and more constricted.

McCann stood emotionless in front of the Russian. He picked up the ball peen hammer slowly with his right hand. Oleg could barely make out what was happening, his eyes hadn't yet readjusted from the chemical tearing. With his left hand, McCann picked up the long spike and reached for Oleg's, small, flaccid penis. As disgusting as it was to do, McCann held back his disgust, pulled at the tiny member and stretched it out. McCann knew, in order to do it right, he'd have to also grab Oleg's testicles and slip them underneath to encapsulate his entire genitalia. Repulsed, McCann grasped Oleg's package in one swift movement, then set the nail at the base of the shaft.

Instinctively Oleg twisted and squirmed, but to no avail. He now felt something, a painful sharp sensation, but still hadn't the full realization of just what was about to happen. It wasn't until he saw the silhouette of McCann's arm rising in the air, drawing back the hammer. McCann drove the heavy metal head down hard and to the spike, nailing Oleg's penis and scrotum to the table and beyond. McCann decided to pound the giant nail a second time for good measure. Oleg wouldn't be going anywhere for a while.

"AAAAHHHH!" Oleg released a blood-curdling scream: part agony, part shock. The pain raced to his brain like a rusted bullet. Everything became terrifyingly real now. His eyes rolled into the back of his head as his brain began to shut down from trauma.

Smack... McCann slapped Oleg across the face. Nothing. *Smack...* he slowly came to again. *Smack...* one more to clear his head. McCann needed Oleg's head clear or all of this would have been for naught.

Oleg's legs were now shaking from the pain, the pressure, and the situation. He could feel blood dripping down his legs, over his feet, and onto the floor. He jerked backward but felt excruciating pain as his tissues tore, then he realized he was, in fact, nailed to the table.

With sleight of hand, McCann pulled out two cigarettes and placed one carefully between Oleg's lips, putting the other in his. He looked to the others and nodded for them to leave. Now it was just the two of them. Oleg braced himself with his hand on the table so as not to create more pain. Over McCann's shoulder, Oleg could see Hammer. He had set the tripod of the wireless video camera, making sure every moment was captured, just as he and the other Russians had done with Ciara.

If Oleg wasn't fully conscious, he became so when the Irishman grasped the gaudy gold chain that dangled from around his neck and yanked it off him, taking it with it half the hair on his chest. McCann lit a sulfur-tipped match off the wooden table and brought it to his own cigarette, it glowed red as he drew in the smoke, taking a long slow draw as if he'd missed the sensation for years. He offered a light to Oleg, but he just shook his head, trying to spit out the unlit cigarette, McCann wrestled free the knife that was buried at the edge of the table. Then took the switchblade, cut Oleg's binds, and placed it into Oleg's hand. Oleg felt the cold steel and thought about slashing McCann's throat with it, but the delay in Oleg's thought process had McCann just out of range before he could react.

"We're gonna give you a chance -- that's more than you gave my Goddaughter," McCann roared. "Her name was Ciara O'Malley!" Oleg stiffened to full alert as McCann's rage sounded like that of his own father's disappointment.

Then McCann looked deep into Oleg's eyes, and patted his cheek like an Italian grandmother. He turned and walked across the warehouse floor, took the cigarette and flicked it skyward.

As though in slow motion, Oleg followed the cigarette as it tumbled from above toward an area where the diesel fuel had pooled. Instantly, the warehouse went up like a Titan Rocket. From the floor to 40 feet high, the warehouse was becoming engulfed in flames. *The oxygen would soon be swallowed up by this hungry dragon,* Oleg thought, *he had mere seconds to react.*

He looked at the table, then to his crotch now swelling with blood at the damage to the vessels, tissue, and cartilage. He quickly assessed his situation, raised the switchblade high above his head, knowing he had only one choice to survive.

Wait. Wait. He ran through the options through his head one more time: *burn to death or slice off the one part he liked the best to save his life.* He grimaced, let out a high-pitched shriek, then brought the razor-sharp blade down hard.

The red light of the video camera flickered for another moment -- then the inferno melted it away.

CHAPTER 46

*T*HUNK. THE LARGE BUTCHER knife came down hard and made a sound like an axe through a hollow tree trunk as it drove through a long length of salami. Victor Rostov carved deep into the sausage and cut another piece for a sandwich. Bandages and small patches of gauze covered his face and hands from the earlier wedding day explosive activities. He was hungry.

All around him people were coming and going, tears and murmurs. Rostov was bored of it all and constructing a plan in his head.

"Aya, Mama!" Oleg's young bride, Ivanka wailed in the room off the kitchen, not knowing she was now a widow. She cried and screamed as her mother comforted her. Rostov walked past his new daughter-in-law and the emotional women toward his study, unconcerned.

"But Mama, it's my wedding night, where could Oleg be?" Ivanka ranted in Russian.

"There, there, little one," her Babushka responded petting her hair and patting her back empathetically.

Rostov rolled his eyes at the yammering of the women, as he walked by. *Where was Oleg*, he thought? *Right where he should be, with Alexei hunting down the cowards who would dare spoil such a blessed event.* They were making their father proud, for once, taking the reins and dominating his opponents to insure his place in the hierarchy.

Rostov couldn't have been happier with his sons, finally. *Sure, they were wild, he had spoiled them for a reason: they were better than others. That was the luxury that America had afforded them. Freedom meant that everyday you should drink your fill of life and let no one stand in your way. Take, take, take, and you will survive and thrive and rule.* This was a mantra Victor lived by, a mantra that catapulted him to the top of his criminal empire and kept him on top. He saw no need for mercy and would give no quarter. Why? To acquiesce was to fail.

Rostov carefully balanced the sandwich in one hand as he reached to close the large double doors of his study. The drawing room was dark, except for the illumination of the LCD flat screen on his desk. Gone were the old CRT's that cast a gray haze over everything like radiation from a Japanese power plant after a tsunami, the new computer monitors were crisp and clean and shone bright white. Who needed lamps when such light was available from a panel?

Victor pulled out the high-back chair from under the large mahogany desk and placed the sandwich on the black leather desk mat next to the mouse pad. He sat down and for a brief moment, he seemed almost giddy at the prospect of being able to eat his snack in relative peace and quiet. It was not often he was left alone, as there was always some sort of problem or challenge he had to deal with in his business. And these past days had been exceptionally stressful.

He sat at his computer and rubbed his hands together feeling a sudden chill in room. He looked at the screen saver of a small dacha in the Volga Mountains he'd remembered as a boy. Although it was a black and white photo, he remembered his father would take him hunting bear in the winters. How he was tasked at an early age to strip and skin his kills, then hang them to dry. He and his father would smoke their meat in a shed they built and their mother would make clothes and rugs from the hides of the slaughter.

An audible bell rang as Rostov received each new email. A red light flashed in the *In Box*. Rostov reached for his sandwich as he depressed the mouse. He saw he had one new message. It was another YouTube video of some sort, probably one the family children sending him another video of their latest antics. Victor Rostov was a serious man, very serious; he did not accept funny cat videos or cute little political segments from colleagues, but he always welcomed communications from the younger family members, as they were why he worked so hard. He though about erasing this one, when curiosity got the best of him. The QuickTime player opened as Rostov brought the sandwich to his mouth. *This better be good*, he thought.

Queued to the exact moment, Oleg suddenly appeared on screen in the warehouse. Rostov's mouthful of meat suddenly went agape as the video played. He could see Oleg standing, naked and impaled to the table, the warehouse ablaze. Rostov watched in horror when his son raised the knife high, closed his eyes, and eunuched himself, as he cried out like a schoolgirl that had scraped her knee on the playground.

Just before the video ended, Rostov watched as the flames engulf his son. Oleg instantly caught fire himself and began to run in circles in a futile attempt to escape.

The sandwich dropped from Rostov's hand when a message suddenly appeared over a freeze frame of Oleg screaming: *OUR MESSAGE WENT UNHEEDED, GIVE US THE KILLERS, OR YOUR MONEY'S NEXT!*

Rostov slammed his fist hard onto the desk, shattering the small plate just as the double doors to his study flung open. Alexei and the head of security appeared in the doorway.

Wires dangled from Alexei's hand. "Papa, I had security sweep for bugs and..." Rostov's fury swelled at Alexei's approached. He put his finger to his lips, signaling for Alexei to shut his yap! By now, Rostov's face had turned from ashen to blood red as his anger intensified. His high blood pressure medication and beta-blockers would not bale him out of this one.

Unable to control himself, Rostov quickly reached into the desk drawer, pulled out a semi-automatic pistol, and pointed it at his son. Alexei stopped on a dime. Suddenly, Rostov turned his aim to the head of security, then fired one single shot point blank. The bewildered security guard took one step backwards, then his legs gave out from under him as he collapsed to the floor. The center of his head opened up and the contents flowed freely. Rostov was a true believer in *Accountability.*

Meanwhile, the video on Rostov's computer had looped, playing again, this time, Alexei was the audience. His eyes widened. Rostov stood, shoved Alexei out of his way, then briskly left the room.

Rostov was beyond consoling now. He marched hard across the marble flooring in the atrium and across to the basement stairway where he had a guard posted. It was late and all the guards had had a busy day. They, too, were torn to bits from McCann's airplane bomb and shards of metal had sliced through their skin.

Unfortunately, the basement guard was dosing on his feet when Rostov approached. "Open it!" Rostov barked. The guard quickly recovered his facilities and fumbled with the keypad. The bolt popped open and the door was swung open. Rostov bounded down the stairs like a young man.

No guard was posted in the basement as Rostov had a much more menacing protector -- Rasputin. He made his way through a corridor similar to the old tunnels of a World War II bomb shelter. Rostov seemed to like nostalgia and felt comfortable with old things. He was most certainly a man from another time.

Rostov could hear Rasputin rumbling around his cage as he sensed his approach. As Rostov got closer and closer to his cage, the enormous bear lifted to his hind legs and stood high. "Roooaarrr!" Rasputin let out a growl that would terrify any man.

"It is me old friend, Victor," Rostov said soothingly. "Do not upset yourself." Rostov went to a long freezer near the cage and pulled out two large salmon. Rasputin dropped back on all fours and approached the bars as his keen sense of smell detected the fish. He slowly quieted. "Where is it, Rasputin, where is it?" Rostov muttered as he threw the salmon into the bear's cage one after another.

Rostov walked to a room that had bars and Plexiglas across the opening. It was a vault, but not just any vault. You could see in, nearly touch the contents inside, but you couldn't go farther than a few inches. Rostov peered through the dense clear plastic. There, inside, he could see the steel cases of money. He counted the cases to himself as his thick finger danced and bounced with each addition. *Hum, everything is right where it should be*, he thought.

Suddenly a number of guards appeared behind him panting from rushing to his aide. Rostov pondered a moment longer as the guards exchanged glances. *What was he doing?* They thought. Rostov snapped his finger and one of the guards stepped forward with a key card. The guard nervously swiped the card through the scanner like he was buying groceries at a check out. *RED*. Nothing. The guard swiped the key again. *RED*. The code had been changed. Lock out!

Furious, Rostov marched to a walled storage unit. He flung open the doors and a vast array of high tech gear appeared. An assortment of infrared goggles, electronic sweeps and scanners, dental mirrors, aerosol spray, night vision, everything a young boy needed to start a war... or prevent one.

Rostov grabbed the infrared goggles and turned back to the vault. He made some tweaks and adjustments on the eyepiece, then gazed into the room. Suddenly, a maze of red crisscrossing laser beams, no more than six inches apart appeared. No human eye could've ever detected them, but in Rostov's business, paranoia was part of his *skill set*.

Rostov continued to scan the room with his goggles. He knew if someone had gone to all this trouble, there would be more surprises. He took one of the telescopic dental mirrors and extended to its three-foot length. He carefully threaded it through the opening, and negotiated the pointer through the labyrinth of trip-wire-type lasers. *Yep, there they were, this room was officially hot.*

Rostov then focused the goggles on the mirror, peering harder to visually bank shot the difficult angle. Then he saw it, a tiny amber light blinking in code, awaiting its final signal. He followed the red, green and blue wires from the source to the tips of multiple silver-tipped blasting caps. The blasting caps pierced deep, inches into numerous brinks of explosives compound C4. Primer cord was wrapped around the plastic explosives to insure maximum damage.

Rostov was very knowledgeable of explosives. When he was a

soldier in the Russian army, detonation was his specialty. Bombs, artillery, ammunition, you name it, Rostov dabbled in it. In fact, Plastique and Semtex, both similar explosive compounds to the C4 before him, made honed his tradecraft making Victor Rostov a fortune in black market sales to the Middle East. He would have to tell his men not to go near his money room, at this point, that money was everything to him and he wanted it safe – better there where no one can to it for a while.

In a great panic, Alexei suddenly appeared behind Rostov. He had a look on his face as though their problems were mounting. "Papa!" Alexei said, not realizing the delicate natural of his father's undertaking. Unshaken, Rostov slowly and steadily removed the protracted mirror from between the invisible beams of light. He threw the mirror down hard, as it crashed and shattered. Rostov's anger was intensifying. His eyes narrowed and sharpened as he leered at Alexei.

Rostov moved toward a small entertainment center across the hall. He stopped, pondered the mechanics of the system, then flipped it on. A faint sound of heavy metal pushed forth from the speakers, then Rostov cranked it up. Now, even Rasputin's roars would be muted by Lars and the other head bangers.

"There is $50 million dollars in that room and you let them rig it to blow up in my face?" Rostov whispered to everyone in the room. "Who are these maniacs? What did you do to them that they would want such revenge?"

Alexei reached his arms out as to plead with his father, "Papa, these *spics* were muscling into our territory, we had to beat them back."

Rostov clenched his teeth together and raised his hand to Alexei, "Why weren't you there to protect your brother?"

Alexei stood silent, knowing he could not respond to that question. If Alexei were capable of any guilt, it would be over the fact that he wasn't there to look out for his little brother, to protect him and avenge him. But Alexei Rostov had no guilt. It meant nothing to him that his brother was dead. Oleg was foolish, a risk taker, he should have stayed closed to him. He got what he deserved. There was no room for failure in Alexei's eyes, and Oleg had failed. He was worthless and not given a second thought.

Rostov took one more look at his eldest son, turned, and stormed back upstairs. *"Ah!"* Alexei screamed in frustration at the disrespect his father had just shown him.

CHAPTER 47

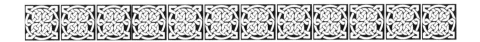

HAMMER KICKED BACK IN Murphy's high back black leather office chair as Sean adjusted the knobs on the surveillance console. He tweaked and turned and tuned the receiver to find a higher frequency as soon as they heard the music in Rostov's mansion. With the heavy metal blaring, it obfuscated any intelligible conversation. *No good for real-time Intel*, he thought.

The work of surveillance is a long, boring process that usually does more for producing hemorrhoids than real actionable results. Hammer sat back and penned an eight-letter word for *Accessing an Application. Hum*, he thought... *Download.* Hammer filled in the empty cubes in the crossword puzzle.

Frank nervously sat across the room and fidgeted, his hands obsessively rolling over and over. He was dying to murder something or someone and could hardly contain his fury. McCann sat across from him waiting for the perfect opportunity, the whole time, anticipating an outburst of unregulated anger.

"Frank, this has all been just an *Eye For An Eye*. America isn't like home, they've a <u>real</u> police force here," McCann said, attempting to reach Frank's sensibilities. "We should let them handle the rest of those bastards." *That was probably not the best thing to say to a bereft father*, McCann thought after saying it.

Frank slowly leaned in toward McCann, standing close to his face, and slowly said, "Did you see what those animals did to my little girl? Don't you try to talk me out of what you <u>know</u> I have to do."

CHAPTER 48

EVEN THOUGH THE CITY of Santa Monica was technically part of the City of Los Angeles, it acted as it's own sovereign fiefdom. It annually accumulated over a $250 million surplus in it's yearly general fund for the city budget: mostly from parking tickets and property taxes, and had the quiet distinction of being one of the wealthiest and healthiest city in the United States.

Santa Monica, having a new, beautiful high-tech police department, often allowed it to be used for television and film crime drama locations. Although the major benefit was that the SMPD wasn't the LAPD and because of that fact, was not bogged-down in bureaucratic red tape.

A black and white surveillance video played as Detective Fitzpatrick, Inspector Tetley, Captain Brink, Special Agent Mancuso and the other Federal agents, as well as half the precinct watched. Chuckles began slowly, then snickers, finally a crescendo of laughter filled the room as Oleg Rostov's wedding was ruined in reality show style.

"I fucking love *YouTube*," one of the officers smirked. A burst of juvenile laughter lit up the room again and again. Even Fitzpatrick couldn't help but get in on the action.

"Enough, Goddamn it!" Mancuso blurted out, forgetting his presence caused considerable irritation to the rank and file. "It's taken years to get this close to Rostov," Mancuso scolded. "He's trying to legitimize decades of corruption through this half-a-billion dollar communications satellite deal. Mancuso turned and pointed a sharpened finger at Fitzpatrick. "… and you could've cost us a federal indictment!" Fitzpatrick feigned a look of guilty. "We've got a multi-agency Task Force in place, right now, that you've jeopardized, with DEA, NSA and the FCC." Fitzpatrick searched his jacket pocket, then pulled out his middle finger, extending it.

"Well, I'm with the F.U.2!" he said, flipping off the head Fed.

Brink jumped off the edge of the desk to intervene. He considered Fitzpatrick a brother, but brothers can have a *love/hate* relationship. "Easy, Fitz, you're on thin ice as it is!" Brink said assuaging the situation. "Agent Mancuso, Detective Fitzpatrick is well within his jurisdiction under the rubric of *serial homicide investigation.* If you guys had *tasked us in,* like you're <u>mandated</u> to do, we wouldn't have stepped on your toes… or even be having this conversation."

Mancuso looked around the room to his men and women, "You know National Security has priority and all this is on a *need-to-know* only! So let's not even go there, Captain." The other Federal agents nodded in agreement, but the cops were having none of it as groans of tedium rose from the polished floor. Lines were starting to draw in the precinct sand with the flatfoots on one side and the Feebs on the other. Tension was mounting.

"National Security, my ass!" Fitzpatrick barked out. "They're fucking gangsters, low-life criminals and now, prime suspects in a serial murder case, Mancuso."

"There is no case!" Mancuso fired back. "As of right this second, you're off it. Anything to do with the Rostovs, forget it, it's all ours. The FBI's in charge now. If you attempt to further complicate things, you'll be looking at Federal obstruction charges to go with a forced early retirement."

As bad as the blood had been between them, Tetley found the threats to be a railroading scenario against his new partner. He decided to speak up. "Agent Mancuso," Tetley interjected. "I've enlisted the assistance of Detective Fitzpatrick to investigate an IRA Paramilitary group that has recently arrived in your city. Captain

Brink has granted interagency cooperation as MI6 thinks this group could be in collusion with the Russians to organize an arms deal through Rostov."

Mancuso, who hadn't been looking at Tetley the entire time, turned his head. "...And as for you, Limey," Mancuso barked with a raised eyebrow, "You've got authorization to investigate shit in the United States!" All eyes jerked towards Mancuso as Brink pushed his way closer to really give this Fed a piece of his mind. *That was way out of order,* everyone thought.

"That's right," Mancuso continued pointing an accusatory finger at Tetley, "I ran a full vet on your story and British Intelligence informed me you're officially on an *extended leave.*" All eyes shifted to Tetley, *was this true?* So whatever you've told these idiots, means Jack Shit! You're lucky I don't throw you in a hole and wait for the *Extradition Papers.*" Mancuso had begun to turn, but snapped back for one more dig. "Another word outta you and I'll have your ass streamlined back in London in time for high tea!"

An uncomfortable hush fell over the squad room, when suddenly a Forensics Division detective burst in. It was Jansen, now all eyes turned toward her. It was true Jansen was smokin' hot with a face to match her body, but at this moment, they all merely desired her professional results. She had a look of excitement as though she were having her own *Perry Mason moment.*

She pumped the manila folder in front of her to clear the crowd. "Sorry, sirs, but I knew everyone here would want to know this A-SAP!" Jansen blurted. "We just ID'd Rostov's son, Oleg." she began to giggle, "… or what's left of him."

"Son-of-a-bitch!" Mancuso blurted as he gritted his teeth and lowered his head. He abruptly turned on his heal and exited the room. His men followed in kind.

"Fitz, you'll love this one," Jansen continued, as she opened the folder to read the dossier. "We found him in a burned-out warehouse off Olvera Street next to his pecker which was nailed to a table." Jansen bit her lip as she fought back a barely controlled urge to laugh.

"It looks like he cut it off before he burned himself up… now is that some guilt-ridden shit or what?" Jansen unnecessarily added.

"Thanks Jansen, but camera-savvy YouTub-er beat you to it. If that's it with the updates, that'll be all," Captain Brink said sternly. Realizing Brink meant business; she nodded and slowly turned and left the room, still a little confused as not being privy to the video the others had already viewed. Bathke, another detective chuckled in a whisper to her so as to avoid Brink's condemnation, "I'll shoot you the link, Jansen, you won't believe it." As the glass door closed behind her, she suddenly burst into hysterical laughter that trailed her down the hallway.

"Fitz, I need you to cooperate on this one… for me!" Brink half-pleaded. "Because of the old *Rampart Scandal*, we're still under scrutiny from IAB and I don't want your name popping up this late in the game. Let the heat die down for a bit. Take a few days of *lost time*, I'll handle the Feebs." Brink was being unusually generous, and no one in the room could figure out why. "And as for you, you've lied to me, mister!" Brink said as seriously as a disappointed father, "just go and get a tan or hit the nearest Hooters before I revoke your visa. I don't want to hear a peep outta either of you until this whole mess is settled!" Tetley knew better than to try and justify his actions and dutifully nodded. His jig was up.

Brink was now as frustrated as a commander with his authority in question could be. Half furious, half in admiration of his man's tenacity, he dropped his shoulders and plodded out of the room. Fitzpatrick, disappointed at his commander's lack of loyalty to his work ethic, was even more furious at faux-partner's dupe. He turned and sneered evilly at Tetley. *This was not going to end well.*

CHAPTER 49

PCH WAS A LONG and luxurious drive and, unless you were wealthy enough to live in Malibu, the Palisades, or the cliffs above the ocean, as the highway was strictly reserved for sightseeing.

It was a clear day, as are most days in L.A., and the Pacific was a deep blue and green under the sand bars near the shoreline. There was barely any wind, and never, ever a single bug to interrupt your day -- one of the quintessential reasons everyone wanted to live there. It was truly paradise.

The tension was palpable in the unmarked Crown Vic as Fitzpatrick had to steel himself from driving off the cliff's edge, just out of spite. He and Tetley were stone cold quite. Like two brothers fighting over the same girl, both men gritted their teeth and looked forward without looking at the other... *who would blink first?*

"God damn it, you fucking lied to me!" Fitzpatrick blurted out, seemingly surprised at himself for being able to be deceived. "You're here on a *witch hunt*, you never even had <u>clearance</u>, are you fucking kidding me?"

Tetley, unfazed, stared out the passenger window at the long coastal highway. "You have no idea what you're talking about," he said in a smug manner. "I'm here doing the same thing you're doing, investigating criminals. We're no different, you and I." Tetley could hear the leather tightening on the steering wheel as Fitzpatrick gripped harder in frustration.

"It may not look like it, but L.A.'s a tough town. We've got plenty of problems, especially gangs and this whole damn mess is just another gang war. It's the Mexicans muscling in on the Russians. Tomorrow it'll be the Triads and the Armenians, or the Zips and the Slants against the Spooks."

Tetley's look feigned umbrage with the detective's prejudicial tone. "Those are very pejorative, and very racist terms." Fitzpatrick squinted as though he were running his last statement through his head again: Zips, Slants, Spooks? "Those are the gang names, you asshole! Besides if I called them pan-faced, bug-eyed monkeys that would be racist. I'm not a *racist*. I hate everyone equally, except maybe you who is topp'n my list!"

Tetley snapped a look toward his driver. "You heard your Forensics woman, that was no ordinary murder, that was an <u>execution</u>!"

Fitzpatrick snickered, probably at the thought of that low-life suffering to no lesser extent than his victims had. "Hell, for all we know, he could've done it himself, you know *Jewish lightening*, a *torch job* for insurance money, Christ, maybe auto-erotic asphyxiation? Oleg and Alexei Rostov are world-class junkies. Oleg probably just had a meltdown. I mean what kind of idiot would want to marry a herpetic sore like Oleg? Anyway, good riddance to that piece of trash."

It was then Tetley seemed to realize that he and Fitzpatrick were really not so different. He decided it was time to speak up, and this time he was undeterred in his persistence of the matter. "The men I'm investigating are ruthless as well and intricately involved in all of this. They've merely begun their campaign of terror on new soil."

Fitzpatrick, who seemed uninterested in politics, blurted out a disagreeable laugh, "What, against Rostov? *Boo-fucking-hoo!*" Tetley did not seem to enjoy being trivialized nor browbeaten, but looking at his surroundings, he realized he had no choice since he couldn't jump out of a moving vehicle at that rate of speed. "I took an oath to protect the people of L.A.," Fitzpatrick continued. "You… you took a vow to protect a fucking <u>queen</u>?"

Tetley could only shake his head in what seemed like disbelief, "You admire those Irish bastards don't you, Detective?"

CHAPTER 50

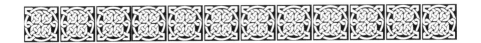

ROSTOV'S MANSION LOOKED LIKE the back up at car wash on Little Santa Monica in Century City, except for the fact that the driveway was filled with the most expensive cars in the world. Ferraris, Lamborghinis, Bentleys; you name it. If you couldn't pronounce it, you couldn't afford it.

All the engines had cooled and there was no movement, except for a single limousine that pulled up and around the secondary lane to exit the compound. Fitzpatrick knew Rostov's men would be distracted with other problems, so he parked Crown Vic up the street and out of view. He and Tetley jumped out and followed their way down a hedgerow.

In the rear of the mansion, acres across the back yard, Fitzpatrick looked over the cliff face as he knelt on the rocky ground. He scanned the beach, yet all he could see was tall windswept grass and kite surfers.

"Hey, if these Irish guys you're so sure did this, and I'm not saying they did -- because there's no proof -- then yeah, I admire them." Fitzpatrick said, finally answering Tetley's earlier question. "Why not? They're helping me rid this city of the worst kind of criminals." He was proud of himself for being more realistic than politically correct. Then he suddenly course corrected. "But that doesn't mean I won't do my job when the time comes."

Gardeners went about their business while Tetley and Fitzpatrick continued to search the hillside as if they belonged there every bit as much as they did. Tetley searched near the fence line. "You'll look the other way, detective, because you're one of them." Fitzpatrick took offense with this statement and arched his back, "one of them, what the fuck are you talking about?"

Tetley straightened up as proudly as any Englishman had ever stood. "Yes, one of them -- you're Irish!"

Fitzpatrick rolled his eyes in boredom. "Yeah, I'm Irish -- Irish-American, Sherlock!"

Tetley was determined to finish his thought. "Humph! Why can't you Americans just be happy with your own little culture instead of trying to be what you're not?" *Oh, now it's gonna be an historical discourse*, Fitzpatrick thought.

Fitzpatrick rarely engaged in long historical or political debates because his blood pressure would shoot skyward. He rarely lost those types of arguments due to his propensity for winning by attrition. "You Brits still don't get it, do you?" Fitzpatrick laughed. "We kicked your sorry asses back to England nearly 300 years ago for pulling the same shit you've been pulling on the Irish since the 11th Century. You've been kicked out of every other country of your so-called *colonies* and since then you can't seem to get over yourselves."

Tetley felt the sting of condemnation. He didn't have much in the way of a come back, as he really was used to one-sided conversations as he patronized others. "Well, I hardly think so. The British Empire spans the world," he said in a grandiose manner, stretching his arms out wide.

"Bullshit!" Fitzpatrick lunged back. "You gave up India, Jamaica, Australia, Canada, Honduras, and Belize just to name a few. And you had the audacity to sell 'em back their own countries that you stole from them in the first place! Your taxes are oppressive and you're just a bunch of socialists in tailored suits!" Fitzpatrick pulled out a pair of tweezers from his jacket pocket and began a micro search. "But not in Ireland, no way! You had a real hard-on for them, didn't ya? They're the thorn in the Monarch's side. Wake up, crumpet-eater, Ireland is your Viet Nam! Cromwell systematically wiped out a million Irish and you call him a saint? You starved over three million more of them by stealing their food and livestock and called *it their Famine*? Hell even Hitler had the good sense not to let his kills suffer. You've tried to starve them out, breed them out, kill all of 'em you could for over a 1,000 years, but they keep kick'n your ass six-ways-to-Sunday. You guys just can't leave well enough alone."

Suddenly, Fitzpatrick peered into a trampled patch of grass noticing something shiny and out of place. He reached down into the moist earth and pushed the tweezers under the lip of the shiny object. The object was oddly shaped: it was seven-sided, an equilateral curved heptagon, and looked like a coin, but weighed more than your usual quarter or half-dollar. On it's head; it showed a harp, the 1970 printing date, and the word *Eire*.

Tetley, stepped up as to notice why Fitzpatrick had stopped hearing himself talk, then moved to investigate. As he peered over Fitzpatrick's shoulder, his eyes widened and lips curled in justification. "That's an old 50 pence coin -- an Irish coin, Detective!"

CHAPTER 51

TOPANGA CANYON WAS MADE famous in the 60s when hordes of hippies and television icons built homes on the treacherous hillsides. The two-lane road that ran all the way to the beach from the San Fernando Valley has so many switchbacks and curves, it seems as though an LSD-possessed engineer had designed the wretched thing. Every week there was some sort of Hemp and Bead Festival or Folk Singer's Concert or something hippie and weird going on, but people seemed to dig it.

Topanga had two things going for it: oceans views and privacy. And that's just what Murphy wanted most in the world. The pad of land had been cleared years before and what stood on the oddly shaped plot was a nearly completed home. It sat atop a mountain peak that overlooked the Pacific Ocean to the west, the Valley to the north, and L.A. to the east, and, of course, Topanga Canyon below. Murphy could always see who was coming his way long before they got to him.

The skeleton frame of wooden four-by-eights and two-by-fours, concrete slab and PVC piping was half-covered by tarps and plastic in case the odd occasional drizzle or on-shore flow might dampen everything.

Murphy stood outside the skinless structure and directed the work like a traffic warden. Liam and Hammer used their talents to frame a skylight as McCann crossed the cement floor, inspecting every detail. He walked the length of what would be the living room until he came to stone fireplace with an ornate mantle. He took a moment to admire the craftsmanship, the stonework, the mortar used to secure it. It was a hearth right out of his childhood in the southwest of Ireland. Tralee, where he was from, was so wind swept and wild, they didn't have an electric light until he was youth.

McCann took a nostalgic moment, then reached into a canvas bag he'd been carrying, pulled out a large wooden object and placed it atop the mantle. It was a hand-carved wooden harp. Murphy and the lads, still not 100% sure of McCann's intensions, had been watching him closely, but McCann knew all-to-well that their eyes were on him.

"While you were liv'n *The Life of Riley*, I was rotting in jail cell making a lot of these," McCann said, sensing Murphy now over his shoulder. He turned to see his brother-in-law, "It's a house-warming present to remember me by." He proudly adjusted the harp on the mantle.

Liam approached and picked up the piece to admire it. "Jesus, I carved enough of these in prison to build me own house."

Hammer, stepped closer to look at the artwork as well. "My arse, Liam! Ya carve like you build, which is crap! You'd need an education just to go back to prison." Hammer laughed, then noticed the look on McCann's face. "You're not still worried about what was done last night, are ya Mick?" The other men leaned in just a bit awaiting his answer.

"Lads, what they done to Ciara was worse than anything I know," McCann lamented. "Your man got just what he had coming to him, but I don't know what will happen if we go any further with this."

Hammer's lips tightened as though he were in a conundrum. "You know Frank wants justice."

McCann's attitude changed quickly. "Frank wants <u>REVENGE</u>!" he shouted. "Don't you see, he's mad with guilt and won't stop until he gets us all killed?!"

Murphy, always the diplomat, could sense the tension escalating, so he decided to diffuse the situation. "Never talk religion or politics

223

on an empty stomach, lads," he interrupted. "Come on, I want to show you something."

Murphy led the group to the backyard through the half-finished house. As they passed under the eaves, a beautiful vista of mountains sloping down to the sea appeared. The view was so spectacular it was humbling. Slowly each man knew how lucky he was to be right there at that moment.

At the base of the drop off, Murphy headed toward a darkened area. He began to run, then leaped into the air, and disappeared from sight. The other men quickly followed to insure he was all right. They stopped at the edge of an enormous hole in the earth and looked down. There at the bottom of the dirt hole he stood, his arms outstretched like the King of Siam.

"Whatcha tink of me new pool, lads?" Murphy shouted up to the others. "The Sultan of Fucking Swing, I am -- a pool, can yaz imagine?"

McCann wanted to laugh, but was still conflicted on just how he felt. "You've certainly done well for yourself," he said sarcastically. "I guess that IRA money you took in Belfast really went to help the needy." Liam took a small step backwards -- this could be explosive.

"Are ya crazy, Mick? I turned that money in long before ever coming here." Playing off the obvious doubt, Murphy returned to his excitement. "I earned this! I scratched together the cash from break'n me bollocks in construction work that bled my fingers raw, then I won a liquor license in a crooked game of poker, and finally found the perfect place for me bar... I've had a run-a-good-luck." McCann sneered in disbelief as Murphy appealed to him. "Mick, you can have this too! Think about it, we're family, you and I."

Murphy looked to the other men and winked, "Sorry lads, no offense!" The others shook it off. "We always worked well together. We'd be partners!"

McCann snickered, trying hard not to warm up, but afterall he was still Irish. "I did 10 years hard time while you were lounging around playing Romeo and building mansions."

Murphy just kept his Dennis Quaid-sized grin on his face. "Jesus Mick, they had us dead-to-rights! You're not gonna blame a fella for sav'n his own arse, now are ya?"

McCann could take no anymore. He took one more long, cold stare and just before he broke into a half-smile, a horn suddenly blasted. Through the bare frame house, the lads watched as Johnny and Sean drove up the dirt road in an old, beaten, pick up truck. Sean quickly jumped out and flung open the back door as the others made their way to meet them.

"Give us a hand here, will ya?" Sean shouted to the others. Johnny jumped out and met them all at the back of the truck. "Frank's been on a bender since yesterday," Johnny said out of breath.

Murphy sneered at the two in disappointment. "I said keep an eye on him, not let him drink California dry!" There, in the back seat, Frank lay like a hot mess, twisting and turning in his soiled suit. He mumbled and cried and carried-on as the men attempted to help this drunken behemoth inside.

"He can't stop mumbling about his daughter," Sean said worriedly. "Look at the state of him, hasn't had a decent pint in years, then makes it all up in one session," Johnny added.

Suddenly Liam stopped and tapped an earpiece he'd had hidden deep inside his head the whole time. He raised his hand for everyone to quiet. Since he was in charge of all communications, it was his responsibility to monitor everything the Rostov's were up to. Liam grinned wide and shouted to the others, "Rostov's on the move, lads." Liam relayed. Then a longer smile drew on his face, "Fancy a day at the races, boys?"

CHAPTER 52

ARASOLS AND WIDE BRIM hats were the order of the day for striking trophy wives with their cigar-smoking, diabetic, soon-to-be-ex-husbands in tow. Money flowed like water here and everyone was here to win. Even though Southern California had fantastic weather year-round, horse racing was still a *seasonal* sport, so anyone who was a serious gambler showed up all day, everyday. On the face of it, Hollywood Park was a clean, wholesome, a Vegas-style gambling emporium, but scratch the surface and the ugliness oozed out like puss.

Alexei Rostov was no stranger to the racetrack as it was always filled with losers, ne'er-do-wells, and the dredges of society, which was a criteria Alexei met in every way, every way, that is except for his $3,000 suits and rolls of $100 bills. He swaggered down by the dirt track, meandered through the clubhouse and smiled at easy women in the bleachers. He had already established his crew in different locations throughout the park. Some were high above looking down; others were placed in strategic positions by entrances and exits. Still others mingled amongst the crowd for face-to-face verification. But this time, Alexei had something different in mind to flush out his prey.

He had ordered three of his men to walk with him as he pushed and staggered through the crowd, spilling drinks and acting the fool amid the pomp and circumstance of horse racing etiquette. After all, at this point Alexei didn't know his brother's killers by face, he only had an idea that they were of a lesser race than he, so, just for that mere fact, needed to be destroyed. As Alexei deliberately drew attention to himself, he cunningly nodded to the men flanking him, who abruptly turned 180 degrees and walked the other way. Now the trap was set. The three men pushed in earpieces for surveillance, then checked the status of them by speaking into tiny microphones concealed in their hands.

"I want you idiots to watch everything that moves, do you understand?" Alexei barked.

"Da!" responded his men in unison.

"I know that these bastards are here, I can feel them, so let's flush them out. Nobody touches them, not now! Just mark them and follow."

Hollywood Park was jam-packed with people enjoying the perfect weather, cocktails, and the high energy of the day. Everyone was having a great time, everyone, that is, except Alexei. The strain of paranoia from cocaine abuse and other assorted drugs was beginning to make Courtney Love look like the Mahatma Gandhi. To calm his anxiety, the Russian angled his head, opened his jacket, leaned in and snorted the hidden bullet of coke.

"The horses are at the gate…" the announcer yelled over the louder speakers. *Bang*, and there off! The ponies raced down the track, dirt and divots flew as the jockeys whipped the crap out of their four-legged runners. Thinking he was still shrewder than his enemies, Alexei had no interest in the horses, but he would be a winner either way.

Yet, as cunning as he thought he was, unbeknownst to Alexei, a pair of eyes spied him through binoculars from the railing above. The reflection from the telescopic glasses followed as Alexei entered the winner's circle. The Russian horse owner handed the jockey flowers and an insincere handshake to congratulate him for his win.

Alexei grabbed a bottle of champagne from the manager, shook it and sprayed everyone as custom dictated, although he looked completely foolish and mean-spirited when doing so. Corks continued to pop and flashes from digital cameras went off for nearly 10 minutes as Alexei used himself as bait to flesh out his enemies.

McCann lowered the glasses and looked curiously at Murphy. "This feels wrong. I don't like how exposed we are." He put the binoculars back up to his eyes and continued, not realizing Alexei's men were ordered to scan the crowd for anything unusual -- anything!

After a few moments, and confident everyone at Hollywood Park had seen him, Alexei exited the track and trailed through the crowd on his way to the stables. Like clockwork, McCann and Murphy made their way at Alexei's six o'clock and dogged him like bloodhounds from a distance. Their haste and overconfidence hadn't help their cause as Alexei's men suddenly caught sight of strange stalkers making beeline, acquired their new targets, and followed in kind.

From the stands, one of the Russians radioed in, "Alexei, you have two assholes following you -- uhm, but..."

Alexei barked at him, "... what the fuck are you trying to say, idiot?"

"They're not *beaners!*"

Alexei nearly stopped in his tracks confused if he had heard his man correctly, but knew that would be a mistake to close the gap on his pursuers. Yet before he could chastise his men again, they clarified. "They're white, they're not Mexican!" Alexei immediately thought they could be Feds or undercover, or worse, contract killers, either way, why wasn't it El Cid's gang? Suddenly the game had become very interesting.

Alexei slowed his pace as he rounded a corner toward the stables and stopped at the pen door. A long, silken black stallion stuck his snout out first, then the rest of his regal head. Alexei began to stroke the animal, speaking to it calmly in Russian. Alexei, the farthest thing from a caring, nurturing animal-lover, used this ploy to buy time, allowing his men to catch up behind McCann and Murphy. He knew the two would have to slow their gate. It worked.

As they approached, Murphy kept it light. "You know, we could cut off that horse's head and put it in the bastard's bed while he slept to send a message, but that's a bit cliché."

McCann never broke his stride or his cover. "I'd like to walk away," he said concerned. "We've sent our message, we should just leave well enough alone."

Murphy's face changed. "Jaysus, Mick, are ya serious? It was Frank's daughter, your Goddaughter! Where's your loyalty?"

McCann turned and sharply glared at Murphy. "Never, ever question my loyalty!" he half-barked, half-whispered. "My loyalty cost me my family and my freedom." Murphy quickly realized his faux pas and the recklessness of his quick tongue, but it was too late, McCann was climbing out of his shell. "I don't recall loyalty keep'n you around Ireland after you fucked-off to America." McCann's eyes turned accusatory. "Why did you have to run so far? Did it have anything to do with that morning in Belfast?"

Still a ways away from Alexei, Murphy knew this was the place that the air would have to be cleared. "Alright, get it off your chest then, Mick!" Murphy said as he stopped dead in his tracks. "I know it's been eat'n away at you since you saw me face again. Say it! Say it, Mick; you think I'm a rat! You think I sold you out, don't you?"

McCann kept walking as he began to back off the issue. "I'm just say'n I'm not going to spend another minute in jail over revenge. Frank's not think'n straight and we should be leave'n this mess to the cops."

Suddenly, a helicopter appeared in the skies above the men. It would not have been out of the ordinary, except for the fact that Alexei, upon hearing the tail-rotor, about-faced, and slid through a gate to an open area south of the track where the helo was landing. Before McCann knew it, Alexei had jumped into the copter and it had begun to take off. *Damn, they'd just lost their chance to take Alexei.*

Still unaware of their tail, McCann and Murphy made a sharp left and headed for the parking lot. They'd been marked and now the hunters had become the hunted.

CHAPTER 53

SAN PEDRO MAY HAVE had a new fresh smell, but just underneath, in the darkened corners and around the back of the liquor stores, you'd find the same seedy, industrial rat-infested harbor town as Raymond Chandler did when he wrote *Farewell, My Lovely* and *The Long Goodbye*.

Steam billowed from the large oil refineries and dry dock warehouses and the dingy yellow low-sodium streetlights produced a ghastly glow at night.

Murphy traversed the oil-soaked streets in Oleg's Hummer: why not, he wasn't going to need it anymore. McCann rode shotgun, but couldn't get over the size of the military-grade SUV. *And to think anyone here could buy one these and drive it to the ends of the earth.* McCann seemed to take comfort at the luxurious freedoms Americans had at their disposal. Frank, on the other hand and the other lads were in the back of the vehicle scoping each intersection for danger.

"You'd think that idiot would've had the good sense to gas up before going to on a killing-spree," Murphy said, semi-serious about the late Oleg's petroleum-based irresponsibility's. In the distance, he saw a lone all-night gas station under bright, fluorescent lights.

"Any of you lads have a 10'er?" Murphy shouted to the back seat. "Jesus, Johnny, this monster's gonna cost a fortune to fill up with petrol," Sean said turning to his friend. Liam dug deep into his pocket and pulled out a note and winked at Murphy in the rear view mirror. As Murphy pulled into the station, Liam jumped out and walked to the attendant sitting behind two-inch thick, bulletproof Plexiglas. He dropped a crisp, $100 bill into the silver tray.

McCann climbed out to stretch his legs and took in the miserable sight of dock-life after dark. He caught a whiff of something as his nostrils flared. He sniffed the air and began to look suspiciously around the area. Nothing: a water-desalinization plant to the left, a power station to the right, and San Pedro Harbor dead ahead. But, still, there was something off; McCann could just feel it in his bones.

Liam returned with a cardboard box heavy with economy-size cups of Joe. "Careful now, boys, that's coffee, except yours Johnny, got ya some Mountain Dew, cause I know you like the serious caffeine," Liam said passing out the drinks.

"Sweet!" Johnny reacted happily.

Frank hadn't spoken a word; he just reached out, grabbed the large cup and returned to the glow of the laptop monitor he was engaged in. Frank moved his finger on the magic pad and scrolled down. He had found a lengthy biography on Victor Rostov and was glued to it. He wanted to know everything about his foe and take full advantage.

McCann's sense of danger was spot-on. What he and the others couldn't see was Alexei and his men a few hundred yards away spying them with night vision goggles from different positions. They had them in a crossfire.

Merely a blip could be heard in Alexei's ear, "Alexei, we've got them," Gregor whispered, even though everyone was wearing earpieces. At least they were starting to catch on. "Yeah, they're driving Oleg's Hummer. What do you want us to do?" Gregor nervously inquired.

McCann quickly turned his head toward the power plant, only to see a parade of cars heading their way. From out of the darkness, El Cid appeared in a low-rider Chevy truck, bedazzled with all manner of ethnic cliché. Behind him, a posse of gang-bangers blasted a mariachi music mash-up of Mexican rock and traditional folk music as though it were *Cinco de Mayo*. McCann realized it was becoming a very surreal scene.

Sean stood mouth-agape just as he topped off the gas tank. The others instantly rallied around McCann in anticipation of trouble. Murphy stepped ahead of McCann as a shield while the others made a wedge of Irish muscle to ward off the approaching horde. McCann placed his hand on Murphy's shoulder as if to say, *it's okay, back off.* He slowly walked forward as El Cid in the lead car stopped while the other cars pulled up in tandem.

Like a *light brigade*, the Mexicans created their own wedge that would certainly have overwhelmed the Irishmen. It wasn't exactly a Mexican Stand-Off, but the Irish weren't known for surrendering even in the face the most hopeless of situations. The Mexicans revved their engines, gunning them through flaming backfires to maximize the intimidation factor.

El Cid jumped from his vehicle and placed his hand in the air. All cars went silent. McCann was near the halfway point in the middle of the gas station lot when El Cid's mood changed dramatically. He'd had a sour, serious look, but as he approached McCann, he suddenly smiled. "Oy ye, Amigo" El Cid shouted, waging his finger, "You gringos are loco!" The lads looked at each other, confused, but still braced for a fight. "Oleg was one bad dude, and to do him like that on his wedding night, *Madre de Dios*, you some fucked-up homies!" Maybe it was the years in prison, or just a cultural difference, but McCann thought, *what the fuck?*

McCann stopped in front of El Cid without an ounce of intimidation or fear. The same couldn't be said of Murphy and the others as they clutched their guns tightly and double-checked that all safeties were in the *OFF* position. El Cid looked past McCann and lifted his shirt, revealing a MAC-10 automatic weapon, with extra clips riddled around his waistband. A loud chorus of bullets being bolted into the chambers of dozens of weapons was almost operatic. McCann knew he needed to calm the situation.

"We just need you to show us Rostov's warehouse, we'll do the rest," McCann said respectfully.

El Cid, although appreciating the sentiment, had his own ideas. "You're right to show me respect, Ese, you're in my hood now. Things are different around here, not like in your country."

McCann noted El Cid's comment and looked around at his men covered in prison ink, sporting wife-beater Ts and pants that hung at their knees. "Oh, I don't know? Looks a lot like Belfast to me," McCann said as El Cid looked around to make sure he was looking at the same thing. "Men with guns and helicopters keep'n a lid on people they don't respect. Never given anybody a break cause they're treated like second class citizens!" Oddly enough, El Cid began to listen closer to this interesting foreigner with the funny accent. "The only difference between here and where we come from seems to be the weather!"

Still taking in the earlier comment, El Cid thought a moment, then burst out, "Hey, I like you, Irish! You some sort of *Ghetto-Defender*, huh?" El Cid took a step closer to McCann, "Listen hermano, you and your crew saved my ass back at my club, and for that I owe you, but *Vatos Locos* are gonna take a big slice of Rostov's pie, comprende?" McCann thought for a moment, then nodded in agreement as the two shared the mutual respect that real men understood.

El Cid nodded his head in response. He smiled wide to reveal a single shiny gold tooth, then threw up his hands and shouted, "Vamanos, muchachos!"

CHAPTER 54

THE RESIDENTS OF BRENTWOOD spent more money on manicuring their lawns, than most people did on a new car. Afterall, this was the former home of not only O.J. Simpson, but also nearly every celebrity and politician worthy of note at one point or another.

The streets in Brentwood were wide and spotless and seemed to be magically hosed down each night, as the flecks in the concrete sparkled from the light of the street lamps. It was reminiscent of old money, old Hollywood, but it didn't feel old, just homey.

Fitzpatrick pushed the antique brass plug on the oversized Spanish door. Tetley took a moment to fill his eyes with the enormity of the estate and the other homes in this neighborhood. He thought these places only existed in movies, boy was this an experience. *Who lived in these homes?* Tetley thought.

Tetley felt a slight pinch on his foot as something; perhaps a pet had accidentally walked across it. Looking down, he saw two children at his feet.

Standing between Fitzpatrick and Tetley stood a young boy and girl. Dej was merely six years old and Siria almost nine. They were dark-skinned and shy holding teddy bears and other toys so close they could barely see where they were walking.

Ringing the bell again, Fitzpatrick was beginning to get testy. Suddenly, the front door flung open and a woman in her mid-40s appeared. She looked at the men, then quickly down to the children. "Oh my God, there here!" she screamed to both men and the guests already inside. The woman reached down and began hugging the two children in a vise-like grip.

Fitzpatrick was used to being ignored, but not by his own sister who was his biggest fan. He continued with the introduction, however meaningless it was as it was falling on deaf ears. "Kate, this is Inspector Tetley," Fitzpatrick said. "Inspector, this is my sister Katie." Tetley nodded obligingly, but Kate was too busy to entertain formal introductions. She quickly scooped up the children's hands and led them inside.

The foyer was grand, complete with black and white marble tile and oil paintings that upon first glance looked like originals. *What did these people do?*

Across the entry into the large living room, an enormous banner draped across the valances reading: *"WELCOME OUR NEW AMERICANS!"* Party guests excitedly turned to look at the new arrivals. Adults were gathered near the portable bar and dozens of children filled the home, running, playing, and laughing. It was truly a heartwarming scene.

Kate walked Dej and Siria carefully up to the other guests. Dej wore a black patch across his face since losing his eye due to damage, then infection in the wake of the Indonesian Tsunami. Siria walked with crutches as her legs had been severely damaged by the weight of the debris that crashed upon her, killing both their parents sacrificed themselves to try and save their children. Siria would have a good chance to walk normally again when the doctors in the U.S. took over her care, but Dej would be blind in one eye until science could catch up.

Dej and Siria's faces lit up at the size of the room and shear beauty of everything wonderful and bright in their new world. The expressions on their faces said it all. In the corner of the room, a priest, Father Delaney, stepped forward to greet the children. He was already half-in-the-bag, as priests get at soirées and opened bars, yet

Dej became curious, having never seen anyone in black with white hair. He didn't know what to make of the man.

Kate knelt at the children's feet and gave them another hug. "Oh, we're so pleased to have you," she said barely able to contain herself. "Are you two hungry? We have lots of food and treats for you." Shelia, one of the other new mothers, spread her arms out to corral another pack of children into the drawing room off to the side. Shelia waved Dej and Siria over to join the group. It was as if the actions of any mother were universally translated, as they children didn't need to understand her words to understand she wanted them to play with the other children. They couldn't have made it over fast enough. As they entered the enormous playroom, the children stood agog at the 120-inch flat screen television, video game consoles, and tables and tables of food. Food of all kinds: hot dogs, pizza, sandwiches, jello, fruits and vegetables and so much more. There was plenty of candy the likes these children could've only dreamed of.

After all the ruckus, Kate stood back up, turned and addressed her brother and his guest. "Sorry, I'm Katie," she said extending her hand to Tetley. "Come on, let's get you a drink!"

Tetley nearly broke a smile and dutifully followed her into the fray. This lovely woman seemed to be the only American who actually knew what proper decorum entailed. "Charles Tetley, Ma'am, at your service," he responded to the back of her head. "You have a lovely home, simply lovely."

Kate winked at her friend Shawna who was heeling the two. "Why thank you, Mr. Tetley," she said, pondering whether or not to curtsy.

"May I say, I think it's a wonderful thing what you and the others are doing for these children."

Four boys shot through the crowd of adults as Dej stopped and nervously tugged at Kate's skirt. "Do you have drink, Ma'am?" Dej said with a heavy Sumatran accent.

Kate reached down and touched his face, "Gosh, they're so polite," she said clasping her hands to her heart. "Now, first, call me Katie, Dej, and yes, we have loads of drinks."

Kate walked toward a long row of drapes, then pushed a remote she picked up from a coffee table. Slowly, two large curtains separated to reveal a giant lighted pool in the back yard. Around the pool, *Tiki torches* burned illuminating more tables with more food and ice-filled tubs of bottled water, sodas, and juice boxes.

Dej's jaw dropped, "Wah!"

Just then a group of children ran from the game room yelping with joy as Shelia tried to divert them from crashing through the French double-doors. The adopting parents could hardly reign in their own emotions watching the children entering what must have been *Candy Land* to them.

Fitzpatrick had already made an end-run around the partygoers and was headed out back to help with the food preparation. He had begun flipping hamburgers at the bar-b-que adorned with a chef's hat and an apron that read: *"KISS THE CHEF"* Tetley followed Kate outside with the children, but seemed uneasy seeing this side of Fitzpatrick. He turned his attention back toward his gracious hostess.

"So, Kate," Tetley said sheepishly, still seemingly uncomfortable with the informality of American etiquette that would allow a newly introduced woman to be addressed by her first name, "How did you learn of these children?"

A smile immediately appeared across Kate's face as she explained. "I work with the Joni and Friends International Disability Center in Agoura Hills."

A curious look tilted Tetley face as if he was searching his thoughts for recollection. Kate decided to edify him before his British charm began to wear off.

"I'm a volunteer there and was fundraising for their *Wheels for the World* and *Wounded Warrior Family Retreat* programs when one of the donors told me about what Ciara O'Malley was doing in Sumatra trying to find homes for all the orphans. So, through backchannels, I was able to contact her and tell her I would personally help her arrange for the adoptions and that we would be blessed if she would bring those poor displaced and disabled children to America where we would love and protect them." Kate took a deep breath as though she had a lot more to say on the subject so close to her heart, when she felt a gentle hand on her shoulder from behind.

Just then, Father Delaney appeared next to Tetley. "Sorry, Katie, I have to take the inspector away from you," and led the inspector to an empty table under an umbrella. "So what brings you to Los Angeles, Inspector?" Tetley had the realization he was now on the spot after being deliberately led to this spot. It seemed everyone there knew who he was, but he didn't have a clue as to who any of them were.

"Yeah, Inspector, tell them why you've decided to grace our shores," Fitzpatrick shouted as he filled a tray with burgers.

"It's just a routine investigation," He replied clearing his throat.

CHAPTER 55

OLEG'S HUMVEE SAT DOCKSIDE near an enormous cargo ship. It was new and trim and looked like a cross between an Arctic research vessel and a luxury cruise liner that could carry thousands of passengers. The name emblazoned on her hull read: *SEA LAUNCH*.

Under giant floodlights, dockworkers toiled as the night shift prepared for the early morning launch. The ship would set sail at high tide as soon as all the cargo was loaded. It would then make its way to the exact longitude and latitude in the Pacific Ocean where the Equator offered the greatest rotational speed, then it was 62 miles straight up, where the planet's boundary ends and suborbital space begins. From there, the payload would be shot into geostationary orbit, safe from overpopulated areas, no air traffic, and no *prying eyes*.

Sea Launch was a joint American/Russian (with Norway and Ukraine) venture developed by Boeing in 1995 to enable private interests to launch rockets carrying their satellites. Rostov knew this and was betting heavily that his communications satellite would revolutionize global telecommunications and the cell phone market. So heavily, in fact, that he was leveraging, not only all his money, but also that of his investors, his own credibility, even his very life. For if the *vore v zacone* backs your play, you had better be sure, without a shadow of a doubt, that you will win… and win big! Needless-to-say, Rostov was under a great deal of pressure.

Inside the Hummer, McCann and the other lads surveyed the area as Frank anxiously awaited the assault. Sean and Johnny were the operational eyes and ears. They had the latest, most sophisticated surveillance equipment money could buy including: high-definition mini cams with color night vision, infra-red detection, blue laser mics, and a host of other toys so no one could catch them off guard. But for now, they could only monitor Rostov's movements while he tooled around his mansion.

"Mick, I haven't heard any crosstalk for over an hour," Sean chirped in, breaking the uncomfortable silence.

McCann shook his head as he peered out across the dock. "I don't like this," McCann said sinisterly. "There are no security guards, why would they leave all this unguarded?"

Frank rustled around in his seat and grabbed the door handle. "Sod that, let's get in there! I want everything that bastard's got burned to the ground." Frank's impatience was now becoming a liability. Suddenly, Johnny raised his hand as he monitored the perimeter -- *quiet.* He turned to look at the lads and then threw a flat hand in the direction he wanted them to look. It was El Cid.

From out of the darkness, El Cid appeared with his men and carefully made their way to the SUV. Frank jumped out too quickly for McCann's liking, but like it or not, they would have to move now. The lads all emptied the Hummer, except for Johnny who stayed behind to cover them. Murphy slowly opened the back gate and slipped a toothpick between the plug to keep the dome light off. He grabbed large, long canvass bags as the other men lined up behind him to grab their own. Frank, the last one to step up, quickly unzipped his bag revealing an array of automatic weapons and explosives. He nodded his head to himself, *check,* re-zipped the bag and carefully closed the back gate.

A wide swath of residual light made a straight line from the dock into the open hangar door. McCann, Murphy, El Cid and the others all made their way inside with the stealth of large predators.

They slipped in and took position as though they would bivouac for the night, but this move was just temporary. It was meant to gain an advantageous position in the unlikely event that a firefight would break out. El Cid and his men were less than patient when it came to these futile paramilitary exercises. Once again, impatience had become a liability. *Strike two.*

From high above the warehouse floor, Rostov and his son Alexei watched every move of the interlopers below as they made their way straight into an ambush. Alexei paid particular attention to McCann, although he had never seen him before, he felt, somehow, that it was McCann who was running the show.

"There they are, Papa, just as I said they would be." Alexei chuckled at his moment of self-worship. "We have them in a *Kill Box.* They're gonna die slowly for what they did to Oleg." Alexei began to mumble expletives in Russian.

Rostov, who should have certainly been impressed by his last son's intuition, but also happy to see revenge taken on those who killed his youngest son – he was not. "Look around you, Alexei," Rostov said in all seriousness. "There's nearly a billion dollars in those crates and in that satellite and rocket." Rostov turned to Alexei, "No shooting, I need them alive! Do you understand?" Rostov was uncompromising. "They changed the code and rigged the money -- my money! We only have 48 hours from the satellite launch to pay the balance. I need those codes!" Rostov's voice went shrill at the end and sparked an odd glance from his son. He had never heard a break in his father's voice and knew he was deadly serious this time.

Alexei bit down hard on his lip, drawing just a taste of metallic blood. "It's gonna be impossible not to kill them, Papa! Let me kill them, please?" Alexei pleaded like a spoiled child, but his father was unyielding.

Meanwhile below, McCann hesitated as he moved alone down a darkened aisle. One gift he'd always had was that of intuition and the red lights were flashing on this one. He thought of the old saying, *"It's not paranoia when they really <u>are</u> after you!"* That never rang more true than at that moment. McCann spied across the warehouse to see El Cid's men cracking open crates with pry bars. They were surprisingly quiet and efficient. As each crate was opened, hand held flashlights illuminated thousands, perhaps millions of knock-off smart phones. Just the kind of cheap, disposable, untraceable, one-time-use, throwaway, *burn phones Al Qaeda* was notorious for using. *Great for the consumer, lousy for Homeland Security!*

McCann made his way through the warehouse, paralleling El Cid, just as one of his men popped open another large container. "We hit it the jack pot, amigos!" El Cid excitedly whispered. He picked one up to inspect and read: *MADE IN MEXICO.* "Look at this, <u>MADE IN MEXICO</u>!" El Cid muffled his laugh and shook his head. "That's what's wrong with this country these days, too many imports. Obama's got to get his shit together."

McCann eyed everyone's movements, seemingly at the same time through his peripheral vision. In another room on the left side of the warehouse lay Rostov's rocket mounted on a platform, ready to be loaded onto the ship. It was majestic, a piece of American ingenuity and technology that the lads had only dreamt about since their childhood. Oddly enough, the rocket was unattended and exposed, no longer covered with the large tarp or secured by sensors and motion detectors. Hammer crept alongside the shiny astro-bound shaft, keenly aware that he could not be seen doing what he was about to do. He ran his fingers across the polished surface and felt the smoothness of sections. The only ripples in the metallic skin were rivets and flat head bolts connecting the pieces. As Hammer came to the nosecone of the rocket, his hand ran over an exterior plate. He smiled, then pulled out an adjustable universal ratchet wrench. Like a blind man reading a book in Braille, Hammer searched the panel door for the right bolts, pressed the wrench down, then drove it counter-clockwise. For a multi-million dollar piece of space hardware, the bolts popped out surprisingly easy. Liam walked up behind Hammer with a small red-lit flashlight. Hammer took off the panel, then faceplate, and carefully removed the gasket to reveal a beautiful, compact gyroscope. Hammer and Liam looked up and smiled at each other.

Suddenly, the whine of the internal overhead crane began to grow louder and louder as the revolutions of it's generator brought it up to speed. Hammer and Liam knew they only had seconds before the dockworkers would be loading the rocket onto the ship. The rocket slowly lifted as a preplanned, auto-timed program had already begun to raise the rocket as it brought it on it's preordained path through the warehouse, outside over the dock and into the hold of the awaiting ship.

In the distance, McCann could see Hammer and Liam running back into the main warehouse and carefully closing the inner door so as not to be seen by any of the workers. *Good. Now what?*

Frank ran up to one of the containers and broke radio silence as he approached El Cid and slapped the cell phone from his hand. "Leave it!" Frank half-yelled. "They're all gonna burn."

El Cid took umbrage with not only the very offensive and aggressive slap, but at Frank's tone, as he was also a guest at this *Thieves Party*. "Listen Gringo, burn what you want, but we help ourselves. This shit's worth more than meth on the street."

McCann moved quickly to intervene. "Take 'em!" He said quickly. Frank stepped up to McCann, "No! I want everything about this guy erased like he never existed." McCann picked up a crate, and struggling with the weight, gave it to El Cid and his man.

Urgently, Sean ran up, breaking the impasse as well as the tension as he suddenly heard *squelch.* He pulled the headphone from his ear so the speaker would engage. *Squawk.* They could all now hear it now. "Feedback, they're close!" Sean yelled in a whisper. Everyone in the warehouse stopped what they were doing and readied their weapons.

Suddenly, floodlights burst bright and instantly illuminated the entire warehouse. El Cid's men froze in place, knowing the value of keeping still during a raid to try and fool the cops. But McCann and the lads knew better, they scrambled to take positions.

"Slowly put down your weapons, Gentlemen!" Rostov's voice boomed from a bullhorn high above the warehouse floor. "Do this now, or you will die." From every vantage point above on the dozens of catwalks that traversed the ceiling, Alexei's men appeared, drawing down their weapons and aiming them at each intruder. It would be like shooting fish in a barrel. Alexei and his men had them *dead-to-rites.*

What Rostov couldn't know is that there was a *dark horse*, a straggler who hadn't yet joined the party -- Johnny.

Johnny sat in the back of the darkened Hummer with a headset draped around his neck and not on his ears, as they should've been. He was blissfully unaware of the unfolding events. He was still young and could be forgiven a lot, but he was not manning his post, and that was something Frank considered unforgivable. The video monitor flashed behind him, but his attention was on the latest issue of *Playboy* as he read mouth agape. "Jesus wept, have ya never seen a more perfect pair!?"

With Johnny clearly asleep at the wheel, McCann quickly took inventory of his surroundings. Even after a decade in prison, his training kicked-in as he surveyed the warehouse for an escape... or at least a distraction. His eyes darted back and forth over and over the complex as Alexei, his father and the other Russians slowly crept down the tall staircases from the catwalks high above. *There!* Across the warehouse, shadowed in a corner were rows of containers that read: *MAGNESIUM, WHITE PHOSPHURUS, FUEL OIL – DANGER*, each more lethal than the other.

Alexei couldn't wait for his father. He eyed McCann, past Murphy, and ended at El Cid. As Alexei made his way to El Cid, Rostov, the elder, focused in on Frank. Now the tension was really flying. "You killed my brother, Oleg, you fucking <u>wetback</u>!" Alexei shouted in El Cid's ear, nearly deafening him. "I'm going to hurt you bad, but I will keep you alive for awhile until you beg me to kill you."

As Alexei worked hard to showboat his tough-guy routine, his men began to round up the straggling gang bangers. Liam, Hammer and the rest of the men were pushed, slammed and beaten to the middle of the warehouse, corralled to the open area. They were disarmed and each one was frisked for additional weapons, but it seemed only the Mexicans carried a variety of killing tools: switchblades, butterfly knives, even belt-buckle daggers. The Russians tossed the killing tools into a pile, careful not to set off any of the pistols. Quickly it grew into what looked like an Afghani weapons bazaar.

Rostov stepped up behind Frank. *Hum, curious, who was this man?* "Before we kill you, you will kindly give us the code for the bomb you rigged to my money," Rostov said, trying to maintain his composure. "Tell me," now shouting in frustration. Alexei bolted a round into the chamber of his Gryazev & Shipunow, Gsh-18, Russian-made pistol. What was so unique, and lethal about the Gsh-18, wasn't that it held up to 18, 9mm cartridges, but the rounds themselves were armor-piercing. You could stop a semi-truck hauling three tons of freight just by shooting the engine block with one of these bad boys.

Alexei placed the pistol to El Cid's head and dropped the safety with his thumb. "Filthy animals!" Frank blurted, breaking the tension with a verbal blow. "You destroyed my little girl." Frank sneered as he lifted an accusatory finger and began pointing it at each of the Russians. He finally stopped at Alexei.

"You, you, you, you… and especially you!" There was fire and rage in Frank's eyes and he didn't care if he lived or died at this point. He was insanely driven.

Rostov maneuvered in front of Frank, closely watching his facials features for tells. "And what of my son, Oleg?" Rostov said in a bland tone, more inquisitive than judgmental. "Who of you killed him?"

Frank locked eyes onto Rostov's, "I wish it had been me!" Frank stabbed Rostov with a piercing glare. "He deserved worse than he got. My sweet daughter never hurt anyone in her life. She was an angel… he was a mongrel."

Rostov viciously pistol-whipped Frank across the face. But Frank was too large, not just in stature, but in constitution, to even feel the pain. It barely fazed him and Rostov couldn't help but take notice of this. Blood began to flow freely from Frank's mouth, staining his lips and teeth red.

Suddenly, Liam stepped up. "Why don't yooz bastards pick on someone your own size… how 'bout it then?" Alexei, never tolerating anyone or anything to interrupt him, marched over to Liam, pointed his pistol at his neck and pulled the trigger. *Bam.* Liam grabbed his throat with two hands from the force of the bullet, slammed into one of the crates as he began to flail, realizing the end of his life was mere seconds away. Gurgling as he fell, he knocked a number of boxes to the ground. Cellular phones spilled out everywhere as blood, silica, packing beads, and carbon composite all melded together in a futuristic looking mess.

El Cid and McCann locked eyes, now was the only moment they'd get. As Liam slowly died a horrible death, El Cid pulled a small blade from his lapel and quickly stabbed one of Alexei's men in the gut, whipping him around to make him a human shield. Even if it was an exercise in futility, El Cid was going to try anything. He was instantly overpowered. Alexei smiled at the gift just presented to him. "I lied, you're gonna die now, Puta!" Alexei raised his pistol again. "Your brother cried like a little girl when he chopped off his own tiny *penito*," El Cid laughed, and yelled loudly, making sure everyone heard it. "He wasn't a man, he was a little <u>bee-otch!</u>"

Alexei became so enraged he hopped up with one leg and front-kicked El Cid in the face, whipping his head backward. This was just the distraction McCann was hoping for. While all eyes were on Alexei and El Cid, McCann slowly reached down to the black canvas bag at his feet. But before he could make his move, one of Alexei's men shot a look and forced McCann to try another tactic.

"He didn't kill Oleg," McCann interrupted before El Cid passed out from another kick. "I'm responsible!" All eyes turned to McCann with a confused look. *Who was this guy?* "It's got nothing to do with them boys, there. Let 'em go and I'll tell you."

Alexei huffed at the thought of McCann having something he could barter. He raised the pistol, and then shot El Cid, square in his chest, knocking him backwards from the force of the high-grain bullet. "You'll tell me anyway!" Alexei responded. El Cid was dead before he hit the ground.

Suddenly, the Mexicans became unglued and started to wriggle and shout at their captures. "*Chinga tu madre!*" one shouted.

"*Puta's Muerte!*" shouted another.

Alexei hardly even noticed the others as his attention was now dead set on McCann. His gun still raised, Alexei walked over and pointed the barrel at McCann's temple, "Tell me or you're next."

From a distance, a strange, high-pitched sound grew louder and louder. All of the men turned toward the source and the awaiting result. *Blam.* Oleg's Hummer suddenly smashed through the wall of the warehouse, accelerating as crates and people began to scatter for fear of getting flattened. Johnny careened the huge metal stagecoach toward the crowd. *Bam.* Down went a Russian, then two more. Johnny's *Call of Duty* score was nothing like this, as his average was getting better with each kill.

McCann instantly reached down into the black canvas bag and retrieved a *Rocket Propelled Grenade Launcher* or *RPG* as they were known. With only seconds to act he quickly flipped the sight up with his thumb, engaged his target, and fired the weapon. McCann followed the rocket with his eyes. He knew to optimize the effect, he couldn't just randomly shoot Alexei or Victor, that wouldn't do. He chose his target so as to have maximum damage. The rocket soared with a flaming trail across the warehouse toward the hanging container. Almost as soon as the missile launched, McCann cracked Alexei in the side of the head with the friction-heated tube. It would now be hand-to-hand from here on out.

Alexei, not a wilting flower, took the hit, but kept control of his gun. McCann realized he and Alexei would have to struggle for dominance. Alexei aimed the barrel at McCann's head, which he turned just in time, but not before taking a round in the shoulder. *At least he was going to make Alexei empty his chamber and not give him time to reload*, McCann quickly thought.

A melee ensued as El Cid's men scattered toward their weapons amid a hail of gunfire that was now filling the warehouse. All hell had broken loose and Johnny seemed more maniacal than the others as he laughed hysterically, driving over every animate and inanimate object he could see. He was becoming so reckless; he even came dangerously close to walloping his own men in the process.

From the floor of the warehouse, smoke rose and diffused the light making it look like a great battle on an Irish moor. Thousands of rounds of ammunition bounced off the dense hulled Hummer as blasts poured from all corners from enemy strafing. The Russians were relentless as they futilely tried to stop the vehicle, hoping at least to slow it down, but quickly realized this was no ordinary vehicle. It was Oleg's Hummer and they themselves had outfitted the brother's SUV like an *Armored Personnel Vehicle*. Nothing was gonna stop that machine. Johnny continued to pick off the Russians one by one as they were now trying to flee the warehouse to safety.

What no one had bothered to see was that McCann's plan was already working. Through the haze, a blue fireball emerged and mushroomed, but not just any old warehouse fire -- this would be more spectacular than a chemical fire!

McCann had hit the container filled with magnesium that, combined with the white phosphorus, the heat of the blast, and the explosion created a reaction damn near impossible to stop, like *Greek fire* saving Constantinople!

Murphy maneuvered through the smoke-filled fray searching for a weapon, but was suddenly clobbered over the head by an enormous Russian. "Ouch, ah fer fucks sake, what was that -- in the ear, really? You bollocks!" Murphy screamed at the monster trying to throttle him when another caught Murphy from behind. Now it was lights out!

The events had unfolded so quickly that neither Frank, nor Rostov had had a chance to move. At their age, they were more mesmerized than willing to run and hide, so the chaos multiplied around them at a frightening rate. It was a miracle that, even in the hail of gunfire, they hadn't been hit, but Johnny was another story. The Hummer broke right towards Rostov. Some of the Russians regrouped around their leader to shield him out of loyalty and routine. At the same time, the other Russians grabbed Frank and dragged him away from the Hummer; they knew Rostov would want him alive. Two others scooped up Murphy over their shoulder and made their way toward the open hangar doors. Their retreat was hasty, but Johnny was going to get his numbers right tonight.

The Humvee skidded to a stop across the concrete floor and Johnny popped open the door with a big surprise. Suddenly, the AK47 in his hand was *rat-a-tat-tatting* faster than a rapper at a *Def Jam* concert. He knew there was a chance he'd hit Murphy or Frank, but he also knew they'd want him to take the shot. He decided to compromise with bank shots and ricochets off the concrete floor. This action might split the bullets and shower the warehouse with even smaller, high velocity shrapnel, but he was willing to risk their lives. It worked... two more Russians caught some superheated lead. Johnny was a wild man.

Alexei reached into his pocket and screamed into a *walkie-talkie*, "Davai, Davai!" Almost instantly a helicopter came out of nowhere and landed near the empty dock. *Sea Launch* had already set sail and was nearly a half a mile out in the channel, so Rostov was thankful his investment would make it – even if he didn't. Alexei ordered three men to carry Frank and Murphy out to their escape and sent the others back to keep the fight going and away from him and his father. Alexei pushed a large red button and the automatic hangar doors began to shut. As yellow caution lights flashed through the thick smoke, the other Russians knew they'd have to fend off the Irish and Mexican hoards by themselves.

The warehouse, now fully engulfed in an unstoppable fire, became filled with toxic smoke. Johnny jumped from the cab and made his way to McCann who had no choice but to play possum. El Cid's men supplied covering fire, which luckily gave Johnny enough time to drag McCann to the vehicle. Just then, Hammer appeared out of nowhere and pushed them both back into the tank with one hand each.

From the passenger's seat, McCann could now get a near bird's-eye view of what was happening. The Mexicans, not retreating due to the honor of their fallen leader, took on the remaining Russians with knives, guns, tire irons, anything they could get their hands on. Then McCann peered through the haze to see one of the Rostov's men had found the bag of RPG's and was pulling one out with his name on it.

"Move yer arse, Johnny!" McCann yelled. Johnny pulled a doughnut over bullets and bodies and hauled ass toward the double doors that were now closing. *Could he make it?* "John-ny!" McCann yelled as the Russian aimed the RPG and fired.

Johnny could see the missile tracking them from the rear view mirror, severely cutting their chances of making it out of the warehouse before the hangar doors closed. "Hang on!" Johnny screamed. He pulled hard to the left just as the rocket zoomed past them. Johnny began to roar hysterically as he watched the Russian, shouting what he presumed would be a tirade of expletives. But they weren't out of danger yet. One of the Russians quickly loaded another rocket into the launcher -- *this time he wouldn't miss.*

Out of nowhere a forklift driven by one of El Cid's men crashed through a load of crates and through the Russian holding the RPG, the blade impaling him to a stack of crates. "Yee Hah!" Johnny yelled like a demented cowboy as he headed for the flaming hole the Russian had shot in through wall.

CHAPTER 56

LEXEI'S HELICOPTER WAS JUST taking off when his dead brother's Hummer came crashing through the warehouse walls, its tires and bumpers ablaze. "Da-vai -- faster you asshole!" Alexei screamed as the pilot punched the stick raising the copter quickly. Johnny turned the Hummer sharply and headed for the flying fortress. One of Alexei's men sitting near Murphy's unconscious body, flung opened the helo's cargo door, threw off a blanket from a piece of hardware, and pulled back on what looked like a floor-mounted Gatling gun. It was a *7.62mm Minigun*; a multi-barreled machine gun that shot up to 6,000 rounds per minute. He pressed the thumb trigger and a burst of flame and lead poured out in frightening streams. At first he did nothing more than shoot up the concrete and heavy equipment, but once he got used to the kick, he directed the barrels towards the Hummer and let it rip.

The Minigun began to heat up and glow red at the tip as the Russian refused to control the bursts into shorter groups. "You idiot, Oleg's Hummer is bullet-proof!" Alexei screamed over the din of the prop wash.

Below, Johnny was having the time of his life zipping around in his new American made monster. This gas-guzzler was solid, maneuverable, as well as being surprisingly roomy! Johnny had thought about a visit Disneyland at some point, but now he didn't have to, as a trip to *The Happiest Place On Earth* could never compare to this whirlwind experience.

He plowed through a row of shipping containers, serpentining around semi-trucks as they went about loading and unloading their cargo for nationwide distribution. Suddenly, he saw the headlights of three more vehicles at his six o'clock. Alexei's other men must have made it to their cars and were gaining ground. Threats from above and now behind, just the way Johnny liked it.

In the backseat, Hammer comforted Liam's body. Although he knew it futile, as Liam had been dead since Alexei shot him in the throat, Hammer's loyalty to his friend was all he'd known for his entire life. He cradled his old friend like a mother with a newborn.

With Hammer busy, McCann had to dig around the footboards with his fingers until he found something. He suddenly retrieved a *12-gauge shotgun* that was just lying under the seat. He scraped together a few shells scattered in and around the seat cushions and began to load them quickly into the side chamber. The pump-action forced the shells into place and McCann was ready. Everyone knew his job and that job would be accomplished.

"I love these wide streets in L.A.," Johnny mused, almost with child-like innocence. "It's a real *driver's town*, don't you think, boys?" McCann eyed Johnny strangely as he pumped a last shell into the scattergun.

Johnny sped around the harbor; Alexei found what he'd been looking for in the helicopter. He pulled the hard plastic tab at one end of a short tube, and it instantly extended with a deep hollow sound. He flipped a retractable sight on the top of the tube and was careful not to touch the trigger button on the top. It was a *Law's Rocket* - a one-shot disposable bazooka. It wasn't the latest in military hardware, but was perfect for the job at hand. "Try to at least hit the tires," Alexei screamed at the Russian manning the Minigun. "Box them in," Alexei continued after throwing on a headset with a wrap-around microphone. He watched as the three cars below split off and maneuvered into position as ordered.

By now Johnny had driven off the docks and was heading into

a heavily trafficked industrial park. Even through the dense doors, Johnny could hear the annoying *beep, beep, beep* of the large transport trucks reversing into the loading docks. Ahead, he could see the side of a long semi that read: *LOWEY'S FISH MARKET.* Big, solid men toiled at unloading boxes and crates filled with ice-packed fish from Alaska and around the world. Johnny headed right for them. He drove up the loading dock ramp, scattering men and fish everywhere. Just then, the mortar from the Law's Rocket exploded near the Humvee and flames engulfed the vehicle. Johnny downshifted quickly at the sound and drove swiftly through the blast unscathed. *Near miss,* he thought.

The cars in pursuit tried a three-way block just as McCann popped his head through the sunroof. The Russians never saw him until it was too late. He fired quickly, but precisely, which was some feat as Johnny was no leisure driver. McCann aimed, fired, then pumped. Aimed, fired, then pumped. The windshield of the lead car shattered. Without even having to see the results, McCann knew the load he used was not birdshot. The car lost control and shot to the left into a large concrete buckle that separated the loading bays -- *one down, two to go.*

The two other chase vehicles quickly adjusted to the fireball that enveloped the road and regrouped in pursuit. Hammer assisted by lowering the back window and pulled the trigger hard on one of the AK47s. It had the desired effect, but these two cars weren't so easily dispatched. One pulled hard to the right and drove behind the palates and cargo bins to a flanking position whilst the other left itself exposed and vulnerable and lagged as the bait car. This worked, Hammer knew he had limited options, but he took the bait and focused his sights on the front grill and tires. It took a moment, but finally, the effects of dozens of armor-piercing, Teflon-coated bullets penetrating rubber tires, gaskets, air, and radiator hoses, not to mention aluminum fuel lines, the big block was finally felled.

White smoke first trickled from the under the hood, then a small flame grew into a raging fire as the car began to careen toward an all-night grocery store. The homeless and ne're-do-wells scattered as the Russians attempted to right themselves, but instead lost control and slammed through the front window of the store. *Two down, one to go.*

McCann had spent so much time concentrating on the chase car and reloading, he never saw the others coming in from the side. The violent collision caused McCann to drop the shotgun to the floor with the barrel pointing at his face. *No discharge, sweet Jesus the jolt could've easily caused the shot to go off... that was close.*

Johnny was doing better than expected. His driving was now in the professional ranks and it looked like they just might make it, when suddenly a *thud* came down hard on the roof.

"What the fuck?" Sean shouted, keeping his eyes on the Russians who were now thrashing the Hummer on one side.

"It came from the roof," shouted Johnny. McCann, knowing it wouldn't be wise to stick his head out of the sunroof again, saw something come down hard again over his head. It was a skid from the helicopter.

"Are ya fucking kidding me?" shouted Sean. "Now I've seen everything. These bastards are trying to kill us with a helicopter!" After a severe beating and numerous bullets, the Hummer's right front tire final gave up the ghost.

McCann and the others knew this fight was seconds from being over. "Right boys, give 'em all ya got – see ya in hell!" With that, Hammer pulled back the trigger on the machine gun and unloaded the last banana clip; jockeying between the car and helicopter above. Unfortunately, Hammer's counter-part in the chase car returned fire, concentrating his blasts on the very spot where he'd last seen Hammer fire. McCann fell back against the seat and shot upward, pumped, shot, pumped again, shot, and repeated through the open moon roof until hot, empty shells began to mound up around his head. Thankfully, the barrage of bullets was too much for the Russians. Now, the last car, as well as the helicopter was critically hit. McCann had clipped the helo's hydraulics and smoke was beginning to billow from above.

No time to appreciate the successes since the helo was done for, when McCann heard Hammer's voice. "I'm fucked, lads!" were his last words as he slumped forward, nearly falling out of the back of truck, that was now perforated by bullets. Sean screamed out to Hammer as he jumped in back to pick up his fallen comrades gun and continue his mission. He half stood, placing the rifle against the rolled down window and fired the *coup-de-grâce* into the driver of the lead car. But just as Sean shot, the Russians fired at the same time like a deadly mirror image. The bullets met Sean just as the lead car swerved hard into the path of a mobile crane. A fireball rose high into the blackness.

"I gotta put us down," screamed the pilot now ascending to 100 feet above the Hummer. Green hydraulic fluid sprayed the helicopter's windshield as he implored Alexei. The pilot fought to keep control of the chopper, but the liquid was blinding him.

A large caliber pistol popped up next at the pilot's temple. "You're paid to fly, asshole, not talk!" Alexei shouted over the din of the emergency alarms and warning lights.

"Look it won't do you any good," the pilot retorted. "If I don't put us down now, we're all dead!" Then another part of the helicopter pounded as if something had just seriously malfunctioned.

Alexei could see below through the open sunroof that Hammer and Liam were dead, and the others were probably seriously wounded. Johnny fought to keep control of the Sport Utility Tank, but they were quickly approaching the end of a pier. Alexei took careful aim, steadied himself, and took one final shot. From the opened driver's window, Johnny's number was up... his head exploded. Alexei laughed manically.

Alexei had kept a ghost car far way from the warehouse just in case. He radioed in to meet the Hummer in the middle. By now, McCann, the only one left wholly intact, took one more shot out the back window. The last shotgun blast aimed true and took out the wheelman. Both vehicles were now without a living driver, or passengers, and were in for a long, cold bath.

No skids, no screeching brakes, no sounds at all came from the Hummer as it crashed through the rusted pier railing with the Russian car following in midair into the dark water.

CHAPTER 57

TRACEY VOGEL'S APARTMENT WAS cozy and lavender; like the millions of cozy lavender apartments so many women in Los Angeles occupied. It had mauve colored walls with taupe drapes to block out the intense California sun, and had the scent of incense and aromatherapy candles permeating the carpet. It was cute, and quaint and perfect for a single, independent L.A. gal.

Tracey was cuddled up on the couch with her dog, Doc, who was snorting and

snoring from his hard day of torturing the cat, eating, and sleeping. Tracey's hand was deep at the bottom of a bag of *Trader Joe's* popcorn and her eyes were wide with skepticism as she made her own computations during *Dancing With The Stars.*

A loud knock at the door startled her. Tracey jumped a good two feet being wrenched from her concentration. "What the heck?" she half-whispered at the door. Doc flew off her lap and raced for the door, barking like a rabid canine. "Quiet, Doc!" she shushed as she peered through the eyepiece. A sudden rush of adrenalin shot through her body as she saw McCann under the bright, porch light. She quickly unbolted all the latches that kept her safe and pushed Doc back with her foot. "Mick, I'm not... you didn't call." Tracey cut herself off when she saw McCann, his clothes still dripping wet, carrying a bloodied, semi-conscious man.

"I need your help," McCann said as he pushed past her, half-carrying, half-dragging Sean. McCann, obviously exhausted from the miles he'd trudged to get to Tracey's, was in dire need of a cup of tea, or worse, but that would have to wait until Sean could be mended… if he could be mended. Tracey, quickly transitioned to the consummate medical technician she was, looped herself under Sean's other shoulder and helped McCann bring him inside. Doc sat curiously by the door and sniffed the air. *Hum, testosterone, that's a rare smell in this household,* his instincts surmised.

Tracey didn't have to give Sean a full medical inspection. "We have to get him to a hospital," she said urgently. "He's been shot! He can't stay here, Mick, he'll die." Tracey and McCann brought Sean toward the couch. For a split instant she thought: *get some towels to put down, so as not to ruin the fabric, or even some plastic maybe, but that wouldn't have been very Christian to have a dying man wait so a mess wouldn't be made.*

"You're a nurse, patch him up!" McCann said in a soldier-like tone. They lowered Sean onto the couch as his body eased into the soft-worn chenille.

Wait, Sean thought and tried to rise again on his own. "Sorry to trouble you miss, I'll just be on my way." Sean said, not wanting to be a bother. He was beginning to become delirious from pain and loss of blood. He was light-headed, and nauseous. Sean fell back hard onto the couch. His breathing became labored -- it was only a matter of time.

Tracey immediately put pressure on the wound. "I've got beta dine and gauze under the bathroom sink," she barked, going into Emergency Room mode. "Bring me a bottle of whiskey. And not the crap I keep on the tray over there, the good stuff under the cabinet. *Shit, where did I put that valium?*" She knew it was crunch time. She always shined in times of crisis, but never saw herself as remarkable as she was during an emergency. McCann was impressed. He had not seen a nurse, or even a woman, for so long that he was bolstered by her exactness and confidence. "What's your name, sweetie?" Tracey said to Sean forcing a smile.

Sean looked up into her big brown eyes and sun-kissed California hair and thought for a moment she might be an angel. "Sean, miss, you've a lovely place here." A tear began to well in her eye as she could see the blood seeping from his body. She pressed harder. "Sean, I need you to know something... this is <u>really</u> gonna hurt!"

CHAPTER 58

ICHIGAN AVENUE WAS PACKED. The annual attendance for the Saint Patrick's Day Parade in downtown Chicago was easily over a million people, but this year seemed double that. Since the recession was turning into a depression under Obama, the U.S. credit rating had been downgraded, true unemployment was rampant, and the American people really needed to get out and feel good about something, anything -- and St. Paddy never let 'em down!

Paddy's Day in Chicago rivaled even that of New York's, or so the locals would have you believe. Festivities would last for days, nearly a week if it fell on a Wednesday or Thursday. Little, if any good commerce would get done during that time. Everything seemed to happen in Chicago, good and bad. This city took corruption and dirty politics out of the closet and draped it in a *Dolce & Gabbana* suit. Everyone was here; Mayor Emanuel and Rod Blagojevich could even be caught hoisting pints of Guinness with the best of them. Oprah was conspicuously absent, but since her network was up and running, she had been spending her days on the beach near her Montecito home, far from the cold winters Lake Michigan offered.

Elmhurst, Schaumburg, Hinsdale, anyone of the dozens of northwestern suburban precincts led the parade with every man and woman in their smartest blues. Police, Fire, CTA, The Elks Club, nearly all the organizations in the city were represented here, with each trying to outdo the next. One of the marching bands came around the corner high-and-tight, pounding out the *Song of Tipperary*. This had an immediate and visceral effect on the crowd. Millions of Christians, Muslims, Hindus, Greek and Polish Orthodox, you name it, all seemed to be Irish this one day each year.

The newly emigrated were wide-eyed and awe-struck at the pomp and circumstance of a parade for a holiday and a saint they'd never even heard of in their tiny part of the world. They sang and swayed, joined hands and laughed happily with the green face-painted patrons and raucous college students that had swarmed in on the *(El)evated* trains. Irish tweed caps, bleeding madras, brightly colored burkas, and good ol' blue jeans filled the sidewalks and skyscraper mezzanines. It seemed all nations and factions were united under the same banner. And, although Irish national flags flew everywhere, respectfully and legally, the *Stars and Stripes* always flew above them. It was as though millions of people had just reached Ellis Island, had been handed a pint and bid, "welcome!" by their new brothers and sisters.

Mary McAleese, a former President of Ireland, was the Grand Marshal and rode through the center of the cheering crowd in a restored 1940s era vintage Cadillac. Even she was overwhelmed at the size and scope of this uniquely American tradition that was, ironically a day meant for prayer and observance, back in Ireland. *None of that here in the States!* She smiled, truly, and waved genuinely, not the typical European *figure eight* fashion, as heads of states had been known to do. Colin Farrell, Saoirse Ronan, Chris O'Dowd, and, of course, Graham Norton were all in attendance. The only question that day: *where was Bono?*

CHAPTER 59

A N AGED THUMB AND forefinger turned the *on* button to the old television. It took a few moments for the tube to warm up, but soon a faded color picture appeared, complete with lines and antennae waves. "Ah, the parade," Yuri said quietly to himself.

There were no high-tech gadgets here, no plasmas or flat screens, no Bose systems, HDMI or blu-ray players, just an old Zenith; it didn't even have a remote. And since there was no cable, one would actually have to get up to turn to one of the two other stations before sitting back down.

An antiqued dressing mirror, long and aged, was none-the-less the centerpiece of Yuri Kalugin's large bedroom. Yuri was nothing if not persnickety about the way he dressed. He was an old school Russian who never forgot his impoverished upbringing and the misery that came with it. He thought back for a moment to when his entire wardrobe consisted of a thick, heavy wool coat and newspaper that plugged the holes in his shoes to keep out the wet snow. Besides, as the head of the largest Russian organized crime syndicate in the United States, he prided himself on being smartly dressed. He was *capo di tuti capo, boss of bosses* of the *Vore V Zacone* and had standards that he not only met, but demanded of his lieutenants, and their underlings as well.

Religious icons filled the room he once shared with his beloved

Elenochka, or Zoya as he called her, who had been dead these past 9 years. Now, only the icons replaced her memory. The Virgin Mother holding the Christ child was his favorite and sat on his nightstand.

Yuri walked back to his drawing table and sat on the tall metal stool with the faded inlaid wooden seat. It felt heavy as he pulled it under himself and fidgeted to get into just the right position. He reached for a long, thin paintbrush in a tray of brushes and dipped the bristles into a clear glass of tap water to dampen it.

The music from the parade was soothing and gave him comfort, and, although it was a singularly American celebration for the Irish, he harkened back to the Soviet May Day parades he so fondly remembered; when Khrushchev and the Kremlin ruled with an iron fist, snubbing their noses at the world.

Yuri dabbed the paintbrush onto an old, weathered palate he'd used for decades. Surrounding him, bookshelves and countertops were filled with Matryoshka dolls of every size, shape and color. Yuri had no real interest in the Matryoshka, but his beloved Nanotchka did. So when she died, he kept them in places of prominence around his old Craftsman home to remind him of better times.

Yuri touched and swirled the brush into dollops of colors: vermillion, mixing with gold flake, mixing with burnt orange. He lowered the large lighted magnifying glass that protracted from a base on the table over his creation and peered through. He was making his own icons. Like that of a true artist, Yuri, softly, lightly touched the tip of the paintbrush to the delicate face of one of the women he was painting. It was a scene depicting Hera learning of yet another of Zeus' infidelities. Her skin was porcelain, her face impossible to read. He moved the brush less than a centimeter over her gown. A single stroke would do the trick.

Suddenly, Yuri's attention was drawn back to the television. The music and pageantry of the parade was interrupted by the deep tones of a local reporter the view from a helicopter hovering above a burning warehouse captured the smoldering corporate logo: *ROSTOV COMMUNICATIONS* as firefighters battled the out-of-control blaze.

"That fire in San Pedro Harbor is still burning out of control," said the field reporter. "Firefighters say due to the large amounts of magnesium and other unknown chemicals in the warehouse, this fire won't be contained for quite some time... back to you in the newsroom."

Yuri's face went pale. He inadvertently squeezed the icon he had so carefully cultured in his hand too hard. His grip broke the delicate work of art into a hundred shattered pieces. He picked up the handset of an old black rotary phone as he wiped the blood from his hand with a rag.

CHAPTER 60

I T WAS A BEAUTIFUL day in Malibu, but Murphy and Frank
wouldn't have known it. Deep in the bowels of Rostov's mansion,
the two men dangled from a large sewage pipe that was large
and sturdy and secured to wooden beams that ran along the top of
the ceiling rafters. Both were strung-up by the wrists and ankles to
insure there would be no Hollywood-esque escape.

There was a sudden *roar.* Murphy looked at Frank curiously.
"What the fuck was that?" Murphy pushed and pulled and somehow
was able to contort and twist his body toward the back. There, just
out of reach, Rasputin sat on his hind legs, then lifted himself to his
full 10-foot stature as Murphy's eyes filled with fear. The enormous
bear growled, rocking back and forth, then came crashing down onto
fours again. Rasputin was agitated at these intruders who smelled of
sweat and desperation and his instincts had naturally forced him to
protect his territory.

"You're, you're alright there, big fella," Murphy said in slow,
deliberate, soothing tones, over and over again. "Jesus, Mary &
Holy Saint Joseph!" Murphy said turning back to Frank. "Frank,
you're never gonna believe..." Suddenly a surge of pain shot through
Murphy's body, shocking his entire system.

When his eyes cleared, he saw Alexei and his men standing by a
table filled with sadistic-looking torture devices. Alexei held a long
cattle prod in his hand. He pressed the button and a blue electrical

charge arced out of the tip. He ran his eyes over Murphy's broken and bleeding naked body. His many holes and scratches oozed blood from the night's prior events.

Yes, that will do. Alexei jabbed the hot shot into Murphy's floating rib as the 8,000-volt current sent his body into another convulsive spasm. Murphy's eyes closed down hard, his neck veins bulged and his head shook violently to the point that saliva drooled from his clenched teeth.

But Murphy was no stranger to torture. The Brits had had their fun at his expense often and cruelly and Murphy knew what his limitations were. The only sound he made was the grunting that accompanied the *grand mal* seizure. Alexei scratched his chin. He seemed intrigued by this large leprechaun.

"Look at this!" Alexei was impressed. "You've met pain before, no?" He searched the room to make sure his men were listening carefully. "Well, I tell you that by the time I'm through, dying will be a gift." Alexei's nose twitched involuntarily as if a timer had gone off in his nostrils. He stopped for a moment, turned and like a drug-sniffing dog, headed to the table where a mound of cocaine sat. He threw the cattle prod to one of his lackeys.

Bending over, Alexei buried his face in the powder and ran his nose through it. An audible sound could be heard as he *Hoover*ed as much yayo as he possibly could inhale like newly refurbished vacuum. His satiation for all things hedonistic had upped his incredible tolerance for drugs. It was a wonder his heart was still beating.

Alexei raised his head from the table to reveal his entire face covered in powder like a white-faced mime or circus clown. He took the sleeve from his expensive shirt and wiped nose, mouth and cheeks in one swipe. "Ah, fuck that was good!" he shouted skyward. Brushing himself off, he returned to the victim at hand. "Oh, I almost forgot - - *Happy St. Patrick's Day!*" Alexei pressed the button once again and jammed it into Murphy's side, seizing his kidneys.

It was just then Victor Rostov descended the basement stairs and walked up behind Alexei. "Alexei, I need the code, God damn it!" Rostov shouted at his son. "It is the only reason they are here. How many times must I tell you?" As soon as he heard Rostov's voice, Frank raised his bloodied head. Acknowledging this, Rostov moved slightly towards Frank. Frank glowered at Rostov, rolled his tongue, and puckered his cheeks. Frank dug deep into his throat to hack up a thick, green lugee. He spit a mouthful of bloody sputum all over Rostov's face. For a moment Rostov was blinded. He could taste the sick in his mouth and instantly searched the room for a towel. *At least I got one good shot in*, Frank thought.

CHAPTER 61

EDERAL AGENTS SWARMED THE dockside where Rostov's warehouse still smoldered. Some fire crews were wrapping their equipment, while others hosed the charred remnants over the side into the bay. The scene looked more like an *Improvised Explosive Device* (IED) had exploded in some far off war zone rather than sleepy old San Pedro. Either way, men and machine had been taxed a heavy toll.

Mancuso and his team of federal agents paced the pier, looking hard for even the slightest clue; inspecting the damage, interviewing any potential witnesses, doing their job. Mancuso wasn't subtle about traipsing over the toes of a multi-jurisdictional crime scene.

Forensic team members Jansen and Washington were hard at work as Fitzpatrick and Tetley pulled up. Tetley was in disbelief as Fitzpatrick just snorted out an, *I told ya so*. He could barely keep a straight face. "I love my fucking job!" Fitzpatrick snickered as he took a high-level view of the damage. Mancuso, on the other side of the dock, stood near a police line where reporters had gathered to scoop the story. The special agent turned quickly to check his appearance in the reflection of a government issued black SUV, oblivious to the fact that nearly everyone saw his ridiculous display of vanity. He spent another moment primping and preening, then about-faced and stepped forward to give an impromptu press conference.

With Mancuso now busy, Fitzpatrick took full advantage of this rare opportunity to get a much needed debrief. He walked pier side just as a rescue diver surfaced and signaled to the crane operator. The cables on the crane stretched taunt and whinnied as they pulled something heavy from the murky depths. First the muddy mess went high above the landing where they had all gathered, moved laterally, and then slowly set down on the concrete before them. It was Oleg's Hummer.

A young, sexy, female reporter, complete with an entire can of Fox News-issued *Aqua Net* in her hair and the hint of tramp stamp under her sheer blouse, stepped up to Mancuso. "Special Agent Mancuso, tell us why the FBI is involved here, was this massacre drug related?"

Mancuso smirked, doing his best, serious DeNiro-like imitation and said, "It's part of an on-going investigation and I'm not at liberty to disclose any information at this time."

The young reporter, obviously frustrated with his lack of a real response, turned on the charm, "Oh please, *special agent!*" She took a deep breath as her breast heaved upwards, catching Mancuso's eye in a not-so-subtle fashion.

Fitzpatrick was impatient, always had been. He wasn't going to wait around for a jurisdictional pissing contest. He reached out and opened the door to the Hummer. Green water and kelp came pouring out like the contents of a rancid bottle of milk. Johnny's pale hand dropped as he was still strapped into the driver's seat, and the *Fianna na hEireann* golden sunburst symbol against a blue background appeared. The IRA tattoo on his forearm was recognizable almost immediately.

"Those are IRA markings!" Tetley shouted. "What does it take for you to see that McCann's behind all this?"

Fitzpatrick squatted down and put his bifocals on for a closer look. He took Johnny's dead hand, rotated it, to see if there was more ink. "Son-of-a-bitch, I told him to stay out of it!"

Tetley huffed, "I want these men to face terrorism charges back in Belfast!"

Fitzpatrick rose and sneered at Tetley as though he were dense.

"Well people in *hell* want ice water! -- You fucking idiot!" He barked, "This is not about *terrorism*, it's about <u>revenge</u>!"

Suddenly, Mancuso caught the dulcet tones of his favorite ass pain from across the pier. He put his hand up and abruptly finished the interview, turned and made a beeline straight for the odd couple. "Agent Maxwell, arrest Detective Fitzpatrick for *illegal trespass at a crime scene* as well as *Obstruction of Justice*, Mancuso screamed at Clark Maxwell, a good looking, diligent young agent. Maxwell turned and locked stepped with Mancuso as he advanced, barreling his way through an array of cops and techies. Fitzpatrick, foreshadowing the agent's move, had no time for this kind of bureaucratic bullshit.

"Back off Mancuso, you're starting to really piss me off!" he said with all seriousness.

"Forget it, Maxwell, I'll arrest him myself!" Mancuso shouted as he reached for the detective.

"You're just dying to show the press over there what an asshole you really are, aren't you?" Fitzpatrick pointed over Mancuso's shoulder to the waiting reporters that had now trained all their cameras on the imminent tussle. Mancuso slowed to a hesitation. *Could he have an Achilles' heel after all,* the detective thought. Mancuso eyed the female reporter who was overly anxious to see his next move.

Just then, paramedics wheeled dozens of stretchers out of the warehouse past the men, each one with a black body bag atop it. Fitzpatrick stopped the lead paramedic. "Where ya go'n in such a hurry, Flash, their already meat sacks," Fitzpatrick said as delicately as only he could. He stepped up and unzipped one of the bags and spread it open in one motion. He shook his head; it was the body of El Cid.

Just then, Jansen and Washington approached from his flank. "Jesus, Fitz, we've got over 40 bodies in there."

Washington said in disbelief. "Man, what a blood bath! This has got to be some kind of gangland massacre shit."

Mancuso stepped in and pointed an accusatory finger at Jansen and Washington, "I don't give a shit what <u>you two</u> think, you don't report to this man! He's off the case." Mancuso knew he'd have to pull the old *whose cock is bigger* card to get any respect now. "Understand?" he shouted in a 360-degree pattern to everyone within earshot. "Nobody talks to this man, and I mean <u>NOBODY</u>!"

Although previously disinterested, Fitzpatrick realized that Mancuso was now fucking with his critical information stream, and he wouldn't have any of that. "Take that extremely large chip off shoulder for once and let's work together on this. This is <u>no</u> gang war!" Tempting, but Mancuso saw right through Fitzpatrick's ploy.

He pulled out his handcuffs from his waist belt under his jacket and feebly attempted to cuff the detective who was easily twice his size. "Nice try! Put your hands behind your head." Fitzpatrick played along with the joke a moment just for laughs, then pulled away just as Mancuso lunged for his wrist. Fitzpatrick stepped back, sashayed to the right, then helped the special agent forward off the pier with his own momentum.

Everyone on the dock could hear the splash as he fell hard into the drink. Suddenly, the reporters broke the yellow crime scene tape and raced to the water's edge. They began snapping photos and zooming in with every video and digital camera in attendance. This would not bode well for Mancuso's career.

CHAPTER 62

TRACEY RACED HER ECO-FRIENDLY Prius down PCH toward Marina del Rey at a higher rate of speed than she'd ever driven. She didn't need to shoot McCann a look that told him she was scared. He knew he'd have to ease her fears. "I appreciate you taking care of Seany back there."

Now she shot him the look. "You owe me an explanation," she said curtly. "Do you think I'm stupid? I read the papers. I know what's going on."

McCann realized he could no longer keep his secrets if he wanted Tracey to trust him. "Tracy, what I'm doing now, I'm doing for a friend," he said sternly, almost fatherly, "don't ask me to explain it. The less you know, the better."

Tracy, knowing she wouldn't get satisfaction on this one, began to sniff as her eyes welled up trying to control her emotions. "I thought you wanted to change," she said with a hint of desperation, "but you don't care about yourself or anyone else for that matter." Harsh words, and McCann got the message loud and clear.

"That's not true," he said defending his decision.

"Then stop this insanity!" she said hitting her hand on the steering wheel in frustration. "Make a fresh start -- I could help you, if you'd just let me."

CHAPTER 63

URPHY'S LAW WAS THE largest pub in Santa Monica and that was saying something in a location where the biggest concentration of Irish and English outside of Europe lived. Inside the bar several volunteer workers were making final preparations for the evening's festivities. Colorful banners with Celtic designs hung, *leprechaun* and *shamrock* cutouts pasted to the walls, and green balloons and streamers floated everywhere.

Fitzpatrick and Tetley entered through the front, hoping to blend in with the others and not be too noticeable, at least not yet. Traditional Irish music blended with *U2* and *The Pogues* was blaring as it kept everyone in the *spirit d'jour*. LCD screens lined the restaurant and bar areas all simultaneously playing *The Quiet Man* in high definition. Tetley was disgusted by the overdone displays of Irishness. He rolled his eyes as he bored of this gauche, typically American, tradition. Fitzpatrick saw this then smile, taking great comfort in his English counterpart's discomfort. He wanted to grab a green plastic bowler or antennae that read: *Kiss Me I'm Irish*, but resisted.

Suddenly, he reached out and stopped Tetley dead in his tracks with his tree trunk of a forearm. "Oh wait, this is my favorite part," Fitzpatrick said looking up a big screen.

Tetley took the opportunity to get a dig in. "Yes, that's right, everyone loves John Wayne in America, don't they?"

Completely unfazed, Fitzpatrick nearly mouthed the dialogue, word-for-word. "This is great, when Ward Bond loses the fish when the guys are fighting -- Priceless!"

"Father, shouldn't we put a stop to it now?"

"Ah, we should, lad, yes, we should, it's our duty!"

From the corner Kelly appeared from under the bar. He had his usual surly face on as he dried glasses with a bar towel. All around him volunteers scurried about.

"Happy Saint Patrick's Day, fellas!" Kelly said, his mood immediately changing. "First one's on the house for the boys in blue. What'll it be?"

Fitzpatrick would've killed to start what he had affectionately referred to as *his Christmas Day*, early, yet he was there for more pressing business at hand. "Where's Murphy?"

Kelly shook his head and immediately soured his puss. "I wish to Jaysus I knew that me self! I'm sick and feck'n tired of carrying the can around here. The busiest day of the feck'n year and that fucker's disappeared! Sure I'll never handle all this mess me-self!"

Unaware of their presence, two of Alexei's men suddenly appeared behind Fitzpatrick and Tetley wheeling a number of beer kegs in on a large dolly. They had nearly passed the bar unnoticed, when the ill-tempered Kelly, with his eagle eyes and sharp tongue, immediately focused in on their poor judgment. "Ah, for fuck's sake, lads!" Kelly barked in frustration. "All deliveries go through the back! Yooz are supposed to know this! Get it right, can't ya see I'm up to me arse here?"

The Russians, not understanding a word of Kelly's bemoaning, simply nodded and continued toward the walk-in refrigerator down the back hallway. "Ah, ya feck'n ejits!"

Paying less attention to the situation than Tetley, Fitzpatrick interjected. "Listen Kelly, this is urgent!" Fitzpatrick bulled. "I need to talk to Murph as soon as he arrives, got it?"

Kelly saw the shift in demeanor in the detective's eyes and course-corrected to the alpha male. "Sure, Detective, sure!" he said acquiescing. "Well, you'll see him yerself tonight. You're still coming, aren't you?" Kelly started listing on his fingers. "We've got dancers from Dublin and brilliant bagpipers, some singers, you know, crooner-types -- Ah, sure it'll be a great craic!"

Frustrated, yet not surprised, Fitzpatrick turned to walk away as Tetley followed dutifully. He was getting used to what he thought of as Fitzpatrick's rude American ways, but stood ready to turn on a dime if need be, if for no other reason than just to keep up.

As the two exited, a victorious *Gaelic football* team entered shoulder-to-shoulder, pushing past them as though they were about to tackle. A large, toothless footballer stepped up to the bar and pounded on the wooden cap. "Give us <u>eighteen</u> pints of Guinness -- and make it quick!"

Kelly sneered, but was careful not to actually sneer too negatively at these monsters. "Alright ya bastards! I'm hurry'n as fast as me bollocks can go!"

Just then an old *Clancy Brothers* tune, *Beer* burst from the speakers and the entire bar began to sing. It was perfect cover for the Russians as they placed the beer kegs carefully into the back of the fridge where no one would be the wiser until it was too late.

A large Russian, with hands covered in *Gulag* ink, reached over the tops of the kegs to a darkened piece of plastic on one of the taps. Delicately, his finger extended and pressed a small keypad. Red LED lights burst bright. The timer was set. The bomb had been activated. The countdown began.

CHAPTER 64

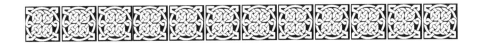

MARINA DEL REY WAS usually quiet this time of year as it was just before Spring Break and the Easter holiday. Normally, the only sounds you could hear where the tinkling of wind chimes, the small hammers on the boat bells, or the wail of a lonely fog horn at the mouth of the channel. Today, though, was different. A local St. Patrick's Day parade was in mid-stride, with plans to end at the fire station near the peninsula. Crowds and traffic choked off Via Marina, Fiji and Palawan Ways, clear to Washington and up and down Admiralty. The only way to get there quickly was to head south, past the main gates on Lincoln Boulevard, then hang a hard right on Tahiti Way. Tracey did just that. She managed to skirt the crowd and drive through marina security, down the dock and nearly onto *The Life of Riley's* slip.

McCann hopped out as quickly as a wounded man could hop out of a Prius, then suddenly stopped, made an about-face and headed for the passenger side window. He placed his hands on the door as Tracey rolled down the window.

McCann reached into his pocket and pulled out something delicate. It was a small bunch of shamrocks on an Easter lily, then dug again, deeper this time, and retrieved a small *Claddagh* ring and handed it to Tracy. "Oh Mick, it's beautiful!" she said in a high pitch.

McCann ran his finger over the ring as he described it. "Don't get any ideas -- it's an *Irish Friendship Ring*: two hands, holding a heart, topped by a crown. The hands mean friendship, the crown means loyalty, and the heart means love." He leaned in and kissed Tracey on the lips. "I'll see you tonight," he whispered, then gave her one last smile, turned and ran down the gangway toward the boat. He had an extra kick in his stride and was beginning to feel something he had not felt in years. A tingling sensation coursed through his body. Endorphins shot through his brain like a pinball just before the tilt. It was exactly these feelings that could cloud a man's judgment, and blur his edge, or maybe even change his life. It was precisely because of these new feelings that he never spotted Alexei's men in the distance watching his ever move through their binoculars.

CHAPTER 65

MCCANN, GAZED UP AT the pristine sky, took a deep breath of fresh ocean air, and admired all the wonderful luxuries the residents of marina had. Suddenly, like every Irishman, realized things were a little too perfect. His senses told him he should become acutely aware – now. He course-corrected as he approached *The Life of Riley*, slowed his pace down the gangway, and cautiously took in all movement and shadows before reaching up to the safety cable to pull himself on board. It was a harder way to gain access to the boat, basically jumping vertically then swinging your body upward like a pole-vaulter, but it gave McCann a stealthy advantage -- just in case.

He moved carefully down the side of the boat, his hand gliding above the portholes to keep his balance and allow him to peak inside before he entered. All clear, so far.

He swung around to the hold door and popped down into the boat with a single leap. He landed on the tips of his toes and threw his hands down, fingers spread, like an Olympic gymnast executing a perfect landing. He quickly surveilled the cabin one last time then crawled under the breakfast nook table. He began to fiddle with the floorboards, then reached up over his head and retrieved a kitchen knife from a place setting above. He jammed the tip into a small fracture in the wood and pried them up. Murphy had built a secret locker into the boat long before and had told McCann about it in case he needed to squirrel anything away.

McCann removed three long planks to reveal a virtual treasure trove of weapons and electronic gear. He grabbed what he could, then suddenly saw a larger, deeper locker that went into the hull of the boat, locked with an industry-strength pad lock. *What could possibly be in there*, McCann thought, then quickly changed gears as he had never been able to figure out Murphy anyway, *why start now*?

McCann's military ring tone burst out of his cell phone, cutting his concentration. He looked at the screen - *Caller Unknown* it read. He pressed the button, but purposely waited to hear the other party speak first.

For a moment there was only silence, he could only hear breathing, then laughter. "I have your friends," a scratchy voice laughed. It was Alexei. "If you want to see them alive again, walk outside and get in the car at the end of the pier." The line went dead. It was a zero-sum move; McCann knew he had no other choice. His greatest vulnerability was now exposing himself and allowing Alexei's men to take him. Conversely, it was his only move to save Murphy and Frank. He knew this to be the cold hard fact, yet he didn't come to the states to start a new life, so he wasn't about to get sentimental now. His old life had nearly haunted him to his death. At least now he could do something and try to save a friend – he was okay with that, he'd already made his peace.

McCann pushed himself off the floor and peered out the cabin window. There they were, Alexei's men waiting at the edge of the gangway for him. He nodded to himself, accepting his fate… then, an idea. He shot down under the table one last time, reached into the locker and grabbed a handful of C4 plastic explosive; a small micro receiver and a key chain with a black garage door opener-type of remote. With his thumbnail, he flipped the tiny arming device to the *on* position and watched for the tiny red LED light to start blinking. It worked. He pressed the chip deep into the C4 and molded it with his hand like a child with *Play-doh*, then quickly concealed it in a pack of cigarettes.

McCann carefully replaced the wooden floorboards, tapping it with his hand for insurance, rose, then hopped off the boat and down the gangway and into the hands of his enemy.

CHAPTER 66

B Y NOW MURPHY AND Frank were weak from torture and blood loss. With his bodyguards behind him in the shadows, Rostov sat alone closely watching every move Frank made. Murphy, ever the clever one, just had to make light of their bad situation, it was just his way. "Your bear over there reminds me of me Auntie Kitty," Murphy started as he coughed out some newly clotted blood from his throat, "Always growl'n and roar'n with a breath that could smite the Philistines!"

Rostov ignored the droll anecdotes as he continued to scrutinize Frank with steely eyes. "You are a stubborn old man," Rostov spoke at Frank. "I run a legitimate business and that money finances it. Disarm the bomb and I <u>swear</u> I will let you live!"

Frank raised is head, his eyes crazed from fatigue, excruciating pain and inexhaustible hatred. He knew Rostov was lying as he, himself, had said those very words to others in his exact position before. "None of that matters now," Frank spoke slowly and deliberately. "My little girl was all I had left in the world."

Rostov's stance softened just for a moment. "We are both powerful men and we both have lost a child dear to us. Let us grieve our loss and go on with our lives." Sweat-diluted streams of blood poured around Frank's ears as he stared like a demon into Rostov's eyes. "Not until your other son is dead!"

That was it, Rostov's compassion ended then and there just as

Alexei approached. "Papa, forget about him. Yuri and the others have arrived," Alexei said as excited as a schoolboy. "The countdown for the launch is about to start. Come on, Papa, we'll get to them later!"

Rostov nodded to his son, then rose slowly from his chair. Alexei, nearly running, bounded up the basement stairs as his father slowly followed, but not before giving Frank one last glare.

Frank had put up a valiant front, but was now becoming despon0dent at the thought of his beloved young Ciara. His head bowed as soon as Rostov left, but he had no more tears to cry. He just hung his head and whimpered like a puppy.

Murphy could not take the sight of seeing this powerful man broken, "Don't you worry now, Frank, Saint Paddy has a little surprise for those fuckers!" Murphy whispered across to Frank as the room went dark

CHAPTER 67

A LINE OF BLACK STRETCH limousines sat idling along Rostov's circular drive like the devil's wagon train. The drivers huddled around the trunk of the last limo smoking their filter less cigarettes and arguing like Arabs in a bazaar, blissfully unaware that Alexei's men were dragging McCann inside the mansion.

At the same time, Fitzpatrick was racing around the Palisades, ascending the old, buckled salt-eaten streets, in an attempt to get to Rostov's mansion quicker. *MapQuest* would've been a big help, but Fitzpatrick, like most men, would be too stubborn to even consider it. Tetley saw movement on the front lawn just as they rounded the turn. He spied through the magnified eyepiece of a pair of high tech binoculars. Through the glasses he saw McCann. He wanted to smile at the thought of McCann finally meeting a slow and gruesome death, but somehow, probably for the first time ever, Tetley felt sympathy for him.

Tetley followed McCann with his eyes, knowing full well it was futile to put up a fight with these Russians, as he was manhandled into Rostov's mansion. "Thuggery!" Tetley said to himself, too low for his colleague to hear.

Fitzpatrick inched the prowler closer, and could now see what Tetley had witnessed. He reacted instantly by gunning the Crown Vic's engine and smashing the wheels into and up the curb, practically doughnutting as he raced toward the large double door entry. Now, he would stop for nothing or no one.

CHAPTER 68

ROSTOV HAD CALMED HIMSELF since his last encounter with Frank and was milling about his drawing room that was wall-to-wall with his investors. There was excited anticipation as they drank and relaxed, awaiting the moment of truth that would define all their hopes and dreams, no matter how devious their journey had been to get there.

In the corner of the room, observing the others like a lion on the high ground of the *Serengeti Plain*, Yuri whirled his snifter of brandy just beneath his nose. He had large hands for a man his size, so the oversized crystal glass was light and easily manipulated. He lifted the goblet, checked the color, yes it was dark enough. The aroma was sweet; he could smell the cask that had aged this fine vintage. Much like a wine expert, Yuri took his time and deliberated his decision, yet after the facts, he couldn't disagree. *Ah, yes, the good stuff* is what Americans would say. Yuri was not given to frivolous compliments, so before giving Rostov any advanced pleasantry, he peered over his glass.

"Victor, Vassili, your taste in brandy is exquisite!" Yuri said to Rostov as he nodded to his plebian. "But how can you afford such luxuries at this point?" Rostov's smile slowly drooped as he attempted to ascertain what Yuri was referring to. *Was it Alexei? Was it Oleg? Was it the disaster at the wedding? Was it the strip club?* He bit the inside of his lip and gave Yuri a flaccid look. "I saw your warehouse on the news this morning," Yuri said slowly and sternly, his eyes lowering as they pierced through Rostov.

Suddenly, all heads snapped at the sound of the other booming voices yelling, "come on everyone, it's about to start!" The investors rushed to grab every couch cushion, love seat and desk chair as they gathered in front of a large, high-definition flat screen. They sat glued to the satellite video link, as the recap of the rocket's assembly was just finishing.

The rocket had already been loaded onto the platform and set to a vertical position. The launch pad lay in a secret location in the middle of the South Pacific just at the equator. Hundreds of digital cameras were placed at nearly every conceivable angle, per the client's request, in order to justify the program to the business managers, CPAs, and future clients. *Camera 38* tracked down the length of the long spacecraft and the words: *ROSTOV COMMUNICATIONS* filled the screen. The Russians began to whoop and cheer as though they were at a Premiere-ship football match.

Alexei grabbed the remote and cranked the volume as the Dolby Digital pulsed out of the internal speakers. "WE NOW BEGIN THE FINAL 60 SECOND COUNTDOWN…" a stoic announcer stated.

It was then Rostov caught a glimpse through the crack in the partially opened drawing room door of McCann being led down the front hallway. McCann looked around quickly, his eyes twitchy, searching the hostile environment for some sort of *Plan B*. He got it. As the men dragging him cleared the study, heading toward the basement, McCann feigned a trip on the stairs. As he did so, he slapped a tiny, gooey amount of C4 onto the shoulder of one of his captures. The Russian, not appreciating the unwelcomed physical contact, turned to tune-him-up for the trouble, yet never noticed the explosives now stuck to his jacket just under his collar. McCann palmed the remote between his inside fingers. *It just might work.*

After McCann passed the drawing room, Rostov excused himself to Yuri and the investors, bowed his head in respect while avoiding any contact with the others, and headed to greet his new captive.

Showing signs of frustration, he now seemed to have another problem on his plate.

"50 SECONDS AND COUNTING TO LIFTOFF…" continued the announcer as Rostov hurried toward the basement.

"Victor, where are you going, our future is about to be written," Yuri shouted as Rostov rushed out of the room.

CHAPTER 69

SPECIAL AGENT MANCUSO SNAPPED his fingers as he peered through a set of his own customized binoculars. Trained on the bay windows, he mentally salivated at the gathering of all these prominent mob figureheads. There they were, all the Russian gangsters he'd been chasing most of his professional career. It was every Fed's wet dream to bag a herd of elephant like this.

Behind Mancuso, dozens of unmarked vehicles sat with dozens of agents looking through dozens of binoculars. "They're all in there," Mancuso mumbled. "Every damn one of them, even the Godfather, Yuri Kalugin himself! It's go'n down today, gentlemen. We didn't get all dressed up in our finest Kevlar for nothing."

Just then, young Maxwell stepped forward. "Luckily they didn't find all the bugs, sir... we still have *eyes and ears!*" Mancuso never dropped his specs for an instant. "Thank God Obama signed off on that *Patriot Act* extension or we'd be screwed!" He lowered the glasses and thought, *Yeah, but nothing yet for any convictions to stick -- I wish they'd just --* Suddenly, Mancuso caught a glimpse of someone driving up the lawn like a bull barging into a China shop.

Damn it, it was Fitzpatrick! Mancuso watched as he tore across the lawn, skidded to a stop, digging a pathway of tire tracks half an acre long. Fitzpatrick burst out of the driver side and began throwing around bodyguards like Mr. T in a midget-throwing contest.

"What the fuck?!" Mancuso screamed in a high-pitch voice like a cat being strangled. "What the fuck did I ever do to deserve this shit?" he fumed. "Fitzpatrick!"

CHAPTER 70

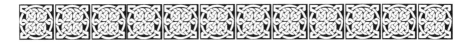

EFORE ROSTOV COULD MAKE it down the basement stairs, Alexei had left the drawing room to meet McCann and his men at the doorway. "In a minute you're gonna join your mates," Alexei purred softly, trying to intimidate him. "These concrete walls are three-feet thick, no one will hear you scream!"

McCann was neither impressed, nor intimidated. He had a job to do and now that job included bargaining for his friend's lives. "Listen you twisted little psychopath, they had nothing to do with Oleg's death, I did it!" McCann said, mustering up his best tough-guy voice. "Release them now and when I know they're safe, I'll let you have the key codes for your money. Keep being a fucking cunt and I'll make sure this whole place goes up with everything and everybody inside, поймите?" McCann finished off like a native Muscovite.

Alexei was shocked, not only by McCann's insolence and disrespect, but by his perfect Russian. McCann had suddenly put him off his game! "You are in no position to dictate terms," Alexei stammered awkwardly as if he were trying to regain his balance. "If I don't have that money soon, you'll join all those little snot-nosed children at the pub. Alexei stepped closer and slapped McCann's face like a grandmother making a point. You're not the only one who knows how to play with things that go *boom*!" Check and mate, Alexei was back. He laughed maniacally as he studied McCann's face that had turned from serious to concerned. McCann knew by now Alexei's threats were not hollow. He never again wanted someone else, especially a child, be forced to pay for his sins, so the stakes were now the highest they would ever be. *Think, McCann, think*, he screamed in his head.

Just then Rostov huffed, "Get him downstairs, davai!"

CHAPTER 71

EXCITED HEADS LEANED IN toward the TV screen like fraternity brothers watching college football. "FIVE, FOUR, THREE, TWO, ONE, WE HAVE LIFTOFF OF THE ROSTOV COMMUNICATIONS SATELLITE ROCKET!" A spray of flame reminiscent of a July Fourth sparkler spewed from beneath the 500 ton, 200 foot tall Atlas rocket as it rose skyward. For a circumference of miles, the calm seas became a torrent from the sheer pressure and heat of the solid rocket boosters.

The investors leapt to their feet, threw their hands in the air and began to cheer as though they were young men again. They turned toward Yuri, their mentor and leader, and nodded in respect over and over again. Yuri, in turn, raised his snifter, lowered his head in acknowledgement as he, too, had broken a smile.

"And what of Victor," one investor shouted.

"Da! Three cheers for Victor Rostov! Hip, hip, hooray! Hip, hip hooray! Hip, hip, hooray!" Rostov could hear the cheers of success as he came up from the basement with Alexei in tow. *This would be his legacy*, he thought.

The cheering continued as all eyes turned back toward the flat screen for updates on the progress.

"AS GROUND CONTROL CONINTUES TO MONITOR THE ROCKET'S PROGRESS, TELEMETRY ARC IS CONFIRMED AT

42,000 FEET. ALL SYSTEMS ARE READING FIVE-BY-FIVE," the announcer said happily.

At that precise point, all eyes were turned away from the front entry, and without hesitation, Fitzpatrick barged into the mansion as Tetley hurried just to stay close. In his wake, the detective had left four guards writhing and moaning in pain on the floor. Rostov had barely opened the drawing room doors when Fitzpatrick was upon him.

At that very instant, Rostov's entire security force descend upon on him. "Back off Boris, or you'll all be under arrest!" Fitzpatrick shouted above the din of investors. Rostov grabbed at Fitzpatrick's lapel, when suddenly a strange sound emitted from the speakers.

The screech of sirens began blaring from the television, "WARNING, WARNING, MALFUNCTION, WARNING, AUTOMATIC ABORT PROTOCOL INITIATED, WARNING!"

The robotic audio report poured from the speakers like a scene from a Science fiction movie. The on-board cameras switched to the area showing the rocket list from its pre-plotted vertical trajectory, first pitching 10 degrees, then yawing 20, 30... until the camera eye caught the blue of the ocean below.

The sophisticated rocket had suddenly gone critical as the safety protocols began to automatically kick in.

"AUTORIZATION TO INITIATE ABORT PROTOCOL AS WE HAVE CRITICAL MALFUNCTION OF THE ROSTOV ROCKET – SYSTEMIC GPS AND GYROSCOPIC FAILURE ALERT! ABORT CODE: ZULU, SIERRA, TANGO, EPSILON, FOX-ALPHA -AT COUNT THREE, TWO, ONE... ABORT SEQUENCE ENGAGED!"

The announcer's voice was cool and calm and felt like a dagger being driven deep into Rostov's heart. Suddenly, the old Russian rushed toward the television. "Nooo!" Rostov screamed as all in the room watched in horror. Rostov's one chance for salvation was quickly becoming a spectacular fireball, exploding mid-air, and dispersing across the clear blue, cloudless sky.

Millions of fiery metal shards rained down, showering the Pacific below with pre-orbital debris. The largest piece of the fuselage fell from the heavens in what seemed like slow motion, as a secondary explosion forced the majestic spacecraft to the bottom of ocean, and to it's final resting place in a watery grave.

Yuri, along the others sat mouth agape, speechless at the sight of this disastrous event. After what seemed like hours, yet were mere moments, the investors one-by-one slowly regained their composure. The sickening realization of what had just happened was now hitting home. Anger soon eclipsed reason as Yuri began to shake his head in disbelief. He mumbled to himself in Russian, as his guttural moans permeated the air while hate-filled eyes turned toward Rostov.

"You swore an oath, Victor, Vassili," One investor shouted above the crowd.

"You told us <u>nothing</u> could go wrong!" another indicted.

"You've squandered all our money. You must pay for this!" The investors began stepping forward, encircling Rostov.

"You must pay with your life, Comrade!"

Yuri, as sick inside as anyone could be, immediately nodded to what needed to be done. It was a very simple *go-ahead* signal to the investors as the men all clawed at Rostov like caged animals at feeding time.

Suddenly, gunfire erupted from the back of the room, as bullets ripped into the crowd. The first three advancing men dropped to the ground, various parts of them flying throughout the room as blood splatter painted the walls. This slowed the next wave of men about to charge Rostov, butt even Yuri wouldn't be able to escape the shower of hot lead that was to follow. The crystal goblet in his hand shattered as he took a single step backwards. Yuri released his grip and dropped the fractured stem, then with his right hand clawed at his jacket as if to remove a smudge. Slowly, blood began to seep from the spot where he was brushing, then more blood, and more. Yuri fell straight down to his knees, raised his head as he gasped his last breath, then flopped to the rug.

It became an orgy of war as each man drew their weapon: investor, bodyguard, cop, it didn't matter, it was now every man for himself.

Any experienced soldier or trained law enforcement officer will tell you, fighting in close quarters is <u>the</u> <u>last</u> thing you ever what to happen. The drawing room now lent itself to a particularly loud and gruesome firefight. There would be no winners.

CHAPTER 72

THOUGH IN THE BASEMENT, the sound was unmistakable, McCann was the first to hear the shots, as he was closer to the top of the stairs. By the time Alexei's henchmen had unwittingly released their prisoner in order to run back up and investigate, McCann had already gotten the drop on them.

Even with guns drawn, these men, inexperienced in the reality of warfare, made the fatal mistake of turning their backs on an old soldier. Before the guards got to the landing at the top of the stairs, the basement door whipped open and Tetley appeared. The Russians quickly drew a bead on the surprised inspector. Just then bullets began to rip past Tetley's temple, one grazing his ear while he stood frozen in fear. Chunks of masonry from the wall next to his cheek explode, ricocheting bullet fragments in all directions.

With no concern for his arch-enemy's predicament, McCann flipped the tiny remote he had palmed, depressed the button and detonated the C4 at the base of the guard's neck. His proximity to his counterpart caused one man to lose his head, while the cast-off and secondary shock wave blew bone, tissue and gray matter through the second man like thousands of deadly projectiles. Both dropped where they'd stood.

Tetley stood motionless, his eyes closed from his near-death experience, seemed paralyzed. He'd seen bullets and bombs before, but this was worse than what Northern Ireland had offered.

McCann had no time for formalities as he shouted up to slap Tetley from his catatonia. "Give us a hand!" he screamed at Tetley, "Give us a hand!" McCann rushed to where Murphy and Frank hung, swaying above the torture table. Tetley gingerly made his way over, through and around the now decapitated and limbless bodies blocking the stairs like a ballerina. *This is bloody awful*, he thought. Tetley now had a new concern, not only had his life just been saved; but saved by a man who was his sworn enemy and his embodiment of evil... *shit*!

From the shadows behind the chaos, Rasputin's ferocious cries sounded like the bellows of death as every one of his sensitive nerves had been shattered. He began to issue an instinctual warning to the new arrivals of their territorial violations and the confusion he felt.

As Tetley hurried blindly into the basement to assist McCann, he nearly jumped out of his own skin and at the sound. His blood pressure shot due north as he cried, "What in God's name?" Rasputin savagely yanked and tore at the worn steel chain that held him captive as Tetley entered his field of vision. All eyes momentarily took heed in case he had freed himself, if that were to happen, the lads would have more trouble than they ever could've imagined. The beast was nearly out of his senses and would rather mutilate himself now, than stay one more instant in chains.

"Come on, Tetley!" McCann shouted, tearing the inspector from his perpetual state of shock. "We've got to get them out of here." Tetley quickly jerked back to reality and ran to McCann. They jumped up onto the steel table, grabbed Murphy to keep him from swinging, then manipulated the bounds that kept him shackled. They only had seconds to do the same for Frank.

CHAPTER 73

THE GUNFIRE THAT HAD erupted in the Rostov mansion resonated throughout the entire neighborhood. If it hadn't been so loud and scary, one could almost mistake it for a Mexican fiesta or an early July Fourth celebration. Mancuso had already radioed to his troops to move by that time, but it wasn't quick enough.

For a large man, Fitzpatrick was unusually agile. This prowess would be no greater surprise than to his victim. Fitzpatrick threw himself into the air, the momentum of his heft carrying him into the largest of the surviving bodyguards. His enormous frame came crashing across his back and shoulders, slamming the Russian guard into the marble mantle. Fitzpatrick was up, recovered quickly and moved like a gazelle. As he stood, he turned with the grace of a dancer. He plunged his index finger into the mouth of one man, then turned it hard and yanked the interior of the man's cheek muscles like a fishhook. He had his attention now and the guard would do anything or go anywhere the detective wanted, or would have half his face painfully torn off in the process.

Fitzpatrick swung the large man in a circle, then released him into a column of the spiral staircase. Another guard, witnessing Fitzpatrick's unorthodox fighting style began to engage him, hesitated, and then turned to run. *Wrong move!* Fitzpatrick reached around the fleeing man's head and dug his thumb into the ear lobe. He squeezed his thumb hard to his hand and yanked, spinning the other into a floor-to-ceiling hall mirror.

Fitzpatrick's carefully calculated movements weren't actually second nature to him, but being a former fighter and avid mixed martial arts enthusiast it sure helped. He fancied himself an American version of *El Guapo, Bas Rutten,* just a little less bald and a lot less sexy.

As the bullets kept flying, Fitzpatrick knew the only way he'd survive was by waiting it out. He dove over the back of huge love seat, as it was a good shield, made from fine solid oak from the Ural Mountains – he felt relatively safe.

CHAPTER 74

TEAR GAS CANISTERS FLEW through the thick beveled-glass windows and into the mansion as fumes began to bellow out of every orifice. You had to hand it to the LAPD, SWAT, SIS, and the other tactical units, as well the rest of the special operations guys. They had some high tech toys and they came to play hard.

Murphy, with the little strength he had, assisted McCann and tried to get Frank down from his bonds, but couldn't help throwing a sneer at Tetley in the process. He knew it wasn't the place or time, but he, like all his countrymen often suffered from *Irish Alzheimer's:* he could forget everything but the grudges!

There was no time for hate-spew or swearing, accusations, or finger pointing. It was all about survival now. As soon as Frank landed on solid ground, the men bolted for the basement steps, just as a thick cloud of tear gas was beginning to float slowly down into the basement, creeping step by step *like Death* arriving to dinner.

McCann turned to warn the others of the blinding cover ahead, when he suddenly realized Frank was not behind them. "Frank, come on!" he shouted at the growing obfuscation. He turned quickly and attempted to grab Frank by the arm and drag him up toward salvation.

"I want that bastard's money!" Frank cried out, fighting his lead.

McCann was taken aback for a split second, but continued to tug at Frank's shoulder.

"Damn it, Frank, we've no time for this." Frank pulled away again, this time taking a swing at McCann to send a message. *Message received,* McCann thought.

"Leave it, Frank, this was about Ciara, remember, only about Ciara." Frank's eyes welled with insanity, but his heart was too filled with hatred for him to be reasoned with. "Frank, we've followed you into battle since we were wee children, but it was always for a cause – this is insanity!"

For a brief instant, Frank understood the separation that was happening, his good friend, loyal above all others, the son he never had would, not follow him no further. With iron resolve, Frank bit his lip in a show of bravado and defiance, and even though it tore the last shred of his heart, and hasten McCann's retreat. He turned, and without saying a word, shot back down the hall. He ran to the door and pressed the keypad to decode and disarm the security system. The red light on the keypad went dark and a tiny green light lit up. McCann would not follow.

Frank quickly opened the door and rushed into the room without a second's delay, scanned the walls, the corners, then ran up to the table of steel cases and frantically fumbled for the key to open them.

Out of a shadowy corner of the basement hall, Rostov suddenly appeared bloodied and battered. "Thank you, gentlemen -- Alexei, kill them all," Rostov shouted as he coughed from the tear gas now filling every corner of the basement like a cloud descending on the trenches of a World War I battlefield. It was then the blood, pouring from the gaping wound in his barrel chest, became apparent.

Somehow, Alexei and his father had miraculously escaped the firefight upstairs and made their way downstairs through the servant's entrance in the kitchen. But they had not come alone.

Rostov waved Alexei to deal with McCann, Tetley, and Murphy, as he would dispatch Frank in his money room himself. It was all coming together beautifully, except of course for the bullets, the blood, the tear gas, and the federal agents. But Rostov would be undeterred. That was his money in that room, he had earned it over the course of his life, and he would be damned if he was going to let anyone else get their hands on it.

Through the dense fog of tear gas, Fitzpatrick appeared like a specter. He had watched patiently as Rostov and Alexei crept down the service stairway and followed as the group upstairs continued to massacre each other. He was longer concerned with Rostov, as much as he hated himself for it, but instead was there to get Tetley out safely, if he could.

The basement had now become a ghostly cemetery, as only silhouettes appeared like gravestones where men once stood. The thick, semi-noxious haze filled every inch and had made its way to Rasputin's den -- the great beast sniffed the air and began to cough and choke. His already heightened senses became overwhelmed and his instinct for survival kicked into overdrive. With all his might, he fought his impending doom.

CHAPTER 75

66 Y OU LOSE, IRISH," ALEXEI shouted as he drew down on McCann. But the Irishman was too quick and dove into the dark. It was then multiple canisters of tear gas burst open and tumbled down the basement staircase from above, to add to the already ridiculous amount of fog. Fitzpatrick, quietly brought up the rear, took it as an omen as he cautiously made his way between Alexei and McCann. He lunged forward, spread his arms and somehow wrangled Tetley and Murphy out of the haze. "Come on, idiots, get up the stairs." Fitzpatrick shouted. The murky smoke enveloped them so quickly; Alexei didn't have time to shoot. No matter, he turned back to search again for McCann, yet, for once, he wouldn't risk shooting indiscriminately as there was always a chance he could hit his already wounded father.

Suddenly, McCann sprang up out of the vapors and clobbered Alexei on the forearm. He had purposely attacked his *lateral antebrachial cutaneous* nerve, knowing full well from his years of prison fights, it would disarm him in an instant. Alexei's hand spasmed, releasing the gun. McCann threw a powerful front kick to his solar plexus, sending him backwards into the fog. It may have been *old-school* warfare, but it was still effective as hell!

For an instant, McCann thought that might be the end of the spawn of Satan. *Maybe he'd passed out from the concussive blast or gone white eyes up from lack of oxygen*, he fantasized. But there would be no such luck, even for this Irishman.

Alexei came out of the cloud like a demon with a round kick that landed hard on McCann's left cheek, whipping his head back. As the fighting crescendoed, the two men moved closer and closer toward the table where Alexei tortured his victims. McCann volleyed *one-two-one* punches as he advance. He'd spent enough time in the joint to practice every fighting technique, but he'd always found the classics to be the best. He aimed high, he aimed low, he fired a left jab to Alexei's face, then followed that by a right hook to his ribs, *upstairs, downstairs*, following quickly with a left upper cut to his jaw. Mike Tyson would've been proud.

But Alexei Rostov was no ordinary foe. As a former *Spetnatz*, the highly skilled Special Forces soldier had trained to kill in covert operations. He was not easily dispatched and the fact that he was hopped up on coke and meth and God knew what, would add a new level of insanity in this fight-to-the-death.

A normal man would've been curled up in a corner pissing blood and calling for his mommy by now, but instead, Alexei jumped onto the torture table to gain height advantage. As McCann advanced, Alexei whip-kicked him, hoping he'd be seeing stars. McCann flew backwards and landed hard on his ass. Alexei reached down and grabbed the cattle prod and hopped off the table in anticipation of the ecstasy he'd get from frying his opponent's eyes out of his head and eating them for a snack.

McCann, realizing he was not only recovering too slowly, but that he really was truly hurt. He didn't know how much more punishment he could take – so every blow would have to count. Alexei pushed the button to the cattle prod as McCann saw the blue arc pulsate from the instrument of misery. The electric noise it made was unmistakable.

In the fog behind the men, Rasputin, heard the *tell tale* sound synonymous with his unending pain. He reared up with all his might, and gave a final, full strength pull. The fractured and crumbling mortar around the faceplate could hold up no longer from the strength the great bear possessed. The steel chain that held the Kodiak could no longer keep him in place. *Snap.* Rasputin was free.

McCann tried quickly to compose himself after last blow to his head and connect the two Alexei's he saw in his spinning head into one target. Alexei peered into McCann's eyes and saw the dilation… he knew he had him. He lunged out and over him with the cattle prod arcing like a tree panther. But just before he made contact with McCann's throat, ending his life in a shocking manner, Rasputin burst out of the thick fog.

As silent and stealthy as any predator that ever lived, 1,200 pounds of fur and flesh descended and came crashing down onto Alexei. If McCann had been woozy before, he was sure-as-shit straighten out now! *What could he do?* He didn't have time to play dead. Either way, he was <u>not</u> going to stick around to see the results. Searching the darkness with his hands, barely able to breath, nearly blind and incoherent, McCann dragged himself away and stumbled to find the handrail that lead upstairs.

"AAAHHH!" Alexei's screams would've filled the entire house, his mortal coil stretched and torn. His cries would've become louder, if it weren't for the fact they were being muffled by Rasputin's enormous body. The great bear began to rip and tear at Alexei's flesh. All the years of torture and sadism Alexei had perpetrated on the giant mammal was now being avenged… one terrifying bite at a time. After mere moments, Rasputin tired of his motionless quarry. With a single stroke of his enormous paw, he tore off Alexei's scalp. The bear sniffed the scent of warm blood beginning to pour, then opened his enormous jaws and snapped them close over his throat to stop the irritating gurgling noise that was coming out.

As the beast rose, he pushed his hind legs backwards, ripping off both Alexei's legs and sending them flying across the room. He stood atop the pulverized body as blood and tissue covered his jawbone and muzzle. If he were human, he would have been proud of his accomplishment, but as it was, he slunk back into a cloud of darkness, as his senses were burning bright for more tasty flesh.

CHAPTER 76

ESPITE THE MELEE OUTSIDE the room in the basement, Rostov trained his gun on Frank as he slowly moved closer toward the steel cases. Frank, still crazed with revenge, picked up a block of Semtex as he caught sight of Rostov nearing him from the polished chrome tabletop. "You have avenged the memory of your daughter and valiantly attempted to destroy my entire enterprise," Rostov groaned and coughed. "But you must understand that with this money, I will rebuild my empire."

Frank lowered his eyes in hatred. "I going to cram this money down your throat until you choke."

Rostov shook his head in agreement, sidling up to the edge of the first case. "Yes, of course you will, my friend." Rostov said, keeping Frank from doing anything stupid with the explosive in his hand. "You will be known as a hero, posthumously, of course."

Slowly a faint beeping sound filled the room, then suddenly beams of light appeared everywhere, crisscrossing the room. A matrix of laser beams clicked *ON* as the electronic timer adjusted to its false delay setting. Rostov and Frank were caught dead to rites in the center. They would have to remain frozen, no sudden movements; they were virtually locked where they stood.

Frank couldn't help but see the irony in what was now happening. He began to laugh hysterically as Rostov focused on the LCD timer on the table flash to 30 seconds, then tick down: 29, 28, 27.

"Switch it off or we will both die!" Rostov screamed at Frank.

"*Das Vi Danya*, comrade!" Frank burst out in maniacal laughter. "See you in hell!" Frank began to tear at the brick of explosive, a hollow gesture in hindsight, as the chemical compound would need a blasting cap or some type of electrical charge to set it off. But Rostov had tired of this irritation. He raised his gun and shot Frank between the eyes, blowing the back of his head against the wall. Frank's knees crumpled and he fell where he stood. Miraculously, his body somehow collapsed straight down, never touching any of the light beams thinly spaced triggers. *Now*, Rostov thought, now he could finally get his money?

The old Russian fumbled to pull a set of tiny keys from his pocket and began to quickly open the first case. *Success*, he heard the click, pressed the thumb releases on both sides and opened the case. His eyes lit up as he stared inside.

It was then a shadow appeared at the money room door. Searching and acquiring his other tormentor, Rasputin growled once, then charged Rostov. "No, no Rasputin, no!" The giant Kodiak broke the first laser beam, then the second, the third, tripping every one of the detonation switches. Rasputin raced up to Rostov, reared up to his full 10-foot frame and filled the entire room. Rostov could feel the bear's hot breath pour over him like a rotted carcass as the great animal came crashing down in a deadly embrace.

CHAPTER 77

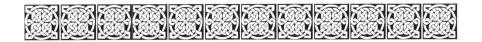

FITZPATRICK AND TETLEY APPEARED out of the cloud of tear gas, coughing and hacking. He flashed his badge as he dragged Murphy outside through a gauntlet of emergency services troops. "Keep your fucking mouth shut and we may just get out of this with our asses intact," he whispered to both Murphy and Tetley. Just then fire, law, and emergency techs ran toward the men. "I got this guy!" Fitzpatrick yelled to fend off the others about to close in and snatch up his prey.

Mancuso and his agents had already systematically rounded up the remaining Russians that were still alive, but had been injured in form or another. The Feds had the easy job as anyone who wasn't shooting or being shot, raced out the front doors into the loving embrace of the Federal Bureau of Investigation as well as the U.S. Marshals Service.

A squadron of paramedics had been dispatched by all the agencies involved, and had taken positions on the street up and down from Rostov's mansion. Each *EMT* had been pulling bullet-ridden bodies out to the front lawn of the mansion, only to find most of the victims had already expired from their injuries.

"Treat this man first!" Fitzpatrick yelled to a paramedic who was leading an injured Russian bodyguard out of the house. "He's with me -- those scumbags can take a number." Fitzpatrick leaned out and kicked one of the bodyguards in the groin, dropping him where he walked. The paramedic gave the detective an odd look, then burst out laughing. Another paramedic had run up to assist the felled Russian. "I said, leave him, and take care of my man! He's a waiter, uh, he's an innocent bystander, so treat this guy first!" Fitzpatrick grabbed the other wounded bodyguard from the arms of the paramedics and threw him toward a large fountain in the center of the lawn. The paramedics knew how powerful a drug adrenaline was and combined with anger, a cop, even a detective, could become extremely volatile.

"Yes, sir, Detective, anything you say!" The medics immediately wrapped their arms under Murphy's and carried him to one of the unoccupied ambulances for assessment. Murphy winked at Fitzpatrick as they carried him away. "Don't let anyone else touch him, or take him, until I get his statement... do you understand me?" The EMTs nodded, then waved in acknowledgement.

Just then, McCann appeared from the mist-filled entry coughing and gagging in an attempt to dispel the gas from his lungs. Officers and Federal agents instantly drew a bead on him as they dropped the safeties of each of their firearms to the *off* position "Put your hands on top of your head, Goddamn it!" Mancuso screamed at McCann.

"Get everybody outta here," McCann began shouting as he waved his arms. "The whole place is about to <u>explode</u>!" These words alone were enough to scatter cops and Feds alike -- the injured, on the other hand, would be *shit-outta-luck*!

McCann raced toward Fitzpatrick who had not yet turned to see him, and, flying in mid air, dove on top of the detective. Suddenly, the ground began to shake at a short rumble, like a medium temblor, then suddenly it turned into a massive explosion from the basement up through the rooftop of the mansion. Fitzpatrick pushed himself over to see what had just happened when he realized McCann was on top of him.

"Stay down, Detective!" McCann shouted to his elder. Flames shot hundreds of feet skyward; as stone, masonry, wood and glass became flying shrapnel. Flaming debris came next, striking dozens of people who tried valiantly to run for cover.

Patrol car windows blew out by the secondary shock wave, or

were smashed by flying debris. Tree limbs, even a garden gnome, flew straight up, then rained down from the sky like holy hell as the pyre of hellfire rose skyward.

McCann turned his head away from the heat, then caught a glimpse of Murphy down the street being lifted into an ambulance, and gave him a look like - *how much explosive did you use?* Murphy smiled at his old friend, then laid his head back onto the pillow as the paramedics locked the gurney down and shut the doors. *He was okay,* McCann thought.

As the last of the fiery debris came raining down, McCann quickly shot to his feet. "We've gotta get to the pub," he implored everyone who could hear him. "Rostov planted a bomb."

Fitzpatrick pressed his large frame off he ground and quickly bounded to his feet. "The kids!"

CHAPTER 78

A CHORUS OF IRISH STEP dancers pounded an elevated stage in unison as festive music and merriment filled *Murphy's Law.* The excited crowd swelled to capacity and the overflow filled Wilshire Boulevard.

Danny Doyle and his band, *Gweedore*, played for the crowd as the fiddle player burned up the strings on her bow like Bridget Regan of *Flogging Molly.* Fans kept time with the dancers and clapped furiously as the newest partygoers, the Tsunami orphans, were rocking out for the first time with their new American parents. It was the biggest party of the year: Saint Patrick's Day.

In the corner of the bar, ICE Customs Officer, Viola Williams raised a glass of green beer with a group of young suitors. They hoisted their pint glasses, toasted each other and sang, even if they didn't know the words. The energy was palpable and all worries of all the patrons seemed to melt away. This was a safe place.

McCann, Fitzpatrick, Tetley, and dozens of Federal agents pushed their way through the nearly impenetrable crowd.

"Follow me," yelled McCann grabbing Fitzpatrick by the sleeve, who, in turn, grabbed Tetley. They broke right toward a small opening in the crowd and ran down the length of the bar rail. Mancuso, shorter than the other agents, quickly lost sight of McCann and took his team in another direction; unaware it would be a dead end.

McCann, the detective and the inspector weaved quickly through the bar, scanning the faces, not really knowing where or what to look for. "Happy Saint Patrick's Day, gents!" Kelly yelled in a slurred, drunken voice, slapping McCann on the back as he passed. "Since that bollocks Murphy's nowhere to be found, the first one's on me."

McCann stopped in his tracks and grabbed Kelly in a tight grip. "Kelly, did you see anyone strange like come in today?" he shouted in the most serious of tones. "Anyone you've never seen before, think, Kelly, think?"

Kelly's broad smile turned down and he looked at McCann as if he were drunk. "Jaysus, Mick, it's *Paddy's Day*, look around at these nutters, whad'ya think?" McCann looked across the wave of people dressed in Irish garb, painted faces, leprechaun hats and beards.

"Yeah, I know what ya mean," he said under his breath. He'd never known that Saint Patrick's Day was so popular over here or that literally everyone became Irish this day. If he had had the time, he would've liked experiencing this truly American custom, but time was the last thing they had.

"Can yaz grab us another keg, Mick?" Kelly slurred as Mancuso appeared with his men. Fitzpatrick raised his hand so as not to be interrupted. "Them delivery boys brought extra beer kegs and didn't even charge us for 'em, God bless their souls." Kelly's eyes suddenly caught an older woman wearing a lace sash and waved to her.

"Nobody gives away beer on Saint Patrick's Day!" Fitzpatrick screamed over the noise of the festivities. "Mancuso, take Kelly and get these people out of here -- move it!"

Mancuso grabbed Kelly and shouted, "Alright men, we've got to evacuate this place, now!" With that, they fanned out quickly flanking the pub-goers and attempted to corral them by closing the ranks toward the front door. Needless-to-say, the crowd was more concerned with drink and song, than being pried away from their well-deserved fun.

As McCann turned to follow Fitzpatrick down the back hall, Tracey suddenly appeared, blocking his escape. Obviously inebriated, she threw her arms around him in celebration, pulling him toward her for a kiss. "Happy Saint Patrick's Day, Micky!" she slurred happily.

"I'm really starting to like you Irish, you guys really know how to party, Woo! Come on, don't be shy, give us a kiss." Without missing a beat, McCann shoved Tracey aside and continued toward the cooler. Tracey's face said it all. First she was miffed, then her face fell, then a pissed look appeared, finally tears welled up in her eyes. "You asshole! You men are all alike.," she whimpered.

Fitzpatrick cautiously pulled the large metal handle on the cooler door when McCann appeared from behind. All eyes focused on the floor loaded with beer kegs.

The three men crept into the cooler, carefully inspecting each keg for something, anything out of the ordinary. Nothing. As they closed in toward the back of the cooler, a single keg sat oddly against the back wall. Fitzpatrick tapped on the keg. *That one sounded hollow.* A beer-less keg was a dead give away as any barman knows that empty kegs get sent to the back alley to be swapped out, not left to clutter a fridge.

Fitzpatrick ran his hand around the base of the keg and felt welding seams that shouldn't have been there, he slowly unscrewed the top of the steel cap to reveal an LCD digital timer. The readout was 2:26… and counting down fast. "Shit!" Fitzpatrick barked. "Tetley, unless you know how to defuse this thing, go help Mancuso get everyone out of here as fast as you can -- you have two fucking minutes!" Tetley nodded and took off.

Maybe it was his lucky day or maybe he was just tired of being around this brash, uncouth man, but either way he was out the door before Fitzpatrick had finished his sentence. "Detective, maybe I can help," McCann said in an eerily calm voice.

Tetley ran back into the bar pushing and shoving his way through the swelling crowd of people. He was a tall, lean man, so he could see over the top of most everyone and could certainly see the futile attempt Mancuso was making to remove the patrons.

Green painted faces, four leaf clovers and green beer, Tetley knew if it weren't an emergency, he'd probably have a seizure at seeing all this. *Everyone was out of bleeding control*, he thought, then suddenly he felt a sharp pain in his bum. He snapped his head to see a beautiful blonde woman pinching him again on his ass. "Ouch!" Tetley blurted like a teenager.

"Where's your green?" the randy woman shouted into his ear. Tetley's face crinkled up, as he certainly didn't have the faintest idea was she was referring too. "You gotta wear green on Saint Patrick's Day or you'll get a pinch, didn't you know that, silly?" she giggled, playfully pinching him again.

"You must leave, there's a bomb!" Tetley shouted, imploring the young woman. Her smiled widened and she brought her face closer to his. "That's sweet," she laughed. "Well you're *DA BOMB*, too. What's your name, Cutie-Pie?"

Frustrated, Tetley rushed toward the middle of the pub, leaving the woman bewildered. It was then a marching band, making the all-day pub-crawl, entered with pipers, fiddlers and a procession of drinkers in tow. Tetley got an idea. He ran up, grabbed the large baton-looking mace from the Major and began marching everyone back outside into the street. He waved at all the parents and bid them stand and follow him like a crazed Pied Piper. The crowd, more drunk than sensible, dutifully obliged their new leader, and allowed him to take them anywhere, all the while careful not to spill a drop of the good stuff. Everyone seemed so overjoyed that it could've been the Romans leading the Christians to slaughter and no one would've cared.

But in the cooler, McCann and Fitzpatrick had their hands full. Sweat beaded then dripped from McCann's brow, even in this subzero environment. Fitzpatrick, with a new *on the job training* skill set, couldn't learn fast enough to defuse this bomb.

"Okay, I need a knife, or something sharp," McCann said in a slow deliberate voice. Fitzpatrick reached deep into his back trouser pocket and plucked out a Swiss Army knife -- *1,001 uses!* he thought, then handed it to McCann.

His brow furrowed as he reached even deeper into the same pocket and retrieved the Irish 50 Pence coin from the hill behind Rostov's mansion and tossed it on top of the keg in front of McCann. "First rule of evidence, *don't leave it at the scene!*" Fitzpatrick said, almost as a conciliatory statement. "Let's pick the damn thing up and just chuck it out back before it blows."

McCann shook his head as he pointed to a clear, thermometer-like tube in the center of the devise. "See that?" McCann pointed. "It's a mercury tilt switch, not to mention a few other nasty booby traps I've never seen before, any movement of this keg after it was activated and its lights out!"

Tetley suddenly appeared in the doorway flustered, sweating, with his shirt stained and reeking of puke. His unexpected appearance startled the two men. "We got them all out, but some drunken fellow just vomited all over me." Tetley whined. "Should I call the bomb squad?"

Fitzpatrick looked Tetley up and down and would've had plenty of sarcastic remarks had they the time, but there <u>was</u> no more time. "Too late! We've got less than a minute," Fitzpatrick said calmly, then turned back to McCann. "Christ, I hope you know what you're doing."

Now it was Tetley's time to lower his eyes in hate. "He's an expert at destroying lives," Tetley said with the venom of a cobra.

"That's ironic, Inspector, as I didn't hear you complain when I saved yours back at Rostov's, did I?" Not expecting that particular realization from his antagonistic partner, Tetley was taken aback.

"Shut the fuck up, Tetley, we need <u>positive</u> thoughts right now," Fitzpatrick barked, then slowly calmed to an almost zen-like state. He knew this would probably be his last act of duty, so he seemed to quickly contemplate how much hazard pay on top of his pension his sister Kate would receive to help with her new kid's college tuition. *He chuckled to himself when he realized the two children she had just adopted would get a kick-ass education, learn to surf, maybe go to a decent UC school, maybe Notre Dame, even Ivy League, and live a long, happy and healthy life, All compliments of their new uncle Kevin they'd known for all of a couple of hours. Oh well, he'd had a pretty okay life afterall.* Now, it's back to business.

"McCann, you disarm this bomb and I'll see you get <u>FULL IMMUNITY</u> for your testimony against the Rostovs," Fitzpatrick excitedly uttered in the fervor of anticipation, "and I'll also make sure you're never hassled by guys like him." He looked back over his shoulder and gave Tetley a glare. "Fuck it, I'll even throw in a GREEN CARD if you move your ass!"

Tetley took offense to Fitzpatrick's last statement. "You can't promise him that," Tetley bristled.

"I can promise him any-fucking-thing I want at this point!" Fitzpatrick blurted. "You still have time to run for it, Inspector!"

Even from the street, McCann could hear the pounding of the Irish *bodhrán* drums beating at a faster and faster tempo like ancient warriors going into battle. McCann could now see a tiny maze of wires as he delicately probed the trigger mechanism like a neurosurgeon. Looking deep into the device, he saw a miniature mirror with two wires: one red, one green. *Which one to cut?*

"Well, Boys this is it!" The digital counter now read 20 seconds, 19 seconds, the drums beat faster and faster. McCann's hand reached for the red wire, then stopped and shot to the green wire and cut it quickly. The drumbeats crescendoed as the timer stopped dead at 17 seconds.

CHAPTER 79

SPECIAL AGENT MANCUSO'S MEN were posted outside the two large oak doors to guard against anyone going back inside Murphy's pub. Suddenly, they burst open as McCann, Fitzpatrick and Tetley appeared in the doorframe looking like they'd each just gone five rounds with Randy Couture. At their feet, kegs of Guinness rolled out into the huge crowd that now clogged Wilshire Blvd. The partygoers had snarled traffic from the beach to Brentwood.

At first sight of the kegs, the crowd went mad, erupting in cheers. Little did they know they were cheering for their own lives that had just been spared. In the middle of the street, Danny and his band had already rewired the amps outside and began to play a fevered Irish jig.

At the edge of the crowd, McCann could see Tracey crying in her beer for having lost yet another man. He approached her from the back, slowly, cautiously, then wrapped his arms around her, pulling her into him tightly. He turned her around to face him, penetrated her gaze with his own, then kissed her deeply. She swooned.

In all the excitement, even Fitzpatrick threw his arm around Tetley and gave him a big kiss on his balding forehead. Then, just as quickly, Fitzpatrick threw him aside when he saw his sister Kate in the crowd dancing with Dej and his sister. He couldn't believe his luck, so he slowly approached to join in as they danced a reel and jig to the rhythm of the music.

Tetley, now half-excited, yet half-rejected, looked up to see the young blonde woman eyeing him and tonguing a straw in her drink. With a devilish smile, she wagged her finger for him to join her. He straightened his hair, or what little of it that was left, then his tie and marched toward her with a renewed sense of honor and machismo.

Standing atop an *L.A. Weekly* newspaper stand, Mancuso looked down on the crowd and couldn't help but smile. "Sir, we just got tip that Whitey Bulger was spotted on Third Street," Special Agent Maxwell shouted up to his commanding officer. "You know he's number one on *America's Most Wanted List* now that Bin Laden's dead."

Mancuso jumped down to address his junior agent. "This Rostov debacle is going to be a paperwork cluster-fuck that's gonna take years to sort out!" Mancuso laughed, knowing he'd been bested, but not exactly hating the results. "Let Fitzpatrick write this one up, he's probably going to get a citation from the mayor for it anyway -- those Goddamn unions!"

Special Agent Maxwell drooped his head and pushed in his earpiece. "Sir?" Mancuso nodded and whirled his finger in the air to gather up his team. As the men started to move, Mancuso began to recite a list of crimes. "Agents, Whitey Bulger has been accused of having nearly 20 people murdered – reacquaint yourselves with his file on the way over." Mancuso stated to his team. "Yes, sir, he's the kind of catch that could get you back to D.C., sir if you don't mind me saying." Mancuso stroked his chin… then smiled.

EPILOGUE

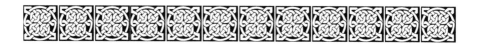

MURPHY'S SAILBOAT, *THE LIFE of Riley* gleamed as it cut through the blue waters of the Pacific. The sun was high in the clear sky and a westerly breeze filled the sails. McCann was at the helm. The sun beat down on his face, but his newly tanned skin could handle it now that he'd begun to acclimate to the Southern California weather and was now getting a proper daily dose of vitamin D.

Forward, Murphy lay in the lap of a beautiful brunette who fed him grapes like *Emperor Nero*. McCann gazed across the deck at all the people he now called friends, and for the first time in a long time, he began to feel truly happy.

"Hey partner, this is the life, huh?" Murphy shouted spewing grape seeds out of his mouth as he spoke.

"Stop callin' me, partner, McCann shouted back, half serious, half-joking.

Murphy smiled and shook his head. "Ah, Mick, this is where ya belong. You're one of *the new Americans* now!" Murphy turned to the brunette. "Get us another beer, will ya, Darlin'."

Slowly a hand wrapped around McCann's waist and Tracey's face appeared from behind him. Murphy, still acting the fool, flapped his arms like a bird trying to fly. McCann looked at Tracey and rolled his eyes. "Permission to relieve you, Captain?" Tracey said as she stood up, front and center, saluting him. She lunged for the wheel and butted McCann out of the skipper's position with her gorgeous hips. She kissed his forehead before he crossed the deck toward the cabin below.

McCann feeling, just the slightest bit proud of himself, allowed the Catholic guilt and his past sins to begin to fade from his soul. He gingerly made his way down the ladder into the hold. The kitchen was unusually clean, for being Murphy's boat, and the fact that there were dozens of people partying topside. He fumbled his fingers through assorted food wrappers and through grocery bags searching for something to nosh on as he had recently started putting on weight and found himself peckish everyday about this time.

Huh, big surprise, no more beer! he thought. He turned and opened the refrigerator to see it was empty, except for a single white cake box. Not being boyishly sneaky, McCann curiously opened the cardboard lid for a wee peak. *Hum, no cake?* All that was in the box was a single green bow. At the end of the bow was a key and sign that read: FOR MICK'S EYES ONLY - ALL YOU OTHER BASTARDS KEEP YER GRUBBY HANDS OFF! It was definitely Murphy's doing. McCann took a knife from the counter as the key was in a sealed envelope. He sliced it opened and pulled out a small note that read: PARTNERS IN CRIME – CHECK OUR LOCKER!

McCann took the key and flipped it meticulously in his hand as he walked to the steel locker, manipulated the key into the lock, and opened it easily. Suddenly McCann's eyes widened as his face turned to stone. There before him, was cellophane–wrapped stacks of cash. He stared in awe at what looked to be millions and millions in US dollars, blank bearer bonds, Chinese Yuan, Japanese yen, Euros, you name it, millions in varying currencies. It was far more money than one man could spend in a lifetime.

McCann, with old paranoia popping it's head up, looked around the empty cabin, then quickly closed the locker. He locked it tightly, and then threw the key in his pocket for safekeeping. Still reeling from the life-changing experience, he then somehow made it back up to the deck without tripping as his head spun wildly.

Murphy watched closely as his ghostly looking friend staggered topside. "Ya didn't think I was gonna let all that beautiful colored paper go to waste, did ya, Mick? I might have lifted a few items the day we visited them Rostovs. After all, we're much more responsible people than them Russkies, don't ya think? We'll put it to good use!" Murphy said with the widest of grins on his face. "I'm kinda hope'n you can find your way to start forgive'n me, *mo deartháir -- mo chara*!" Murphy turned back quickly to plant a kiss on the lovely brunette awaiting his affections. "Why don't you stick around awhile, brother? I promise, no shenanigans, just a nice, quiet life. I'll help you get established as a proper American, and you can help me make a few risky investments!"

McCann looked aft at Tracey's alabaster skin beginning to pink in the hot sun, then gazed back to Murphy, then back to Tracey again as she blew him a kiss. He leaned over the railing, just slightly, to catch a glimpse of a pod of dolphins riding the pressure wave ahead of the boat... then exhaled a long, overdue breath as though he was exercising a demon, and slowly, very slowly, he began to smile.

THE END

__Special Thanks__ go to those who helped cultivate this novel in various ways (whether they knew it or not) including: Ian Pozin for Cover design, Editors: Betsy Schell & Terry Rubenroit, Áine, Andrew Fallon, Shannon & Pat Fitz, David Brown-Warner Brothers, Starbucks A.M. Gang, Kesicks, Fosters, Soukups, the WLV B&N folks, Michael Altenhofer, Andrea Bari, Buttaccios, The Great Sean Feeny, Hugh Hefner, Lori Jo and Jane, Bryant Humphrey, Jacobskinds, Klones, McD, McGovern, all the Mics, Alan & Yvonne O'Neill, Brandy & Mike, M.A.T.E.S., Claudine Schooley, Julia Escova, Mike & Ursula Hansen, Tim & Lori Carhart, Marc Madnick-Final Draft, Nikki & Di, Pat Muldoon, Poseys, Jeff Queen, Tami Ravsten, Denise & Mike Romance & Vom Fass, Jeff Ross, Smiths, Pat Stack, Conor, Anar, MVP "Blackout", Fitz's Pub, Fitz's SpareKeys & Fitz's Bulldog, Creighton Prep & Westlake High 81'Alumni, Hollywood Prep, Mary Jones, Jackie Connor, Terry & Howard Rubenriot & the Virtuals, Timothy V. Murphy, all the Murphs, all the Fitz's, Todd Bathke, Lady KMB & David, Jesse Nicassio, the UFC Gang, Jameson's Whiskey, Bob Hilgenberg, Eric & Amber, & Phil Narutis for the beers, Baltic DNA for the Oscars, Ireland: ('Free State' & North,) Malibu (the North end,) Omaha & Chicago, Santa Monica and everyone in it, the good people of Hollywood (but just the good ones, which are few), The City of Oak Park, WLV Cisco's & Paul Martin's, Bob Hamer, Katye Baddeley, Johnny Horvath, Steve & Jana Covell, & The Back 9, OrthoPro, Mark Brito, The Ventura County Sheriff's Dept., Academy, & D.A.R.T. Team, JCOC83: The Secretary of Defense & The Joint Chiefs of Staff, Rene Bardorf-Dep. Ast. Sec.Def. PA, Rose-Ann Lynch OSD, Dave EvansOSD, the Pentagon staff & personnel, the DOD, Wounded Warriors, Regina Cross, CGS & Alice Kottmyer, AA at The State Dept., all U.S. Armed Forces, & anyone else I couldn't fit in... you know who you are!

ABOUT THE AUTHOR:

KYLE C. FITZHARRIS IS the best-selling author of the political thriller, *The Eighth Plague*. Fitzharris worked intelligence under Non-Official Cover (NOC) in Central America and Mexico, and at one point led a task force of eight-federal agencies. His efforts helped indict international conspirators responsible for drug smuggling, money laundering, murder-for-hire, & terrorist funding. He is currently working to bring *The Eighth Plague* and *The New Americans* to the big screen.

In 2012, Fitzharris was handpicked by the US Secretary of Defense, and nominated by the Joint Chiefs of Staff & the DOD to the prestigious *JCOC & DOCA*. At the Pentagon, Fitzharris was assigned liaisons, briefed, and then flown by C-17 to Army, Navy,

Air Force, Marine Corps, & US Coast Guard bases up and down the Eastern Seaboard. He was honored further by being tasked with the mission of bringing greater attention to our Wounded Warriors, as well as creating awareness of the struggles and needs of the families of deployed and post-deployed men & women of the U.S. Armed Services.

Fitzharris resides in Southern California, but visits Ireland often.

For more information on *The New Americans, The Eighth Plague*, or the author, please visit www.kylefitzharris.com.

CPSIA information can be obtained
at www.ICGtesting.com
Printed in the USA
FSHW010104261218
54692FS

9 781475 991079